THE COZY CORGI COZY MYSTERIES

COLLECTION ONE: BOOKS 1-3

MILDRED ABBOTT

Cover, Logo, Chapter Heading Designer: A.J. Corza - SeeingStatic.com

Main Editor: Desi Chapman

2nd Editor: Corrine Harris

Recipe and photo provided by: Rolling Pin Bakery, Denver, Co. - RollingPinBakeshop.com

Visit Mildred's Webpage: MildredAbbott.com

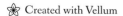

Created with Vellum

COZY CORGI COZY MYSTERIES
BOOKS 1-3

Cruel Candy
Traitorous Toys
Bickering Birds

CONTENTS

CRUEL CANDY

TRAITOROUS TOYS

BICKERING BIRDS

for
Nancy Drew
Phryne Fisher
and
Julia South

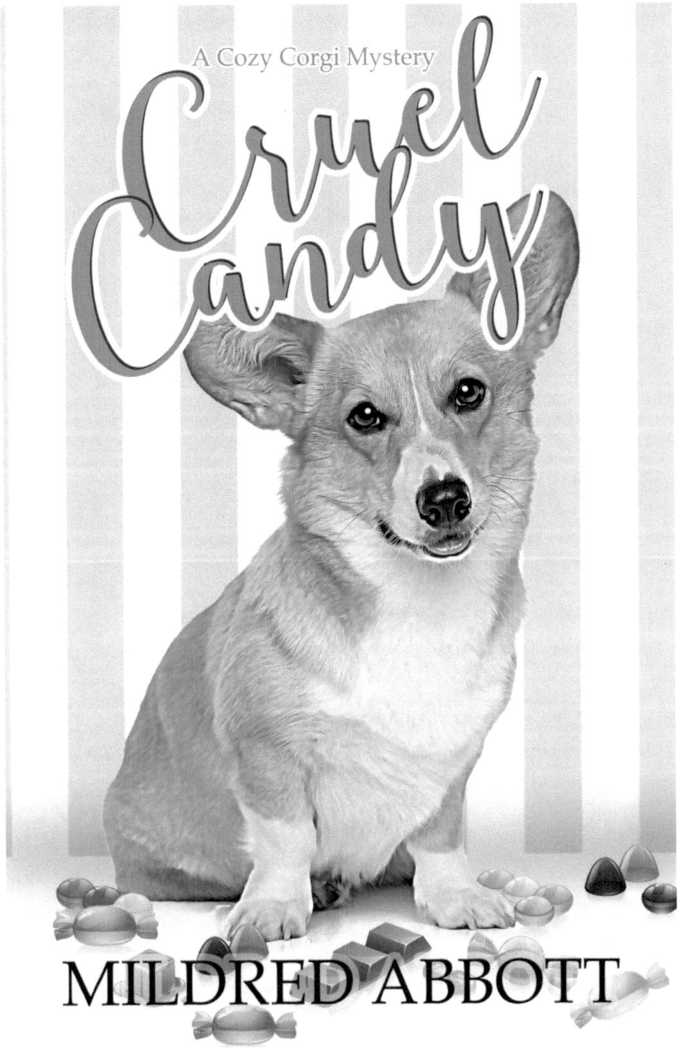
A Cozy Corgi Mystery
Cruel Candy
MILDRED ABBOTT

CRUEL CANDY

Mildred Abbott

"Oh, Watson, what have I gotten us into?" I stared at the shop through the safety of my car window. It was smaller than I remembered. I leaned forward, bumping my forehead on the glass. Fairly tall, though, at least two storeys. With the dark-stained log siding and forest-green trim and shutters, it looked like a log cabin had been sandwiched between the other stores of Estes Park.

And it was mine.

The thought ushered in a wave of excitement. A tingle of nausea too, but more excitement than anything. At least that was what I told myself.

The death grip I had on the steering wheel of my Mini Cooper said otherwise. I tore my gaze away and turned a forced smile toward the passenger seat. I needed to be brave for Watson.

He arched a brow lazily at me, not bothering to lift his head from his curled-up position. Managing to pull one of my hands free from the steering wheel, I slipped the car into Park, then scratched behind his pointed fox-like ears.

"We're here. It's been a long day, and you've been a great copilot." A grumpy copilot, but that was normal for

Watson. A quality that probably wouldn't be as endearing if he wasn't so stinking cute. "I'd say you deserve a treat. What do you think?"

At what was unquestionably his favorite word, Watson bounded to a standing position and began bouncing on his two front legs. His stubby corgi legs didn't make him that much taller, though the bouncing helped.

"And this is why we work, you and me. Food is king, behind books, of course." I snagged a dog bone out of the glove compartment, started to request for Watson to sit first—demands never worked—then decided it wasn't worth the effort, and held it out to him. Despite his voracious appetite, which even a shark would envy, Watson avoided removing my fingers and made short work of the snack.

After a couple of minutes, Watson cocked that judgmental brow of his once more. His thoughts were clear: *The prolonged staring is creepy, lady. But I'll forgive you for another treat.*

He had a point. I was putting off the inevitable. Which was silly. I was excited, happy. Time to launch into an adventure.

I turned toward the shop again, took a breath, and opened the car door. *Here goes nothing.*

My knees popped as I stepped onto the sidewalk, and I sucked in a breath at the tweak in my back. I supposed a drive halfway across the country was a reasonable excuse, even if I was still two years away from forty. I glanced back at Watson, who had curled back into a ball. "Seriously? The ten-hour nap wasn't enough?"

After a few more seconds of glaring, Watson acquiesced, stood, and stretched. He raised his knobbed-tail of a butt in the air, just letting me know he was still in charge, and then leisurely crossed the console and hopped out beside me.

"Thanks for joining me, your highness." I shut the car door and looked up at the shop. It seemed a little larger once I stood in front of it. It would be charming. My gaze flicked to the sign above the door that read *Heads and Tails*. *Would* being the operative word. Who knew what horrors lay behind the papered-over windows. I'd never envisioned a behind-the-scenes look at a taxidermy business, but it seemed I hadn't been aware of a lot about my future. Well, whatever. If it was too horrible, I'd just pay one of those junk companies to come in and haul everything away.

That thought brought a sense of relief, but then another swept it away. I was thinking like a city girl. I doubted a town the size of Estes Park had a junk-removal business.

And again, I decided, whatever.

I had a feeling I was going to be saying that a lot.

Movement caught my eye from the store window to the left of my shop. Before I could make out a figure, I was captured by the crimson script over the glass, *Sinful Bites*.

Perfect. Some fortification would be needed in the very likely chance I was getting ready to walk into a store filled with petrified dead animals. I veered off to the left, giving a quick pat to my thigh. "Come on, Watson. Mama deserves a —" I almost said treat. "—reward too."

A pleasant chime sounded as I opened the door to Sinful Bites and allowed Watson to waddle through. I cast a quick glance around. The store was done in my favorite colors—the walls, cabinets, and displays all in various shades of rich earth tones. It felt homey, comfortable. Exactly what I would be going for when I redid the god-awful taxidermy shop. That boded well for my relationship with my neighbor.

A woman with short, spiraling brunette hair looked up in surprise from behind the cash register. Her brown gaze glanced at me in confusion, then moved to the front door, and back.

I offered a hesitant smile, feeling like I'd messed up somehow. "Everything okay?"

"Yes!" The woman smiled back, wide and bright. "I'm so sorry. We just closed. I could've sworn I locked the door," she said, her tone apologetic.

"Oh. Well, I can come back another time." Despite myself, I couldn't keep my gaze from traveling over the gleaming cases filled with candy.

"Not at all! My fault for not locking the door, and I haven't started putting things away yet, so I insist." Another smile.

"Thank you. I promise I'll be quick." I moved closer to the cases, unsure if I would be able to keep that promise. Though slightly picked over, the display was magnificent. Gleaming fruit tarts in golden brown crusts, hand-size brownies filled with nuts, caramel, and chunks of candy. Fudge of every flavor, truffles of various shapes and colors, and chocolate. So much chocolate that I was suddenly aware I'd smelled it since I walked in the door. No wonder I felt at home. Chocolates done in nearly every imaginable way—almond bark and turtles, covering pretzels, marzipan and nougat.

Heaven, I decided. I'd died and gone to heaven. I managed to tear my gaze away from the smorgasbord of delights and look at the woman. "I think I'm in love."

The woman chuckled good-naturedly and held out her hand. "I'm Katie. Always nice to meet someone who appreciates dessert more than cardio."

I stiffened for a heartbeat, wondering if I should be insulted. But at the twinkling of Katie's eyes, I couldn't help but laugh. I felt an instant kinship with the woman. "Yes, I'll take dessert any day over fitting into a size eight. Though my real weakness is carbs, not candy. Give me a hot loaf of fresh bread and I can die a happy woman." I took Katie's hand.

"Me too, actually. I might work in a candy shop, but bread is what I do best."

"Then I am definitely glad to meet you, Katie." I released her grip and gestured down to Watson, who stared up at me, salivating. "My little corgi friend is Watson, and I'm—"

"I'm telling you, Lois, if you would just use actual sugar in your baking instead of all the stupid substitutions—" Two elderly women walked through the back door of the shop, cutting me off. They both halted at the sight of Watson and me. The blonde cast a quick glare at Katie. "I thought we closed."

Katie flushed. "I apparently didn't lock the door. Sorry. But I believe—" It seemed she was searching for my name. "—our friend here is in need of some chocolate."

The blonde looked at me and cast another glare down at Watson, but by the time she met my gaze once more, her smile was wide, even if it didn't reach her eyes. "Well, of course! You've come to the right place. Sinful Bites has the best chocolate in town."

The other woman's eyes narrowed, but she didn't say anything.

Katie cleared her throat, cutting the brief tension that had filled the place. "Do you know what you'd like? If you're not sure, I can get you a sample."

Getting-to-know-you time was most definitely over. Which was doubly sad, as at any other time I would've taken Katie up on the offer of samples. Under the inspection of the blonde, however, I didn't dare. "You know, I just drove into town, and I really should get home. Why don't you give me an assortment of the ones you like best." Chances were high such a thing would end up being more expensive than I'd intended to spend on candy, but since I was going to be neighbors with the shop, it was clear I needed to put my best foot forward as quickly as possible.

"Home?" The third woman finally spoke. "Do you live here? You must be new in town. I don't think I've seen you around."

"I just moved in. Quite literally, in fact." I smiled at the woman, who seemed nicer than the blonde. "I've visited several times. I have family who live here." I nodded at Katie as I spoke, trying to include her again and continue the introductions. "I'm Fred, and this is Watson. We just made the long drive from Kansas City to Colorado. This was our first stop in town."

The woman gave a chuckle. "Fred? I don't believe I've ever met a woman named Fred." She gestured to herself and the blonde. "I'm Lois Garble, and this is my sister, Opal. Opal owns this candy shop, and I own the one two doors down, Healthy Delights."

"It's a pleasure to meet you both." *Sisters?* The two women definitely didn't look like sisters. Although, now that I thought about it, they had the same features. It was only everything else that was different. Lois had naturally graying hair, a clean and wrinkled face, and she wore a plain cotton dress. Opal had dyed, highly stylized blonde hair, copious amounts of makeup, a brightly colored dress, and tons of jewelry. “My true name is Winifred Page, but everyone calls me Fred.”

“Well, I think that is simply adorable. And it suits you.” Lois shrugged playfully. “Like I said, I’ve never met a woman named Fred, but if I could imagine one, she’d have beautiful auburn hair just like yours. I’ve always thought Opal would look ravishing in that color.” She cast a sidelong glance toward her sister’s coiffed blonde hairdo.

Opal didn’t comment about becoming a redhead. “Page? Your last name is Page, and you have family in town? I don’t remember a family with that name.”

I nodded, though for some reason I was tempted to lie. “Yes. My mother grew up here. Phyllis Oswald, though now she’s Phyllis Adams.”

Both Katie and Lois seemed to take a step back, but Opal didn’t budge, instead folding her arms over her ample bosom. Any semblance of welcome or friendliness vanished, not that there’d been much from Opal. “I thought I’d heard your name before.” If looks could kill. “So that means you’re the one taking over Sid’s taxidermy shop.”

Again, lying seemed the intelligent thing to do. “Yes. Though I won’t be doing taxidermy. I’m going to be changing it to a bookshop. It’s going to be called the Cozy—”

“I’m sorry, but we’re closed.” Opal sniffed, nostrils flared. “And for future reference, I don’t allow dogs in my business.”

I halted, unsure what to say. One of the things I’d always liked about the town was Estes Park’s dog-friendly nature. I started to glance at Katie and then thought better of it. The last thing I wanted to do was get the shopgirl in trouble. I gestured back toward the door. “Sorry for....”

What was I sorry for exactly? "Watson and I will just be going."

Lois gave a loud good-natured laugh and swatted playfully at Opal, which Opal avoided with a glare. "Please forgive my sister. It's her intake of sugar and butter and things the good Lord never intended us to eat. It makes her cranky." She managed to deliver the line with a cheerful air, making it sound more like an endearing quality than an insult. Lois headed around the counter and slipped a birdlike arm through mine. "You come with me. I'll get you some sweets that are natural and nourishing, and I have homemade dog-bone biscuits." She looked down at Watson, then back at me. "I didn't notice. How adorable. He's a redhead like you." Without waiting for a response, she looked back down once more. "What do you say... Watson, was it? Do you want a treat?"

Watson bounced on his two front paws again at the word, causing Lois to chuckle. The only thing I really wanted to do at that point was get away, but Watson's reaction settled it. Plus, how could I deny the woman without seeming rude?

I allowed myself to be led toward the front door and cast a glance back, offering a quick smile to Katie and a final apologetic grimace to Opal.

Lois led me out of the shop, around the front of Heads and Tails, then pulled out her keys to usher me into Healthy Delights. "Sorry, I already shut the place down, but I'll get you an assortment of things from the back. Give me one second, dear." She flicked on the lights and then headed through the back door to disappear with a small wave.

The tingle of nausea rose again. My shop sat directly between these two sisters. Lois seemed sweet enough, but Lord knew what I was getting myself into with these two.

Pushing the thought away, I spared a glance at Lois's store. It was the exact same layout as Opal's, just flipped, but the similarities stopped there. Where Opal's candy shop felt cozy, warm, and friendly—despite the woman herself—Lois's was done in a garish combination of pastel colors, sickeningly sweet pinks, and yellows. My stomach gurgled.

Watson didn't seem to notice. He chuffed and looked up at me.

"Your treat is coming. Calm down." I shook my finger at him. "And I blame you for pulling me into this."

He chuffed again, and this time bounded so his paws landed on my foot, clearly telling me to shut up and get on with the treat giving.

"You're ridiculous." As if watching a car crash, I looked back at the shop. It didn't make any sense at all. How could the sister who owned the cozy and delicious-smelling candy shop be so irritable, while the one who designed the monstrosity that looked like Easter on speed was the kind one?

Before the color palette had a chance to permanently scar my corneas, Lois returned with a large brown bag in one hand and a massive dog bone in the other. "I'm sorry I have to rush. I'd love to get to know you and your precious pup, but Opal and I have dinner plans, and I don't want to keep her waiting." She thrust the bag into my grip. "For future reference, I make everything Opal does, just a healthy, all-natural version. It's fun to mix and match."

I forced a smile. I hadn't been able to identify what smell seemed to linger in the air, but it wasn't pleasant. If the desserts were edible, I'd be shocked. "Thank you. I appreciate your kindness. I'm sorry if I did anything to offend—"

Lois waved me off, whipping the dog bone in the air, a

large crumb flying across the room. In a rare show of speed, Watson zoomed away in pursuit. Lois didn't seem to notice. "Never you mind. That's just how Opal is. You see, she and I were hoping to purchase the taxidermy shop after Sid passed, but your mother wouldn't consider selling. Said her daughter was taking it over." Though her chipper tone didn't fade, Lois's smile did, a touch. "I won't hold that against you, dear." Another hand pat. "But if you decide you want to sell, we'd appreciate it if you would let us know." Leaning closer, her voice dropped to a whisper. "Lots of people move to Estes Park, captured by its beauty and charm, only to discover they feel a little trapped in the mountains and constricted by small-town life. Chances are it will happen to you too. Of course, I hope not, but"—and yet another pat—"when it does, remember my sister and me."

I opened my mouth to respond, but was utterly at a loss for words.

Words didn't seem to be required. Lois wrapped her arm around my shoulders, which was no small feat, considering I was several inches taller than the woman, and led me toward the door. She shoved what was left of the dog bone at me. "This is made from peanut butter I ground myself, and organic grains. They are five dollars apiece, but this one's on the house." She opened the door for me and stood aside. "Welcome to town, Fred."

"Thank you, Lois." I clutched the paper bag and waggled the dog bone in Watson's direction, capturing his attention. "Come on, buddy. Let's go." Watson tore off from where he'd been sniffing in the back corner of the shop. I nodded my thanks to Lois once more, then walked to the car. I changed my mind a few paces away from my burnt-orange Mini Cooper. Turning around, I headed back toward the front door of the taxidermy shop. I'd been so excited to see inside, to get lost in the planning of what my bookstore would look like, that I had driven straight here when we got into town.

After locking her front door, Lois crossed in front of Heads and Tails, gave a final friendly wave, and disappeared into Sinful Bites once more.

Pushing the odd sisters out of my mind, I addressed Watson as we stopped at the front door. "I'm sure you'll love all the smells you're going to find in there, but just remember, if we come across a dead animal and I scream, you're forbidden from telling anyone. If you do, there won't be any treats for a week."

Watson gave a quick, sharp bark.

"Crap. I said treat, didn't I?" At the repeated word, Watson resumed bouncing, his dark brown eyes wild with excitement and looking like a deranged bunny.

I couldn't help but chuckle as I lifted what was left of the dog bone. "Luckily, we have one. You can get it as soon we're inside."

I paused at the lockbox hanging from the door handle, then set the bag of healthy candy—*what a thought that was*—at my feet. Catching my reflection in the window, the paper behind the glass causing it to act nearly as effectively as a mirror, I couldn't help but scowl. My hair was a complete mess, and a sheen of light caught the gleam from dog hair. I glanced down at my peasant blouse. Life with a corgi meant I was in constant need of a lint roller, but after the day in the car, things had gotten to a nearly ludicrous level. To make matters worse, I gave my brown broomstick skirt a flick with my wrist and sent a fresh wave of dog hair spiraling around me. Wonderful. So much for putting my best foot forward. Meeting three of my neighbors while looking like I was part corgi myself.

Well, whatever. Too late to be helped now. Besides, it wasn't like I'd ever actually be dog-hair-free anyway. Pushing the concern away, I pulled out my cell and scrolled through text messages from my mother until I came across the lockbox code. I punched in the four digits and gave a yank. There was no click and the lock didn't budge. Clearing it, I tried again. Same reaction. I checked the text, confirming I had the numbers right, then tried a third time. When I was still denied, I tapped my mother's name and lifted the phone to my ear.

It rang several times, then finally clicked to a message saying my mother's voice mail was full and could no longer accept messages. What else was new? I tried the lockbox one final time. For a moment, I considered breaking the window on the front door and reaching in. It was my shop, after all.

What a way to start a new adventure, breaking and entering. Patience had never been a virtue I fostered, but letting out a resigned huff that sounded more like a corgi than a woman, I stuffed my cell back into my pocket. "Looks like we're thwarted at the moment, Watson."

Retrieving the paper bag, I led us back to the car, held the door for Watson to hop in, then followed.

I'd been so ecstatic about opening the bookshop, I hadn't even considered who my neighbors might be. Being directly between Lois and Opal was going to be.... Well, I was afraid I didn't have a word for exactly what that was going to be. I doubted it would be all that pleasant.

Watson chuffed.

"You feel it too, don't you, boy? Who knows what we're

going to have to face with those two. At least we have each other."

He let out a long pitiful whine.

"Aww, look at you being all empathetic. What's gotten into—"

I realized Watson's frantic gaze was focused on my hand, not looking deep into my eyes and sharing a moment. "Oh, I forgot." I handed him what remained of the all-natural dog biscuit with a sigh.

When the combination on the front door of the cabin didn't work either, I had half a mind to leave the bag of all-natural candy on the porch for the squirrels, toss Watson into the Mini Cooper, and hightail it back to Missouri. Or anywhere else, for that matter. As far as hitting the Reset button of life, this was turning out to not be so smooth.

This time, however, Mom answered her cell on the third ring. I sat on the ancient driftwood bench while Watson plopped down on the corner of the porch and observed a couple of chipmunks scampering over the roots of a nearby evergreen.

Though only a little after six in the evening, night had fallen, and the November air was brisk. As we sat waiting, my impromptu uprooting of my entire existence began to feel right once more. I'd forgotten how vibrant the stars seemed in the mountains, overlooking rocky peaks and massive forests. They were so clear a person could almost believe she could reach out and pluck one from the sky. Even the swirls of the Milky Way were visible. Not to be outdone, the soft breeze whispered gently through the bare branches of aspen trees, carrying the fresh scent of pine, earth, and snow. The gurgling of the partially frozen Fall

River, several yards away from the back of the cabin, was nearly hypnotic.

This was good. So very, very good.

I'd forgotten how beautiful it was in Estes Park. Forgotten the way my pulse slowed and my mind relaxed. It didn't matter that the bookshop would have a cranky candy-store owner on one side and a fake candy store on the other.

After nearly ten minutes, I also realized I'd forgotten just how far removed my grandparents' old cabin was. There was a new development of designer houses to drive through to reach it, but they were a good quarter mile away and not visible through the trees. At any other time, that would be a pleasing thought, but not when I couldn't get into the house. My grandfather always said bears were more afraid of us than we were of them. I never wanted to test his theory.

Just as my brain began to turn the sounds of the surrounding forest into something sinister and I was about to suggest to Watson that we take refuge in the Mini Cooper, headlights cut through the trees, flashing across the porch and then disappearing again as a vehicle came up the winding road.

The massive truck barely missed my rear bumper and slammed to a halt. Mom practically threw herself out of the passenger side, giving a graceful leap to the ground, which, considering her diminutive stature and age, was impressive.

"Winifred!" She hurried across the small distance, met me before I'd made it off the porch, and wrapped me in her arms. "Welcome home, baby!"

"Hi, Mom." As always, at barely five foot tall, she felt like a doll in my embrace, so tiny and fragile.

She pulled back after little more than a moment, then scurried over to the front door and began punching what seemed like random codes into the lockbox. "Come on. Let's get you inside. You must be freezing. You're not used to these Colorado winters."

"You've only been back six years, Mom. Surely you haven't forgotten that Midwest winters are much worse than anything you all have out here."

Watson bounded up and let out a happy yip, then rushed toward the truck.

"Well, hello there, little buddy." Barry Adams leaned his tall lanky frame down to rub briskly at Watson's sides. "Good to see you again." They'd only met two other times, but for whatever reason, they'd bonded. Each time Watson saw Barry, it was like Barry was a walking dog bone. After a few seconds, Barry stood once more and gave me a tentative hug. Despite that hesitation, his deep voice was warm and full of affection. "Glad you're here, Fred. Your mother's been over the moon knowing you are going to be near once more. And I think you'll be happy."

I returned his hug. I liked the guy. A lot. Not to the same level as Watson, but still. However, it was odd to think of him as my stepfather now, so I didn't. "Thanks, Barry. I think it'll be good."

"Barry!" Mom called out, not bothering to look over her shoulder nor pausing in her frantic pushing of buttons. "Do you remember the combination I put on this?"

"Pretty sure you put the key in your pocket, didn't you?" He winked at me.

Mom threw up her hands and then shoved one deep into her pocket. "Sure enough! I swear, I don't know how I manage to remember a thing." She slid the key into the lock, twisted, and threw open the door. Then she turned and handed me the key. "I guess this is yours now. Don't worry about the lockbox. I'm sure the combination will come back to me at some point."

And then the four of us bustled in. Mom and Barry made quick trips around the house, flicking on lights.

Watson looked up at me, his tongue hanging out in a grin.

"Go on." I waved him off. "Go explore."

He was gone, nose to the ground and snuffling here and there like he was guaranteed to discover a treasure.

After shutting the door, I glanced around the cabin. It was smaller than I remembered—probably eight hundred square feet. But also cuter than I recalled. Most of the furniture needed replacing, but the design was good, and the log walls and beams crossing overhead gleamed golden in the light. I peered into the kitchen. It hadn't been updated since the sixties, but my grandmother had kept it in pristine condition until she died. It seemed the renters over the past decade had done the same. I liked the mint green of the refrigerator and the oven. It suited me.

"We came out here yesterday and cleaned a little. It wasn't in too bad a shape. We were hoping to have time to clean out the shop as well, but we didn't quite get around to that." Mom stroked the curtains over the small kitchen window, like she was petting Watson. "I found the time to make these yesterday, though. I thought the kitchen needed some freshening up."

I stepped forward, narrowing my eyes. "Are those flamingos?"

Mom nodded. "Sure are. I think the pink makes the kitchen look happy."

"I hope you like them." Barry shrugged good-naturedly. "I picked out the material."

"I couldn't tell." I had to stifle a laugh. The background

of the flamingo material was a lemon-yellow and lime-green tie-dye print. Other than at his and Mom's wedding, I had never seen Barry out of his tie-dyed T-shirts and loose-fitting yoga pants. "They are lovely. Thank you."

He beamed.

"Well, we would've done more, but we didn't expect you for another six weeks." Mom turned back from the curtains, concern etched over her face. "I thought the agreement was for you to stay at the publishing house for the transition to go smoothly."

The room suddenly felt hot. "I changed the agreement." The last thing I wanted to talk about was Mysteries Incorporated.

Mom swiped a lock of long silver hair behind her ear as she crossed the kitchen and took my hand into hers. There were still streaks of auburn in her hair, the last vestige of the only physical trait I'd inherited from her.

"I know what she did was awful, honey, but Charlotte was your best friend since you two were little. I'd hate for a little thing like money and business to come between you."

My mother could find the good in a rabid wolverine if given the chance. "Don't worry about Charlotte. Trust me, she's not worrying about us." Mom opened her mouth to protest, so I switched the topic as I turned to Barry. "I met the neighbors. I don't think Opal was thrilled at my arrival."

Barry groaned. "She is a piece of work. If I had other property I could give you besides the taxidermy shop, I'd do it in a heartbeat so you wouldn't have to put up with her every day."

Mom swatted him. "None of that. Opal's a fine woman. Sure, she may be a little grumpy at times, but she's got a heart of gold. Everyone knows that Lois's business would've had to close its doors within a couple of weeks if not for

Opal. Sinful Bites has supported Healthy Delights since they opened. Anyone who's willing to do that for their sister can't be all bad."

I sucked in a little breath before Barry could protest. "Oh, I forgot. Lois gave me a bag of candy. I left it on the porch. I better go get that."

"Probably a good idea to leave it right where it is, dear." Mom offered a guilty smile.

"It's really that bad, huh?"

They both nodded. It was Barry who found the positive that time. "But Lois is a fine woman. Couldn't ask for nicer."

Mom smacked the counter. "That reminds me. I made Tofurky stew. It's in the car. I'll be right back. I figured you'd be famished after your drive. I wish Verona and Zelda weren't on a cruise. We could've had our first family dinner."

We stared after her as she hurried away. Barry grinned at me awkwardly. Several silent moments passed before Watson pattered in, accepted a pat on the head from Barry, and then settled at my feet.

Barry cleared his throat. "You like the flamingos, huh?"

"Barry!" Before I had to lie another time, Mom's raised voice drifted in through the front door of the cabin. "Where did you put the stew?"

He flinched, scrunched up his face in concentration, then his watery blue eyes grew large. "Oh, crud. I forgot she asked me to put it in the truck." He grimaced. "Be right back."

I couldn't help but smile after him. I'd always held my mother and father's relationship up as the perfect marriage. They'd balanced each other out. Mom was flighty, forgetful, and fun. Dad had been serious, kind, and brave. I had to admit, Mom and Barry together? They didn't balance each other out in the slightest; they were nearly two identical peas in a pod. But happy. So very happy. I loved that my mother got to have two good marriages in her lifetime when most of us couldn't even find one.

Mom poked her head in through the front door. "Seems like you and Watson are coming to our house for dinner this evening." She plopped the paper bag from Lois just inside the doorway. "Here, in case you get a desperate craving in the middle of the night."

THREE

Sleep didn't come easily, which was no great surprise. I'd left Kansas City in such a rush that I'd dropped a small fortune for a moving and packing company to do it all for me and then drive everything out later. The delivery date was still two weeks away. A long time not to have my own bed, but the sense of freedom of hitting that Reset button was more than worth tossing and turning for a while. Between the lumpy mattress and excitement over starting on the shop, a full eight hours wasn't in the cards. I doubted I'd even gotten five.

As a result, I poured nearly half a pot of freshly brewed coffee into a large thermos, coaxed a bleary-eyed Watson to the car, and drove downtown before the sun had even considered coming up.

Mom never remembered the code she'd used for the lockboxes, but she'd given me eight different keys off her ring, swearing that one of them would be the correct one. Chances were low, but this whole move was about hope, so I decided to latch on to that as I parked in front of Heads and Tails, sparing a glare at the awful wooden sign above the door. "That will be the first thing to go, Watson. Disgusting name, considering." I winked at him. "The Cozy Corgi is much better, don't you think?"

Watson didn't even bother to sigh.

"You're no fun."

After managing to convince Watson to leave the warmth of the car, I stood in front of the shop door, trying key after key. By the fifth failure, hope was fleeting. As I tried to decide if I would drive directly to Mom's and wake her up so I could get her whole ring of keys, the seventh key slid in with ease, then produced a little click as I twisted the door handle.

Look at that—hope paid off. Removing the key, I unlocked the deadbolt, then paused. This was it. I was about to see my future bookshop for the first time, enter the place I hoped would bring fulfillment and meaning back into my life.

I cracked the door, and Watson stiffened to instant alert, shoving his nose into the narrow opening.

His reaction startled me, but it only took a second to remember what the store was. Currently my dream future was filled with stuffed, dead animals. Maybe I should've waited for daylight.

Watson pushed against the door, shoving his muzzle in.

"At least one of us is going to enjoy this." I opened the door, and Watson rushed through. "Remember our deal. If I scream, it's our secret."

He didn't bother to reply. With the windows covered in paper, no glow from the streetlamps illuminated the place, and I felt around on the wall beside the door until my fingers found the light switch. Taking a steadying breath, I flicked it on and looked around.

For a ridiculous moment, I wondered if I was in the wrong shop. There was a large central area, with smaller rooms on all sides, so I couldn't see everything, but from what was visible, there wasn't a taxidermic animal in sight. Furniture and cabinets here and there, but not even a solitary furry creature. Letting out a sigh of relief, I stepped all the way in and shut the door. Watson's claws clattering over the hardwood floor sounded from somewhere in the back.

I started to walk in farther, then paused, pulled a tie out of my pocket, and twisted my hair into a quick ponytail. I might not see any animals, yet, but the place was filthy. The last thing I needed was spiders getting in my hair.

I moved through the rooms, flicking light switch after light switch. With each room I entered, my excitement grew. I might be sandwiched between Opal and Lois, for better or worse, but this little shop was everything I'd hoped for and more.

At least it would be.

Barry had mentioned the shop had been designed as a little house ages ago and had never been renovated to a more open concept, which would better suit a store. I had planned to hire a construction team to remedy that. As I explored, I changed my mind. Each room was connected to the other, surrounding the central area. All I needed to do was take off the doors. Each room could have a different theme. Kids' books in one room, cookbooks in another, romance, mysteries—every genre would have its place.

My entire goal for the shop had been to create a warm, inviting environment where people could not only shop for books but also hang out and enjoy reading them. A cozy sanctuary from the rest of the world, tucked away in an adorable tourist trap of a mountain town. This was turning out even better than I'd envisioned. A couple of the rooms even had fireplaces in the corners. I could get a few mismatched armchairs and sofas to spread around. The Cozy Corgi was going to be something special.

Near the rear of the main room, a beautiful wooden staircase led up to the second floor. I could just make out the spindled banister running around the circumference. I knew the previous renter had lived up there, and I hadn't decided if I was going to rent it out or make it part of the bookshop. Probably would have to use it for storage and inventory.

From Watson's reactions, it was easy to tell where the taxidermy had been. He was especially interested in the corners of the rooms, sniffing around, then looking up the wall as if he could see what had been there. In most of the places, I could just make out an imprint in the dust of where something had hung. The previous tenant had passed away in the summer, and the shop had stayed empty. I could've sworn Mom and Barry said they hadn't had a chance to do anything to the place, what with my moving the date up so suddenly, but maybe they had just been referring to a deep clean. Finding it all in good shape was a nice surprise. Deep cleaning I could handle myself. Trying to figure out what to do with mounted bears, foxes, cougars, and Lord knew what else would have been a completely different story.

There were two closed doors at the back of the shop. I opened the first one, and flicked on the light to reveal a bathroom much in need of updating. I checked to see if the toilet worked; it did, a good sign. The other room opened into a tiny storage space—not nearly enough for what a bookstore would require. Which only reinforced the possibility that upstairs would need to be used for storage. Just as I started to close the door, Watson barged in, continuing his sniffing exploration. He made his way around the circumference of the room, then paused at what appeared to be a small deep freezer in the corner.

He stuffed his nose between the wall and the back of the deep freezer, then shoved against it with a wiggle of his butt. With a whine, his attempts grew more frantic.

Something about his reaction caused my skin to prickle into gooseflesh. "Come on, boy. Let's check out the upstairs."

Watson looked over his haunch at me, let out another whine, and returned to pushing against the deep freezer.

Feeling like the first victim in a slasher film, I crossed the room and stood in front of the appliance. I was being ridiculous. If anything, the freezer was probably just full of meat which Watson could smell.

The sensation of being nervous about a deep freezer overrode feeling like the dumb bimbo in a horror movie. I threw open the lid with a flourish just to get it over with and move on, then glanced inside.

Two huge black eyes gleamed up at me from the darkness. With a scream, I released the lid and practically threw myself backward. It shut with a bang.

With all the commotion, Watson let out a startled yelp and rushed past me.

I nearly turned tail and follow him out of the storeroom but couldn't rip my gaze away from the deep freezer. What had I just seen? An animal, obviously. I was in a taxidermy shop, for crying out loud. Granted, I didn't know they put animals in deep freezers, but I supposed that made sense. Those eyes, however, were unlike anything I'd ever seen.

It was an animal. Right? Had to be. I didn't need to look at it again to figure that out.

I turned to leave the room again and found Watson

staring at me warily from the doorway. "Well, you were absolutely no help."

With a sniff, he padded back into the room and returned to sniffing at the base of the deep freezer. He managed to get his head all the way behind it—apparently slamming the lid had moved it a few inches from the wall. He let out a growl, wriggled his butt some more, and then popped back out, looking the epitome of satisfied.

Watson was nearly out the door again when I realized he had something in his mouth. Without thinking, I reached down and snagged it, fearing it could be poisonous or harmful.

It wasn't. Just a feather. Angling it toward the light, I gave it a twist. It was a soft brown with white spots across it.

Watson growled softly.

I looked down to find him glaring up at me. "Not for you, buddy. Sorry." His gaze remained focused on the feather, so I stuffed it in my jacket pocket, hoping it would be out of sight and out of mind. "We'll go get you another of those dog bones when Healthy Delights opens later this morning."

He didn't seem impressed.

I looked over at the deep freezer once more, a strange sense of dread wriggling in my gut. "Oh, for crying out loud." I was being ridiculous, again. Reminding myself that I was a self-made businesswoman and the daughter of a cop, I stomped back over to the deep freezer. I paused long enough to pull out my cell phone and flick on the flashlight. With another steadying breath, I opened the lid and angled the light inside. This time, I didn't make a noise, but was still unable to repress a shudder.

A large owl stared up at me.

Just an owl.

Nothing dangerous or even all that surprising. I supposed when Barry and Mom got rid of all the other taxidermy, they hadn't thought to check the deep freezer. Though who in their right mind would? You expect to find dinner or ice cream in a deep freezer, not whole animals. Though the owl was frozen, obviously, I couldn't quite tear myself away from its gaze. Even in death, its eyes were huge and gleaming.

Behind me, Watson growled again.

It was enough to break the spell. I closed the lid, softly this time, and turned to Watson. He started to head back to the deep freezer, but I scooped him up. It always surprised me how heavy the little guy was. "No way! We're getting out of this room, shutting the door, and neither one of us is coming in here until I find someone to do whatever you're supposed to do with dead owls."

Watson hated to be carried, and he thrashed in my arms until I placed him on the floor outside the storeroom. He continued his reproachful glare as I shut the door. Letting me know just how over me he truly was, Watson waddled into the main room, cast a dismissive glance in my direction, and galloped up the stairs.

The second floor. Crap. Maybe Sid What's-his-name had several deep freezers filled with animals upstairs.

Might as well get it over with.

Keeping the light on my cell phone on, I walked up the wide staircase. To my surprise, the steps were in good shape, not even a creak. I found the light switch easily enough and turned off the flashlight and stuffed my cell phone away once again, then looked around. The upstairs was the same size as the first level, but here the layout was open concept, like a studio apartment. Sid's old bed, sofa, and entertainment center spread out in different clusters. Against the north wall were two separate rooms. The first one stood open and revealed another bathroom. The second door was closed, and Watson lay happily in front of it, knob of a tail wagging as he chomped down on something.

"Seriously? Again?" I hurried over to him and attempted to pull whatever it was out of his mouth. He jerked away and shuffled back several feet. From his deepened glare, it was clear I'd be getting attitude from him for my rudeness for the next several days. At my feet, where he'd been, were two pieces of wrapped candy, and an empty piece of ripped cellophane. I scooped them up and inspected them. They were round and hard, almost looking like gumballs except for their deep black color. I sniffed one to make sure it wasn't chocolate. Although in that small quantity I doubted it would hurt Watson if he managed to eat one. Even as I thought it, I could hear him crunching on the piece he'd successfully gotten out of the wrapper. The scent was instantly recognizable. Licorice.

I pocketed the candy as well, simply to get it out of the way, and gave Watson a glare of my own. "Never mind. I don't see a large all-natural dog bone in your future today, after all." At least it hadn't been chocolate. I loved Watson, but his food obsession drove me nuts. He refused to eat dry dog food of any kind, yet absolutely anything we found out in the world was surprisingly edible—even if it wasn't.

Deciding not to do battle to try to get what remained of the licorice out of his mouth, I opened the door, flicked on the lights, and stepped into a large kitchen.

The floor was littered with candy. More of the hard licorice scattered among pieces of chocolate, marzipan, and peppermints. An overturned pan of brownies was scattered across the countertop. A cardboard box was stuffed with something, and another was overturned, spilling out a variety of copper cookie cutters.

Something brushed against the hem of my skirt, causing me to jump, and I looked down to see Watson sneak past me into the room.

"Oh no you don't. No more candy for you." I started to reach down to scoop him back up, but he let out a low, dangerous growl.

I flinched back. I'd only heard that growl, which sounded surprisingly vicious, a few times, both occasions when some stranger was at the door. He'd never growled at me like that.

It took me a moment to realize he still wasn't growling at me. His front shoulders were drooped down and his back was rigid, rump in the air as he showed his fangs. He crept toward the counter, still growling.

For the second time that morning, gooseflesh broke out over my arms. This time, however, as I followed him, I felt even more like the first victim in a horror movie.

As Watson rounded the corner, he sank lower, his growl deepening.

At his feet was a large wooden rolling pin, the end of which was stained a dark red.

I moved a little farther in to see behind the L-shaped counter, and sucked in a breath.

Opal Garble lay on her side, between the counter and a metal island laden with cooking supplies. She was in a deep-purple bathrobe, her perfectly coiffed blonde hair spread out on the floor in a pool of blood.

It was rare that another woman could make me feel small. Truth be told, it was rare that a man could make me feel small, but next to Officer Susan Green, I might as well have been a petite waif. Though I'd inherited my father's strong build, adding my own softness and curves to the equation, Officer Green was every ounce as sturdily built as I was. But she looked like she spent every weekend carrying boulders up the side of the mountains. In addition to her girth, she matched my five-foot-ten height, and her gaze leveled with my own. Her pale blue eyes were narrowed and hard.

"You're the one who called in the murder, correct, Ms. —" She glanced at her notepad. "—Page?"

"Yes, that's right." The floorboards above our heads squeaked, and I glanced up. At least three officers were taking care of Opal, while Officer Green stayed with me. She didn't seem overly happy with the arrangement. "I'm the only one here, well, me and Watson." I motioned down to where Watson lay at my feet, his muzzle resting between his stretched-out front paws.

Officer Green made another note without looking at Watson and spoke as she wrote. "Why exactly were you here?"

"I'm opening a bookshop."

"In Heads and Tails?"

I nodded. "Yes, though it will be called the Cozy Corgi."

She lifted her pen and cocked her head at me. "I was under the impression Opal and Lois Garble were going to take over the lease and expand their businesses." It wasn't a question.

"Honestly, I wasn't aware of their desire to do that until I met them when I got into town yesterday afternoon."

"You just moved to Estes Park?"

"Yes, ma'am." The police officer had to be a good ten years younger than me, but being deferential seemed the best way to go.

Impossibly, her gaze grew colder. "Let me get this straight. You're telling me that you just moved in from out of town, and yet you managed to snag the lease of a coveted piece of property away from two local women who've lived here their entire lives? One of whom is now lying dead above our heads."

Again I glanced toward the ceiling. I could almost hear Opal applauding the accusatory tone in the officer's voice. "Well, this piece of property is owned by my mother and stepfather, so...." I licked my lips. "I didn't know anyone was interested in the property when I decided to move out here. My stepfather is a native as well, and my mother was born here, though she only moved back fairly recently."

It seemed having native ties to the town was important, though I wasn't quite sure why I shared all that information. It wasn't like I had done anything wrong, even if Officer Green seemed to think differently.

And it appeared I'd only scratched the surface of how cold both her gaze and her tone could become. "Your stepfather is Barry Adams?"

Suddenly I wanted to lie. It wasn't a sensation I was used to, but since driving into town, it was starting to feel like a habit. "Yes, ma'am."

"And your mother is Phyllis Adams?"

I nodded.

She rolled her eyes. "Of course. Well, that explains a lot."

"It does?"

"Yes. It does." She scribbled some more notes. "My brother owns the magic shop."

I waited for an explanation of that statement, then realized none was coming. I also realized I probably didn't need one. Barry had inherited a ton of property from his family. My mother helped him manage them. They were both wonderful people, and I loved them dearly, but I often pitied their tenants. Despite their good intentions, I was certain that forgetting the code on a lockbox and not knowing which key opened the door was the tip of the iceberg of what their management style was like.

The officer checked her watch, appearing to do some mental calculations before speaking again. "You reported that you got here around five in the morning?"

I nodded again. "Yes, ma'am."

"You can call me Officer Green."

"Yes, ma'am." I shook my head, wondering if I was intentionally trying to channel my mother in that moment. "Sorry. Yes, Officer Green."

She grimaced. "And yet you called dispatch over an hour later. What took you so long to report the death?"

"I called less than five minutes after I discovered Opal. Probably less than three." I gestured around the shop. "Watson and I were inspecting the place. Making renovation plans and how to lay out the bookshop."

She cocked an eyebrow. "Watson?"

I pointed down at my feet.

"Oh." Another eye roll. "Is your dog a master of renovations, or just a literary scholar?"

"Neither, I'm afraid." The officer wasn't a dog person, obviously. Why wasn't that a surprise? "He did discover an owl."

"An owl?"

This time I pointed toward the back room. "In the deep freezer. There's an owl. Watson found it." What was wrong with me?

"Miss Page, a beloved member of the town has been murdered in your shop. Do you really think I have any concerns about an owl?"

"No, ma'am—err... Officer Green." I needed five minutes to clear my head, maybe then I could stop answering questions like a maniac. No, actually, breakfast. I needed breakfast.

She let out a long-suffering sigh, then leveled her stare at me once more. "And where were you before arriving here this morning?"

"At my house. Sleeping." I almost added that it wasn't so much sleeping as trying to sleep, but then reminded myself that I didn't need to ramble incessantly. And that I needed to get ahold of myself, hungry and tired or not. Very few people made me nervous. It was ridiculous that I was allowing Officer Green to get to me. Though, I rationalized, it wasn't every day I stumbled across a dead body. I supposed I was allowed to be little thrown off.

"Can anyone confirm that?"

I pointed at my feet again.

She glanced down at Watson and then returned to her notepad. "Okay then." She scribbled something, then opened her mouth to speak again, but the sound of footsteps on the stairs caught her attention.

I followed her gaze and managed to keep my jaw from going slack. It was a testament to just how overwhelmed I'd been at the sight of Opal that I'd somehow missed this police officer, who carried a briefcase, coming into the shop. At well over six feet tall, he looked like he'd just stepped off the set of some television police drama. I placed him at around forty years old. His stunningly handsome face was all sharp angles and chiseled features. From the way his body moved beneath his uniform, it seemed the chiseling kept going below his neck.

I kicked myself mentally. There was a dead woman upstairs. The last thing I needed to notice was how handsome one of the police officers was. Or that his swept back raven-black hair made him look like an old-time movie star. On top of all that, the last thing I needed or wanted in my life was another man.

He flashed a smile at Officer Green which didn't meet his eyes, and then his bright green gaze flicked my way. He appeared to halt for a heartbeat, his gaze making a quick trip down my body, then back up, and then his smile did meet his eyes. "You must be Ms. Page. You made the initial call, correct?"

"Yes, that's true." Look at that. I *could* speak. And do so without drooling. "My name is Fred."

This time, when he halted a few feet away, his pause was more obvious. His eyes narrowed, but it seemed more out of curiosity than anything. "Fred?"

"Winifred Page, Sergeant." Officer Green's eye roll could literally be heard in her voice. "She's the daughter of Barry and Phyllis Adams."

I started to correct her, but the sergeant stepped up to us and held out his hand for Officer Green's notes.

She gave them over reluctantly, a slight blush rising to her cheeks. Anger, I thought. Not embarrassment.

He flipped through before handing them back. "Thank you, Officer. If you'd help the others, I'll take over with Ms. Page."

For a moment, it looked like she was going to argue, but then she cast an accusatory glance my way. "Yes, sir." She stomped off.

He held out his hand to me. "I'm Sergeant Branson Wexler. Nice to meet you... Fred." A wry smile played at the corner of his lips. "Though I'm sorry it's under these circumstances."

Though his tone stayed professional, I was certain he was flirting. Which was ridiculous. Men like him didn't flirt with women like me. Maybe one more symptom of skipping breakfast.

Granted, he was several inches taller than me, but men like him wanted the blonde bombshell or dark-haired maven. And if they took a walk on the wild side, it would be for the redhead vixen type. Not the curly redhead bookworm. I took his hand, offering him a firm shake. "Nice to meet you as well, Sergeant."

He held my hand for just a moment too long. Long enough to confirm the lack of breakfast had nothing to do with what was happening between us.

Maybe just an interrogation technique?

He motioned toward the counter in the main room. "I noticed some chairs in there. Care to have a seat?"

"Sure. Thank you." I started to head that way, but the sound of his masculine gasp caused me to pause.

"And who's this?" Sergeant Wexler squatted down and

extended the back of his hand to Watson, who gave a tentative sniff, then cocked his head, allowing his ears to be scratched.

Not instant love, but not revulsion either. From Watson, it was almost a ringing endorsement.

"This is Watson. He's a corgi." I wasn't sure why that second detail was needed. Nor was I sure what was wrong with me. I'd gone from nervous with Officer Green to completely flustered with Sergeant Wexler.

And who was I kidding? I knew exactly what was wrong with me.

His smile was genuine, and his gaze stayed on Watson as he stretched out his other hand to offer further scratches. "Watson, huh? Like the little guy who helped out Sherlock Holmes?"

"Yes, exactly. He...." I started to tell him where Watson's name had come from, but for some reason held back. It seemed too personal, considering I'd just met the man. No matter how attractive he was, or that he was making my pulse do stupid things.

After a few more seconds, Watson pulled away, and Sergeant Wexler let out a chuckle. "He's not exactly the cuddly type, is he?"

"Depends on the moment."

He stood. "I suppose the scene of a murder isn't exactly cuddle time." He tipped an imaginary hat toward Watson. "Good call, sir." Then he motioned back toward the main room and smiled at me again. "Shall we?"

We took seats in some folding chairs that were behind the counter. Sergeant Wexler took out a yellow legal pad from his case and placed it on the counter as he scrawled a quick note across the top. "I know you just went through this with Officer Green, but I like to hear things for myself when I can." He paused in his writing and met my gaze once more. Though still friendly, any hints of flirtation had vanished, and he was all business. It put me more at ease. Probably a sad commentary that official police interrogations were easier to handle than possible flirting. "Care to walk me through how you found the body?"

"Certainly." I folded my hands in my lap and decided to give him the quick version. He could ask more questions if needed. "Watson and I came to check out the store. I'm converting it to a bookshop, so I wanted to get an idea of what work I have to do. When we made our way upstairs, that's where I found Opal. Well, where Watson found Opal, actually. I saw the bloody rolling pin and then saw her. I think I probably stared at her in shock for a few minutes, and then I called 911."

As he wrote, he nodded a few times, then looked up again with the next question. "Did you touch anything when you went in? Accidentally knock over the candy or check for a pulse?"

I shook my head. "No. She was very clearly dead. And the room was like that already. Candy everywhere. It was what we found first. Or what Watson found first. There were a few pieces of candy outside the door, and he snagged one before I could get to it." I dug in my pockets and pulled out the two wrapped pieces of candy. The feather fell on the floor, but I snagged it before Watson could get it and shoved it back into my pocket. I held out the candy to Sergeant Wexler. He took them and lifted them to his face for inspection. "You said you found these *outside* the door?"

"Yes."

"The door to the kitchen was closed when you and Watson went upstairs?" He looked at me over the candy.

"These two pieces were on the floor outside the door, and then you went in and found Opal?"

"Yes." I nodded. "Actually there were three pieces, Watson ate one of them."

The corner of his lips quirked into a brief smile, and he made another note. "Any idea what Opal Garble was doing in your shop?"

"No, I…." I sat up a little straighter. In all the hysteria, that question hadn't even entered my mind. Probably because the store didn't feel like mine yet. That and considering it was my first time walking in on a dead body, I probably wasn't thinking too clearly. "I have no idea. Although, it looks like she was baking or…." I thought of the boxes. "Packing?"

"Yes, it definitely seems that way. Strange that she would be cooking here. Obviously I've never inspected it, but I would assume Sinful Bites has its own kitchen. Any thoughts of why Opal would need to bake in your kitchen?" Sergeant Wexler's tone wasn't accusatory or dismissive like Officer Green's had been, but there was definitely a different feel to it now. I couldn't quite put my finger on what it was.

"Like I said to the other officer, I just got into town yesterday. And I've only met Opal once. And this morning was my first time to ever walk into the shop. I wouldn't have been able to tell you what the kitchen even looked like, or where it was, much less why someone was using it."

"But your father and mother own this property, correct?"

"Yes. Though Barry is my stepfather. My father passed away several years ago."

His expression softened for a moment. "Sorry for your loss."

I nodded but didn't offer anything else.

"Do you think your stepfather or your mother were allowing Opal to rent the space for extra cooking room or something?"

"I don't—" I cut off my explanation. Somehow, answering Officer Green's questions had been easier, despite her obvious dislike. Sergeant Wexler's charm and good looks were throwing me off, which was frustrating. I didn't care how charming and good-looking the man was. I wasn't going to say anything incriminating about my stepfather if I could keep from it, not that I had the slightest worry that Barry would do such a thing. The man refused to even use mousetraps, let alone bludgeon an old woman with a rolling pin. Nevertheless, I wasn't going to offer up that he hadn't cared for Opal Garble.

"Not that I know of. It was their idea that I open the bookshop at this location. Granted, I arrived a few weeks earlier than I'd intended, but they'd made it very clear the shop had been vacant since the previous tenant's death."

"Very well, then. Thank you." Another note. "I'll need to speak to them, of course. Do you have their number handy? If not, I'm certain I can get it easily."

"Of course." I pulled out my cell to retrieve their numbers. There was no reason not to give him those.

Before I could answer, another police officer approached. "Sergeant, I think you'll want to see this."

"I'm in the middle of questioning a witness, Officer Jackson. Give me a moment please." His tone was dismissive, almost arrogant, and at odds with how he'd spoken to me.

The other policeman hesitated and then motioned over his shoulder. "Sorry, sir. But we found something rather important in the basement."

There was a basement?

"Is there another body, officer?" Again, Wexler seemed irritated to be interrupted.

"No, sir."

"Then please give us—"

"The basement is a grow house, sir. A large one."

Sergeant Wexler sat up straight, and I gasped. Both he and the other policeman looked at me. His green eyes showed surprise. "You know what a grow house is, Fred?"

I nodded. "Yes. An illegal marijuana-growing operation."

More surprise, and this time obvious suspicion.

At the look, I figured a little more explanation was in order. "My father was a detective. One of the cases he was working on was bringing down an illegal drug ring." The last case he worked on. The one that had gotten him killed.

As Sergeant Wexler got up to follow the other officer, I stood as well. We'd taken a couple of steps before he looked back at me, a thick, perfectly shaped brow cocked, and an air of amusement in his tone. "And where do you think you're going?"

I hesitated. "To the basement...." As the words left my lips, I knew it was ridiculous. Of course I wouldn't be allowed to go.

"Did you already know about the basement, Fred?" He turned toward me fully, his professional demeanor back in place. "Did Watson sniff that out as well?"

I shook my head. "No. He's typically on the search for food, not drugs."

Sergeant Wexler's lips twitched once more. "I'll make sure to document that in my notes, just so suspicion doesn't fall on your corgi." There was that flirtatious tone again.

The officer who'd discovered the basement snorted out a little laugh. "I doubt he would smell it, especially if he wasn't trained for such smells. The room seems to be extremely well insulated."

When Wexler spoke again, any hint of flirtation was

gone. "Be that as it may, I'm afraid I'll have to ask you and Watson to stay up here."

I started to nod, then a wave of claustrophobia seemed to wash over me. "Actually...." I motioned toward the front door. "Do you mind if I get some fresh air? I need to get out of here for a little bit."

He hesitated, considered, then smiled. "Of course, but don't go anywhere, please."

"I'll stay right outside."

He gave another nod and then followed the other policeman to the back of the store.

I didn't bother to look down at Watson, just patted my thigh and headed toward the door. "Come on, boy."

I blinked as we stepped outside, the sunlight hurting my eyes after hours in the dim shop. I checked my watch. Nearly eight in the morning. The other stores were opening, and though it was winter season, a few tourists already wandered the sidewalks, most of them pausing to inspect the police cruisers in front of the shop, then glancing at me.

I considered going back inside to avoid the curious looks, but the thought made my skin crawl. Instead I leaned against the wall of the shop and folded my arms, trying to look unapproachable.

Now that I was outside in the brisk November air, the strangeness of the situation became more pronounced. There was a dead woman in the top floor of my soon-to-be bookshop. A murdered, dead woman. And as if that wasn't enough, a marijuana-growing operation was in the basement.

How had Mom and Barry not noticed it when they'd removed the taxidermy? Although, knowing them, they wouldn't have thought to check a basement. Who knew if they were even aware they owned a basement.

A basement! What a nice thought. I wouldn't have to use the top level for storage after all. I realized I was smiling and then shook my head. Dear Lord. I couldn't allow myself to be that awful. Being happy about a basement when a woman had lost her life? Although, I supposed it was okay to try to find a bright side. I glanced at Watson who was staring up at me. "Don't look at me like that, Judgy."

At the sound of the door opening beside my right shoulder, I jumped and turned around to see someone looking up at me.

"Fred!"

It took me a second to put a name to the pretty round face. "Katie, hi." I glanced behind her into the interior of Sinful Bites. The cases were still filled with candy and sweets. My stomach rumbled. Then I recalled that the owner of Sinful Bites was currently getting a chalk outline above us.

"I didn't realize you were here. Do you know what's going on with all the cop cars?" Katie stepped fully outside. "I arrived about fifteen minutes ago. They were already here."

"Yes, unfortunately I do. I hate to—" Katie's words sank in and I paused. "You just got here?"

She nodded, looking confused.

"Don't most bakers have to get up in the wee hours of the morning to get the day's treats prepared?"

Watson whined, causing Katie and I to look down. He lifted a paw.

"Oh, I said the word, didn't I?" I reached down offering an apologetic pat. "Sorry, boy." I grinned at Katie. "I said the T-word."

"I caught that." Katie sighed, her demeanor shifting to something like annoyance. "And you're right. Most bakers do exactly that, and if it was my shop, that's what I'd do as well. But Opal doesn't like me to come in outside of business hours. I'm supposed to do the baking in between customers during the day. She's very strict about the times I can be here." Katie attempted to look over my shoulder, though it didn't do her any good, considering the windows were still papered over. "The police are in your shop?"

"Yes."

Katie looked up at me expectantly, waiting for an explanation. "Are you okay?"

"I'm fine. Thank you." We stood awkwardly for a few moments while I considered what to do. I was certain I shouldn't tell her anything, but it felt strange to know her boss was dead inside my shop and to just stand out here and pretend everything was normal. I glanced around, making sure no tourists were nearby, and lowered my voice. "Actually, Katie. I'm sorry to tell you this, but...." I swallowed. Crap. What was I doing? I'd never had to break the news of anyone's death before. Although now I'd started, I couldn't think of a way to finish without simply telling the truth. "It seems that... Opal was killed in my store this morning. Or last night. I'm not really sure which."

"Opal was...." Katie took a step back and bumped into the doorframe. She shook her head as if to clear it. "Are you serious?"

"Yes. I'm sorry."

"Opal is dead." Katie shook her head again, then repeated the phrase. "Opal is dead." Her brown gaze flicked up to me. "Killed, you said? As in... murder?"

I nodded, something about Katie's reaction seemed off.

"Wow." Katie blinked a couple of times, her voice seeming far away. "Wow. Murdered. That's really... wow." She glanced back into Sinful Bites and cocked her head.

"Huh. Maybe that means...." Her words trailed off, so I didn't get to hear what that might mean, and when she looked back, there was a blush over her cheeks. "Sorry. That's awful. About Opal."

I couldn't keep from saying, "You don't seem all that upset."

She let out a snort and a half laugh, though it was a dark sound. "You have to forgive me." She gave a little shrug. "I tend to be blunt. And that can throw people off sometimes. But no, I'm not all that upset. Surprised, definitely. Upset? No. Opal wasn't a very nice woman. Wasn't a very nice boss either."

"Yeah, I noticed that yesterday."

Katie's eyes widened at my words.

"Well, I did." I gave a shrug of my own. "I tend to be blunt myself, most of the time." Growing up with a father who was a detective, death wasn't a new topic in my world. Not that he shared his cases with me that much, but he'd never been one to live by the notion that a person shouldn't speak ill of the dead.

Something passed between Katie and I, an understanding perhaps. Once more, I felt the kinship with the woman that I'd sensed the day before. "I'm sure this is absolutely horrible, but I've been up since before dawn, and with all the drama, I haven't had a chance to eat anything. I think my blood sugar is crashing. Any chance you have something more substantial than chocolate in there?"

She beamed. "I do! I have this amazing ham-and-cheese roll that I baked at home last night. I brought it for my lunch. But you can have it if you want. Opal never lets me bake things like that for the store."

"Oh my God, you're a godsend!" I glanced back toward the front door of my bookshop, hesitating. Whatever. I wasn't under arrest, and I wasn't exactly wandering off. I was right next door. And I needed breakfast and to get out of the cold.

Katie hung up the Closed sign and warmed up the roll.

Despite myself, I was unable to keep from making almost embarrassing sex noises as I ate it. And not just because I was ravenous. The thing was pure perfection. A stunning combination of buttery, flaky crust, salty ham, and creamy cheese. Proving just how much I loved Watson, for every two bites I took, I ripped off a piece and tossed it to him. He seemed to enjoy it as much as I did. "Katie, what are you doing working in a candy shop? You need your own bakery."

"Tell me about it. I've been trying—"

At that moment, a door slammed somewhere in the back room, and a second later, Lois Garble stepped into the doorway, her long gray hair wild and her eyes wide. She looked between Katie and me, and when she spoke, I could hear the fear in her voice. "Have either of you seen Opal? She wasn't at home when I woke up. And then I get here to find police cars outside."

Katie and I looked at each other. "Why don't you sit down, sweetie?" The tone and gentleness Katie used when she addressed Lois made it clear she held completely different feelings for the owner of Healthy Delights than she had for the woman's sister. "We need to tell you something."

"I swear, Mom, it was one of the hardest things I've ever had to witness." Watson and I were snuggled together on the couch in Mom and Barry's living room. "Lois completely broke. Screaming, crying. She was hysterical."

"It makes sense." Barry gave a serious nod. "Not only were they sisters, but Opal did everything for Lois. Everything. From managing the money to handling conflict. Not that there was much conflict with Lois, with as gentle as she is. I don't know how she'll cope without Opal."

"She'll be fine." Mom's soft voice seemed miles away, as did her expression as she stared unfocused over my shoulder. "It's amazing the pain a person can go through and survive. How we keep living even when our world crumbles." Again I couldn't help but notice how small Mom was. She'd always been petite, a trait that had gotten squashed by my father's genes, but she seemed more and more fragile.

Barry reached across the coffee table and squeezed her hand, then held it gently.

I knew the moment Mom was reliving. Over the course of the afternoon, I'd relived it several times myself. It hadn't hit me when I'd seen Opal's body, not during the interview with the police, not when I told Katie. But Lois's reaction? I'd seen it before. I'd been with Mom the night the officers came to our door about Dad.

She was right. I wouldn't have guessed Mom would've survived with how broken she was. Much less that she'd move back to her childhood home and marry her childhood sweetheart barely a year later.

The afternoon had drained me. I was beyond exhausted. I had no doubt any sleep I'd missed the night before would be more than made up for the second my head hit the pillow. I didn't plan on setting my alarm.

"They're not letting me back into the shop for several days. They're not sure how long. Though that's not surprising, considering the shop is the scene of a homicide and a secret drug den." I stroked Watson's back, and he let out a long, contented sigh. "Not a great beginning for a place I was going to call the Cozy Corgi. There's not much cozy about murder and drugs."

Mom smiled, seeming to come back to the moment. "Chances are it'll make your opening week so much more successful. I guarantee you everyone will want to drop by, probably take a bunch of pictures and post them online with some murder-hashtag thingy."

"Murder-hashtag thingy?" I chuckled softly, the laughter relaxing me a bit.

"You know, that social media stuff. They use hashtags. Personally I can't stand Twitter, too much drama. But Instagram is fun. Although I don't use too many hashtags on my posts."

Look at my nearly seventy-year-old mom being hip. "I didn't know you had an Instagram account."

"Oh, sure. Verona and Zelda got me going on it. It's a lot of fun. Mainly I just post pictures of the jewelry I make, but sometimes I post about the grandkids on there."

I could just imagine Barry's twins trying to teach Mom how to use social media, I wished I'd been a fly on the wall.

Barry smirked. "Remember that time you accidentally posted the naked picture of me? You nearly lost your account."

Mom rolled her eyes and gave me an exasperated sigh. "I was simply doing it to use the filters. They really do make a picture a thousand times better." She patted Barry's hand. "Not that you need filters, of course." She looked back at me. "I swear, in this day and age you'd think this country would be a little less puritanical. Half the world has a penis. I'm not sure what the big deal is."

"No. No, no, no." I waved my hands in front of my face, letting out a sound that was somewhere between a scream and a laugh. "It's enough that I had to walk in on a dead body today. I cannot handle these mental pictures on top of it all."

"Does that mean you don't want to see the photo your mother and I took this morning? We're sending it out next month as a Christmas card. We're both wearing Santa hats." Barry couldn't keep the smile off his face. "*Only* Santa hats."

"Argh!" I waved my hands again. "I swear you're trying to kill me. Please tell me you're kidding."

Barry opened his mouth, but I cut him off.

"On second thought, don't answer that. It's better not to know. And please take me off your Christmas card mailing list."

Barry shrugged. "Fine. No Christmas card for you." He focused on Watson. "But you will get one, won't you, buddy? You don't want to be left out on Christmas."

At attention from Barry, Watson leapt off the couch and hurried over to get petted.

The place where he'd lain against my thighs suddenly felt cold.

As the two of them had a love fest, Mom turned back to me. "On the bright side, now that you're not going into the store for a few days, we can spend the time getting the house together. I know your things aren't scheduled to arrive for a couple more weeks, but I'll help you do some cleaning, and maybe we could go shopping for some new items before your stuff gets here. Start fresh."

Though it killed me to think about postponing getting the bookshop ready, she had a good point. It would be nice to get the house done as much as we could. "I don't think we need to do much shopping. This house is so much smaller than what I had in Kansas City. I'll be getting rid of a good two-thirds of what I own as it is."

She fluttered her hand in dismissal. "I already said I thought you should leave it all there to begin with. Why you would want anything in your house that Garrett touched is beyond me. There's no reason to bring that negative energy all the way to Colorado."

"Why are you doing this to me? What have I ever done to you?" I rubbed my temples. "First Opal's dead body this morning, then I'm scarred with images of you and Barry engaging in a dirty Christmas photo shoot, and now you bring up my ex-husband."

"What? I'm just saying that there's only so much healing that sage and crystals can accomplish." Mom shrugged. "But if you don't want a fresh start, that's your choice. I'll bring over the crystals and sage anyway."

I latched on to the subject change, more out of desperation than anything. "Speaking of a fresh start, I really appreciate you guys handling the taxidermy. I can't tell you how much I was dreading walking into all those dead animals."

Mom and Barry exchanged looks, and then both turned back to me. Mom stared at me quizzically. "What do you mean, dear?"

I wasn't sure how to answer that. "Well, just what I said. Thank you for handling cleaning the bookstore out. I wasn't sure what I was going to do with the taxidermy that—" I had to recall the man's name. "—Sid had left."

Barry shook his head slowly. "We told you, darling. We hadn't made it down to the shop. We barely had time to pick up at your place and hang the curtains."

I studied them like they were playing the world's most boring, unfunny joke. "Are you serious? You didn't get rid of all the taxidermy?"

They both shook their heads again, and Mom answered

this time. "No. You're saying it wasn't there when you went in this morning?"

Before I could answer, a loud knock sounded at the door.

The three of us jumped, and Watson ran to the door, letting out a vicious bark.

Barry stood with a groan and chuckled. "I swear, as long as a potential robber never sees that little guy in advance, you've got yourself one hell of a guard dog." He walked across the room, patted Watson on the head, and opened the door.

Mom and I leaned around to look, and I sucked in a little gasp at the sight of Sergeant Wexler illuminated in the doorway.

He glanced into the house, gave a little wince and a nod as his gaze met mine, and then refocused on Barry. "Mr. Adams?"

Barry nodded. "Yes, sir. What can I do for you?"

Again Sergeant Wexler grimaced. "Sorry to say, but I need you to come with me to the station for questioning in regards to Opal Garble's murder."

If it hadn't been clear that I'd moved to a small village of a town, sitting with Mom at the police station clarified it instantly. The times I'd visited Dad at the station in Kansas City, the place had been a madhouse, bustling with activity, noise, and chaos. In the middle of it, stood my father—tall, strong, capable of handling anything that came his way.

As we sat waiting for some word, the little police department in Estes Park was nearly as quiet as a hospital waiting room, save for the ringing of phones. There was even one of those inspirational posters of a cat hanging on a branch that was in classrooms when I'd been in school. From the yellowed tattered edges, I figured it was about how long the poster had hung on the wall. If not for the officers in uniform, I probably wouldn't have been able to identify where we were.

Mom kept her hand in mine, forcing me to acknowledge how much more frail she had grown over the past six years. I'd noticed on our visits, but I was shocked that her skin was paper thin, and the bones underneath felt as fragile as a sparrow's. She looked at me with red-rimmed eyes.

"This is taking forever. It's ridiculous. Like Barry could ever kill anyone."

I squeezed her fingers. "We've been on the other side of this a million times, Mom. I'm sure it's just protocol." I spared a glance at the open box of doughnuts on the counter. They'd disappeared gradually as we'd sat waiting. "Things don't seem to be in a hurry here." Nor did they seem to care about stereotypes or leaving their snacks in a break room.

"I can't imagine what they possibly could've found linking it to Barry. We haven't even been in that shop since Sid died. I doubt we've been in it for a couple of years before that, actually."

"Probably best not to speculate. We'll get our answer soon enough." I attempted to keep my tone neutral, even though I wasn't sure why I bothered. "However, it would probably be best to call someone other than Gerald Jackson. I know he and Barry go back to childhood—"

"There's no point discussing it, Fred." Mom cut me off, and there was a touch of steel in her exhausted tone. "Gerald, Barry, and I all go back to childhood, and there's no one else Barry would consider representing him. No one."

"But Gerald? Seriously, Mom? Can you imagine what dad would—" At the sting in her eyes, I shut up. Not the time.

Actually, it was the time. The only time, but bringing Dad into it wasn't going to help.

There was movement down the hall that caught my attention. Officer Green. I was surprised to see her still on the clock. I started to call out to her but then thought better of it. She'd made her feelings about Barry and Mom very clear.

Maybe she was the reason Barry had gotten pulled into this.

Thankfully, she didn't notice us and walked out of sight.

As I was getting ready to return my attention to Mom, and come up with some other argument about Gerald, Sergeant Wexler stepped into the hallway, sipping something out of a Styrofoam cup. The sight of him brought a flash of anger and a sense of betrayal. Even as the emotion cut through me, I was aware it was preposterous. We didn't know each other. He hadn't betrayed me. Still, I went with it. I spared Mom a glance. "I'll be right back."

She followed my gaze and nodded. "Finally. Thank you, dear. You and your father were always better at handling things like this."

It took an effort not to bring up Dad in terms of Gerald again, but I called out to Sergeant Wexler halfway down the hallway and realized the loud echo was coming from me stomping. I slowed, forcing calm into my voice as I approached him. "May I speak with you?"

He hesitated. And I could see some sort of struggle in his beautiful green eyes. *Beautiful green eyes*? The thought only managed to increase my irritation.

"I'm sorry, Ms. Page, but I'm not quite ready to speak to you and your mother yet." He offered a smile, one that I was certain he practiced and used with every family he encountered. Handsome, measured, and cool. My irritation sparked further.

"Then let us see Barry. I'm sure he's a wreck, and it would definitely help my mother."

"Ms. Page, I know you aren't aware of how all this works, but trust me—"

"My name is Fred, not Ms. Page." Even as I hissed out the words, I was aware that no matter what he said, I would've been annoyed. If he'd called me Fred, I'd probably have taken his head off and told him to call me Ms. Page. But I didn't care. "And maybe you haven't been told, but my father was a police detective. Rest assured my mother and I are well aware of how all this works. And I know, especially with as slow as things are around here, you can expedite this if you had half a mind. The very idea that Barry is involved in this is absolutely ludicrous. Anyone who's spent more than two seconds with the man would know that. The fact that you're considering his involvement only shows how incompetent you must be."

Well, that was a dumb move. It was rare that my temper got the best of me, but his handsome face was making me want to bash it into the wall. Or kiss it. Which made me want to bash it even harder.

To my surprise, when he spoke, he didn't sound offended. "Barry Adams was a police detective? I don't think we're speaking about the same man, *Fred*. I might not have lived in Estes Park very long, but I'm fairly certain that detail wouldn't have escaped my attention." Not only did he not sound offended, but if anything, there was an amused twinkle in his eyes. Which was also irritating.

"See, right there. I gave you this information earlier today. Barry is my stepfather, not my dad. Obviously if you can't keep such a simple detail straight, it explains how you could accuse Barry of something so absurd." In the back of my mind, I knew my father would turn me over his knee to hear me speak to another police officer that way. That or die laughing.

Sergeant Wexler's annoyingly twinkling eyes studied me, as one of his stupidly charming grins formed at the corner of his lips. Finally he motioned with his cup to an empty room next to us. "Well then, by all means, why don't you let me know how to do my job."

I stepped in, waited for him to shut the door, and took a

place by the table. I was not going to sit down. "First off, I don't appreciate the sarcasm, Sergeant Wexler."

Yep, full-blown grin. "Branson, please."

"What?"

He shrugged one of his shoulders. "You're the one who insisted we be on a first-name basis, so the name's Branson."

I stared at him. "Are you actually flirting with me right now?" Those words I *hadn't* meant to say.

He opened his mouth to speak, then gave another shrug. "I'm not in control of how you interpret my words, Fred."

I gripped the edge of the table. It didn't wobble. Bolted down, it seemed. Probably best for both of us. I took a calming breath, at least it was supposed to be calming. My temper wasn't going to help Barry.

"What in the world do you have on my stepfather? I don't actually think you're incompetent. I was impressed with your skills today." I figured I'd get more with flattery than anger. And as much as I hated to admit it, I had been impressed with him. "You can't possibly think Barry killed Opal Garble. I don't believe you'd make such a stupid mistake."

"It seems you're the master of the compliment and insult combination." He took a sip of his drink, his grin never faltering. "And since your father was a detective, you're obviously aware I can't share that information with you. You also know I wouldn't bring him in if I didn't have cause."

I did. It didn't make sense, but he was right, mostly, and I knew it. "You can hold him for twenty-four hours without any real cause. It happens sometimes, when the police don't have any real leads but it makes it look like they're doing something."

His grin finally faded. "And that was pure insult. I can

promise you, Fred, I am not that kind of cop. I'm good at what I do." His eyes narrowed. "I will let you know, considering the information I do have, I will be keeping your stepfather overnight."

I balked, and guilt bit at me. Sometimes my temper helped; other times it made matters worse. "Don't do that just because you feel insulted by me. It's beneath you."

"Obviously we don't know each other." He took a couple of steps toward me. Considering the glower on his face, I supposed I should feel threatened, but I didn't. I did feel something, however, even if I didn't want to admit what it was. He held my gaze before continuing. "I can assure you, your critique on my professionalism and skills have nothing to do with why I'm holding your stepfather overnight."

Probably five minutes too late, I opted for keeping my mouth shut. I didn't want to make matters worse than I already had. And strangely, I believed him. He wasn't simply trying to prove a point. As nonsensical as it was, he'd found some connection.

When I didn't speak, Branson's posture relaxed and his tone softened. "I am sorry for what you and your mother are going through. Especially considering you're part of the police family."

His sincerity was clear, and it dampened my anger somewhat. "Thank you." I cleared my throat. "I'm sorry for letting my temper get the better of me."

"I have to admit, I'm a bit surprised that with your connection to how things work that your family has chosen Gerald Jackson." Actual concern laced his voice. "I'll happily call you a better lawyer. You could open the yellow pages, close your eyes, and pick one at random and get a better lawyer."

Tell me about it. "Gerald and Barry are old friends." I attempted to infuse some confidence in my tone. "Barry has complete faith in his abilities."

His eyes narrowed. "Then why isn't Gerald having this conversation with me right now?"

"He stepped out to get a kombucha. He needed some energy." I wanted to crawl in a hole. "Some natural energy."

He smirked, considered for a moment, then nodded to himself. To my surprise, he let the topic of Barry's choice of legal representation drop. "Here's what I can do. Why don't you get your mom, and I'll bring Barry in." He pointed toward the mirror. "I'll be listening in of course." His green eyes twinkled again as he cocked that perfectly shaped brow. "I can trust you to stay away from funny business, right?"

"Unfortunately I didn't come prepared with a nail file. I think we're good this time." To my surprise, I heard the tenor of laughter in my voice. "And thank you. I appreciate you allowing us to speak to him."

"If you want to wait for your lawyer, then—"

We probably should. Gerald might be able to make it where we could have a private conversation, but, I doubted it. We'd be waiting for nothing.

He studied me a bit longer, his smile changing and softening yet again. He started to speak, then stopped with a shake of his head and took a step back. "Get your mom. I'll be right back."

Mom burst into tears as soon as Branson shut the door, leaving Barry with us. She wrapped her arms around Barry and shook.

I didn't resent Barry. Nor had I ever had any feelings of

betrayal that Mom had married him so soon after my father's passing. However, sometimes I wondered whether Dad's death affected Mom less than it did me. Seeing her now took any notion of that away. She'd always been flighty and silly and tender. But she'd also been a cop's wife. There wasn't much she couldn't handle. This wasn't the same woman who'd raised me.

For his part, Barry's eyes were also red-rimmed, and his hands trembled as he smoothed her hair. "It's okay, my dear. It's okay."

I gave them a minute or two, then patted the metal table in the center of the room. "I don't know how much time Branson—Sergeant Wexler is giving us. So let's talk." I waited for Mom and Barry to shuffle over and take seats beside each other, their fingers remaining intertwined. Then I leveled my gaze on Barry. "Trust me, I know you had absolutely nothing to do with this, but I also believe the police have something on you. They wouldn't be keeping you overnight if they didn't."

Mom sucked in a breath and gripped Barry's hands tighter. "They're keeping you overnight?"

Barry turned to me. "They are?"

"Yes. Sorry, but they are." Well, crap, I could've handled that better. "They might not have told you that yet, though I'm certain they've informed you on why they are holding you on Opal's murder. What in the world is going on, Barry?"

He glanced between Mom and me. I swore I could see the guilt in his eyes grow as he looked at Mom. My gut twisted.

Apparently Mom could see it too. "Barry?" Her voice trembled. "Surely you didn't have anything to do with this?"

"Of course not. I would never hurt anyone. Even Opal."

I cast a fleeting glance toward the two-way mirror, though I'd promised myself I'd give Branson the impression I didn't care that he was listening in.

Mom relaxed, already convinced. As was I. I couldn't picture Barry hurting anyone. But neither could I imagine him having that tone regarding anyone who'd just been murdered. There was definitely something there.

I reached out and tapped his arm, holding his attention. "Fill us in."

Again guilt crossed his face, and he lowered his gaze. "You're not gonna like this. And I'm sorry."

Mom flinched but didn't pull her hand away—some of her old resolve showing through. "Then tell me already and get it over with. Whatever it is, we can't deal with it until we're all on the same page."

"Why don't we wait for Gerald. He can't be much longer. He might be able to make it where we have a bit more privacy before we get into this." Another glance towards the mirror. "How hard is it to find kombucha?"

Barry turned wide eyes on me. "He makes his own. He probably had to drive out to Glen Haven. He actually lives across the stream from Verona and Zelda."

Of course he'd live by my stepsisters in a place without cell reception. And of course he'd have to drive all the way there to get his homebrew when Barry needed him. I started to suggest waiting, but really, what was the point? Like Gerald could do anything, even with all natural energy coursing through his veins. "Fine. Go ahead."

I could swear I heard Branson laughing behind the glass.

Barry nodded, then took a long slow breath before launching into a story. "Opal had a side business of making edibles." He fluttered his free hand. "Edibles are baked goods or candy with pot in them. Marijuana."

"You know Charles was a detective in the drug enforcement unit. I'm well aware of what an edible is, Barry." Though she still didn't pull her hand away, Mom's voice was hard. "You also know how I feel about drug use."

"I know. I'm sorry. That's part of why I've never told you." His eyes widened, and he rushed ahead. "And I promise that's all I do. Just some edibles to help me sleep at night. I'm not addicted to heroin, or meth, or anything like that."

Mom rolled her eyes. "I know that, stupid. You mean to tell me you've been using edibles in our house?"

He nodded. "I'm so sorry. I—"

I tapped the table. "Guys, focus. You can figure that out later. What does this have to do with Opal's murder? How does consuming edibles get you arrested? I thought pot was legal in Colorado."

Mom shook her head. "Not in Estes Park. They still don't allow it to be sold."

"But is it legal to use it here?"

They both nodded.

I glared at Barry. "Are you telling me you were selling it? You became a drug dealer?" Maybe we should've waited for Gerald.

Mom gasped, and Barry shook his head emphatically. "No! Never! I just bought edibles from Opal. Or at least I used to." He grimaced. "I started buying them from the store in Lyons after Sid died."

There was a brief knock, and the door opened. Branson stuck his head in. "We need to wrap this up, folks."

"Give us a few more minutes." I met Branson's gaze and softened my tone. "Please."

He nodded. "Just a few more minutes." Then he pulled back out and shut the door. He didn't even smirk. Impressive.

I refocused on Barry. "Cut to the chase. If it's not illegal to use marijuana here, then you're not in trouble for it. What's the catch?"

He turned to Mom, his tone and expression channeling a wounded dog. "A couple of months ago, right after Sid died, Opal threatened to tell you I was one of her customers if I didn't agree to sell the shop to her." He shrugged pathetically. "I wrote her and told her that I wouldn't be threatened or blackmailed, that there was even less chance I'd sell the property to her now, and I would be taking my business elsewhere."

Mom looked at him expectantly, like there was more to come. But I saw where this was going. "You wrote Opal a note? You actually put it in writing?"

He nodded.

It took substantial effort not to roll my eyes. "So the police have a note from you to Opal, one which announces she was attempting to blackmail you and that you weren't having it. It also confirms you were at least partially involved in her illegal business." One part of this didn't make sense, though I was learning things about Barry that I hadn't expected, so who knew? "So you were aware she was using the kitchen in Heads and Tails? It makes you a part of it. At least I'm assuming she was making her edibles there. Did you know about the marijuana plants growing in the basement?"

The disgust that crossed his face left no doubt about his sincerity. "No, I most definitely did not. I have no idea how she's had access to the store. I assumed she was making edibles in her bakery with the rest of the candy. And I'd forgotten the store even had a basement. Though if I recall it right, it was nothing more than a crawlspace, not actually a basement."

Thank goodness for that, at least. Though I wasn't sure if his awareness could be proven one way or another. Even if they couldn't get Barry on murder charges, his property was being used as a grow house and distribution center. "Is there any other connection you can think of that would tie you to Opal? Anything at all?"

He considered for a few seconds and then shook his head. "No. I really don't think so."

I believed him.

Barry turned to Mom. "Phyllis, I'm so, so sorry. I swear it's the only secret I've been keeping from you. You know I'm nothing more than an old mountain hippie. Some habits are hard to break." Tears rimmed his eyes once more. "Even for the love of your life."

Tears slid down Mom's cheeks, but she straightened and squared her jaw. "This is a discussion for another time. We'll figure it out." She sniffed. "Are you going to be okay here tonight?"

"I'm not worried about that. I'm sure I'll be fine." Barry glanced over at me. "Will you and Watson stay with your mom tonight? I don't want her to be alone."

"Of course we will."

As if he'd been listening in, another knock sounded on the door and Branson stepped inside. "I'm sorry, but I really do need to end this now."

"Thank you. We're done here." I smiled at him, genuinely grateful for this small gift. And if I put myself in his shoes, or put my father in his shoes, I didn't blame Branson for what he was doing. "We'll call in the morning to see when we can pick him up."

He hesitated. “Well, that will depend on what we might find—”

“You won’t find anything else.” I intentionally hardened my gaze at him. “And as far as a murderer, you’re wasting your time. Eating a magic brownie before bed and killing someone with a rolling pin are very different things. And again, anyone who’s met Barry for more than a minute, knows that the second one would never be possible.”

Surprisingly, he allowed me to have the last word and nodded as he stepped aside, holding the door open for us.

I stood, then leaned down to kiss Barry on the cheek. “See you tomorrow.” I waited for Barry and Mom to say their goodbyes, then took her hand, and led her out of the police station, intentionally not looking back over my shoulder at Branson.

Just as we walked outside, Gerald rushed toward us. For such a short, round man, he was able to move pretty quickly. I opted to let Mom speak to him while I warmed up the car, otherwise, there might be another murder on our hands.

When we finally pulled out of the police parking lot, Mom finally broke once more, tears streaming, and her frail hands trembling. “I know it’s stupid to say, but I wish your father was here. He’d know what to do. You and I both know that if they can find an easy target to pin this on, they will. You don’t get much more of an easy target than Barry.”

She was right about that. About everything. I took one of my hands off the steering wheel, and clasped hers once again. “I’m not going to let that happen. I promise.”

When Watson and I had driven into town that first evening, I'd taken a wrong turn and entered Estes Park a different way than the usual route. Normally we drove up the Big Thompson Canyon, all the while marveling at the massive stone walls that left a person feeling rather insignificant. Instead we'd entered off Highway Seven, which twisted and turned through the forested mountains and then suddenly opened to such a spectacular view I had to pull the car over and get out.

From high above, safely nestled in the valley of several different mountains was Estes Park. I could see the entire little village. The highway continued down, cut through a huge lake, and then into the heart of Estes Park, the quaint little shops and restaurants the center of it all. Houses and neighborhoods spread out from there to the base of the surrounding mountains. The sky had acted as a huge dome, silvery clouds offering a thick blanket of protection over the town. Snow had been softly falling, and the rays of the dying sun cut through here and there, causing bright patches on the earth below. It looked like Watson and I were entering a magical little world contained in a snow globe. It had been such a good omen to the start of my new life. Of the hope I was pinning on this little town and on the Cozy Corgi.

Now as I stood on the sidewalk looking down the rows of shops, wondering where in the world to begin, I could almost picture myself standing on that outcropping of rock once more. Had it really only been two days ago? Things inside the snow globe weren't exactly how I'd envisioned. Far from it. I'd left behind my life in Kansas City after multiple betrayals. I never would have dreamed I was trading betrayal for murder.

Even with murder and some of the stores closed for the winter season, I couldn't deny the town's charm. It was a storybook. The countless shops that filled several blocks of Elkhorn Avenue were a mix of styles, from mountain chalet to log cabin facade and retro fifties and sixties structures. Maybe retro wasn't the right term, since these hadn't been designed to resemble that time period. They'd simply endured over the past six decades. Vintage… that was better than retro any day.

I'd hoped to wake up to find that Mom and I could go down to the station and pick up Barry. No such luck. They were only halfway into their twenty-four-hour cutoff mark, and for some reason, they were going to use Barry as an example. Probably not a fair thought. Branson didn't seem the type for unnecessary power plays. But what did I know? Although, he had me thinking of him as Branson instead of Sergeant Wexler. That in and of itself was a troubling development.

Mom had opened her collection of wires, strings, beads, and healing crystals. I knew she could get lost in her jewelry making for hours. I couldn't sit still. Nor did I have any desire to get my cabin arranged. My brain might've grown comfortable enough to be on a first-name basis with Branson, but it didn't mean I trusted him to keep from pinning all of this on Barry if he could. I wouldn't sit by and watch that happen.

True, maybe I didn't know what I was doing, but I wasn't entirely clueless either. My father had been a detective, my ex-husband a police officer, and my best friend and I had built a multimillion-dollar publishing house solely focused on mystery novels. I could do this.

I pushed aside the tiny voice that whispered I hadn't seen the signs of my husband's affair nor had I realized all those years later that my best friend was getting ready to shove me out of our business. I couldn't dwell on those things, or I wouldn't have a chance of being a lick of help to Barry.

At the end of the day, it didn't matter if I knew how to do this or even if I could do it. I simply had to.

But where to start? I wasn't sure why, but I felt like the answer was somewhere in one of the shops. Maybe simply because downtown was where Opal had been murdered, but anyway, it seemed as good a place as any. That didn't narrow it down too much. Which shop screamed, "We sell clues about murder"? The shop with knitting supplies, the taffy pulling store, the bread bakery, the T-shirt seller, the magic shop that sat right behind the large wooden waterwheel? I discarded the last notion quickly. At least not yet. Officer Green's brother. I couldn't handle any more hostility, at least not so early in the morning. I stared at the waterwheel, though. The river that cut through town was frozen, so the wheel wasn't turning. I knew the feeling. My wheels weren't turning either.

I glanced down at Watson. "I need you to take over, buddy. I'm making emotional connections with the waterwheel. I can't be trusted." I gestured with his leash down the street. "Lead on."

Watson twitched his ears, sniffed the air, then headed out. I was relieved when he passed the magic shop. It would've been just my luck for it to be his first choice. We passed store after store, not pausing at the Native American jewelry shop, the toy store, or scrapbook supply. To my surprise, Watson only wedged his nose under the doorframe of the delicatessen and gave a great sniff before moving on. The same was true with the cheese shop.

Though the sky was bright, it was cloudy, and the day was cold. It lacked the biting humidity that made the winter in Missouri so much worse, but I still pulled my jacket a little tighter around me. "It doesn't have to be the perfect place, Watson. We just have to start somewhere. Somewhere warm."

He didn't bother looking back and kept right on trotting down the sidewalk. A couple of tourists paused and started to reach out to pet him, but Watson angled away and avoided their outstretched fingers.

I gave an apologetic smile. "Sorry, he's grumpy before coffee in the morning."

They laughed good-naturedly, then ducked into a dress shop.

Coffee! No wonder my brain was foggy. I'd been so antsy to get going I hadn't even taken the time to make a pot. There was a coffee shop a little farther down. We'd stop there.

We were three shops away from caffeine salvation when Watson paused, lifted his nose in the air, then backtracked a few paces and stood in front of a door. I glanced up at the sign, *Cabin and Hearth.*

"Here? Really?" I pointed the way we'd been headed. "We almost made it to coffee."

Watson blinked.

So be it, I was the moron who told my dog to lead the way. The least I could do was actually listen to him when he played his part. "Fine. Have it your way." I pulled open the door, allowing Watson to walk in, and then I followed. The scent of spiced cider wafted over me, instantly making me feel warmer.

A quick glance around threw me off for a second. I'd stepped inside of someone's home. Someone's expensive home. The sensation passed quickly, as the layout wasn't quite right. A large canopy bed made of massive logs sat next to a driftwood bench upholstered in fawn-colored leather. Lamps made of artfully aged metal had cutouts of elk and wolves and glowed amber through their stained glass shades.

There was a commotion somewhere in the back, and a short round woman with cotton-candy, white hair and wearing a gingham dress popped out from behind a display of river rocks that been painted to look like cats. "Hi there, dear! I thought I heard someone come in." Her eyes widened as she took in my height and then warmed at the sight of Watson. "Well, aren't you just the cutest little thing?" She sank to her knees and held out both hands toward Watson. He barely hesitated before accepting her affection.

Strange.

"Carl! Get one of the dog bones," she called out over her shoulder and then refocused on Watson. "And hurry quick. You've simply got to meet this one!"

Dog bones. Of course. How he did it, I had no idea.

Though he was smarter than me, obviously. I should've realized he wasn't looking for clues, just a snack.

The woman seemed to remember I was there, looking up at me again once more. "I should've asked; is it okay if he has a doggy bone?"

"Yes. It is. Thank you." I motioned toward a hall tree made from nothing but antlers. "Your store has quite... unusual things."

"We try. Many of our items are one of a kind. Just because Estes Park has countless houses and cabins doesn't mean they should all be decorated the same." She gave Watson another quick rub, then placed her hands on her knees so she could stand. "You must be visiting. I'm certain I would've remembered this little guy. What's his name?"

"This is Watson." I held out my hand. "I'm Fred."

"Oh goodness, I'm so bad about that. I'm so sorry. I should have introduced myself. I see a dog and just get all wrapped up." She quickly shook my hand. "I'm Anna. And welcome to town. How long are you visiting? Where are you from?" She rattled off the questions without any real interest. She probably asked them a billion times a day to every customer who walked through the door.

That might be me soon enough.

"I actually just moved to town. Into one of those cabins you're speaking of."

Her blue eyes brightened with interest. "How wonderful! Cabin and Hearth can be your one-stop shop. If you have something in mind you don't see in our store, we can order it or have it custom-made for you."

Just then a man carrying a dog bone emerged from the back of the store. He was short and wide, nearly the exact same build as Anna. The hair lacking on the top of his head was compensated for by his fuzzy white beard. Between the smell of cider and the cute chubby couple, I felt like I was meeting Mr. and Mrs. Claus.

Anna snatched the dog bone out of his hand and waved it around as she spoke, causing Watson's head to whip back and forth. "Carl, this is...." Her eyes narrowed in a look I knew too well. "*Fred*, you said?"

I nodded.

She shrugged and kept going. "She just moved into town. Has a little cabin and is looking for a.... What are you looking for, dear?"

"Sorry to say, I'm not looking for anything at the moment. All of my things are being shipped from back home. I'll have to get rid of things the way it is. Downsizing and all."

Both of their faces fell.

"But I love your store. I'm sure once I get everything arranged, there'll be something I'm missing. From looking around, it looks like there's an entire log cabin lifestyle I wasn't aware of."

"That's true." Anna only looked partially satiated. "You might want to reconsider having your things delivered. I always say, when starting a new life, there's no reason to bring all the things from your old one with you."

I couldn't help but laugh. "You know, my mother was telling me something similar just last night."

Another sweep across the room with the doggy bone. "Sounds like a smart woman. Bring her in, I'm sure she'll help you figure out what you need."

Watson whined.

"Oh, look at me. I'm so sorry, sweetie!" She bent slightly and offered a familiar-looking dog bone to Watson. "These are made locally, right across the street at Healthy Delights. Goodness knows, you won't find much else good there, but dogs definitely love Lois's baking, poor dear."

"Anna!" Carl spoke for the first time. Squeaked, rather. "What a thing to say!" He gave me an exasperated look, and though his tone softened, he still sounded rather like a mouse. "Lois is a lovely lady. And if you're looking for healthy alternatives to sweets, that is exactly the place to go." He patted his belly. "The missus and I obviously aren't prone to such sacrifices."

It looked like Anna was going to argue, so I jumped in. Plus, it seemed like the perfect segue. "This will actually be Watson's second bone from Lois. And you're right, he loves them." I pointed to the window. "I'm getting ready to open a little bookshop where Heads and Tails used to be. I met Lois when I arrived in town a couple of days ago."

"You?" Like I predicted, it was all the encouragement Anna needed. She let out a gasp and clutched her hands over her breasts. "I heard someone was moving into that shop." Her eyes widened once more, and her tone grew scandalized. "And what a way for you to enter town. I heard you found Opal, not to mention that drug den growing in the basement."

I'd pegged Anna as loving a good story, but I hadn't thought she'd be aware of all those details already. Maybe the stereotype of living in a small town wasn't all hype.

Before I could think of what to say, Anna grasped my hand. "Tell me all about it. I heard she was hit on the head with one of those meat tenderizers. Gladys told me that yesterday. But *I* told *her* it didn't make any sense. What use would a candy maker have for a meat tenderizer?" I marveled at Anna's apparent ability to not need a breath. "I mean maybe she used it to pound nuts or something, but that doesn't seem very efficient for operating the business.

Not that I would put much stock in anything Opal Garble does. Or *did*, God rest her soul. The murderous tramp."

"Anna!" Carl's squeak caused Watson to let out another whine, despite still chewing on the dog bone. "The woman was murdered. Don't say such things!"

Anna's tirade had been so frenzied, I barely had a chance to take it all in, and before I could consider what to say, she launched in yet again.

"Don't you get me started, Carl Hanson. Just because the woman is dead, doesn't mean she was a saint." She pointed a ring-encrusted finger in my direction, as if I'd been about to take her husband's side. "Believe me, she had it coming for a long, long time. Why, to tell you the truth, I can't believe it didn't happen years and years ago."

Carl *tsked* and cast an irritated glance at Anna, then refocused on me. "Please excuse my wife. It's a small town, and there's not a lot to do here. Sometimes she can get a little caught up in the rumors floating around about people."

Anna planted both fists on her hips and glared. "Don't you dare act innocent. Wasn't it you, just last night, telling me about Peter Miller—" She glanced my way interjecting with a mock whisper, "He owns a glassblowing shop in between downtown and the national park, and is a happily married man and father of three." Then she turned back to her husband and continued at full volume. "—and how you caught him sneaking around with Gentry Sawyer?" She paused to suck in a quick breath and offered another stage whisper my way. "Gentry owns the Christmas shop, which is close to the glassblowing place. He is *also* a happily married man and a father of one. He also has a very cute beagle named Snoopy. Not very original as far as beagle names go, if you ask me, but adorable nonetheless." Then back to full volume and addressing Carl. "So don't you talk about me being the one to get caught up in rumors. Not when you're the one making them." With the last few words, she tapped against her husband's chest.

At the look of scandal across his face, and Anna's heavy breathing, it was all I could do to keep from laughing. I decided to milk it and play along. Swiping a page out of Anna Hanson's playbook, I took a step toward them and lowered my voice. "Since you brought it up, I must admit, I did meet Opal the other day as well. She struck me as rather... abrasive."

"Abrasive?" Proving everything his wife just said was true, Carl's soft-spoken voice lilted and slipped into hyper-drive as he did a complete one-eighty. "I'd say that's a gracious word for Opal." Anna nodded along. "The woman was evil. Pure evil. And a murderer." Unlike his wife, Carl didn't bother with pretending to whisper for effect. "She was known as the black widow around here. She's been married three times."

"*Three* times!" Anna bugged her eyes out. "Three. What kind of respectable woman gets married three times, I ask you?"

"As if that's the point, Anna." Carl cast her an annoyed glance for her interruption. Then back to me. "All three of those husbands? Dead! Every single one. A heart attack here, a car crash there. Black widow, I'm telling you."

"Like I said. Opal Garble had it coming." Anna crossed her arms and lifted her chin.

With his frenzy spent, Carl looked suddenly remorseful. "Well, I still say it's a step too far. One shouldn't speak such things about the dead." He stretched out pudgy fingers and lightly touched my hand that gripped Watson's leash. "What else did you notice when you met Opal the other day?"

I needed to figure out a way to inquire about what happened without becoming known as a town gossip. Although with these two, I doubt it mattered what I said. They'd probably tell any story they wanted about me. So I decided to go for it. "Not much. Just that she was rather rude to Katie, the girl who works for her, and a little dismissive of Lois. Not sure if that's the right word for it. Though I've heard she was the one supporting Lois, so I suppose it makes her not all bad."

They both nodded, but this time it was Anna who spoke. "I have to agree. It was her one redeeming quality. Lois is such a sweet, gentle lamb. Again, her candy making is only fit for... well...." She cast a glance down at Watson. "But even so, Lois deserved a kinder sister. I'd say Opal knew Lois was the one good thing in her life. And the only one who would love her despite her horrid personality. But yes, she was good to Lois, even if it was self-serving."

A gust of cool air swept through the store as the front door opened and a family entered.

Though she looked irritated at being interrupted, Anna raised her voice, sounding cheerful once more. "Welcome to Cabin and Hearth. We'll be right with you. Feel free to look around." When she turned back to me, her smile remained. "Sorry to cut this short, Fred." She bent to pat Watson on the head, but he backed away, his ulterior motive now achieved. "Well, anyway. Welcome to town. It's good to know someone will be taking over the taxidermy shop. Wait, no, you said you're opening a bookshop, didn't you? That's a much better choice. Just remember, we're right across the street. We'll keep an eye out for you. Just let us know if there's anything at all you need. And bring your mother in. We'd love to help you get your cabin in tip-top shape." She looked over at Carl as if suddenly remembering he was there. "Good grief, what are you still hanging around for? We just got that new shipment of decorative pillows in the back. They're not going to unbox themselves."

Carl gave me a little nod, his gaze not meeting mine, before he walked away.

"Nice to meet you again, dear. I hope you and Watson will be very happy in our little town." Anna offered another smile and a little wave before she headed toward the family.

As we stepped back out onto the sidewalk, the day had grown brighter but no warmer. "If I didn't need a coffee before, I sure do now." I smiled down at Watson. "And you most definitely earned yourself another treat. Granted, those two need a whole bucket of salt to go along with anything they say, but nice choice, Mr. Watson. Nice choice."

I wouldn't have pegged Opal as a murderer, but if all three of her husbands had died unexplained deaths, maybe that had led to her being bludgeoned. If nothing else, it was a different angle than the edible business she was running. And about as far away from Barry as I could get.

After a large dirty chai and a cranberry-orange scone, I felt ready to go again. The Black Bear Roaster hadn't had dog treats, but I'd given Watson a couple bites of my scone. He'd more than earned it.

Not only had the time inside the coffee shop given me a chance to warm up, but after replaying some of the conversation I'd had with Anna and Carl, I was feeling hopeful. Maybe I actually could do this. I didn't have any real hope of solving Opal's murder, but I was beginning to feel more confident that I could at least get enough leads to punch holes in Barry being the main suspect.

Rebundled against the cold, Watson and I stepped outside, then hurried across the street and began to walk back up the other side of shops. Finding out about Opal's three dead husbands was unexpected, but it didn't narrow down which shops might offer the best leads. I hadn't seen a casket shop among the bunch. Where did one go to find out who was angry about dead husbands? I turned it over to Watson again. But he didn't stop anywhere, just dipped his head and trudged past countless shops. Until we arrived in front of Heads and Tails. At least that was where I thought we were stopping, figuring that Watson recognized our shop. Instead he came to a pause in front of Healthy Delights.

I glared down at him. "Seriously? A huge dog bone and nearly a fourth of a scone, and this is what you have in mind? Granted, I agree, the scone was a little dry and could have used some more white-chocolate chips, but still."

I glanced in the window. The store was dark, just like Sinful Bites. No sign of Katie or Lois, nor did I hear any commotion from inside my shop either that would lead me to believe the police were still there. But I'd been given strict instructions not to enter until I'd received an all clear.

"Sorry, buddy. Your favorite shop is closed." I motioned forward. "Lead on. Where to next?"

Watson simply blinked up at me, then returned his attention to the door of Healthy Delights.

"Fine." I stepped around him. "I suppose you've done enough this morning. We'll see how I do." I led Watson past a shop that did old-fashioned tintype photography, an ice cream parlor, a shop with nothing but cupcakes, and a pet store. The last one, I had to drag him away from. Doubtlessly, he could smell the dog treats inside.

With none of the shops calling to me, we ended up across the street from the waterwheel. Directly in front of Victorian Antlers. I'd expected to drop in later in the day to say hello, but there was no time like the present. Plus, though not at Anna and Carl's level, Percival and Gary could gossip with the best of them.

We were barely ten feet inside the antique store when there was a squeal, and a tall thin man, wearing a deep-purple fur coat, rushed from behind the counter waving his arms in the air, then wrapped me in a huge hug. "I've been waiting for you to drop by!"

I hugged him back. "Hi, Uncle Percival. It's good to see you, as always."

He pulled away, holding me at arm's length as he inspected. "Hair, gorgeous and flawless, as always. Eye makeup"—he waffled his hand—"better than when I saw you last year, but we need to work on a stronger cat eye. Good lip, though. I'm glad you remember it's all about a dramatic eye and a subtle lip gloss." His gaze traveled down my body, and he grimaced. "Still, Fred? Really? Do you really need another lecture? How you can share my genes and still think a broomstick skirt is ever appropriate, I simply can't understand. I swear even Barry's daughters have a more innate sense of style, and I'm fairly certain that man has tie-dye in his veins." He picked a dog hair off my shoulder, and then a smile broke through, and he patted my cheek affectionately. "But nevertheless, you're family, so I must love you despite your fashion taste." His eyes narrowed. "At least tell me you're not wearing cowboy boots under that monstrosity."

"Fine. I won't tell you."

He let out a howl, and I couldn't keep from chuckling.

"That's a lot of criticism from a man wearing a purple fur coat. What animal in the real world is purple, anyway?"

He gasped. "Darling, it's faux fur. I may live in the mountains, but I'm not a heathen. And the color is boysenberry, not purple." Next to her older brother, my mom seemed the epitome of common sense and restraint. His brown eyes twinkled in affection as he looked at me, and he raised his voice once more. "Gary, baby, get out here! Our prodigal niece has returned to the fold!"

A man the exact same height as Percival lumbered from somewhere in the bowels of the overly packed shop. Though he was the same height, the similarities stopped there. At sixty, Gary was ten years younger, soft-spoken, somehow managed to retain his physique from his pro-football days, and was about as excitable as a possum playing dead. His dark face spread into a handsome smile as he pulled me into an embrace. "Good to see you, sweetness." His deep baritone rumbled through me.

They both said their hellos to Watson, who received them with familiar ease but not much more, and then they turned their attention back on me. Percival grabbed my hand and held on. "I talked to your mother earlier this morning. She told me all that was going on. And she said you were doing your own investigation."

"No." I shook my head. "I'm not investigating. I'm not pretending like I'm Dad or anything. But it's ridiculous that they think Barry had anything to do with it. I figure I might as well find out anything I can if it helps clear his name."

"You always were your daddy's girl." There was such affection in Gary's tone that I couldn't help but smile at him as I tried to hold back the burn behind my eyes. Gary had gotten along with my father like gangbusters whenever they'd visited. Mom and Percival chatting about fashion and food and movies, while Dad, Gary, and I talked sports. I never cared all that much for sports, but knew if I waited long enough, Gary would get Dad to start talking about his open cases, and after a few beers, Dad always said a little more around me than he would've at other times.

I decided to cut through the pleasantries. "What do you guys think about Bran...er... Sergeant Wexler?"

"Branson, huh?" Percival's brows shot up, always too quick for his own good. "I'd say he's a handsome devil."

Gary rolled his eyes, but nodded. "He seems like a good man. We've not had too much interaction with him. He's only been in Estes for the past three or four years. Seems like a fair guy, though." He shrugged. "Unless, of course, he keeps Barry in there much longer. You just have to meet the guy for two seconds to know he's not going to do anybody any harm."

I hesitated for a heartbeat, trying to determine if I was betraying Barry's confidence, but figured it was more important trying to find out any other details which could exonerate him than to keep his secrets. Even so, I glanced behind me as if there were customers in the store. "Did Mom tell you why they're keeping him?"

Percival and Gary exchanged glances, and then Percival pinched his forefinger and thumb together and held them up to his lips while making an exaggerated sucking sound.

It was my turn to roll my eyes. "Yes. Something like that."

"I do hate how your mother found out like she did. She's a gracious woman, but she's never been the most open-minded about substances. Of course being married to your father didn't help the situation, I suppose. I always worried what she would think if she found out about Barry."

"You knew already?" It wasn't like Percival and my mother to keep secrets from each other.

My uncles exchanged glances once more. "Darling, it wasn't exactly a well-kept secret that Opal could get a guy what he needed, at least for those of us who needed it. Granted, we didn't know where she was making them, not that it would've mattered."

"Or that she had a small fortune of pot growing in the basement." Gary let out a low whistle.

I nearly asked if there had been confirmation on the amount of marijuana she'd been growing, but then realized the implication of their words. "Wait a minute. You guys too?"

Gary had the decency to look a little embarrassed. "It's legal now."

Percival let out a snort. "Oh yes, we waited until it was legal." He squeezed my hand before letting it go. "Darling Fred, not everyone grew up in a police state household. Some of us were children of the sixties and seventies. And trust me, edibles barely register. Yesterday's pot is today's kale. Now, if you really wanna have a good time—"

I held up my hand. "Unless you think this can help Barry, please, spare me the details."

"Exactly." Gary glared at his husband for a second, then looked back at me. "Besides, Barry quit going to Opal quite a while ago. True, at the time we didn't know it was because Opal was threatening to spill the beans to Phyllis. Barry just told us he liked the product in Lyons better."

Percival waved him off. "So fill us in. What have you discovered so far?"

"Not much. In fact, outside of stopping for coffee, the only place I've been is Cabin and Hearth."

Gary let out an uncharacteristically loud whoop and slapped his knee. "You started with Anna and Carl? Girl, you hit the ground running!"

Percival rubbed his hands together in anticipation. "Chances are whatever they said was a bunch of hogwash, but I'm sure it was delicious. What did they tell you?"

Again I hesitated, feeling like if I really was going to look for clues, I needed to keep things to myself. But they were family, and who knew, maybe what I'd heard would trigger something one of them knew but hadn't thought was important. "Well, have either of you heard the rumors of Opal being a black widow?"

"Black widow?" Percival's face fell. "That's all you got out of the Hansons? Sweetie I could've told you that. Everybody talks about her being responsible for killing all those men. Of course nobody's offered a shred of proof. Lord knows, she was mean enough to do it."

"Nah." Gary grimaced. "She wasn't the nicest woman around, but she wasn't a murderer. And I always got the impression she loved every one of her husbands. At least as much as Opal could love anyone outside of Lois. She wasn't a killer."

I glanced at Percival for confirmation. He shrugged as if the admission cost him. "Yeah. I have to say I agree."

Like in the cabin furniture store, we were interrupted by a gust of cold air, and the four of us looked over at the tiny woman who entered the shop.

I did a double take when I recognized Lois Garble underneath the black veil of her hat. It took her longer to recognize me, but when she did, she halted for a heartbeat and then hurried toward me. "Oh, Fred." She shocked me by throwing her arms around me, at least as far as she could reach. "I was planning on trying to find you today. You were so sweet to me when I was such a mess yesterday. It was the worst moment of my life, but I'm so glad I had you and Katie there to hold me together."

I patted her back and glanced at my uncles, wanting salvation. She really had been hysterical, but Katie had been the one to hold and soothe her. I'd been utterly clueless on what to do and only mumbled some nonsense as I patted her shoulder.

After a second, Lois pulled back and noticed Watson. "Oh, and you, sweet baby. I don't have any of my bones with me. I'm so sorry." She rifled through the basket in her hands, then pulled out what looked like a gingerbread man and looked at me. "Not exactly a dog treat, but it's all natural. No chocolate or anything. Do you mind?"

Watson left out a chuff which clearly meant I'd better not screw this up for him. "Of course. That's very kind of you, Lois."

She handed him the cookie, and Watson took it, then began to prance away. He glared back at the end of his leash. I dropped it so he could wander behind the counter and eat his treasure in peace. Lois pushed the basket toward Percival and Gary. "I've been baking up a storm. That's how I cope. If I stop for even a second, I just end up sobbing. But now I don't know what to do with all the things I've made. I can't bring myself to open the store. I just don't have it in me. Even the thought of going by the shops makes me want to die. It just makes me want to die."

Percival slid the basket of baked goods on the counter with a distasteful look on his face before he and Gary gathered around Lois, comforting her like the wounded little bird she was. "You're not alone in this, Lois. You've got the whole town behind you."

"Percival's right, sweetie. We're all your family now. All of us."

"You are both wonderful." She sniffed, and through the veil, a tear glinted on her cheek. Lois turned to me. "I'm so sorry, how rude. You were here, and I just walked in and interrupted. Please don't let me keep you if you're shopping or need help. I know you have a new house to furnish. I'm sure you need some beautiful antiques. You couldn't find better than Percival and Gary here."

"Oh no, Lois, you're not interrupting at all." Despite myself, I was tempted to pat her on the shoulder again. Lord knew what good that would do.

"Fred is our niece. Her mom is Percival's sister." Gary's smooth voice somehow made such an innocuous statement sound comforting. A skill I most definitely didn't have.

It took her a second, but then Lois let out a little chirp. "Well, that shows you what a mess I'm in. Of course she is. We talked about that when we met the other night. You're Phyllis and Barry's daughter." Another chirp and she left the embrace of my uncles and grabbed both of my hands in hers. "Oh, Fred. I wasn't even thinking." She sniffed. "I heard about poor Barry. Of course I called them instantly and let them know they had the wrong person. Barry's the sweetest man. There's no way he would ever do anything like that to Opal."

I'd already liked Lois, but she stole my heart in that moment. "You did? You called the police station?"

"Well, of course I did. I want justice for Opal, but not at the price of an innocent man."

"Thank you." It was all I could say before my throat constricted.

She squeezed my fingers before letting go, looking back at my uncles. "And actually, I have to thank you for receiving me so kindly. I've taken a couple of baskets to a few of the other proprietors downtown. Not everyone has been so welcoming. It's so embarrassing I almost just went home. But I can't stand to be by myself right now."

Gary's muscular chest puffed up. "Who's not been welcoming to you, Lois? I can't even imagine."

Lois sighed, the noise making her sound sickly. "I can. I understand it completely. I've never been so embarrassed in my life." She sniffed again. "One minute I'm a sobbing wreck because I don't know how to get through a moment without my sister, and the next I'm just so mad I'm shaking. So humiliating. To find out that some people knew. This whole time, they've probably been looking at me, thinking I knew about what Opal was doing. About the"—she dropped her voice so it was barely audible—"drugs."

Not having any of Gary's skills at comfort either, Percival nearly squawked. "What! You mean you didn't know?"

Lois started to cry.

I stood several paces away while Gary and Percival tried to put Lois back together again. Right when it sounded like her breathing was becoming close to normal, my cell vibrated in my pocket. It was Mom. I hit Accept and held it to my ear. "Are you okay?"

"Yes!" Her voice was a million times brighter than when I left her that morning. "They just called. They're releasing Barry on bail. But I'm too worked up to drive. Will you please come get me, Fred? We can pick him up together."

"Those cots at the jail are surprisingly comfortable. The food left a lot to be desired, but it was a great night's sleep." Barry grinned happily at me in the reflection of the rearview mirror.

He and Mom wanted to sit together, so they were crammed into the back of my Mini Cooper. Watson had his typical place beside me in the passenger seat. I'd expected to pick up a frazzled, haggard-looking Barry. Instead, he was chipper, obviously well rested, and bright-eyed.

"Oh, and you'll never guess who my cellmate was last night." Barry clapped his hands together once. "But try. Guess."

Mom giggled and seemed to give it some actual thought. "The first person I can picture in jail would be Mark Green, but I don't think you'd seem so pleased by it if it was him."

He shuddered. "Dear Lord no. I would've had to sleep with one eye open."

I glanced at the rearview once more. "Who's Mark Green?"

"He owns the magic shop." Mom's tone took on an apologetic tone. "I know it's ungracious of me to say, but he's not the nicest of men."

Green. Of course. I should've realized. Officer Green's brother. It seemed the dislike went both ways.

Before I could ask for more details on that, Barry nudged my shoulder from the back seat. "Your turn, Fred. Take a guess."

"Seriously, Barry? You just got out of jail and are playing guessing games?"

He *humphed*. "Fine. I'll just tell you." He turned his attention to Mom, since she was actually interested. "Simon Faulk."

"Who...?" Before Barry had a chance to reply, Mom sucked in a surprised breath. "Oh, Simon! The new manager of Day of Lace. I've only met him a couple of times. But he seemed like a nice young man."

"Very! I was charmed by him. I must say, it was a pleasant way to spend the evening. It seemed he and Rion got into it about a new shipment of wedding dresses, and Simon punched him. Which, honestly, I can't see him doing. He really is a gentle soul." Barry let out a long-suffering sigh. "He got out before me this morning. I must say, the few hours after he left simply dragged by. I never would've guessed there was so much behind-the-scenes drama in the wedding dress business."

Mom made a knowing *cluck*. "Capitalism, dear. Not good for the soul."

I couldn't hold back my laughter, and dared to glance into the back seat. "You do realize you two own at least a fourth of the properties downtown, right?"

Mom furrowed her brows. "I don't see your point, dear."

I knew better than to wade into that murky pool. Though I turned back to the road, I addressed Barry. "And I'm glad you felt like it was a vacation, while Mom and I were worried sick about you last night."

"No need to worry. I have to say, Sergeant Wexler obviously thought I was up to no good, but he was kind with me. I hated he wasn't there when I left. Maybe I'll bring him back a thank-you card or something."

"Don't you dare! I don't care if Opal was trying to blackmail you. And I don't care if Branson was right to hold you on suspicion. We do not give thank-you cards for someone putting us in jail."

"He let me out again, Fred. That counts for something."

I glared at him in the mirror. "Because he was pushing the twenty-four-hour mark, Barry. You're not cleared of anything yet." I loved them both, but sometimes their easy-breezy nature rubbed me the wrong way. "And while we're at it, why didn't you guys fill me in on the rumors about Opal? Maybe this whole thing has nothing to do with her making edibles or growing pot. With three dead husbands, surely there's some angry extended family out there who blame her and want their revenge."

Mom chuckled. "That's just silly, darling. This isn't a Lifetime movie. And those are just rumors. I won't say Opal was my favorite woman in the world, by any means, but she wasn't a killer."

I nearly asked what kind of movies she'd been watching on Lifetime, but decided it was beside the point. "Just because you think so, doesn't mean someone who cared about one of those husbands feels the same. Even if we can't figure out who it is, it's a completely different direction on this case, one that would prove it has absolutely nothing to do with Barry." I turned off Elkhorn Avenue and onto the road leading to their house.

"Oh, Fred." Mom reached up and squeezed my arm. "Please be careful."

I glanced back at her again, startled. "What do you mean?"

"You just referred to this as a case. You sound just like your father. I'd like to tell you to leave it alone. Let the police handle it. Barry's innocent, it will come through. Whatever's happening, someone killed Opal. And if you're treating this like a case, it means someone's not going to like that you're snooping around." She sighed. "But I also know you are your father's daughter. It wouldn't do any good to ask you to stop, or even beg. So be careful. I can't lose you. I won't."

I didn't know what to say to that. My heart warmed at being compared to my father, which I knew was silly as I was constantly being compared to my father by anyone who knew him, but it still made me feel like he was near every time it happened. I hadn't thought I'd been putting myself in danger. Maybe that was silly too. Asking questions about a murder? Obviously it wouldn't be appreciated by the actual murderer. I ignored that thought as I pulled up in front of their house.

"Maybe you're right. Maybe it has nothing to do with Opal being a black widow. But I'd like you guys to think about those husbands, if you knew them. If they have any family in town. Maybe you might find an option of someone who is capable of killing someone with a rolling pin." After I put the car in Park, I swiveled back to look Barry in the face. "What's the name of your dispensary in Lyons? Or is there just the one?"

He cast a guilty glance toward Mom but answered, "Green Munchies."

Mom rolled her eyes.

Barry refocused on me. "You're going there? I'll come with you."

"Oh, no you don't!" Mom clamped a hand on Barry's thigh. "The last thing we need right now is you being caught buying more edibles."

The insulted expression that crossed Barry's face was nearly funny. "I'm not going there to make a purchase. You just got done telling Fred to be careful. I'm going as backup." He scrunched up his nose and lowered his voice to mutter. "And if I did buy something, it's legal there."

I pointed my finger at them. "Number one, this isn't a case, no matter what I said. Therefore, I don't need backup. I'm just going to check it out and ask questions. Number two, and most importantly"—I gave an unwavering stare at Barry—"you're not going."

"But—"

"You're not going!" Mom and I chimed in unison, and then chuckled at each other.

It began to snow in earnest over the half-hour drive to Lyons. I'd wondered if I'd have to get a new car, considering winter in the mountains. But so far, the front-wheel-drive seemed to be cutting it. I found Green Munchies easily enough. I'd never been in a dispensary before, and had expected to pull up to a dilapidated building that was probably close to being condemned. Instead, the new construction was a modern square of concrete, glass, and lightly colored wood.

During the drive, I convinced myself that my growing nerves were more about the snow and possible slick roads than where I was headed. But the self-deception faded along with my nerves as I looked at the place. It didn't feel like walking into a dangerous drug den at all.

As we weren't in a crowded area, I didn't bother with

the leash, letting Watson keep pace beside me as we exited the car and walked up the pristine sidewalk.

I was unable to stop myself from gawking when we entered the store. It was like Whole Foods and Apple had a night of passion and produced a drug-wielding baby. Like the outside, the space was sleek and shiny. The open concept was minimalistic yet had high-end finishes. The cases however, were space-age, massive plastic white ovals which glowed softly. No wonder Barry said things had been more expensive here.

Watson and I slowly passed the first couple of cases. An endless array of what I supposed were pot leaves were labeled with names I would expect at a high-end coffee shop. And on the other side, the baked goods put the stunning display I'd seen in Sinful Bites to shame. I addressed Watson even though I didn't take my gaze from a red-velvet brownie. "Don't even think about getting a snack here. If you keep going as you are, you're going to be so fat you'll be nothing but a ginger-furred log." Not to mention I couldn't imagine how expensive a dog treat in this place would be.

A soft chuckle from behind caused me to jump, and I whirled around. I blinked at the handsome man behind the counter. At least I thought he was handsome, behind the costume. I had to remind myself that Halloween had been a couple of weeks ago.

"Sorry, I didn't mean to startle you." The man smiled gently. "I didn't hear you all come in. Do you often have conversations with your dog?"

Conversations with my dog? I glanced down at Watson, who peered up at me. Huh. I hadn't actually thought of that. "You know, I suppose I do."

"He's a cute little fella. And we do have dog treats here.

I know you're worried about him becoming a log, but he would be an adorable log."

Watson yipped at his favorite word.

I ignored him. "No, thank you. He's had enough. And as funny as it might be, I wouldn't consider myself a very good corgi mama if I got Watson high."

Confusion crossed the man's features, and then he shook his head. "Oh no, the dog treats are just boring old dog treats. None of the good stuff in them."

Another yip from Watson.

The man pulled on his handlebar mustache. "Well, even if your dog can't have a treat, we've got lots of treats for you. Any you'd like to check out?"

Watson growled. I glared at him, then cast the same expression on the man. "You've got to quit saying that word."

More confusion. "What word?"

I pointed at Watson as I mouthed, "*Treat.*"

His bloodshot eyes widened, and then he smiled. "Oh. Of course. Sorry." He considered for a moment, pulled on his mustache again. "Well then, any *delicacies* you'd like to try?"

With the second pull of his handlebar mustache, the full picture of his costume came together, and I realized it wasn't a costume at all. The brown fedora with a small red feather, skintight goldenrod-colored shirt under an equally skintight silk vest, gray scarf, and vivid tattoos covering his thin arms, which were revealed by his rolled-up sleeves. He was a hipster. But not like the ones we had back in Kansas City, at least not like any I'd seen. I tried to focus on the task at hand.

I was disconcerted enough being in a dispensary, but the unexpected combination of designer ambience and an updated version of Mark Twain as a drug pusher was throwing me off. "I... er... honestly, I've never been in a store like this before. I'm not really sure where to start."

His eyes glinted. "A virgin. Looks like school is in session." He gestured to different locations around the store. "What do you think you are most interested in? Smoking, vaping, tinctures, oils, edibles?"

Tinctures? "Uhm... edibles?"

"Edibles!" He nodded sagely. "That's what I thought. You look like an edibles type of girl."

Again he took my words away. I looked like an edibles type of girl? I wasn't certain if it was a commentary on my weight or not. And as I was at least fifteen years older than the guy, I wasn't sure he should be calling me girl.

He didn't seem to notice my discomfort, talking to me as he turned and headed across the store to the case with the red-velvet brownie I'd been eyeing. "Edibles are a great place to begin. A lot of people are less nervous around them. You do have to be careful with consumption, though. It's easy to get too much if you don't know what you're doing or if you're not sure of the quality or quantity of marijuana in the product. I can guarantee you everything we sell here at the Green Munchies is the highest of industry standards, and I'll be able to guide you on the right dosage on whatever you choose." He came to a stop behind the counter, placing both hands on the glass, the lights from the overarching oval casting strange shadows over his features. "The name is Eddie, by the way."

I was still trying to process his spiel, and it took me a moment to land on the appropriate response. "I'm Fred. And this is Watson." I had a moment of panic, wondering if I should have come up with an alias. Too late now, and probably silly to even consider. It wasn't like I was under-cover or anything. Or that I was a detective at all, for that matter. I was an ex-professor, turned ex-publisher, turned bookstore owner. That was it.

Eddie pointed at small squares of fudge which had a layer of pecans, swirls of caramel, and crystalline chunks of salt. Mouthwatering. I was going to have to give myself a similar lecture about treats as the one I'd given to Watson.

"These are one of our more popular items. And what I would recommend to someone trying edibles for the first time. It's easy to cut off the amount you need. You can freeze it, and it's just as good later on. That's not always true with some of the baked items." He then pointed to a smooth glistening bar of chocolate. "Of course, this is the same sort of deal, if your tastes run more simply. We also offer a punch card. You get twenty-five percent off a future order once you've spent five hundred dollars. Enrolling is free, and I highly recommend it."

I suddenly felt like I was being pressured to sign up for Amway or getting a membership to Costco. This was what buying pot was like?

My father was killed before marijuana became legal anywhere in the country. I was certain none of his under-cover drug dealings had ever resembled this. I couldn't even fathom what he would say or think if he stepped into Green Munchies, or what he'd make of Eddie.

The thought made me want to bolt. Dad had been on my mind too much over the past day. It made sense, I knew, but it was leaving me shaky. Maybe coming here had been a mistake. At least at the moment. I'd buy something quickly so I'd leave a good impression and get back to Estes. "I'll just get whatever you recommend."

No sooner had the words left my mouth than I could swear I felt my father's disapproval. Or maybe it was just

Watson still glowering at me after denying him a treat. Either way, I couldn't waste this moment. But how to turn the conversation without causing suspicion?

The answer was obvious. "My stepdad, Barry, recommended your shop. However, he didn't tell me what he normally gets. Chances are low you remember him or his order." That was a lie. If Eddie had ever been in here when Barry came knocking, I had no doubt he would remember. Although, who knew? Maybe in the dispensary business, characters like Barry were a dime a dozen.

"Barry?" Eddie's voice brightened and lost every ounce of its professional tenor. "Tie-dyed, hippy Barry from Estes Park? That Barry?"

I nodded. Apparently not a dime a dozen.

"Dude! That old guy is dope! Like he's the real thing." Eddie cocked his head, studying me. "Wait a minute, you're his daughter? And you've never tried pot before?"

"*Step*daughter."

"Ahhh." He nodded. "Right. That makes sense, I suppose. Well, I will definitely hook you up. And to top it off, I'll go ahead and give you the twenty-five percent discount today. I love that guy. Meant a lot that even though he could've purchased in Estes, he'd drive all the way down here to the source. A percentage is a percentage, don't get me wrong, but it helps me out when customers come directly to my place." Eddie pulled out what looked like an expensive candy box, and began to fill it with an assortment of brownies, chocolate-covered pretzels, a few cellophane-wrapped hard pieces of candy, and gummy bears. "I assume you want his normal?"

This was his normal? If Barry was buying this much, I marveled he was able to keep his stash away from Mom. "Sure. That's great."

He continued to fill the box as he spoke. "But seriously, Barry is awesome. Super chill, and like straight-up legit. I swear he taught me a thing or two about how to smoke up."

Good God. If he kept going, I was afraid I was going to learn things about Barry I definitely didn't want to know. Something Eddie said echoed in my mind as he prattled on, and I sucked in a little gasp.

Eddie glanced at me. "You okay?"

I nodded, trying to determine how upfront to be. I decided to go for it. "You said Barry comes to the source? Does that mean Opal got her... supplies from you?"

Eddie jerked, his expression growing dark. Apparently he hadn't realized how much he'd said.

I'd already messed things up. That was fast.

He considered for a moment, then shrugged, though he didn't look any happier. "You're Barry's girl, so you're dope by association." He leaned forward, his voice lowering not so much to whisper but in anger. "Don't get me wrong, I'm a pacifist, but I'm not going to lie. I heard what happened to Opal. I'm not shedding any tears. People like her deserve what they get."

I pressed a little further; why not? "Yeah, Barry seems not to be her biggest fan either. Which, you've met my stepdad. He likes everybody."

"Exactly!" Eddie practically snarled. "Sid and I had a good thing going for years. I'd grow the stuff, give him a fair price, didn't demand too much share of the profit. It was chill. Easy, cordial. Granted, what he did with all those animals wigged me out. I'm a pacifist, like I said." He shuddered but kept going. "Then he started dating that candy woman, and she convinced him they could make a ton more money if they started growing their own product." He straightened, holding his arms out as if he was being crucified. "You know how much I have to pay for the license to grow? How much inspection I have to endure? And she thinks she can just walk in, do it all behind closed doors, and reap all the profit? Like I said, I didn't do her in, but she had it coming."

She had it coming. That seemed the theme around Opal Garble. And she'd been dating Sid? That was news, but I didn't want to let on I hadn't known that part. "She was stealing business from you and getting away with it without having to pay any of the fees and go through all the red tape. Why didn't you turn her in?"

"Believe me, I threatened to. Course that evil woman just laughed. Told me to go ahead. Said she'd bring me down with her."

"How could she do that? You said yourself you're already paying the fees and going through inspections."

Behind his handlebar mustache, Eddie's cheeks turned bright red. "Yeah, but I was also supplying Sid with product. And Estes Park, with its holier-than-thou attitude, still refuses to let a dispensary inside its town borders." His snarl was back. "As much as I hate to admit it, there was no way I could take Opal down without doing the same thing to myself."

"Ah. I suppose that makes sense." It really did. And it looked like Mom and Barry were probably right. With Opal seeming to be comfortable blackmailing and threatening people, the three dead husbands probably weren't even on the radar. I refocused on Eddie, remembering I needed to play the part of Barry's dope stepdaughter, not that I was really sure what it meant. "Man. That really does suck. Well, at least you know you did things the right way and you don't have to worry about Opal anymore."

"True story." Eddie smiled and relaxed again, another

twinkle glowing in his eyes. "Plus, I'm betting another bakery will open to replace whatever shop Opal had. Maybe I'll get my foot in the door once more."

I forced a friendly shrug. "One can hope."

"No doubt!" Eddie held up the box that was nearly filled to running over. "This look all right for you?"

What in the world was I going to do with all of that? "Looks great, thanks!"

"Awesome." Eddie beamed like he'd expected me to say no. "Good thing I'm already giving you a twenty-five percent discount. You're gonna get your money's worth today!" He shut the box and pulled out a green ribbon to tie around it. Definitely not what I expected from a dispensary. "I almost feel sacrilegious for asking this of Barry's step-daughter, but do you want me to go over how to use this and figure out portion size?"

I shook my head, feeling queasy at the thought. "No, but thank you. I'm sure Barry will make sure I get it all right."

An alarm clock that probably wasn't much younger than me blinked large red numbers from across the dark bedroom. Nearly three in the morning. I was tempted to get up and turn the clock to face the wall so I couldn't see its taunting, but Watson's soft snores drifted up from beside the bed. I didn't want to disturb him.

At least one of us was sleeping.

I kept reminding myself I didn't need to solve Opal's murder. That hadn't been the point. I simply needed to get enough information to cause probable doubt against Barry. Even if it felt like simply meeting Barry once was enough probable doubt in regards to murder. I felt like I already had more than enough. I could take it all to the police, offer it up on a silver platter—or better suited, in the designer box with the green ribbon—and let them have at it.

If it was that simple, I probably wouldn't be tossing all night, turning over endless possibilities in my mind. What little research Mom and Barry had done on Opal's dead husbands while I'd been at Lyons revealed nothing. At least no more than what everyone else already seemed to know. Three husbands over the span of decades—three *dead* husbands. And while casual gossip held Opal responsible, no genuine allegations had ever been laid at her feet. Plus, the most recent death had been long enough ago that if the husband's families were going to raise a stink, they would have done so before now. Mom and Barry both thought it was a dead end. However, the saying was that revenge is best served cold. Maybe in this case it got served with a rolling pin.

In the dark of night, something about that scenario didn't sit right with me. I couldn't put my finger on why. I simply didn't think her black-widow status had led to her death. After talking to Eddie, I had one more person Opal had either tried to blackmail or threatened. And I'd only been asking questions for a little over a day. My hunch was the list would end up being a long Who's Who of Estes Park. Recreational marijuana use might be legal in Colorado, but it seemed Estes Park was its own entity. Sheltered on all sides by the mountains and secluded in its own way of life. It was one thing to threaten a guy like Barry. Mom would be the only one to be surprised or to care that he partook in magic brownies from time to time. But what other secrets were out there? Who else might Opal have blackmailed? Maybe she had finally crossed the wrong person.

Watson let out a long whine in his sleep. Probably dreaming of treats. He'd given me the cold shoulder as we drove back to Estes.

I twisted again and readjusted to curl around one of the pillows. And maybe it had nothing to do with threatening or blackmail. Eddie didn't seem any more capable of murder than Barry, but he was definitely angry. Maybe he'd been a little too emphatic about being a pacifist. I thought I was fairly good at reading people, but who knew? I'd never spoken to anyone with a handlebar mustache before; maybe it had thrown me off my game. And at *that* gem of a thought, I realized I was doing myself absolutely no good. I needed sleep. And I needed to quit trying to figure out who killed Opal and just be satisfied I had enough evidence to take the spotlight off Barry.

Though, did I really? I didn't actually have any evidence. Just gossip and hearsay. Sergeant Wexler had a physical note from Barry refusing to give in to Opal's blackmail. I needed something more. Much more.

Watson's whimper brought me out of a dream about chocolate bars with tiny handlebar mustaches waving pot leaves in the air. I glanced at the clock. Not even half past three. I glared down at him. "Really? I literally just fell asleep."

He whined and bounced his front paws.

It took me a second; Watson never interrupted my sleep. Then I remembered where we were. With a groan, I threw back the covers and twisted out of bed. "First thing tomorrow, we're finding a contractor to install the doggy door, and a dog run." I scratched his head. "Come on. It's not your fault."

Watson scampered ahead of me and took his place by the front door, still bouncing and whining pitifully.

I started to open the door, then remembered it was mid-November in the middle of the mountains, and grabbed the coat off the hall tree as I shoved my feet into the snow boots I'd left by the entryway. Watson whined again as I tried to fasten the buttons. Giving up, I reached for the door handle. "Fine. Fine. We don't all have fur coats on, you know." I had barely cracked the door before Watson barreled through.

I was surprised when I joined him outside. Despite the heavy snowfall, there was no wind, the sky was clear, the moon full, and stars illuminated the entire scene. Again I was swept up in the impression of living in a snow globe. I breathed in the crisp pine-scented air and felt myself relax. The move had been the right decision. I just needed to get through this part, help Barry clear his name, and then as soon as the police were done with the store, I could begin setting up my bookshop and building my new life.

Watson trotted over, seemingly content after finishing his business.

"Go ahead and sniff around. I'm not ready to go in yet. But stay close."

He looked at the cabin, then back up at me.

"Oh, good grief. How did I end up with such a finicky, grumpy little man?" I bent down to scratch his ears, but he scuttled away toward the door. Shaking my head, I followed, opened the door once more, and let him inside. I leaned against the wall, suddenly enjoying the view even more framed through the silhouette of the overhang and log columns of my front porch. It was paradise. Though Thanksgiving was still a week or so away, I had the sudden urge to get a Christmas tree. Soon, I could be sitting by the fire, reading a book, while the tree lights twinkled happily in front of the window where snow fell outside. I stuck my hands in my coat pockets and squeezed around me, relishing the notion.

After a tickle on my hand, I withdrew something from my pocket and held it up to catch the moonlight. The feather. I'd forgotten. What a strange thing to have stuffed in my pocket.

The feather! An entirely new option crashed over me, somehow combining with what I'd learned from Eddie earlier in the day. What if none of this had to do with edibles or Opal's attempted blackmails, or her overall unlovable personality? What if it barely had anything to do with Opal herself? She'd been dating Sid.

I twisted the feather again, considering. No doubt the police were taking care of the owl in the freezer, but what if it all centered around that? Weren't owls an endangered species? I was fairly certain I'd heard something like that. Maybe only certain species of owls. Those big black eyes flashed in my memory. There had been a lot of death in Heads and Tails. Opal, Sid himself, countless animals.

Wonderful. Just what I needed. Some other bunny trail.

I stared at the feather a few more minutes, considering, then stuffed it back into my pocket and went inside. By the time I entered the bedroom, Watson was already asleep in his doggy bed beside my four-poster. "You've got it so good, you don't even know."

I tiptoed across the room and slipped into bed, rearranging the pillows and pulling the covers up to my chin.

The red flashing lights mocked me from across the room, reminding me I'd forgotten to turn the clock around.

Watson let out a contented, dream-laden sigh, and I rolled my eyes.

Well, whatever. It wasn't like I was going to get any sleep anyway.

I didn't have internet service at my cabin yet, so I considered going to the library or Mom's to do a little research first thing in the morning. However, I doubted I'd be able to identify what kind of bird the feather belonged to on Google. There had to be countless brown feathers with light spots. I'd noticed a bird shop downtown the day before. It looked like nothing more than endless birdfeeders and seed, but maybe they would know.

Bundled up for the cold, Watson and I hopped in the Mini Cooper and took off. We were halfway to downtown when I realized I was missing the obvious. I lived in Estes Park, which cuddled up next to Rocky Mountain National Park. I had a whole forest full of animal experts at my fingertips.

I took the time to stop by Black Bear Roasters to get a dirty chai and try my luck with a different pastry. Maybe the bear claw would be a little moister. Made sense, since the place had the word *bear* in its name.

No such luck. At least for me. Watson, on the other hand, thought his half was perfection.

We drove through downtown and up the couple of miles of winding road that took us through various neighborhoods until we neared the entrance of the national park. The snow had stopped, and the day was bright. The end result had turned Estes Park and its outlying scenery into a Christmas village. It would've been much more fun to be at home decorating the Christmas tree than trying to solve a murder.

The thought gave me pause.

Well, I supposed I might as well admit it to myself. Mom was right. I wasn't simply trying to clear Barry's name. I wanted to solve the thing. Wanted Dad to look down on me, grin, and whisper, "That's my girl!"

And truth be told, setting up a Christmas tree didn't sound near as fun as solving a murder.

With an odd sense of giddiness, I pulled the car up to one of the tollbooths that looked like tiny log cabins. I rolled down the window and waited for the ranger inside to look my way.

He didn't.

After a second, I decided to knock, and reached

forward. The seatbelt held me back. With a growl, I unfastened it and tried again, rapping on the cold glass.

The ranger jumped and gave a sharp holler as he whipped around to look at me.

Though his eyes were wide in surprise and his features relayed shock, I had an out-of-body experience, or at least as close to it as I'd ever come. Oscar De La Hoya stared back at me.

In other words, my dream man stared at me. The only time I really enjoyed the sport conversations Gary and Dad had was when Oscar De La Hoya had one of his boxing matches on the television. I pretended not to notice, but the man was beautiful. And I could never understand how someone with a face like his made his living by getting it hit.

Oscar slid open the window, and his shocked expression turned to a smile as he gave a little laugh. "Sorry about that! I was totally in my own little world there. Glad the window was shut. You probably would've heard me scream like a five-year-old girl."

I think my mouth moved, but I wouldn't swear to it. Whatever it did, it failed to make any words. He was even more beautiful in person than on screen.

His dark eyes narrowed in concern. "Ma'am? Are you alright?"

And that word was a brick to the forehead. A needed one. The man in front of me was Oscar De La Hoya back when I was in seventh grade. This kid was probably twenty-five and saw me as a *ma'am.*

And here I hadn't even bothered with Percival's lessons of a dramatic cat eye and simple lip gloss that morning.

Oscar leaned out the window and touched my arm. "Are you needing assistance, ma'am?"

From up close, I realized that Oscar De La Hoya was

more beautifully cute than actually handsome. Attractive, to be sure, but there was more of a boyish quality to his good looks than the dark sultry edge that Branson Wexler seemed to possess in spades.

"Do you need me to call someone? Maybe a doctor?"

"Has anyone ever told you that you look like Oscar De La Hoya?"

Oh my God! Oh. My. God!

My mouth had worked, only, not really.

He flashed a brilliant smile. Why would anyone with a face like that allow someone to come at it with boxing gloves? "Yeah, I get that all the time. Although that guy's pushing fifty, so I'm not exactly sure if it's a compliment or an insult."

"How old are you?" And again with the mouth vomit! Maybe the staggering amount of edibles in that stupid box from that stupid shop had permeated the air while I lay in that stupid bed. I had to be high as a kite; that was the only explanation.

"Thirty-one." His beautiful smile turned playful. "How old are you?"

"Thirty-eight." I said it like I'd just been given a birthday present. He wasn't twenty-five. There was only seven years between us. That wasn't so....

And again—*Oh. My. God.*

I turned to Watson, desperate for him to save me from myself.

He blinked at me.

Traitor. Then I realized I could save myself. I snatched the feather from the cup holder and held it out for Oscar to take. "Is this from an endangered owl species?"

He flinched back, and I realized I'd bumped the feather

against his nose. Still smiling, he took the feather and inspected it.

I had the impression that his smile had transitioned from the genuine kind to the type someone used when confronted with a crazy person who they feared might eat their face.

Oscar ran a finger over the edge of the feather, his brows knitted. Finally he looked back at me. "I have no idea."

"You don't?"

He shook his head. "Sorry to disappoint you. Unfortunately we disappoint a lot of tourists. We're always getting feathers, rocks, leaves, sometimes little portions of twigs. While I know the names of more items in the park than your average bear, I'm not actually an encyclopedia."

"Oh." So not only had I just made a complete fool of myself, I'd done it for no good reason.

He chuckled softly. "I gotta say, I've never had someone look so disappointed when I didn't know the answer to something like that. Do you and the feather go way back?"

Probably because I already felt like the biggest fool in the world, I bristled at his teasing and snatched the feather from his fingers. "No. Not all that long. Sorry to have bothered you." I turned to face the road, ready to pound the gas and drive away as quickly as possible. I might just keep on going. After this, it might be a good idea to start a reset on life somewhere else.

"Ma'am." I deflated at his use of that word once more and looked back at Oscar to see him motioning over the top of my car toward a larger cabin a little ways off the road. "I have a computer in there. We can look it up if you really need to know."

"No, thank you. I don't need to waste your time. I'm

sure I can do that part on my own. But thank you again. That's very sweet of you, Oscar."

I realized my mistake as his eyes bugged once more and his smile returned. He leaned forward and whispered, "Would you be disappointed if I told you I've never been in a fight in my life, much less in a boxing ring?"

I couldn't help but laugh. "Actually, that makes me feel better. I've never understood why someone with a face as cute as Oscar's would allow himself to be hit."

And once more, the expression on his face let me know that I'd messed up again. "Cute, huh?"

I felt my cheeks burn.

He didn't give me a chance to peel out and drive myself over the edge of a cliff. "I'm Leo Lopez. And your face is too beautiful to let people punch as well."

He rendered me speechless, again. Beautiful?

Leo angled around so he was looking into the passenger seat and addressing Watson. "Would you let your mama know that in polite society it's customary for the other person to share their name as well during an introduction?"

To my surprise, Watson crossed the console and stood with his front paws on my thigh and stretched out to Leo, allowing himself to be petted.

Though they looked nothing alike, it seemed there must be a little bit of Barry Adams in Leo Lopez.

"Um, this is Watson, and his mama who can't seem to string two intelligent words together this morning is Winifred Page. But everybody just calls me Fred."

"A beautiful woman named Fred?" His brown eyes met mine again, and though there was a teasing glint then, I was surprised to see sincerity as well. "You're definitely the first of your particular species I've ever met." He paused long enough for there to be a spark of heat, unless I was imagining things again, and then motioned over the car once more. "Seems like that feather is pretty important to you. I may not know what it is exactly, but I probably have ways to find out quicker than you. May I save you some time?"

I nodded, not trusting myself to try to use the English language again, and he motioned once more.

"Go ahead and pull in on the side of the road. I'll meet you there."

By the time I parked, Leo was already out of the toll-booth and nearly to the cabin. As I approached him, I realized he was also several inches shorter than Branson, and was almost the exact same height as myself. He seemed a little surprised as well as I approached. I didn't think the glint in his eye dissipated, though.

He held the door open for us. "Just remember, the next time you're in the park, make sure you have a leash on Mr. Watson, here. Not only is it the law in the national forest, it's simply good practice. I'm constantly hearing about coyotes and mountain lions darting out to get people's pets. Just the other day a cougar got the family cat in the back-yard during their daughter's birthday party." He shuddered, but chuckled. "That's going to be some expensive therapy later on."

It felt like he poured ice water down my back. I could envision Watson out in the moonlit snow the night before. It hadn't even entered my mind, which, looking back, was beyond stupid. We lived in the mountains now, not the upscale Plaza of Kansas City. I mentally redesigned the dog run I'd been planning for Watson. I didn't care about the cost; that thing was going to be top-of-the-line and as safe as I could possibly make it.

"Sorry. Didn't mean to startle you." Reading my mind, he bent down to pet Watson, who was still acting like he was in love. "No harm done. Your little guy is safe. And it's common for tourists to make that mistake. Like I said, what happened to the cat was someone local who should have known better. Don't feel too bad."

"No, don't be sorry." I forced a smile, though the sense of guilt still bit at me. "I'm glad you mentioned it. I'm not a tourist. I just moved to town. I'm opening a bookstore in the old taxidermy shop. And I've been planning on installing a dog run for Watson at my house. I wouldn't even have thought...."

"Oh, welcome to town! And don't stress about it. I'll give you the number of one of my friends who does construction. He's more than able to design something for your corgi that will keep him safe. It won't be cheap, but it'll be worth it. In fact—" His expression changed suddenly, and his gaze focused on the feather I held in my hand. "Wait a minute, you're taking over the taxidermy shop? I heard about Opal." He looked up at me and then back at the feather again. "Is that from there?"

I nodded. "Yes, I found it behind a freezer. There was a dead owl inside. But I'm not sure if this feather belongs to that particular bird or another. Or if it even matters."

"Oh, it matters." He plucked the feather out of my hand and crossed the room to sit in front of a computer. "We do the best we can, but poaching is a constant problem. Sometimes worse than others. I've wondered if Sid played a part in that, not that it matters anymore since he passed, but I'd still like to know. I raised my concerns with the police about his shop, but without any evidence, there was nothing they could do."

I took my place over his shoulder and watched as his fingers flew over the keyboard. He definitely knew where he was going, and images and lists of species flashed across the screen. If I'd been on my own, I would've spent hours trying to decipher all the information, probably to no avail. But within three minutes, Leo clicked on an image and rolled a few inches away to give me more room. "Does this look like the owl you saw?"

The owl was beautiful. Warm dark brown with white spots covering it, causing it to look like it was caught in a snowstorm, with darker striated feathers near the tail. And huge black eyes. I supposed all owls had huge black eyes. "I think so. Granted, you could probably put up a lineup of five different owls and I might not be able to tell the difference, but I think so."

"It's the Mexican Spotted Owl, not endangered but federally threatened." Leo held the feather between us again. "Do you mind if I keep this? I'd like to do a little more research on it. Ask my supervisor."

For some reason I hated to let it go. But I nodded anyway.

"Thanks, I appreciate it. Any help we can get stopping poaching is priceless." Leo laid the feather by the computer, and when he looked back at me, that unnamable twinkle had returned to his eyes. "May I get your number? Just in case the feather is useful? I figure you'd like to know."

I'd come to Estes Park to hit Reset on my life. In every aspect. And one of those aspects was leaving behind a world that was constantly connected to my ex-husband. This new life didn't have room or the desire for a relationship. Or for men in any sort of romantic entanglement. This life was about Fred Page, Watson, and creating my dream bookstore. Simply having a calm and pleasant life. I didn't want anything more complicated than having to search for rare first edition books for persnickety shoppers.

Yet here I was, barely two days into that so-called reset

of a life, and I was investigating a murder. Even more terrifying, I found myself giving Leo Lopez—the Oscar De La Hoya of the Rocky Mountain National Park Service—my phone number.

I didn't remember Watson and me walking to the car or driving back out of the national park. The fog lifted on the way to downtown. I stared at Watson in accusation.

"What was that? You were all over the guy like you'd known him for years. Letting him scratch your ears, looking at him like he was Barry's long-lost brother. He didn't even offer to give you a treat!"

Watson's ears perked up at the word, and he turned expectant eyes on me.

"No way, you Benedict Arnold. You only get treats when you stop me from acting like a complete moron and attempting to ruin our new life here. Absolutely no treat for you."

He whimpered and looked longingly at the glove compartment, then back at me, his adorable large brown eyes full of pleading.

"Oh, fine!" Steadying the steering wheel with my left hand, I punched the button for the glove compartment, treats and paperwork spilling out everywhere. Watson had a heyday.

Watson and I drove back to downtown. If I'd been thinking clearly, I probably would've gone home and taken time to write down my thoughts and things I'd discovered so far, minimal though they were. It would've given me a chance to process through new possibilities and come up with a game plan. However, that would have required clear thinking. The combination of discovering the feather might belong to a threatened owl species, which pointed away from the edible connection, and Leo's reaction to me made any chance of thinking clearly an impossibility.

Or maybe it was *my* reaction to Leo that was throwing me off.

Or maybe it was my reaction to *Branson* that was throwing me off.

I wasn't supposed to be thinking about any man, let alone two. If any clear thinking was happening at all, I would've put a pin into my investigation and found out if there was a nunnery near Estes Park and taken vows of chastity as quickly as possible.

Probably well enough I didn't check. I doubted they let new nuns keep corgis with them in the room. But seriously?

I hadn't had a tingle of romantic notions since my divorce six years before. Well, before that, truth be told.

Telling myself it had nothing to do with shoving thoughts of Branson and Leo out of my mind, I hooked the leash to Watson's collar and we strolled the downtown once more. Proving my brain hadn't turned into complete cotton candy, my first stop was to Wings of the Rockies, a store specializing in wild birdseed, feeders, and so much ornithological paraphernalia the place felt a little like a cult headquarters. With one mention of the Mexican Spotted Owl, the owner demonstrated her ability to sound like an Animal Planet documentary. But ultimately she offered nothing useful to anyone who wasn't covered in feathers.

We paused to grab a burger and fries from Penelope's for lunch, before checking out the pet shop. I didn't have much hope that a pet store would offer anything helpful with any aspect of my leads, and I was proven correct. But the owner, Paulie Mertz, a peculiar little man, owned two corgis of his own. Flotsam and Jetsam. It seemed he was also an avid Little Mermaid fan. Before I managed to leave the store, I'd inexplicably allowed myself into promising a corgi playdate a week from Friday.

As we walked out the door, I crashed into someone and accidentally stepped on Watson's paw as I attempted to backpedal. He let out a shrill yip and I shuffled to give him space, once more bumping into the person.

"I'm so, so sorry. I was rushing and I—" My words dried up as I looked into cold blue eyes.

Officer Green glared at me, her hatred clear. She was in her street clothes, a surprisingly feminine sweater and skirt. She looked different enough that if it weren't for her eyes, and her revulsion, I might not have recognized her. "What are you doing, *Fred*?" The amount of disgust she was able to muster at my name was impressive.

"I'm just asking questions to—" I shut my mouth, biting my tongue in the process. I really was thrown off, if I was actually going to answer that question honestly. I had to take a second to remember where I was. Flotsam and Jetsam. Unwanted playdate. Pet shop. "I was asking if there was any way to special order Watson's preferred dog food. They don't carry it here."

Her eyes narrowed as she glanced over my shoulder toward the door, then sneered at me again and gestured toward Watson. "Watch where you're going. And I hope your *dog's* tags are up to date. I'll have to check on that the next time we run into each other." And with that she was gone.

I stared at her as she stormed off. I don't think anyone had ever hated me so much. How could anyone hate a near stranger so deeply? Maybe she'd killed Opal. Just for fun.

Watson and I had barely taken a step away from the pet store when I pictured Officer Green returning to ask if I'd really been checking on special order dog food. With a sense of dread, I turned around and walked back in.

A hundred dollars of special ordered dog food Watson would doubtless refuse to eat later, we ended by walking a block or so away from the main strip to the Christmas shop and the glassblowers. Likewise, I didn't truly expect any connection to Barry, but given that the owners had come up in Anna and Carl's gossipfest, I figured I should at least drop by. Neither owner was in.

By three in the afternoon, Watson and I had nothing to show for our efforts besides getting to know more of the townspeople and possibly burning off a third of the calories from the burger I'd devoured at lunch. Feeling like a complete failure and that I'd wasted several hours on nothing, I pulled out the number of the contact Leo had given me for Watson's dog run. To my surprise, he agreed to meet me in less than an hour at my home.

Leo hadn't been wrong. I nearly choked when presented with the written estimate for the job. Though, I couldn't argue that the man was thorough. I suppose there might be a chance he was milking a newbie and her love for her dog, but I didn't care. I agreed to burying the dog run a foot and a half into the ground, a reinforced roof, complete with an additional overhang that matched the existing roof on the house to provide shelter, and a triple layer of mesh fencing, that was guaranteed to keep out any predator. To top it all, the construction could start in three days. Watson would be safe, and I could sleep through the night. I decided it was priceless.

Between the hours of unproductive questioning and waving goodbye to thousands and thousands of dollars for Watson, I decided comfort food was in order. Within an hour, I was back from the grocery store, had tomato soup bubbling away in a pot on the stove, and was slathering the bread for grilled cheeses with butter. I'd already stoked the fire and set my Kindle on the arm of the recliner nearby. I needed a night to turn my brain off. No thoughts of men, past or present, no twists and turns of murder or investigations. The only thing that could make it better was having my actual books in the house, and my own overstuffed armchair by the fire. But this would do in a pinch. I'd already decided I was going to reread *Anne of Avonlea*, a childhood favorite. I had enough mystery for the day. It was time for comfort.

A knock sounded on the door just as I placed the grilled cheese on the sizzling pan. I glanced at my cell—no missed calls. Chances were it wasn't Mom or Barry. I didn't want to see anyone. I was officially peopled out.

A second knock, barely ten seconds later.

With a grumble, I removed the grilled cheese and turned off the burner. Someone had driven all the way out to my cabin; they weren't going away easily. And with my Mini Cooper gathering snow outside, I couldn't pretend I wasn't home.

Watson followed me to the door, growling the whole way.

I started to look for the peephole, then realized there wasn't one. That wouldn't do. One more thing to pay for. I nearly threw open the door, then realized how stupid it would be. Especially with everything going on. And while Watson's growl sounded vicious, he wasn't exactly the best guard dog. I paused with my hand on the door handle. "Who's there?"

"Sergeant Wexler. I just need a little moment of your time."

I recognized his voice instantly. It didn't pass my attention he used his formal name and his tone didn't sound overly friendly. So much for not thinking about men that evening. I opened the door, and the breeze ushered in a small gust of snow. I stood aside to make room. "Come in out of the cold."

"Thanks." He stomped his feet on the porch, then stepped in.

Add doormat to the things to purchase.

I shut the door and turned to look at him. Watson growled softly a few more seconds and then let it fade away. Words left me for a moment. It was my first time seeing

Branson out of uniform. He made quite the picture in the uniform, don't get me wrong, but Branson in civilian clothes was just as arresting. Flecks of snow glistened in his black hair, and his body seemed impossibly more fit and male under a green flannel shirt, brown leather jacket, tight dark-wash jeans, and snow boots. The stern expression on his handsome face helped cut through my unintentional admiration and helped me find my voice.

"What can I do for you?"

"You can explain why you're harassing the shop owners of downtown, for starters."

I flinched. "Harassing?"

His eyes narrowed. "What would you call it?"

I started to say that I would call it investigating, then realized that probably would sound even worse. I allowed my gaze to travel over his body once more, this time intentionally, and making sure to take any attraction away. "I'm not sure it's any business of yours, *Branson*. It doesn't seem like you're here on official business."

"I came like this as a courtesy, Fred." He glowered, the expression suited his thick brows and angled jaw. As did his low rumble. "However, if you need it to be official, I can happily put on the uniform and call you down to the station." He shrugged. "It's up to you."

Watson growled again, drawing Branson's attention downward.

"Your mom is safe, little man. Don't get your hackles in a bunch." His gaze flicked to mine, though he still addressed Watson. "She'll always be safe with me."

My heart gave a little flutter, and I felt the truth of his words. If he'd been in his uniform, I could've chalked it up to that. I equated the police with safety, with my father. But standing there in his flannel shirt, with his wide shoulders and barrel chest, I couldn't deny my instincts told me I was indeed safe with Branson Wexler. No matter his mood.

My stomach rumbled, and I latched on to it. Maybe there hadn't been a heart flutter after all, just a reminder my dinner was waiting. I considered for half a second, then decided I was tired of overthinking, and motioned back toward the kitchen. "I was just making dinner. Tomato soup and grilled cheese. Want some?"

Those bright green eyes widened in surprise, and some of his apparent irritation dissipated. "I... uhm...." His gaze flicked to the fire, then back at me, and for the second time that day, I saw a spark of heat in a man's eyes.

More as a reaction to myself than Branson, I waved him off and headed back toward the kitchen. "Don't make a deal out of it. I'm hungry. You interrupted dinner. You can either join in or watch me eat as you accuse me of things I've not done."

He chuckled as his footsteps trailed after me. "Grilled cheese and tomato soup sounds perfect. Thank you."

A mix of thrill and *Oh my Lord, Fred, what are you doing*? shot through me. "Great. Do you like mayonnaise on your grilled cheese? Or do you not know how to eat it correctly?"

Another laugh, this one full. "Didn't know you had such a sick sense of humor."

I turned the burner back on and glanced at him. "I wasn't kidding."

He paused as if waiting for a punch line, then gave a slow nod. "Well, all right then. No, thanks for the offer, but I will take my grilled cheese incorrectly, it seems."

"Your loss." I started buttering bread for his grilled cheese. Was I flirting? Surely not. "But don't you dare ask for a bite of mine when you see how much better it looks." Someone shoot me. I was flirting.

"Don't worry. I think I will be fully satisfied." Branson crossed the kitchen, slid out of his jacket, which he hung on the back of a chair, and leaned an elbow on the counter. "Can I help you in any way?"

Despite myself, I did an actual double take, then simply shook my head and refocused on unwrapping the cheese, fearing my reaction would convey too much. Such a small thing. A thing I knew should barely be noticed, let alone cause warmth to spread through my body. It was an offer my father would have given my mother, one that Barry gave her now. But it was an offer Garrett had never given me in our eight years of marriage. "Thanks. The glasses are in the cabinet to the right of the sink. If you'll fill them with ice, that would be great. There are trays in the freezer."

"You got it." And without hesitation, Branson began to fill the glasses. "Cute kitchen. I like the retro style. However...." He chuckled softly. "I know I've only met you a couple of times, but I consider myself a very good reader of people. Not in a million years would I have pegged you the type for choosing tie-dye curtains with—" His eyes narrowed, and he leaned forward slightly. "—flamingos?"

Giving in to the ease I felt with him, I offered a smile. "You'd be right. Those were a welcome-home present from Mom and Barry. At the time, I planned on replacing them as soon as possible, but they're already growing on me."

"Ah, glad my skills aren't fading away. You keeping them because of your family also matches my impression of you."

I couldn't tell whether it was flirtation or not, but I opted to take it as a compliment.

Dinner was ready within a matter of minutes, and we

settled in at the small sea-foam green wooden table in the center of the kitchen.

Branson let out a long satisfied groan at his first bite of grilled cheese, which he dipped into the tomato soup. "Boy, does this ever hit the spot. It's been a long day, and I haven't eaten since breakfast."

I held my sandwich midair as I responded. "It'd be better with mayo." Then I took a bite. He was right. It did hit the spot. We ate in silence for a few minutes, some of the ease that had existed while I cooked evaporating. "If I recall, you came here to say not nice things about me. Might as well get that over with."

He sighed, like he'd rather skip the whole thing, but then his expression hardened slightly. "I had reports that you've been going around downtown asking questions to all the shop owners. What's that about?"

He'd had reports? Officer Green flashed through my mind. Yeah, I was willing to bet I knew exactly where those reports had come from. I took another bite of the sandwich, more to give myself a few moments to consider how to best respond. I hadn't done anything illegal. "I'm a shop owner myself now. Don't you think it's a good idea to get to know my fellow business owners?"

He rolled his eyes, though his expression spoke more amusement than irritation. "How about this, Fred. Don't treat me like I'm an idiot, and I'll give you the same courtesy."

I couldn't help but laugh. Nor could I help feeling even more comfortable with him. "Fine. We were just going around, simply asking questions, putting out feelers. Opal was killed in my shop. Right in the heart of downtown Estes Park, surrounded by businesses and people she'd worked with for years and years. It only makes sense that someone, somewhere, might know something."

Branson started to speak, then paused to chew and swallow. "We?"

I gestured toward Watson with my sandwich. "Yes. We."

Watson's ears perked up as Branson looked over at him, probably hoping he was about to get some of the grilled cheese. Branson chuckled again. "Of course. We." He refocused on me, his tone growing a little more serious again. "If it's so innocuous, why did I get a call from Myrtle Bantam squawking about being interrogated about endangered species of owls?"

The fidgety owner of Wings of the Rockies flashed through my mind, and I gave an unladylike snort. "You totally did that on purpose."

"I don't know what you're talking about." The corner of Branson's lips twitched, giving him away.

"Squawking? The owner of the bird store was squawking?"

He shrugged, all innocence. "You met her. Wouldn't you say it's an apt description?"

I would actually, not that I was going to give him the satisfaction. "I'd say it was low-hanging fruit, and you can do better."

He leaned closer to me across the table, his eyes twinkling. "Her last name is Bantam. Did you know that's a type of chicken? I mean, come on. Talk about low-hanging fruit."

I hadn't known that, and I laughed again. "That's pretty wonderful. It's a good thing I'm not a police officer. I'd probably abuse my power and check to see if she'd altered her name."

He leaned closer still. "Oh, I have. And the delicious part? She hasn't changed her name. She truly might be part chicken." He let his gaze linger a few seconds longer, causing my traitorous heart to beat a little faster, and then he leaned back once more. "So back to my question. Why, if you're doing nothing more than meeting your competition, is Myrtle Bantam calling to squawk at me again?" He took a spoonful of soup.

"I didn't say I was meeting my *competition*." Genuine irritation sliced through me, though not at Branson. So it wasn't Officer Green after all. At least not *only* Officer Green. "And I don't know why she's calling to complain. If anyone was harassed, it was me. She... *squawked*... on and on for nearly forty minutes about owls. Believe me, if you've ever wondered about all the interesting things that can be found in owl pellets, I can fill you in. And if you're not sure, an owl pellet is the mess of leftovers the owl vomits up when they're done eating. And again, I'll remind you, it was forty minutes. Forty! About owl vomit. Would you like to take my formal complaint now, or should I come down to the station?"

Branson leaned back in his chair and howled with laughter. When he finally looked back at me, he had to wipe away the tears from his eyes. "Welcome to town, Winifred Page."

I glowered at him and mentally promised myself I would never direct business toward Myrtle Bantam if I could keep from it.

"After her call"—though there was still humor in his tone, his expression grew serious once more—"I checked in with a few other shops. It sounds like you've been busy. I don't think there was one you haven't gone in."

For all the good it did me. "Like I said, I'm getting to

know my neighbors. You still haven't listed anything harassment-like."

This time, when Branson's expression shifted, it grew darker. "I also got a rather vexing call from one of the rangers in the national park. He was quite adamant he had proof, after a visit from you, that I'd been lax in taking his unfounded claims seriously." He leveled his stare on me. "You're a smart woman, Fred. I'm fairly certain you realize the national park isn't one of the shops downtown."

Leo had called Branson? Though baseless, something about Myrtle Bantam made it easy to picture her calling to complain; that wasn't true about Leo. "Don't ask me to believe Leo said I was harassing him. I simply had a suspicion I needed some help verifying."

"No, he made no such claims." Branson's eyes narrowed, and though I thought it was at the mention of Leo's name, I couldn't be sure. "But while we're at it, that's one of the other things I wanted to talk to you about. It seems you took evidence from your shop with you the other day. I'd be willing to chalk it up as not realizing the importance of what you had with that feather. Do you make a habit of taking things from crime scenes? I would think the daughter of a policeman would know better."

I stiffened, his words feeling like a slap. "That was a low blow, Sergeant Wexler." My temper spiked. "And no, I don't. I stuffed the feather in my pocket before I found Opal's body. I didn't even think about it again until last night when I felt it in my pocket. And as far as what I'm doing? You've accused my stepfather of murder. And as the daughter of a policeman, I understand why, I understand the steps, and won't hold those against you. However, I also am aware that sometimes *low-hanging fruit* is the easiest thing to grasp at, and that overworked and under-budgeted police stations might see an easy way to close a case." My volume rose, I tried to reel it back in, but to no avail. "And furthermore, judging by what Leo told me, it sounds like I have reason to be concerned. Sid had a federally threatened owl in his deep freezer. Maybe Opal's murder had nothing to do with edibles at all, or with her attempting to blackmail Barry, and doubtless other people. Perhaps it has everything to do with her poacher boyfriend."

Branson's expression shifted several times over my tirade, but his eyes widened in surprise at the last revelation. "Opal was dating Sid?"

"Yes."

He shuddered. "Now that was a visual I never wanted to have in my head."

My irritation didn't allow me to find humor in it. "See, right there. Just by asking questions, I uncovered something you had no idea about."

Branson sighed and offered a small smile, and for the first time, sounded condescending. "A detail which doesn't help your stepfather at all. Sid died months ago. A heart attack, not murder. Opal was killed in the kitchen where she was making edibles. In a building where she was growing a forest of marijuana plants in the basement. A building owned by your stepfather, who we know Opal attempted to blackmail. I can guarantee you Opal wasn't killed because of a *feather*."

"You can't really believe Barry would kill someone." My fingernails dug into the soft flesh of my palms.

"No, I don't." Branson's tone didn't soften. "But despite being good at my job, I've been wrong before. And because I'm good at my job, your stepfather is still on the suspect list. The very short suspect list."

"Exactly. Good at your job or not, you're making

mistakes and not looking in the right direction." I squared my shoulders and lifted my chin. "Someone has to do the legwork. And if I can't trust the police department to do it, then I will."

"Fred." Branson spoke through gritted teeth. "I understand you want to clear Barry's name, and I also understand your father was a detective, so you feel somewhat... entitled to pretend like you're one as well." He almost looked apologetic as he said his next words, though his effect didn't weaken. "Like I've said, I'm good at my job, and because of that, it doesn't matter whether or not I like you. I will charge you with hampering an investigation if you continue. You need to back off and leave this to the police."

"Were you even aware that Sid started the edible business? He was getting his marijuana from the Green Munchies in Lyons, and that Opal was the one who talked him out of it. Did you know it was Opal who decided they could make a lot more if they began growing their own product?" Whether it was due to my temper or needing to feel justified, the words fell from my lips before I could bring them back. I'd promised myself I wouldn't bring up that detail to anyone unless I had good reason to believe it could clear Barry's name. I didn't exactly know what the consequences would be, but I didn't want to be responsible for getting Eddie and his business in trouble, not with as kind as he was to Barry and myself. Not unless I had to.

Fury crossed Branson's face, and he gripped the soupspoon so tightly it trembled and clinked against the bowl. "What?"

"You heard me." I wasn't going to repeat it. I wasn't.

His nostrils flared as he spoke. "That little weasel was the one filtering drugs into *my* town?"

I wasn't completely sure why I felt protective of Eddie,

but I did. "You're missing the point. Sid was the one who set up the operation, and then Opal took charge. Who knows what else she was doing, or how many enemies she made. The least of whom is Barry. And my point remains, I'm clearly discovering things the police department has no idea about, just by talking to people over a matter of days. So don't tell me to back off when I'm doing a better job of it than you are."

Branson had appeared muscular and strong in a model, man-in-uniform way before. But as he trembled with rage, that illusion faded. Combined with his anger, physical power seemed to radiate off him. And while I didn't feel necessarily unsafe with him; I wasn't entirely certain he was as predictable as I'd assumed.

After several tense moments, still trembling, Branson stood with clenched fists. "Thank you for dinner. And regardless of what you think about me, my abilities, or the Estes Park Police in general, you will leave this well enough alone. I will not hesitate to formally charge you, Fred. The best thing you can do to help your stepfather is to let us handle it. You will only get in the way."

I started to argue, but he was already storming toward the front door. Just as he touched the handle, he glanced back. Though unsuccessful, it seemed he was attempting to infuse some kindness into his tone. "The other reason I came was to tell you that we're done at Heads and Tails. Maybe it seems as if we've been sitting on our thumbs, but we've had a murder scene to deal with, as well as a grow house. We've been focusing our attention there. I knew it was important to you to get your business going." The accusation in his eyes was obvious. "So it's done. You can take possession of it again tomorrow." And with that, he was gone.

I sat there, stunned, too many emotions, thoughts, and possibilities tumbling around in my mind and gut. After a while, I tossed what little remained of Branson's sandwich to Watson and took a bite of my own. Whatever he said, if he thought I was going to sit back and let the cards fall where they may regarding my family, he was sorely mistaken.

When I got up in the middle of the night to take Watson outside, this time on a leash, I was still so angry I promised myself I'd march right back downtown, barge into every single store, and become even more direct with my questioning. *Nobody* told me what to do. Not even a police officer.

By the time dawn crept through the windows, however, my temper had abated somewhat. I didn't have any follow-up questions to what little I'd discovered the day before, so it made more sense to wait. Selfishly, I wanted to get into my shop. To really spend some time there and begin to plan its future. The benefit was that I'd found I often thought more clearly when I was distracted with other work. Maybe in mapping out the layout of the Cozy Corgi, something in the back of my mind would click.

Packing a lunch of tomato soup and a freshly made grilled cheese for myself and a baked chicken breast for Watson, we headed downtown again. By lunch, the soup and grilled cheese would be cold, but I thought I could manage. If I couldn't, there was a fully functioning kitchen upstairs. Just because a woman had been killed there didn't mean the stove couldn't heat up soup and grilled cheese.

I didn't bother with the leash in the short distance

between my car and the shop, and no sooner had I opened the door than Watson took off like a bolt. Not a big deal; if he wanted to explore, he could. I flipped on the light downstairs and suddenly realized I could hear the pitter patter of his little feet above my head.

Of course he would go to the floor where we'd found a dead body.

I'd planned on working myself up to checking out the second floor again. But no time like the present. I supposed it didn't matter if Watson was up there or not. It wasn't like it was disrespectful, but it still didn't sit right. I marched up the steps and flicked on the light, illuminating the second story. He was nowhere to be seen.

"Watson?"

There was a snuffling, and he popped his head out the doorway of the kitchen.

Where else would he be? "Come here."

He let out a little whine, took a tentative step in my direction, then scampered around and disappeared once more.

"Good Lord, you are such a little brat." Might as well get it over with. I walked toward him, took a deep breath, chastised myself for being ridiculous, and stepped into the kitchen. "What are you doing in here? Looking for clues?"

Watson ignored me, scurrying here and there, his nose shoved to the floor. He hurried to the door, sniffed around it, both in the kitchen and outside in the main room, and then darted back into the kitchen once more.

Then it hit me. "You're looking for candy, aren't you? More of that licorice stuff you had last time." So much for clues. Well, I was already there, might as well look around. There was nothing to find. No chalk outline, no stain of blood, no rolling pin—not that I'd expected there to be. It also didn't look like the aftermath left from an inspection. The place was spotless. Even the appliances looked like they'd gotten wiped down, not even a trace from where they'd surely dusted for fingerprints. Now that I thought about it, I realized the same had been true for downstairs. The place was remarkably cleaner than the first time I'd seen it.

My irritation at Branson lessened further. I had no doubt it was thanks to him.

The kitchen wasn't anything special. Though more updated than the one at my house, it lacked any amount of charm. And despite Opal creating her edibles here, none of the equipment was high quality. I looked down at the floor where I'd found Opal's body. I could still see her lying there.

"I'm going to figure out who killed you, Opal. Although, let's be honest, I'm doing it for Barry more than I am for you." That was an understatement. "I am sorry for your loss. But just so we're clear, I'm using the kitchen to warm up my lunch later on. If you have a problem with it, you better start haunting me now."

Sorry for your loss? Is that what you should say to someone who'd been murdered?

And if that thought wasn't enough to let me know I needed to be elsewhere, I didn't know what was. I realized I still had my bag in my hand, so I went over to the refrigerator and put in my soup, the sandwich, and Watson's chicken.

I gave Watson the cold shoulder as I walked out of the kitchen, not that he minded. "I'm going to eat your lunch, by the way. Good luck finding candy." I wouldn't do it of course, but it would serve him right.

After returning downstairs, I decided to get all the

unpleasant tasks over with, so I looked in the storeroom. I was certain the deep freezer would be empty. To my surprise, the freezer was gone. That seemed a little presumptuous. Maybe they'd seized it for evidence, and I'd get it back once they were done? After another moment of consideration, I decided to tell Branson to dispose of the thing, if possible, the next time I saw him. It wasn't like I'd keep food or anything in it. I'd never be able to open the lid and not see a dead owl staring up at me.

I wandered from tiny room to tiny room that surrounded the large open space in the center. Once again my excitement built as I pictured how charming the place was going to be. Even if it was dreary and rather depressing at the moment.

But I could fix that part easily enough.

As I walked to the windows, I considered. Everyone would be staring in, trying to catch a glimpse of the place Opal Garble was murdered, or to get a look at the woman who found her. Well, whatever. Just like with the kitchen, might as well get it over with. In less than five minutes, I'd ripped down all the paper covering the windows, and the morning sunlight filtered in, brightening up the place.

If I hadn't been excited before, I was then. The shop almost glowed in all its wooden wonder. There was some damage from where taxidermy had been hung and age spots here and there, but nothing that endless bookcases wouldn't fix.

Whatever irritation I still held against Branson faded away with him giving me the gift of getting in here quickly. I truly was ready to begin my new life. So ready, I had a moment's thankfulness to Charlotte for stabbing me in the back. I shook the thought off quickly. I most definitely didn't owe her any gratefulness. But the end result was enough money I could live on, if I was frugal, for the rest of my life. And Lord knew, there was no other way a person should open a physical bookshop in this day and age. Still, she'd stolen my career, and even though the settlement was substantial, it was nothing compared to what the publishing house would make by the time we hit retirement.

A friendly round face smiled at me from the window, startling me and ushering me back to the present. I'd been so caught in the past, it took me a moment to recognize who was waving at me. When I did, I hurried to the front door and let her in. "Katie! What are you doing here?" Dumb question. "Taking a break from the shop?"

Katie stepped inside. Before I could shut the door, Watson let out a torrent of barks from upstairs and then barreled down the steps, probably preparing for an intruder. He barked a couple more times, then pulled to a stop when Katie knelt and held out the back of her hand. With a sniff, he inspected, nudged her fingers with his nose in way of approval, and padded off once more. She smiled at me as she stood. "He's not the most affectionate of little guys, is he?"

"Not hardly. Although he is with some people." I rolled my eyes as I noticed him disappear back up the steps. He was determined, I'd give him that, at least where food was concerned. "He's even affectionate with me at times. Typically when I have food. But he's captured my heart, the little monster. He thinks I'm here to serve him. Which, at times, I think is right."

"Well, he's cute, that's for sure." She glanced around, scrutinizing, then returned to me. "No, the shops aren't open yet. Everything's up in the air." She sighed. "It's part of why I came downtown. I had to get out of the house.

Then I saw the paper was down from the windows. I thought I'd say hi, see how you're doing."

For a heartbeat, I wondered if Katie was doing some of her own investigation, then realized I was being paranoid. "That's sweet of you. I'm doing fine. Glad to be able to get back in here. It's going to take a while to get everything set up, but I think it will end up being beautiful. A cozy little bookshop."

"It's a great place. And it'll be a lot better now that it's not filled with taxidermy."

I shuddered. "At least the bar is set low."

Katie fidgeted, nervous. She licked her lips before speaking again. "You redheads are able to wear the most god-awful colors and look wonderful. I simply don't understand it."

I wasn't sure what I'd been expecting, but most definitely not that. "Excuse me?"

She made a waving motion over my body. "You've got on a mustard-colored sweater over a pea-green and drab-brown speckled skirt. All of which are colors of baby vomit. And yet somehow, it makes your skin glow and your hair practically shine."

She was right. Earth tones were most definitely my color, but still. "Uhm, thank you. I think."

"Take me, for instance. If I put on any one of those colors, I'd instantly look sick, like I was dying. I have to stick to blues and greens and other jewel tones. Luckily, they're my favorite anyway, so it doesn't matter."

What in the world was happening? "Well, your skin is already tanned and glowing the way it is, so I suppose that makes sense."

She nodded. "I'm of Sicilian heritage." Her gaze flicked around the shop. "We have good skin."

"Katie." I opted for bluntness. "What's going on? It's nice of you to come by and say hi, but we've entered this weird conversation of colors and fashion which I'm not really sure what to do with."

She practically sighed in relief. "Ah, you're right. I'm so sorry. I've just been starved for adult conversation. Anything. Even if it's only about your horrible choice in colors." She waved over my body again. "Not that you don't look absolutely wonderful in them. But I needed to talk to someone who could offer some sort of mental stimulation greater than a five-year-old. I've been staying with Lois since Opal's death, and I'm afraid I'm just a little... desperate."

"It's nice of you to stay with Lois during this hard time." Katie had spoken so fast I had to replay some of the finer points before I could take in their meaning. "If I'm not mistaken, I was placing Lois to be quite a bit older than a five-year-old."

Katie rolled her eyes. "I would've thought so too. I've worked around her for two years, and I had no idea she was like she is." She bugged her eyes. "I have a whole new respect for Opal, and that's saying something. If I'd been Opal, it probably would have been Lois you found dead up there."

What a strange thing to say. Lois... and what a thought. An interesting one. "Well, you've got me now. Want to have a seat and tell me about it?" I motioned toward the folding chairs Branson and I had sat on just a few days ago.

"Oh, no, I couldn't dream of it. I know you've got a billion things to do." Even as she spoke she headed toward the chairs and plopped down. "But if you have a second, I won't turn it down. I'm sure it's horrible to make a joke like this, but you might just be saving me from murder."

I sat in the other chair across from her. I desperately wanted to hear what Katie had to say. As scattered as she was, it felt important, but the way we were seemed a little awkward. Like a police investigation or something. "We can go up to the kitchen. There might be tea or something to eat up there. If nothing else, I have some tomato soup we could share. If that doesn't make you too nervous."

Katie looked at me puzzled. "Why would that make me nervous?"

"Well... the kitchen is where I found Opal."

Her eyes brightened. "Oh! Right! That's where Opal was making all her edible pastries and things. Maybe there's still some supplies up there." She was beginning to sound like I'd just given her a Christmas present. "Do you mind if I bake something while we chat? I'll do something easy and quick. While living with Lois, I've not been allowed to make anything outside of vegan recipes that don't allow any sugar." She shook her head. "No sugar!"

Some of the affection I felt for her before returned. She was a strange woman, but I liked her immensely. "Absolutely. I love that you're not timid about being in the same room where a woman died, and I suppose you're offering to share whatever you make?"

"Of course!" With that, Katie practically launched from her chair, and though unintentional, did a nearly spot-on impression of Watson as she bounded up the stairs.

As I suspected, all ingredients had been stripped bare. Katie said the same was true for Opal's shop.

Proving just how desperate she was, Katie made a run to the grocery store and was elbow deep in flour and powdered sugar as she made the crust for lemon bars.

I liked Katie already, but I was fairly certain that by the end of the baking process, I would practically be in love with the woman. I gave her a chance to lose herself in the process before I began questioning. "So tell me, what's so horrible about living with Lois? She seems like such a sweet old lady."

"She is! She's a darling little lamb." Katie spoke freely as she measured, then poured powdered sugar into the mixer. "But that said, she is one intense little lamb."

Funny, Katie was the second person to compare Lois to a lamb.

She motioned down to Watson, who hadn't left her side since she started baking. "She's quite literally been so under my feet that I practically keep tripping over her. She's always been nice to me, but it's like we're suddenly best friends or sisters." She angled a telltale glance my way. "*Conjoined* sisters more like."

Katie chuckled at her own joke, and I chimed in. Lois definitely sounded more intense than I would've expected, but she'd been fairly shattered when she'd come into Victorian Antlers two days before, so maybe it was to be expected. "She does seem rather fragile. Don't you imagine she's just afraid to be alone?"

"I'm sure that's it, of course it is. And I feel horrible being critical. But I haven't had a moment to myself. Thank the Lord she had a hair appointment, and those always take her hours."

I started to nod, then hesitated. "Her hair appointments take hours? I could see that for Opal, not for Lois. Her hair looks natural."

Katie rolled her eyes. "It is. But it's still a process. Believe me, I've heard about it in detail. She goes to this homeopathic hairdresser. First there's an oatmeal bath, next they do something with mayonnaise, but it's the homemade, egg-free kind, of course. After that—"

"Okay, I got it. That makes sense. Sort of." I winked at her. "If you're really conjoined twins all of the sudden, I'm surprised you're not getting an oatmeal treatment for yourself."

She shivered. "Oh, she tried. Even broke down and cried a little bit. But I had to put my foot down at something." Katie fingered her spiral locks, leaving a trace of flour behind. "My hair was that something. But you would've thought I was killing her. I'm telling you, Fred. I take back every bad thought and word I've ever had about Opal. No wonder she was angry all the time. Lois is sweet, but the woman is possessive! I dated a guy like that once, for about two weeks. Worst two weeks of my life. It's like she owns me."

I couldn't even fathom it, but a horrible thought entered my head. "Did you know Opal and Sid were dating?"

Katie smacked both her dirty hands down on the counter and gaped at me. "You're kidding? Opal hated him." She glanced around the kitchen. "Although, I didn't know she was making edibles either, and if she was doing it in Sid's kitchen... who knows? Opal acted like she hated everyone except for Lois. And I've heard she'd been married several times, so maybe it was just her idea of romance."

Katie popped a small glass pan into the oven and returned to the mixer and began beating some eggs, before looking up at me suddenly. "Where did you hear about Opal and Sid? I never would've suspected."

"From the guy who owns the Green Munchies in Lyons. I drove down to talk to him the day before yesterday." I wasn't sure if it was residual from my conversation with Branson the night before or not, but as I made my admission to Katie, I was surprised to find myself a little embarrassed. "I've been asking around. I thought maybe I could find something that would help clear Barry's name."

To my surprise, Katie cocked her jaw and grinned. "Doesn't surprise me at all. No wonder I like you." She let out a girlish laugh, one that didn't quite fit her. "I actually went and saw Eddie myself yesterday."

"You did?"

She nodded. "Yes. I snuck out of the house for a couple of hours. Came back to Lois being a complete sobbing mess. I can't even say why I went there, but I just felt so stupid, all this coming to light and it's been right under my nose. I know people think that I knew about it, about Opal making edibles. But I swear I didn't. Lois didn't either. She's completely devastated. I just needed to know how big a fool I'd been to not notice. Eddie was sweet. Assured me the way things had been set up, there would've been no way I could've known. And he didn't have one good thing to say about Opal."

"Tell me about it." Guilt bit at me at the thought of Eddie. I had no doubt that I'd caused him some sort of trouble with what I'd told Branson. Maybe I'd drive down later in the afternoon and apologize. Or give him warning.

"Did you know a few years ago, in North Carolina, a bunch of newborns were testing positive for being addicted to marijuana?"

Katie's question was so out of the blue it drove Eddie out of my thoughts. It was almost as though she was trying to distract me. "You know, I can't say I did know that."

Katie nodded sagely as she zested a lemon. "It's true. And then the nurses would have to call social services, of course, because the newborns had to have become addicted to marijuana from someone, and it had to be their mothers, obviously." She looked at me expectantly.

"Obviously." If she was playing me, her acting skills were stellar, and I couldn't shake my innate sense of fondness for the woman.

"Well—" Katie dipped a finger in the bright yellow mixture, stuck it into her mouth, and gave a pleased smile. "—it turns out, that none of those baby mamas were using drugs of any kind. After an investigation, they discovered certain brands of baby soaps and shampoos, while not actually getting the babies high at all or even containing THC, were causing the babies to give false positive on drugs tests."

I waited for the story to continue. It didn't. "Oh, that's... something."

Katie nodded again. "I know, right."

Again I hesitated, but no further explanation was offered. "Katie, does that have something to do with Opal?"

"I don't think so." She seemed to consider as she removed the crust from the oven, then peered over at me expectantly. "Do you?"

I shook my head, trying not to laugh. "I doubt it, but I thought maybe you did since you brought it up."

"No, that was just a little tidbit about marijuana for you." She shrugged. "Sometimes, when I get a topic on my mind, I do a lot of research. Granted, with Lois over my shoulder, I've not been able to do as much as I normally would, but I managed a little. It was just one of the interesting stories I found out."

"Well, okay then. You never know when you might need a random fact. They might make all the difference." The lady was a hoot.

Katie poured the lemon mixture over the baked crust, and shoved it into the oven with a contented sigh. "I can't thank you enough, Fred. I almost feel like myself again."

"I'm the one who should be thanking you. I get fresh-baked goodness, have a pleasant memory in this kitchen, and someone to bounce ideas off of." It would be silly to say out loud, but I truly did feel like I'd made my first friend in town. "And maybe this sounds horrible, but as nice as it is to do what you're doing for Lois, surely you can't take it all upon yourself to stay with her. That's too much for any person. Even if it was a role Opal filled for her."

Instant guilt cut across Katie's features, and embarrassment weighted down her tone. "I have a confession." I lifted my eyebrows, and she continued. "Commercial rental property isn't easy to come by in Estes. Especially the kind I need, since I'm a baker. Opal and Lois are listed jointly on both shops' leases, Sinful Bites and Healthy Delights. I'm hoping Lois will let me take over Opal's side of the lease. I can finally open my own bakery like I've dreamed." She grimaced. "I truly did like Lois, and I'm sure I will again when I don't want to strangle her, but the lease is one of the main reasons I'm still staying with Lois. That makes me horrible, doesn't it?"

I laughed. "For some reason, Katie dear, it makes me like you even more." It was true. But, it also could be a reason for Katie to want Opal out of the way. Though I simply couldn't see Katie doing such a thing.

She beamed in relief, but her eyes widened, and she turned and set the timer above the oven. "Barely remembered." She moved to the sink and began to wash up as she continued to speak. "Any other fun factoid you'd like to know about marijuana? I discovered a ton. I can even tell you what wattage of lights is best for optimal growth."

I sat up straighter, Katie's words triggering something. "I forgot, I haven't checked out the basement, where Opal and Sid were growing all their product. Barry said it was nothing more than a crawl space." I motioned to the door. "Want to check it out with me?"

"You know I do!" She gave little more than a cursory wipe of her hands with the dishtowel, and we hurried down to the main floor.

Near the back, in a hallway close to the storage room, another door led down to a long flight of steps. I flicked the light switch by the doorframe, and we wandered down. I gaped as we arrived into a huge room, nearly half the floor space of the level above, with the ceiling two inches above my head. I lifted my hand, touching the underside of the floorboards of the main level. "They've put some work into this place. Maybe Barry didn't remember, but a crawlspace definitely doesn't have six-foot ceilings." The room was empty, nothing but the lights overhead, no trace of plants, pot or otherwise. A tingle of excitement went through me, and I looked over at Katie. "You want to hear what makes *me* a horrible person?"

A smile spread across her face, and she nodded.

"I love that whatever Opal and Sid did, they did all the backbreaking work, and I now have an actual storage room."

THIRTEEN

Katie cut the cooled lemon bars and sprinkled powdered sugar over the top before choosing four of them to bring over.

"It's a good thing I'm not a salad kind of girl. There's gotta be two days' worth of calories in this thing." I picked up one of the lemon bars, sniffed it, and managed to offer up a cloud of powdered sugar which combined with the snow lightly falling outside the window and made a perfect holiday moment, despite all of the turmoil.

Katie chuckled. "Nah. I almost made my gingerbread recipe, which I serve with ice cream. Lemon bars almost count as dessert."

I started to laugh, but the sound turned into an awkward orgasmic groan as I took a bite. Bright, tart, and sweet, and even better than it smelled. "Oh my God. I think I'm in love with you."

"Just wait until you try more of my savory dishes. They're my specialty." She giggled. "You'll be asking me to marry you."

"I'm close to that already." I took another bite; it was just as good as the first.

Watson had already devoured his chicken, and was staring up at us expectantly. I pretended not to notice.

"Do you think it says horrible things about us, when we're able to enjoy eating in here where Opal passed?"

Katie shrugged. "Not at all. The kitchen is for cooking and eating. Not for killing someone. Or for dying, for that matter. It's the killer and Opal who made the faux pas, not us." She took another huge bite as if to prove her point.

"All right, seriously now, where have you been my entire life?"

"If I told you, I'd have to kill you." She started to giggle and then cut herself off. "Okay, even I have to admit that's a little too far."

Our gazes met over our perfect desserts, and we both burst out laughing. God, it felt good to laugh. Felt good to be normal and happy. A wave of affection washed over me, and I reached out to squeeze Katie's forearm. "Thank you for this. I can't tell you how much I needed it. It feels like I haven't laughed in ages."

"You've been under a lot of stress since the moment you moved into town. I'd say that's understandable."

"It's been a lot longer than that." A hint of shadow filtered back into my mind. "Part of why I came here to begin with. So thank you."

A pleased blush rose to Katie's cheeks, and she smiled. "I'm thankful too. Trust me, there weren't any moments like this with Opal. Whatever brought you to town, I'm glad you're here." She started to take another bite, then paused. "Still... I must admit, I'm curious why you chose Estes Park. I know your mom is here, but we don't get many single women in the prime of their lives moving to Estes."

"You're here, aren't you?"

Her kind eyes flashed panic, and for the first time, her smile seemed forced. She shook her head, curls bobbing. Despite what I noticed, when she spoke, Katie was back to her normal, cheerful self. "Oh no you don't. This is about you, and I asked first." Her brown eyes sparkled. "And I told you when I'm curious about things, I like to find out stuff. So far, I've discovered you founded your own publishing company. Is your bookstore an offshoot of that or something?"

For a moment I was thrown off at the thought of Katie researching me on the internet. Then I remembered her odd factoids about marijuana. Maybe this was just part of Katie.

She backpedaled quickly. "Not that you have to tell me, of course. I'm sure it's none of my business."

It wasn't any of her business, but suddenly, I needed it to be. Or at least needed to share with someone who wasn't obligated to take my side through the bonds of family. There was something off about Katie, or something she was hiding. Maybe it made me as big a fool as Barry with Gerald, but I couldn't shake the feeling that I could trust her. "No, it's okay. I can talk about it. And no, the bookshop is not an offshoot of the publishing house. My partner and I had a falling out. I'm no longer a part of the company."

Katie hesitated like she was judging if she should ask the next question or not, but I already knew her well enough to know that she would ask whatever it was. Sure enough, she proved me right. "I have to say, I'm surprised. Honestly, my guess was that you'd gone through a divorce. Felt the need to have a life switch or something."

"You're closer than you know." Goodness, was I that much of a stereotype? Single woman moving across the country to start her life anew. "The divorce was six years ago. It's the other version of the tale as old as time. Husband replaces his wife for a younger model, complete with *enhanced* features."

Katie chuckled, but more in commiseration than humor. "I can just imagine."

"I did a life change then too." Yes, it seemed I truly was a stereotype, in duplicate. Might as well own it. "I was a college professor, specializing in American and British literature. After the affair, I left teaching. My childhood best friend, Charlotte, and I joined together and opened a publishing house. To both our surprises, within a year, it was a smashing success. To this day, I can't tell you why, when so many other small publishing houses are closing. Maybe just dumb luck. Whatever it was, those six years working with Charlotte were the best of my life. I was honestly grateful Garrett had the affair and wanted a divorce. It made my life so much better." A sense of loss cut through me. I really had built such a beautiful life. I hadn't wanted anything more.

"I'm sorry, Fred." This time Katie reached across with the companionable squeeze. She let a few moments pass before asking more questions. "You said you and Charlotte had a falling out?"

I couldn't hold back a bitter laugh. "That was a polite way for me to put it. It turned out, I was a fool, and Charlotte found fortune much more enticing than friendship."

"No!" Katie's tone grew defensive. "Don't refer to yourself like that. Just because someone is a horrible person, doesn't make you a fool."

"In this case, it does. Long story short, Charlotte was better with the numbers. I was better with the creatives. It was part of what made us such a great team. She handled contracts and finances. I handled going over submissions and choosing the writers and books I thought had the best chance of being successful. We were both extremely good at what we did. She'd formatted our business agreements in such a way, from the very beginning, that when the time came, it was easy to push me to the side. I should've had a separate lawyer look over our contracts when we founded the company. But she was my best friend. It never entered my mind she only had her own interest at heart. A much larger publishing house came along and wanted to incorporate us into their business. I resisted, not realizing I didn't have much of a say. Now Charlotte and our company are part of the big five, and I'm here, opening a bookshop."

Katie looked furious. "You should sue!"

I laughed again, once more there was no humor. "The past nine months have been nothing more than litigation. But that's part of why I showed up so much sooner than expected. All of the sudden, I was just done. I could see the lawsuit spreading out for the next years of my life. It's no way to live. So I settled. For a very good chunk of money, to be sure, but nothing compared to what should have been." I motioned around the kitchen. "I can't say I'm glad it happened, but I *am* glad I'm here. And I'm excited about what the Cozy Corgi will become. I'm ready for a simple, beautiful, easy life. Just Watson and me, my family, my bookstore, a beautiful mountain town—" I gave Katie a heartfelt smile. "—new friends. The perfect life. True, a different version than what I had envisioned. But who knows, maybe it will be a better one."

"I hope so." Katie returned my smile, but then hers became teasing. "Not to be a naysayer, but I'm not sure what it says when your new adventure begins with a murder. I'm impressed you're still here. I think I would've tossed my little bundle of fur in the back seat and got myself right back down the mountain."

This time, my tone was genuine once more. "Like I said. It seems I like to play the part of a fool. And even though there are no books yet, I'm going to fight for this little place. Whatever it takes, I'm going to make it work. You wait and see. The Cozy Corgi is going to be the best little bookshop you've ever seen in your life."

"You know, Fred, I don't doubt you in the least." She eyed my empty plate. I didn't even remember finishing it. "Want another piece?"

"Are you kidding? The first two were the size of small icebergs."

"Well, I want a third." She narrowed her eyes. "I think you should have another, just to make sure that ex-husband and ex-best friend of yours know you're going to enjoy every second of your new life."

Who could argue with that? I slid the plate forward. "Fill me up, my friend. This new life doesn't come with the calorie counter!"

I enjoyed my time with Katie so much I nearly suggested she stay as I continued making plans for the layout of the shop. I didn't. Not because I didn't trust or like Katie, but I needed this store to be my own. For better or worse, I wanted every decision to be mine. No more business partner. This shop would be entirely Winifred Wendy Page, and no one else. Well, no one else besides Watson in any case.

Between the early hour of sunset, thanks to winter, and me losing track of time, it was dark by the time Watson and I left the Cozy Corgi.

After my time with Katie, Eddie continued to be on my mind. I didn't count him a friend, definitely not in the same way I did Katie, but I truly did feel guilty about selling him out to Branson so quickly. Or maybe the emotion had very little to do with Katie and revolved more around Charlotte. Not the same thing by any means, but it was most definitely not the type of person I wanted to be.

Though the early evening was dark, it had quit snowing, and the roads were clear. I was halfway to Lyons when I realized I should've at least called. I had noticed Green Munchies stayed open until ten every evening, but it didn't mean Eddie would be there. As there was no cell reception between Estes Park and Lyons, Watson and I just kept going.

We arrived a little past six thirty. Once again, I didn't bother with a leash, so Watson followed me up the sidewalk and into the front door. Like before, the place was sleek and clean, the massive plastic ovals casting a soft glow through the place. Eddie was nowhere to be seen. No one was anywhere to be seen. Other than soft music, the place was silent.

I nearly called out, but didn't want to be rude, so I decided to wait. Instead of going to the edibles like we had before, I wandered around the other section of the shop, checking out the various paraphernalia, most of which I was clueless to what they were.

The assortment of pipes was rather fascinating, ranging from simple clear glass to intricate ones shaped like dragons and fairies. My favorite was a combination of glass and metal, complete with wheels and dials, designed in a steampunk style. It looked more like a piece of art than a pipe. I'd have to ask Eddie to show me if the wheels and gadgets actually did anything or if they were just for show.

As I perused the store, a tingle of anxiety began to gnaw at me. Something was off. "Eddie?"

Watson flinched at the sudden sound of my voice. Strangely, it was even startling to me. Things were too quiet.

Not pausing to consider, I stepped behind the counter and headed toward the door that to led into the back. "Eddie?"

The lights were on but dim, revealing a small stockroom with a warehouse feel. Like the front of the shop, it was clean, modern, and organized. Still no movement or sound.

"Eddie?"

Watson whimpered and lowered his head. With a whine, he glanced up at me, then returned his attention to the ground. He headed off in the direction I'd just noticed. A door in the back wall. Watson reached it a few paces before me, paused with his nose pressed to the crack of the door, and let out a low growl.

I reached for the door handle and hesitated. What was I doing? Playing the part of a fool, to be sure. There'd already been one murder in a dispensary; now here I was, in another one, alone.

For some reason, whether it be stupidity or stubbornness, the idea of rushing back to the car and calling the police seemed weak. I gripped the door handle, turned it, and gave a push.

The room was dark but a newly familiar odor hung in the air.

The volume of Watson's growl increased.

Hand trembling, I felt beside the doorframe, found the light switch, and flicked it on.

This time when I found a dead body, I didn't gasp. Somehow, I'd expected it.

Eddie lay facedown on the office floor. His feet were nearest me, and I couldn't see his face, but I knew it was

Eddie, even without confirming his handlebar mustache. Although different, his clothes nearly matched what he'd worn before. If not on the floor, his tall, lean frame could almost have passed for being asleep, his arms and legs straight and relaxed. Blood matted the back of his head, and a large pool had grown around him. Some insane part of me demanded that I go to him and check to make sure he was dead.

Maybe I didn't gasp, but I couldn't bring myself to touch him either. There was nothing to check. I'd never seen a gunshot wound, but I was certain that was what I was looking at, and something about the blood made me feel like he'd been dead for a little while at least.

Still growling, Watson slinked toward him, sniffing at the soles of Eddie's shoes.

I smacked my thigh. "No! Stay back, boy." Once again, the volume of my words startled both of us, and I froze. Here I was being loud with a dead body at my feet. What if the killer was still around?

No sooner had the thought flitted through my mind than I tossed it away. If there was anyone else here, I would've heard them while I was in the front room.

Not taking the chance that Watson was going to get into one of his stubborn streaks, I scooped him into my arms, carried him to the car, and got inside. I dialed 911 and told them I would wait for them outside the shop.

Poor Eddie. Poor, poor Eddie. The only person who seemed to be grieving about Opal was Lois. Somehow, I knew that wouldn't be true for Eddie.

In a crazy thought, a part of me was relieved he wouldn't be getting into trouble from Branson. He wouldn't know that I'd so easily thrown him under the bus. I shook my head at the thought. What a horrible notion.

One thing was for sure, though. With Eddie's death, it most definitely narrowed the motive. This didn't have anything to do with dead husbands or owl feathers. I supposed it might still be connected to blackmail, but I couldn't see Eddie being involved in that.

Part of me wished Barry hadn't been released on bail after all. Then, at least it would've been simple to prove he hadn't committed this murder either.

"I'm telling you, Sergeant Wexler couldn't have been nicer." Barry paused from where he was scrubbing the wall. He kept forgetting to wring out his sponge after dipping it into the sudsy water, and as a result, his pink-and-blue tie-dye shirt was nearly soaked from the mess running down his arm. "When he came by the house this morning, it was like he'd never truly thought I'd done it at all."

I didn't really believe Branson had thought Barry killed Opal. Which was part of my frustration with him. He hadn't come to the Green Munchies the night before, so I hadn't been able to get a feel from him on what he was going to do about Barry.

Mom looked over from where she was sponging the opposite wall, without halfway drowning herself. "Well, of course not. No one in their right mind would think you could hurt anyone. And he *should* be nice. All the trouble he put us through. I'm just glad we had an alibi for that drug dealer's death in Lyons."

"His name was Eddie, Mom. He was a nice guy." I still felt a twinge of guilt at the thought of Eddie. Though the notion made no sense. There was nothing I could've done.

But still, while Katie and I had been gossiping over freshly baked lemon bars, Eddie was being shot.

"Yes, he was." Barry cocked an eyebrow my direction. "You thought so too, Fred?" At his feet, Watson pranced through a puddle of water, leaving footprints trailing behind him.

"Watson!" Percival's cry was a little shrill. "I just finished mopping."

"I told you to save mopping till last." Gary shook a putty knife in Percival's direction, then transferred the piece of candy he was sucking to the other cheek before speaking again. "I'm going to leave a mess behind after I scrape the putty off these patches when they're dry. And I don't want to hear a word about it."

"Fred said she didn't care about the holes. They're going to be covered by bookcases anyway." Percival and Gary had been bickering since they arrived with my parents to the Cozy Corgi over an hour before.

"Okay, you two. I don't want to be responsible for the bookstore causing quarrels." I refocused on Barry, more to avoid further sniping than any desire to continue to talk about Eddie. "Granted, I only met him that once, but Eddie seemed very sweet. And he absolutely loved you."

Mom let out a long-suffering sigh. "Well, he should. Barry informed me just how frequent his trips to Lyons were and how extremely unfrugal they could be."

Barry muttered something under his breath.

The four of them had insisted on doing a deep clean now we had the store back. The process made much easier by Branson and the police department. Before Mom could retort, I switched the conversation again. "So you feel like Branson—Sergeant Wexler truly believed your alibi?"

Mom answered for them. "The four of us were having

our monthly spades tournament yesterday. We were all together. So Barry has three alibis."

"I'm surprised he didn't find that a little too convenient." Was that irritation I was feeling? I thought so, but the term didn't feel quite right.

Percival grinned at me from where he followed Watson around with the mop. It seemed Watson was enjoying the game. "You can quit calling him Sergeant Wexler, darling. We all know the two of you are on a first-name basis. And now he's not threatening to lock up your stepfather forever, I'm certain you have the entire family's blessing to take that hot man on a date!"

Before I could protest, Barry joined in. "I think you should. He obviously likes you. He even asked about you this morning. Wanted to know if you were okay after discovering Eddie's body."

"He did?"

Barry nodded.

And with that, I realized *irritation* hadn't been the right word for what I was feeling. I was hurt. Branson knew I discovered Eddie's body, he had to be aware I'd be worried about the police trying to pin a second murder on my stepfather, and he hadn't so much as called.

The realization made me want to hurry over and pick up Barry's bucket of dirty water and dump it over my head. I had no business feeling hurt, or any other sentiment, for Branson Wexler. "Well, I'll believe it when I see it. It wouldn't surprise me at all if he swings by here any minute to take you in for further questioning."

"He won't. He was very clear that as far as he was concerned, the case against Barry was closed." Mom dropped the sponge into her bucket, wiped her hands on her jeans, and crossed the room to pat my cheek. "It's over, sweetie. And I can't thank you enough for all you tried to do for Barry. You are most definitely your father's daughter. But you can relax now. It really is done. Sergeant Wexler said he couldn't give us details of course, but that Eddie's murder had to be linked to Opal's. They were both involved in some shady business and must've made a common enemy." She dropped her hand and offered a sweet smile. "Percival is right. Branson is a very handsome man and obviously a very good cop, just like your father was. I think he would suit you."

I knew Mom was desperate for me to have another relationship. See me as happy as Barry's daughters were with their husbands and children. As much as she was thrilled I was in Estes taking over my grandparents' old cabin and opening the bookshop, I knew she didn't believe I was really fine on my own. And as far as the case being closed....

"I was thinking that way, too, last night. About Opal's murder and Eddie's being connected... not about Branson." I cast a warning glance at Percival, who had lifted a finger toward me and looked on the verge of a sermon. "But the more I think about it, the less it makes sense. None of you saw the bodies. They were different, completely. Eddie was shot in the back of the head. His body was lying there like he was asleep. Opal was beaten with a rolling pin, for crying out loud. She was sprawled on the floor. If it was really drug-related, and if the same person killed her, why in the world would they use a rolling pin if they had a gun handy?"

Four pairs of blank eyes stared back at me. Clearly the thought hadn't occurred to any of them.

Gary pulled a piece of candy out of his pocket, causing Watson to hurry over at the sound of unwrapping cellophane, and he popped it into his mouth before offering a comment. "That's a good point, Fred. But you accomplished what you set out to do. Barry is no longer under suspicion. The police can handle it from here." He smiled at me, his affection clear. "Your job now, is to turn this empty store into the most adorable and cozy of all bookshops the world has ever seen. That's it."

How wonderful that sounded. If only it were that simple. "I hardly think I accomplished anything with Barry. I never cleared his name. It was just happenstance."

"You discovered Eddie." Barry beamed at me. "That led to clearing me."

"That would've happened anyway. Someone would've found him. It didn't have to be me." I wished it hadn't been. For whatever reason, after discovering Opal's body, I had to make a choice to recall the scene. With Eddie, the sight of his lifeless body kept flashing behind my eyes.

"Well, either way, it's over. And we're all safe and sound. I call that a success." Mom gestured up the steps. "I'm glad you decided to get a refinisher here to do the floors before you have the bookcases installed. I think you should do upstairs too, while you're at it, even though you're not sure you want to extend the bookstore up there. At least that way it's done, and you'll have more options."

It took some effort to focus on the bookshop. "You're probably right. Might as well do it all the first time, just in case."

"Good." Mom clapped her hands. "Well then, Percival, I think we're about done here after you get one more pass with the mop, if we can get Watson to sit still, that is. I say we all go home and have dinner. I have a huge pan of enchiladas in the fridge, just waiting to be popped in the oven."

"Oh sure, leave all the backbreaking work to the older brother. I see how it is." Percival winked at Mom. "But you've got Grandma's recipe for enchiladas, so you know I'll do about anything for those."

Gary fished another piece of candy out of his pocket, but it slipped through his fingers and bounced across the floor. Watson scrambled for it.

"Oh no you don't!" To both of our surprises, I made it there first and snatched it from between his teeth. I grinned at him in satisfaction. "You're going to have to up your game, little one." I started to hand the candy to Gary, then stared at it, something trying desperately to click in my mind.

"You okay, darling?" Gary pulled another from his pocket and held it out to me. "You can have a fresh one."

"No, thank you. It's just that...." And then it snapped. Licorice. I looked up at Gary. "Where did you get this?"

"We have about a billion of these back at Victoria Antlers." He rolled his eyes. "Lois keeps bringing us a new basket of candy every single day. We've thrown everything away so far, except for these. These little hard licorice balls are the one thing the dear woman ever made that are any good. Maybe the only thing in my life that doesn't have sugar which was worth eating."

I stared at the licorice. Lois....

I refocused on Gary and then cast my gaze around at the rest of my family. "Did Opal make these too?"

It was Barry who answered. "No. She didn't make hard candy of any kind. Not even her edibles. It was one of my complaints about buying from her. You either had to consume them quickly or freeze them. Which is fine, but if you freeze things, then you have to plan ahead to defrost them. Things like these are much easier to just unwrap and pop in your mouth without"—his gaze darted guiltily to Mom—"people knowing."

My heart began drumming out a rocketing rhythm, and I held the candy like it was a piece of evidence in the courtroom. "This is what Watson was eating the morning I found Opal's body. The one he got was from outside the kitchen door, right upstairs. And then there were others inside the kitchen as well."

I'd expected gasps of awe and understanding, but again, those four pairs of eyes stared at me expectantly, without any spark of comprehension.

I shook the candy at them. "You said yourself Opal never made these. And Lois said that she had no idea Opal was making edibles or using this kitchen." Still no reaction other than staring. I shook the candy again. "If Lois is the only one who makes these, then what were they doing in the kitchen when Opal was murdered?"

Flames of understanding began to flicker, but just barely. Gary's low voice was only just audible as he considered his words. "Could be just like what happened here. Maybe Opal had some in her pocket like I did and spilled them."

The others nodded in agreement. And I had to admit, it made sense. But not quite. "I got the impression Opal didn't like Lois's baking." I was certain I wasn't making that up, but I wasn't sure if I'd actually heard someone say it or if it was just what little I'd seen of how Opal treated her sister.

"I doubt she did. There's not much to like. But maybe she liked these." Gary shrugged again. "Trust me, it helps to have something you genuinely like to be able to brag about when Lois is around."

Mom came up and slipped her arm into mine. "Let the police handle it, honey. I'm sure everything is fine. Let's wrap up here and go home to dinner."

Giving an excuse that I needed to stay and do a couple more things upstairs, which I didn't think anyone believed, I sent the family on their way with the promise that I would be at Mom's shortly.

I needed to think. Without other voices around.

Though I couldn't quite make sense of all the puzzle pieces, my gut told me I was right about Lois. I couldn't truly picture her doing it, but now that the thought had entered my mind, I couldn't quite *not* see her doing it either.

But what to do?

Watson followed me as I paced, and after a couple of circles around the shop, I realized we were leaving footprints in Percival's mop job. I took a second to feel guilty about that, then wondered why we'd bothered with mopping at all. I was going to have the floors refinished.

I shoved the thought away, not important and obviously not the point, and continued pacing. My family was wrong. Even if I couldn't explain why. They just were. For whatever reason, it had been Lois. As soon as I saw that licorice, I knew. I just knew.

But Mom was right about something. This was the police's responsibility. What was I going to do? Trudge over to wherever she lived and do a citizen's arrest? Call Katie and....

Katie.

If I was right, then Katie might have a lot more to worry about than Lois being codependent.

Despite my surety, as I pulled out my cell to call Branson, I couldn't help but feel foolish. The sensation increased as he answered the phone. "Fred, how are you?"

It took me a second to respond as I realized he must've saved my number in his phone. I decided not to read into that. And again, not important and not the point. "Hear me out." I opted to skip pleasantries so I wouldn't lose my nerve. "I know who killed Opal."

There was silence on the other end of the line. When he spoke, Branson seemed hesitant. "You do?"

"Yeah, I do." I stopped pacing and stood still, closing my eyes even as I worked through it again. "The morning Watson and I found Opal's body, it was because of these little licorice candies. Watson found them outside the kitchen door, and that's when I went in and found her body. They were scattered across the floor in there as well."

"What—"

I barged on, knowing that if I paused, I might not have the chance to get it all out. "It turns out Opal never made licorice candy. Only Lois. And Lois claims that she never knew Opal was operating an edibles business, or even that she was cooking in Sid's old shop. So what were the licorice candies doing in that kitchen?"

Once again, if I expected a barrage of trumpets of understanding at the end of my spiel, I was sorely disappointed. "So... you believe that Lois killed Opal because some of her licorice candies were at the crime scene?"

From the tone of his voice, I knew I was wasting my time. "Yes."

"Why couldn't Opal have had some of Lois's candy with her? Maybe she liked it."

"Opal didn't like anything Lois made." Even as I said it, I still wasn't sure whether I'd actually heard someone claim that or if it was just my gut instinct.

"Fred...." Branson's sigh didn't sound irritated, but it felt like he had shifted to speaking to a small child. "I know your dad was a great detective. And I know you're a brave, intelligent woman. But I think you might be in a little over your head here." His voice brightened somewhat. "I thought you'd be glad your stepfather is no longer a suspect."

"I am!" Stupidly I tried again, remembering one of my other points. "What about the murder scenes? They're completely different. You saw them. Opal was hit with a rolling pin and was splayed out over the floor. It was messy. Eddie was shot in the back of the head, and his body was... I don't know, different somehow. How do you explain that?"

"I didn't see Eddie's body. Lyons is in a different county than Estes Park. However, I've seen the pictures and read the report." He was back to sounding like he was explaining things to a child. "Though the weapon might be different, it's very clear the murders are connected. These two individuals were dealing drugs illegally. They had a direct connection and a hostile relationship. Their being killed within days of each other is not a coincidence, Fred. Or did Lois kill Eddie too?"

"I don't know! Maybe?" My temper was getting the best of me. "No, I don't think so. Not that I know Lois, but I don't know why she would kill Eddie."

Branson's tone softened into a kind of soft pity, which only irritated me more. "Why would she kill Opal?"

"I don't think she knew about Opal and Sid dating. It turns out that Lois is a little bit possessive."

"Sid died months ago, Fred."

Oh, right. I kept forgetting that part. "I don't know the motive, all right. But my gut tells me Lois did it. And the clues point that way as well. The licorice candy was right there. Lois's licorice candy."

He sighed again. "Okay, I'll... look into it."

I knew that tone. I'd used that tone countless times. When speaking to an agent, sometimes directly to an author, as I tried to tell them I wasn't interested in the manuscript but they couldn't take no for an answer. That placating "I'll look into it, I'll consider it, I'll give it another try." Everyone knew it was hogwash, but it was polite and made all parties feel better. Kinda.

"Thanks. I appreciate it." I disconnected the call before Branson could say anything else. Before *I* could say anything else. I knew he was just doing his job, and I knew there was a low chance he believed my theory; even my family dismissed it. But still.... If we kept talking, I'd say something I'd regret.

Well, he could think what he wanted. I wasn't sure how I was going to prove my theory, but I would. It was past being about Barry now. Some part of me knew I should at least claim it was justice for Opal that drove me, but it wasn't. Not really. I wanted to solve this. Needed to. Probably for a bunch of reasons, but I didn't bother to try to figure them out.

I looked around the shop. I was antsy. I needed to do something with my hands. But nothing else needed to be done, and I'd kept the rest of the family waiting long enough for dinner. I spent a few minutes scratching behind Watson's ears, so long that he rolled over, demanding belly rubs. As always, by the time I was finished, we both felt better. Calmer. I didn't have to take care of anything else at this moment. And Lord knew, if I tried, I'd do something rash.

I locked up the shop, and Watson and I started toward the car. Before I made it five feet, I noticed light coming from the back of Healthy Delights.

I paused, considering. Maybe a light had been left on, though I didn't remember noticing it before, but it had still been daylight when we'd started cleaning. Maybe it was Katie, stealing some time away from Lois, though I doubted she would do it there of all places. Maybe Lois?

Maybe Lois.

And at that possibility, all other thoughts fled. In the back my mind, I could feel the tingle of *What are you doing? Do you really think you're going to get her to confess? What do you do if she does?* But they were fuzzy and easy to ignore.

I walked right up to the door and knocked.

There was no answer, no movement inside. I knocked again.

Still nothing.

Maybe the light had been left on from another time and no one was there. Even so, I knocked one more time. There was a shadow in the back, and then a small form emerged and walked through the store. Even silhouetted, it was clearly Lois. As she drew nearer, my blood began to pound in my ears. I focused on remaining calm. As far as Lois knew, there was no reason for me to suspect her.

Lois leaned close to the glass, the streetlights illuminating her face. After a second, she brightened in recognition. With a twist of the lock, she threw open the door.

"Well, Fred! Watson! What a pleasant surprise." Her

eyes narrowed, but not in a sinister way as much as I tried to imagine it. "What are you two doing here? It's freezing outside."

I went with the truth. It was simple and relaxed me. "I was just next door getting things ready. We're going to have the refinisher come soon for the floors. Then I noticed a light on in the back of your shop as we were walking to the car. I thought I'd make sure everything was all right."

"Oh, yes dear. I wanted to do some baking this evening. It soothes my soul, you know?" She relaxed a little more. "I so appreciate you checking on me, and my shop. But all is fine."

I could hear the dismissal in her voice. In another second she'd bid me good night and lock the door. I couldn't let that happen, even though I still had no idea what I was doing. I'd just landed on asking Lois for a dog treat for Watson as an excuse to come in when Lois saved me the trouble.

"Actually, Fred, I hate to be an inconvenience, but Katie's been coming down here with me when I bake. Helping me sometimes. She said she didn't have it in her this evening. Her words. So she stayed home. I think she's growing tired of me already." Her eyes grew hopeful. "Would you like to come in for a bit?"

I hesitated for a heartbeat, asking myself if I was truly going to do this, even though I already knew the answer. "Of course. Maybe you can show me the secret to those dog bones Watson loves so much."

Lois stepped back from the door, making room for me even as she shook her head. "I'm sorry, dear. I'm sure it sounds completely awful of me, but I never share recipes. Although I allow people to watch. But I'm not making those this evening, I'm afraid. Tonight is apricot-and-prune brownies. I use them as binding agents for the flour and chocolate. As you know, I only cook vegan, so there's no eggs or milk. But the apricots are a spot of brightness and the prunes give a nice tang."

I could use that sentence alone as evidence that she had the soul of a murderer. "Sounds.... I'd love to... see you in action."

"Wonderful! I'm so glad!"

After she locked the door, Watson and I followed her back into the kitchen. As dog friendly as Estes Park was, I expected her to make a comment about him being where she cooked. She didn't. Instead she gave him one of her massive dog treats.

Now that we were back in her kitchen, my common sense began to scream at me. If I truly believed Lois was the murderer, what in the world was I doing alone with her away from the sight of anyone else? And I was putting Watson in danger as well. Though, I could picture Lois as a murderer, I couldn't imagine her hurting an animal. Surely a vegan wouldn't kill a dog. But even if I was right, even if she was the murderer, I was at least five times stronger than Lois, easily. A stiff breeze was stronger than Lois. Unless she really was Eddie's murderer as well and there was a gun lying about. I couldn't think about that. I'd made my choice. Time to see it through.

Lois returned to her so-called brownies, which were currently a brown glob in the bottom of her mixing bowl. As she started to work, her conversation turned back to Katie. "It's lovely to have you here, Fred. You're such a bright, warm addition to Estes Park. I'm so glad we get to be neighbors." She cast narrowed eyes on me, the kind that told me to keep secrets. "I have a confession. I'm considering having Katie take over my sister's shop. She's been just the sweetest thing since Opal died. Or at least I thought. But she seems to be pulling away. So I'm not sure. We'll have to see how the next few days play out." She gave an apologetic shrug. "I know the girl is desperate for her own bakery, and she has talent. Just like Opal, she uses too much sugar and animal byproducts, but there's talent there. I think I can mold it into something truly wonderful. But I don't see the sense in being neighbors and sharing a lease with someone who looks for excuses to have time away."

Despite knowing it would be best to simply agree with everything Lois said, I couldn't help but defend my friend. "I think Katie would be a wonderful person to pass on the legacy of Opal's baking skills. I'm sure she'd do a fine job."

Lois tossed some sort of seeds into the brownie mixture and nodded at me as if I'd hit the nail on the head. "That's just it. Katie wants her own bakery. She won't recreate Opal's legacy. I need someone who will follow Opal's recipes exactly. Nothing on the menu needs changing. It should stay exactly as it was. I thought Katie was that person. That she could step into the place Opal left behind in the shop."

Intense little lamb was right. I decided to push. "And maybe into the place Opal left behind in your home too?"

"Yes. Exactly." Lois nodded and actually looked relieved that I understood. Giving no hint of awareness of how morbid that truly sounded, she brightened. "I'm so glad you understand. Katie just doesn't seem to." She paused in her movements and turned to me, a new light in her eyes. "Fred, do you bake?"

"No." I did, not at all to Katie's standards, but I wasn't going to say so to Lois.

The look of disappointment barely lasted three seconds. "That's okay. I can teach you. Honestly, Opal's more traditional way of baking is much simpler. You could take over her shop. We can even expand into Heads and Tails. You and Watson could live with me. It would be beautiful."

Now my skin truly did crawl. How Katie had managed one night in the same house as this woman was beyond me. She seemed to transform from a sweet little woman to Norman Bates in a long wig and a dress. But this was definitely the rabbit trail to follow if I planned on getting the confession out of her. But what good would a confession do if it was her word against mine? I really should have thought this through. "Well... I was considering what to do with the top floor of the shop. You... might be onto something."

She almost looked pretty and innocent in her delight. "I knew I liked you." Lois motioned me over. "Come here. Let's finish this recipe together."

My phone. Somehow, if I could get it out and hit the Record button. Did the phone have a Record button? I'd never been great with technology. Maybe if I made a video. I could hit Record on the video and then put it back in the pocket of my skirt. Now how to do that without Lois noticing....

I joined Lois at the mixer. She scooped up a small spoonful and held it out to me. "Here. Taste."

I started to decline but thought better of it, so I reached for the spoon.

She held it away from me. "No, taste."

Nearly feeling violated, I lowered my hand and opened my mouth.

When Lois spoon-fed me the mixture, it took every ounce of my willpower not to shudder, both at the disgusting flavor and texture of the brownie batter and at the sensation of being fed by Lois. I forced a swallow, then a smile. "Very good."

"Thank you. See, you don't need to have sugar to make things sweet. I don't like things unnaturally sweet." She inspected me for a second. "What do you think? Could it use more honey?"

It ought to be thrown in the garbage. "No. I think what you've done is perfect." And I could really use a hot shower.

"I agree." Her smile let me know I'd said the right answer. "I'm so glad you stopped by tonight. It clarified what I was feeling, but didn't want to admit. I've been debating with myself on what to do about Katie. She's constantly making suggestions every night when I'm here baking. As much as I missed her company this evening, it was nice not being told how to improve on my creations." She looked at me adoringly. "And now I know why things didn't feel right. You're a godsend, Fred." She started to turn back to the brownie mixture, then narrowed her eyes at me once more. This time there was no illusion of kindness there. "You're single, right? No husband or boyfriend?"

I shook my head.

"Are you hoping to find one later?"

"No. I've been down that road. I think I'm done." Even though I was doing nothing more than playing a role at this point, Branson flitted through my mind. "Definitely done." Leo flitted through next.

Good grief.

"Smart girl. That's how it should be. Glad I don't have to worry about that."

I knew it. I knew that was why she'd killed Opal. Even if it had been months after Sid passed. I regretted not having had the time to figure out how to record the conversation on my phone, but there was no time like the present. "I imagine it was hard for you when Opal started dating Sid, wasn't it?"

She stiffened slightly. Then kept right on going. “No. Men were Opal’s weakness. She had horrible taste in men. Sid was no surprise. He wasn’t any better or any worse than the losers that came before. And he didn’t last any longer than the others.” She handed me a lemon. “Here, let me get you the juicer. Will you do this for me? Pushing it always hurts my hands.”

The switch was so abrupt that it threw me off. “Sure. Of course.”

“Thank you, dear. You’ll need to cut it in half first.”

I retrieved a cutting board from beside the nearby sink. Lois’s words replayed through my mind. *Didn’t last any longer than the others*. Did that mean...? Maybe I could get her to expand on that. “You weren’t a huge fan of Sid, huh? I suppose it makes sense, with him being a taxidermist and all. It seems being a vegan, you would have a problem with—”

I turned to look at her just in time to see her swinging the heavy glass juicer up toward my head. But not soon enough, as it crashed into my temple.

My head throbbed, and when I attempted to open my eyes, the bright light of the kitchen caused me to groan. Something wet wiped across my face.

"Goodness. You weren't out very long."

Despite the pain, I blinked several times and forced my eyes open. Watson's black nose was all I could see as he whimpered and licked my face.

Then the picture came into view. I was lying on the kitchen floor. I started to attempt to stand, but something held my hands behind my back.

Lois stood behind Watson, glaring down at me. "You are such a disappointment, Fred. I've heard about the way you and that policeman look at each other. I wondered. Even when you showed up here tonight, I wondered. But you had me convinced, for a few minutes; you really did." She gave a bitter laugh. "To think you could ever replace my sister." She took a step toward Watson, a knife in her hand catching a glint in the light.

I tried to move him aside with my head, but he just licked more ferociously. "Please don't hurt him. Please, Lois."

"How dare you?" Lois halted, looking scandalized. "I

would never hurt your dog. Watson hasn't done anything wrong."

Insane or not, relief washed through me. "Thank you." Then I noticed the knife again, and all semblance of gratefulness vanished. I flinched as she stepped toward us again.

"Oh, stop that." She sounded irritated, not at all the gentle tone I'd heard from her up till now. "I'm not going to kill you. At least not here. I learned that with Opal. I wasn't strong enough to move her. I was still trying to figure out what I was going to do with her body when you found her. I'm not going to make that mistake again. That's why I didn't tie your feet. We'll go somewhere else."

I relaxed somewhat at that. I couldn't tell what my hands were tied with, but there was no wiggle room. Lois had done a good job. But if my feet weren't tied. It should be easy.

Why waste time? I whipped my body around, attempting to knock her legs out from under her with my right foot, but only succeeded in sending Watson scrambling away and partially flipping myself over to my stomach.

"Such a disappointment, Fred. I'm not an idiot." Even so, Lois took a step back, still clutching the knife. "Do sit up, dear. There's no need to drag this on."

I rocked, managing to get back on my side, then cast a glance down at my feet. Though not bound together, they were each tied with an extension cord that left only a few inches of slack between them. Enough to shuffle along but not enough to run or kick.

"We don't have all night, so move it along. Sit up." She considered. "Maybe we have all night, but I doubt it. I've learned not to take time for granted."

I lay there, still trying to figure out a new course of action.

"I said sit up!" Lois let out a scream as she stomped her foot.

The way the knife trembled in her hand, I wasn't certain how in control she really was. She might change her mind about Watson, or change her mind about needing to get me somewhere else. And she was right about time. I needed as much of it as I could get.

Not wanting to push her any further, I sat up, making a much greater show of it being difficult than it actually was. Hoping I could use that for when she told me to stand. Give me the time when it happened to look for any chance of attack. With as birdlike as she was, it shouldn't be too hard to shove her into a wall hard enough to do some damage, though doing so without tripping over the extension cord or falling into her knife could be a challenge.

She nodded in approval as I finally rose to a seated position.

"Good. Now stand."

She really wasn't wasting time.

Time really was the thing, wasn't it?

How to get more of it....

Countless mysteries I'd read through the years, and just as many submissions to our publishing company, flitted through my mind. It was a trick as old as the first mystery. One even used on Inspector Gadget, for crying out loud. But if it was good enough for all of them....

"So you killed Opal because she was dating Sid?"

If a person can get the killer talking, it was always their downfall. At least in books.

Maybe Lois hadn't read as many mysteries as I had, because she took the bait.

She sneered at me. "No, of course not. I would never kill my sister because of a man. Why would I kill her because she dated those horrible men? That would be stupid."

Despite needing to think of a way out of this, Lois's words ended up distracting me. "You mean *you* killed Sid?"

"Of course I killed Sid. He was taking her away from me."

She said it so nonchalantly, as if it was the simplest, most obvious thing in the world. The man in her sister's life was eating up her sister's time, so he had to die. No, not man... *men*.

"You killed her three husbands too, didn't you?"

Again her look said the answer was obvious. "They were easy. And planned. They weren't as juvenile as what accidentally happened to Opal. Or what is even happening with you right now. Gradual poisoning is not inventive, but it works. Fiddling with a car, a live wire on a wet floor. No cleanup needed at all."

I most definitely hadn't seen that coming. "I can't believe Opal would cover for you."

"She didn't know. Of course she didn't know." Her watery eyes grew wide and desperate. "But she would've. If Opal had known, and I was in danger of jail, she would've covered for me. She would have." She waved the knife in my direction. "Now stand up. This isn't a show-and-tell. Get this done." As she spoke, she took a step back. She might be crazy, but she was aware enough to know I wasn't going down without a fight.

And again, I made a show of standing, though it truly was more difficult than sitting up. With my ankles tied so closely together, I had to lean against the wall to push myself to my feet.

And there was no opportunity to attempt anything.

As soon as I was standing, Watson seemed more at ease.

He still cast wide eyes in my direction, but he left my side and began to prance around the room in agitation.

"Just to be clear, Fred." Lois waited until I met her gaze. "No funny business. I don't want to, but if it keeps you in line, I will hurt Watson. And if I have to, I'll end you here and now. Figure out how to clean up your mess later."

She meant it. Not that it surprised me at this point, but it was clear there was nothing she wouldn't do. Now that I was standing, my panic rose, and I attempted to keep a clear head. There had to be a simple way out of this. She was a frail old woman. But one who was obviously insane. One who had already killed at least five people. Keep her talking. Just keep her talking. "Why did you kill Eddie?"

She flinched, and for the first time since I'd awoken on the floor, she looked like Lois again. "Who?"

"The owner of Green Munchies?"

Her confusion was genuine.

"The dispensary in Lyons. Where Sid and Opal first got their start to grow their own marijuana plants."

She looked pleased. "I didn't know him, but serves him right. Corrupting my sister that way. I'm glad he got what was coming to him. I wish I knew who it was. I'd bring them a candy basket."

I'd known whoever killed Eddie was different from the person who had killed Opal.

Watson was still skittering around, darting between me, Lois, and the front of the shop. He stood in the doorway of the kitchen, staring at me and whining.

Lois wheeled on him. "Be still, Watson. Be a good boy. I don't want to hurt you, but I can't have you getting loud." I'd just started to attempt a step toward her but halted when she whipped back around to me. "And you, enough of this."

She motioned toward the back door with the knife. "Get moving."

I took a few shuffling steps. Watson hurried to my side, then paused. Time. I still needed time. "Then why Opal? If you didn't kill her because of Sid? Then why?"

Despite Lois's desperation to get me moving, her lips snarled at my question, hurt and anger crossing her features. "I never meant to kill Opal. She was my sister. My world. I just...." A tear ran down her cheek, and she wiped at it with the back of her hand, the knife coming dangerously close to her forehead.

Watson went back to the doorway of the kitchen, trying desperately to get me to follow him.

More tears made their way down Lois's cheeks as she glared at me. "I assumed she had a new man. She was sneaking off every night. She thought I didn't know, but I did. So I finally followed her. Followed her right into Sid's shop and up to that kitchen. I confronted her. And she admitted it all. What Sid had introduced her to, how she had turned it from the crackpot idea he'd had to the full business it became. How she'd made a small fortune from those poor dead animals Sid had left behind, and never shared it with me. And the whole time she was talking, she just kept packing. Just packing and packing, because you were in town and going to take over the shop. Telling me I should be glad, that it was helping keep my store afloat." Lois's cadence grew more frantic. "I tried to talk her into letting me be part of it. We could do the cooking right there." She gestured around the kitchen with the knife. "If anything, it would make more sense to come from me. That the business would really take off with my all-natural recipes. She just laughed. I didn't mean to hit her. I really didn't." Even as she shook the knife at me, her expression and tone begged for my understanding, for my forgiveness. "I would never hurt Opal. But she was laughing. At the idea of me making her business better. Not even caring that she'd kept this whole part of her life a secret. That she left me out of it."

The tears had become rivers, and she wiped across her eyes again.

As the time-tested ploy of buying time proved true, I saw my chance. With the knife lifted to her own face, and Watson scurrying back toward me from the kitchen doorway, just behind the back of Lois's feet at the exact right moment, I launched myself toward her. Springing, I smashed into her chest with my shoulders. At the force of my impact, she stumbled back and fell over Watson, who let out a high-pitched yelp, and we crashed to the floor.

I landed on my right shoulder, the pain taking my breath away and causing my vision to go white. I blinked quickly, trying to scurry backward.

But there was no hurry. Lois had hit her head on the counter, or something, on the way down. Her eyes were closed, and the small pool of blood was already growing beneath her head.

Dead. I'd killed her.

There was a flash of panic, a wave of guilt, but I shoved both away.

This time, standing up was harder. Between the pain in my shoulder and my feet getting caught on the hem of my skirt, it took considerable effort. Watson was back at my ankles, whimpering like he was in trouble.

I started to soothe him, but heard a jingle and the scrape of metal at the back door. I attempted to shuffle into the main room, to try to make a run for it. Though, who I was running from, I couldn't say.

Before I'd managed even a step, the door swung open, and Katie stepped inside. "Lois, I'm sorry. I feel horrible, and I shouldn't have—"

Her words fell away, and her eyes grew huge, staring at Lois bleeding on the floor. Then she looked at me, taking in my tied feet and arms. "Fred! Oh, Fred!"

Without sparing another glance at Lois, Katie rushed into the kitchen and began to untie me.

"Fred! What in the world? Are you okay? What's going on?"

With my hands untied, I motioned toward Lois and bent to work on my legs. "Check on her. Is she dead?"

Katie only hesitated for a moment before going to Lois and kneeling. She paused one more second, then pressed two fingers to her throat. A heartbeat passed and then another. She looked up at me. "She's not dead. There's a pulse."

"Thank God!" I nearly sank back to the floor in relief, then refocused on Katie. "Call 911, will you?"

I watched through the window of Healthy Delights as Lois was strapped to a gurney and wheeled through the front doors toward an ambulance. She still hadn't regained consciousness.

Branson raked a large hand through his thick dark hair and shook his head at me. "You are something, Fred Page."

As irritated as I'd been with him earlier, I had to admit I thought the same about him. He'd shown up mere minutes after the first two police cars. He'd clearly been off duty, as he wore a sweater, jeans, and snow boots. He'd stepped in and taken charge, the whole time keeping a protective hand on my shoulder or a watchful eye over me as he spoke to the others.

I glanced over at Katie and handed her my cell. "Would you call my mom? Fill her in on what happened and let her know you'll be joining us for dinner."

"Sure thing." She gave a knowing glance toward Branson, took the phone, and walked away.

Turning back to Branson, try as I might, I couldn't keep the *I told you so* out of my tone. "I told you it was all about the licorice candy." It seemed the *I told you so* wasn't only in my tone.

"That you did." He grinned, started to reach for my hand, but then seemed to think better of it. "I'm sorry about that. It appears I should have given your gut feeling a little more credence."

"Remember that in the future."

His brows shot up. "Do I need to? Is there another murder you're plotting to solve?"

"No." Just the thought made my stomach clench. I narrowed my eyes at him. "But what about Eddie? You thought he and Opal were connected. But Lois genuinely didn't seem to know who he was."

"I was wrong." He shrugged. "I guess they weren't connected. But now that they're not, I really won't be on the case at all, since Eddie isn't part of Larimer County. But I've heard they already have a suspect in his murder." This time his eyes narrowed. "Fred, even if they didn't, you can't go investigating Eddie's death. This was enough."

I liked his protective nature, and I also appreciated how quick he was to say he was wrong and apologize. Again, it set him apart from my ex-husband and more into the category of my father and Barry. But still....

I poked him in the chest. "Maybe you haven't caught on, Sergeant Wexler, but I don't like being told what to do. In the future you might remember that, or I promise you won't find a quicker way to solve a case."

He threw back his head and laughed, the same full, hearty sound he'd let loose in my kitchen. It did things to my heart I would rather it not do. When he looked back, his green eyes were bright and full of affection.

"Noted. Don't tell Fred what to do. Got it." His smile changed slightly. "As a demonstration of that, may I request you reconsider and go to the hospital? If you don't want to take the ambulance, I can drive you."

I started to argue, but the throbbing in my head let me know I was being stubborn for a stupid reason. "I'll ask Katie to take me before we go to my mom's for dinner."

I glanced down at Watson who blinked up at me from where he sat on my foot. He hadn't moved in probably half an hour. I wouldn't be able to say he wasn't affectionate anymore. I'm not sure why I looked at Watson, maybe asking his permission, hoping he'd tell me to reconsider what I was about to do. I didn't find either in his gaze, just corgi adoration. So I made the decision myself and looked back at Branson.

"Would you like to join us after? For dinner? My mom made her grandmother's enchilada recipe. And I know for a fact she picked up her hatch green chilies from some vendor in the canyon, so it should be good and spicy."

He shook his head, the tickle of disappointment clarifying exactly what I was beginning to feel for Branson. "No, thank you. I think your family has seen enough of the police for a little while." That time he did take my hand. "Rain check? When you feel up to it. Perhaps dinner with just you and me?" He gestured down to Watson with his chin. "And little man too, of course. I know you're a package deal."

I nearly said yes, then shrugged. "We'll have to see, Sergeant. This might've been your one and only chance. Ask me later and find out."

Branson shook his head and gave a forced exasperated eye roll. "You really are something."

The entire family had demanded to meet Katie and me at the hospital, and by the time I was released with a clean bill of health, Mom had to rewarm the enchiladas, causing them to be unusually dry, but still delicious. With five people I loved surrounding me at the table, and Watson still snuggled at my feet, I felt at ease for the first time in days. And with the aroma of home-cooked food combining with the soft glow of the lights, the gentle background sounds of Christmas carols that Mom always put on before Thanksgiving arrived, and snow falling lazily outside the window, I knew I was home. Truly and completely home.

I stayed up a little longer after Katie and my uncles left, simply needing to be in my mother's presence for a while. The twins were returning with their families in a few days, so I needed to soak up as much solitary Mom time as I could before the grandkids took over. At the doctor's urging, I agreed to stay the night, just to have Mom and Barry near.

The next morning, Barry walked Watson and me out to the car. Mom was still asleep, but I needed to be home. Strange how quickly my grandparents' cabin had become home, even without any of my belongings.

"Hold on for a second, Barry, will you?" After I opened the door and let Watson hop in and over the console to his spot, I leaned inside and reached under the passenger seat.

When I handed him the black box tied with a green ribbon, Barry's gaze grew large and darted back toward the house.

I chuckled. "We both know Mom is not going to make a big deal about it. Not really. She might pretend she wasn't aware, but you've known each other since you were kids." I tapped the box. "Consider this a last gift from Eddie. He really did love you."

Barry gave me a long hug, and when he spoke, emotion snagged his voice. "Glad you're all right, kid. I don't know what we would do if anything ever happened to you." He pulled back to look me in the eye. "I only met your dad a couple of times over the years, but with as proud of you as your mom and I are, I can only imagine how proud he'd be of you right now."

And then the emotions were gripping around my throat. I didn't attempt to respond, just squeezed Barry's shoulder in thanks. Somehow in all the mess of things that night, for the first time since arriving in Estes Park, Dad hadn't entered my mind. How strange. Maybe because I was doing exactly what he would've done. Well, not exactly. I'd made a near mess out of it all at the end, but still....

Barry's typical wacky smile returned, and he kept his voice low. "I might know your mom is okay with this"—he shook the box gently—"and you might know that your mom is okay with this. But that doesn't mean your mom knows she's okay with this."

"It'll be our little secret." I gave him a wink.

My shoulder, neck, and head ached something fierce, but after a hot shower and a few pain pills, it was manageable. If I hadn't already booked an appointment to have the internet hooked up at the Cozy Corgi, I would've crawled into my own bed and slept a couple of hours. Why they could get it to the shop two days earlier than they were willing to schedule it at my cabin, I had no idea. One more thing I decided I would chalk up to small-town life. But as it was, it felt good to get up and move. It wasn't like there was anything to do yet. My things from Kansas City wouldn't be delivered for a while, so I had nothing to do at the house. At least with the internet working at the shop, I could get my first inventory order in. The whole store wouldn't be murder mysteries, but my first order most definitely was going to be nothing but.

I paused as Watson and I walked from the car to the store, and I stared into the window of Healthy Delights. Who would've thought? I gave a little shudder and then spared a glance toward Sinful Bites. I supposed I'd have new neighbors. Hopefully they wouldn't be killers. Another thought hit me and warmed my heart a little. Maybe Katie would get her bakery, after all. It would be lovely having her next door.

Barely ten minutes passed before there was a knock. Watson barked more hysterically than normal. Probably a little traumatized from the night before.

We made our way back downstairs when there was another knock. I could see a man in uniform outside the glass front door. Surprise, surprise, apparently there were some advantages to small-town life. You'd never get an internet provider showing up early in the city.

When I opened it, I realized my mistake. Not the internet provider. Instead a cute young man with his brown delivery uniform showing between the folds of his jacket. He held out a tablet. "If you'll just sign this, I'll bring your delivery inside. It's heavy."

One look at the large box, and I knew what it was. My heart began to beat like mad. I scribbled my name and thrust the tablet back into his hands. "Thank you so much! Have a good day." Then I practically shoved him out the door.

As I began to rip open the box, I gave Watson what was probably the most foolish of smiles. "Wait until you see this. I ordered it last week before we headed out."

Despite all the cleaning we'd done the day before, I

ripped into it like it was Christmas morning, chunks of cardboard flying and packing peanuts acting like snow.

With a grunt, I pulled the huge wooden board free. The deliveryman had been right. The thing was a heavy beast. Which was good. It was quality. At least it better be, considering what I'd paid for it.

After ripping off the final layer of plastic, I inspected it and let out a happy sigh of satisfaction. The edges of the wood were scrolled so they made the outline of an open book. The interior had been painted white but artistically aged, and arching blue letters near the top of it read: *The Cozy Corgi*. Beneath the letters, in the same aged blue, was a stack of books with a corgi sitting on the top. It was perfect.

I angled the sign so Watson could see. "What do you think? It's you!"

Watson leaned warily closer, and gave a little sniff. Some of the packing pieces went flying, and he shook his head. Then he inspected once more, and there was a furrow between his eyes as he studied the corgi.

He didn't like it.

"I know he's a little bit fatter... er... fluffier than you, but I thought it made him cute." I tapped the chubby corgi sitting on the books. "Let's be honest. With the amount of dog treats you've been getting lately, this silhouette is only a matter of days away."

And at that word, that magical, ridiculous, annoying word, Watson's displeasure disappeared and he began to pounce on his front paws.

I sighed. "If you are anything, Watson Page, you're predictable." I leaned the heavy sign against the wall, then motioned toward the door. "Well, come on. I'm sure I have some treats in the car."

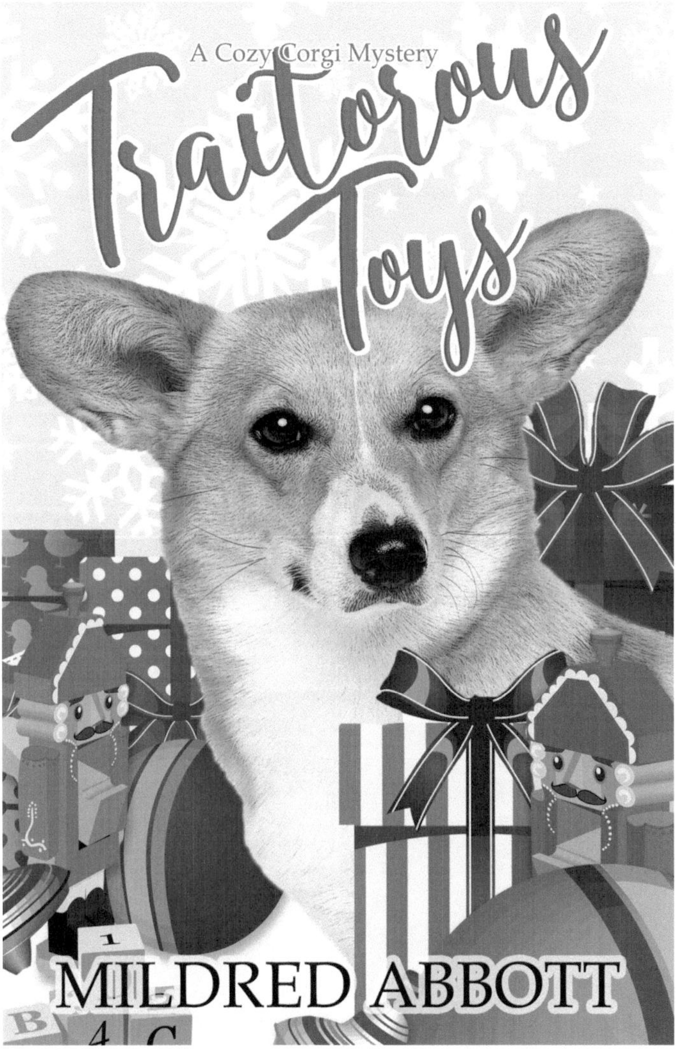
A Cozy Corgi Mystery
Traitorous Toys
MILDRED ABBOTT

TRAITOROUS TOYS

Mildred Abbott

ONE

Despite Watson's sensitive nose, and the smell of recently varnished floors, we spent the entire day in the Cozy Corgi bookshop. When the motherlode of all deliveries arrived before noon, the majority of the books were at least within the walls of my store, and I now owned more than an empty building. Progress!

After having the sign hung, the floors and walls refinished, and all of the bookcases installed, I'd thought my dream shop was becoming a reality. But with mountains upon mountains of boxes of books taking up most of the large center room, it finally began to feel real. And that realness doubled down. Transforming the place seemed nearly impossible, especially considering the timeline I'd set for myself, but even so, excitement thrummed. It was happening. Finally.

I spent the rest of the afternoon pushing boxes to the center of the smaller rooms that ran around the perimeter of the main floor. The more I worked, the more manageable it seemed. I already knew my favorite space. The corner room in the back left side of the shop. It was the one with the largest river rock fireplace. My uncles' store had a Victorian sofa and antique standing lamp with an ornate fabric shade I'd been eyeing. Those would go there, and it would be my mystery-themed room. Each little nook would have its own genre. The largest offshoot would be the children's book area, and while I was going to make every inch of the store as spectacular as I could, the mystery room was going to be just a touch more special.

By the same time next year, I'd have the entire shop decked out for Christmas. As it was, I used some of my illusive time to cut out paper snowflakes and tape them to the windows looking out on the tourists passing by. Next year, lights, trees, and maybe I could even brew some spiced cider for customers. But, for now, wonky snowflakes would have to do for holiday cheer.

"If you keep glaring at me like that, I'm going to leave you home tomorrow." I glowered at Watson, who peered up at me as I taped the final snowflake on the glass. His corgi eyes doubtlessly did a better job of glowering than mine. "It's not like you'd be unsafe. With the fortune I just paid for your dog run, the abominable snowman himself couldn't break in."

The threat to leave him home was an empty one, and we both knew it. Even with the Fort Knox of dog enclosures, I'd worry about him the entire day and get absolutely nothing done. Never mind the fact that since he'd waddled into my life a little more than a year ago, we'd been inseparable.

Watson's intense look was interrupted by a sneeze, a second one, and then he went right back to glaring.

"You know, buddy, the Cozy Corgi bookstore is named after you. We're going to have to work on your disposition before we have living, breathing customers."

I was fairly certain his brown gaze darkened. Watson

was persnickety about which strangers he would allow to fawn over him.

A few seconds longer of our staring battle and I admitted defeat. We had both known I would. The only way I could change his disposition in the moment was to offer him a treat. And I'd already given him five since coming to the store a few hours ago. Since moving to Estes Park, Watson had steadily required more treats, and he was just a bit "fluffier" than was healthy. Not that I had much room to judge. My newest friend, Katie, was a baker, and I felt fairly certain she was intent on me buying an entire new wardrobe, with all the fresh carby goodness she continually shoved my way.

"Fine. You win. But this bookstore isn't going to put itself together, you know." I strode to the counter, slipped into my jacket, and grabbed my purse and an incorrectly delivered letter. It seemed I got someone else's mail every other day. I wondered how much of my own ended up somewhere other than with me. At least all the books had come to the right place.

I couldn't blame Watson. The smell of stain, varnish, and all the other chemicals used to refinish the wooden floors of the two-leveled shop a couple of weeks before had finally faded. We'd had an entire day and a half of getting the Cozy Corgi ready without runny noses and stinging eyes before the newly installed bookcases that filled nearly every room on the main floor had their turn at a beauty treatment. I was planning on opening the store in January, but that was only two weeks away. If I started stocking the books on the shelves too soon, I feared no one would buy them due to their absorbing the chemical smell.

After slipping on his leash, I stepped outside with Watson, paused long enough to lock the front door of the shop, and then began walking down the sidewalk. The two stores on either side of the Cozy Corgi had been candy shops, but now sat empty, waiting. While some of the stores had closed for the winter season, these were the only ones that felt desolate. I was certain it wouldn't last for long.

"One more stop, and then it's family dinner night."

Watson turned his unimpressed gaze on me again.

"Barry, buddy. You get to see Barry."

And with that, his eyes lit up and he gave a little hop. My stepfather was Watson's favorite human in the world, outside of myself. And there were times I wasn't entirely certain I outranked Barry.

Though it was barely four thirty in the afternoon, the sky was dark and only a small pink glow remained over the rim of the mountains. Snow fell in thick soft flakes, and while it was cold, there was no wind, so it was a crisp pleasant sensation. The weather mixed with the garlands, light-festooned streetlamps, and the ropes of glowing tinsel across the street made me marvel at my new life.

When we first moved to Estes Park from Kansas City the month before, I'd felt like we'd landed inside a snow globe. Now, with the holiday barely a week away, I was convinced we lived in a Christmas village. The sensation was compounded by the endless rows of shops on Elkhorn Avenue, all of which were either vintage fifties and sixties mountain style or those, like mine, that looked like small log cabins.

Within five minutes, we walked close to the end of the next block, and I checked the address on the envelope. The return address showed that it was from a Denver law office. There was no business name, but the numbers matched those under the silver script that read Rocky Mountain Imprints on the glass door.

A bell chimed as we walked in, and Watson let out an irritated snuff seconds before the smell hit—not overly unpleasant, and less harsh than what my own shop currently smelled like, but it was a weird mix of heat, plastic, and something I didn't have a name for. Endless racks of T-shirts and hoodies filled the store, and every inch of wall space was papered in square designs, ranging from cute forest animals, to Smokey Bear, to borderline risqué logos about hiking naked.

"Welcome, and Merry Christmas!" A cute blonde woman waved at me from behind the counter.

I nearly jumped at the sudden sound of her voice. I hadn't noticed her amid all the cacophony of fabric colors and images. Not to mention she was nearly pixie small.

"Thank you! And Merry Christmas to you." I motioned down at Watson. "I hope you don't mind that my dog is with me." Estes Park was extremely dog friendly, but Watson and I had encountered the rare shopkeeper who didn't appreciate animals in their store. In their defense, Watson tended to leave a cloud of dog hair wherever he went, as evidenced by every article of clothing I owned.

"Of course not!" The woman's bright voice was nearly as cheerful as a pixie. "He's adorable. We actually sell T-shirts for dogs." Her eyes narrowed as she inspected Watson. "He's... a basset hound, right? I don't think we have any of those, but I do a lot of the art myself. I can custom-design something for you. Maybe a basset hound wearing reindeer ears or something for the season?"

I shook my head and managed to smile instead of grimace. "Thank you, but no. Watson would murder me in my sleep if I tried to put clothes on him. Once in a while, he'll let me get away with a little scarf, but even then he gives me attitude for days after. And he's a corgi." A basset hound and a corgi both were long and short, but really couldn't look more different, with basset hound ears nearly dragging the floor, and a corgi looking for all intents and purposes more like a chiseled fox.

"Well, if you change your mind, let me know. I'll happily create something for a corky. I've never tried to do anything with scarves, but it could be a fun adventure."

A *corky*? I was going to have to remember that one. Maybe that could be a new nickname when Watson was being a snot.

As we walked closer to the counter, the woman seemed to get smaller. Granted, that wasn't an unusual sensation for me upon meeting petite women. I was a healthy five foot ten, which seemed like a good size to me, but anytime I was around women the stature of my mother, I grew the tiniest bit self-conscious. At thirty-eight, I'd expected to outgrow that particular insecurity. Maybe by the time I was forty....

"I am actually not here to shop. Sorry." I held out the envelope. "This was delivered to my store by accident. It's addressed to a Sarah M. Beeman, but it had your shop's address."

The blonde's eyes narrowed as she took the envelope, and then she glanced toward the back of the store before flashing me another smile. "Thank you. I'll see that she gets it." She cocked her head. "Wait a second. You said it was delivered to your store? I don't think I've met...." Her gaze left me once more, flicked to Watson, and then I saw understanding. "Ah! The Cozy Corky, the bookshop that's coming. I saw your sign. It's adorable."

She might not know her dog breeds, but with that comment, she won my approval. I was particularly proud of the wooden sign above my door with a corgi sitting on a stack of books. I held out my hand. "That's me. My name is Winifred Page, but everyone calls me Fred."

"Fred! That's almost as adorable as your shop sign." She slipped her tiny hand into mine. "I am Peg Singer." She tilted her head toward the back. "My husband, Joe, and I own the shop." She broke our hands' embrace and then gasped. "I have the best idea! That logo would be amazing on T-shirts and hoodies, we can even put them on hats. If you buy them in bulk, I'll give you a discount, and then you can mark them up and sell them at your store." She gestured behind her at a row of trophies. "Each summer we locals have a softball season. There were so many shop owners by the end of last year, we talked about splitting into two teams. You could lead the new one, and your little dog could be the mascot. Joe does really wonderful things with jersey imprints."

I shook my head, a little more emphatically than I'd intend. "I'm so not a sports person. Any team I'd be on would be guaranteed to lose. And Watson is about as athletic as a beached whale." I reminded myself I needed to get off to a good start with the other business owners, so I paused, considering. "The Cozy Corgi logo on shirts and stuff might be cute, though."

"I promise you it would be."

"Let me think about it, but...." I fished around in my purse for my newly printed business cards "Let me leave you my information and you can send me the details. Will that work?"

"Absolutely!" The card went the way of the letter. "I'll send you some options and quotes in the next couple of days."

I hadn't figured out what I was going to do with the top level of my shop, it had been an apartment before—and the scene of a murder. I hadn't wanted to extend the bookstore up there, preferring to keep it more of an intimate space, but maybe Cozy Corgi merchandise could be fun.

Watson pulled on his leash, obviously done with another smelly location. I followed his lead. "It was a pleasure to meet you, Peg. We should probably get going, though. My little guy is getting hungry." I loved Watson for all that he was, even his often grumpy disposition. But one of my favorite parts of puppy motherhood was always having a ready excuse to leave.

"It was great to meet you as well, Fred." She gave a finger-wiggling wave to Watson. "And you too, Walter."

I truly did like the idea of the Cozy Corgi merchandise, but I made a mental note to double and then triple check spelling on any proofs she might send my way. The Cozy Corgi could easily end up being the Grumpy Goat or some such nonsense.

The snow had picked up, and as Watson and I stepped outside, the cold fresh mountain air was such a contrast to the plasticky smell of the T-shirt shop that I stood there for a second to luxuriate.

I turned back the way we'd come, and the store next to Rocky Mountain Imprints caught my eye. I wasn't sure how I'd missed it to begin with. Toys filled the window, and like my shop, the outside was a log cabin façade. The arched wooden sign over the door read Bushy Evergreen's Workshop. Unlike the T-shirt store, even from my spot on the sidewalk, it was easy to see the place was completely decked out for Christmas. I gave Watson an apologetic grimace. "One more stop before Barry. But this is the last one. I promise."

Before he could sit down and refuse to move, I pushed open the door and ushered him inside.

Sure enough, the place was as charming as it seemed from the outside. I'd toured all the stores when we first moved, but I'd been so focused on all the drama, I hadn't paid too much attention to aesthetics. Bushy Evergreen was an unfortunate name choice, but *workshop* was appropriate. It felt like Watson and I had stepped through a portal and landed in Santa's workshop in the North Pole. The tiny place practically overflowed with toys. For a second I couldn't figure out what was unusual about it, but then it hit me, only increasing the sensation of being in a place owned by Santa. Most of the toys—much like Estes Park itself—seemed to be from a time long ago. Tops, jack-in-the-boxes, wooden train sets and cars, and endless rows of stuffed animals. Many of the wooden toys and figurines looked expertly hand carved. In all the chaos of toys, three different Christmas trees were stuffed here and there, twinkling brightly. Garland was roped around every available surface, looping over the perimeter of the walls and outlining the shelves and tables.

"Wow." I stood in awe and forgot that I was nearly forty. This place was Christmas morning—smells of hot chocolate and molasses, the feeling of rushing down the stairs to find brightly colored packages under a sparkling tree.

There was a warm chuckle from somewhere to the left. "Never get tired of seeing that expression on people's faces. I don't think I've ever noticed one on a dog before, but even your furry friend appears enchanted."

I glanced at Watson. Sure enough, Watson's gaze flicked from one thing to another and he seemed captivated by it all, rather than irritated at keeping Barry waiting. Talk about a Christmas miracle. Maybe we really had stumbled upon Santa's workshop.

Catching myself, I looked toward the voice, and seemed to misplace my own. The man standing behind the counter was no elf. Nor was he Santa. He was a tall, rugged mountain of a man. Dark red hair and stunningly handsome. Where Peg had made me feel like a giant, this man made me feel like... well, probably how Peg had felt next to me, I assumed.

He flashed a bright white smile, somehow increasing his good looks, which shouldn't have been possible. "You all right?"

I nodded and had to lick my lips so I wouldn't drool, more than anything. I pointed to the garland strewn magically over the store. "Yes. I've just never seen garland that lights up before." That much was true, the crystalline garland was a constant shifting rainbow of colors. It almost looked like it was made from shards of glass or snow, and somehow glowed in countless sparkling hues.

His thick brows creased. "Yeah, it was my idiot brother's idea. Pretty spectacular stuff, unless you're the one hanging it. I think I bled for a week." Whatever irritation he felt vanished. "Looking for a gift?"

I shook my head. I was not looking for a gift. Although, since I was in a toyshop... "Yes, though I have no idea what to get. I have nieces and nephews. Two who are fourteen and two who are eight. Two boys, and two girls." He had a small dimple in his chin. Not too deep as to be distracting, but just enough to highlight how chiseled his jaw truly was. "Well, they're my stepnieces and stepnephews actually. I'm not very good at this whole aunt thing. My stepfather has two daughters; they're twins." His blue eyes might actually be made from sapphires. "And of course they married twin brothers, because Verona and Zelda weren't identical enough, they had to marry twins. And they each have a fourteen-year-old and an eight-year-old, and I have absolutely no idea what I'm supposed to do for presents. Judging from the way they reacted the last few Christmases, I'm a horrible gift giver."

Watson yanked at his leash, pulling my attention to him. He cocked one of his puppy brows at me and sat down.

He'd just earned himself another treat.

If I'd kept going, I probably would've told the man my entire family history. I turned back to him but focused on a carved bear over his shoulder. Maybe he was like an eclipse, you could function if you didn't look directly at him.

"I can definitely help you out with the eight-year-olds, but I doubt we'll have much to offer the teenagers. They seem to want nothing more than cell phones, iPads, and cash." He gave another chuckle, proving that the sound of his voice was just as distracting as his appearance, no matter where I looked. "Depending on what they're into, I just got a new shipment of...." His voice trailed off momentarily, causing me to look him full in the face again. "Wait a minute. I recognize you, and your dog. You're—" He snapped his fingers a couple times. "—Fred Page, the one opening the bookshop where the old taxidermy place used to be. Where Opal was killed."

For a moment I was beyond flattered that he had not only recognized me but recalled my name. Then I quickly realized chances were he'd been much more captivated by the murder and investigation that had swirled around me upon my arrival in town than he was about me personally. And that, more than keeping my focus away from him, helped me to quit acting like a complete fool. "That's me.

For better or worse. Watson and I are the ones opening the bookshop. You must be... Bushy?"

Even as I said it, I knew it couldn't be. A man like that didn't have the name Bushy.

He shook his head, and once more there was a flash of irritation like there'd been about the garland. "No. This was my father's store originally. He still carves a lot of the toys, but it's mine now. Bushy Evergreen was one of Santa's original elves. He was a woodcarver and was in charge of the toyshop. My father felt a kinship with him. I would love nothing more than to put a sensible name on the place, but we've been here for over fifty years. Doesn't make good business sense to change it now." His charm was back. "My name is Declan, thankfully, not Bushy."

Before I had the opportunity to somehow put my foot in my mouth again, there was a slamming of a door, and a voice rang out from somewhere in the back. "Declan, you're never going to believe what I just found. I was just driving back from the grocery store and there was this old chest sitting beside a dumpster." A man rushed through the doorway carrying a wooden box that looked like it had been kept at the bottom of the ocean for the past century. At a glance, I almost thought he was Declan's twin, but it was a fleeting notion. He had the same height, coloring, and hair, but even though he had similar features to Declan, everything seemed off somehow—not malformed, just not as pleasing. Even so, he was very clearly related to Declan. "I was thinking I can clean it up, and Dad could—" His words fell away as he noticed me, and halted. "Oh, sorry. Didn't mean to be so loud. Didn't realize we had customers."

Two other figures emerged from the back. I wasn't sure if they'd been there the entire time or if they'd arrived with the strange Declan look-alike. An ancient-looking man with snowy hair, who was clearly Declan's father, and a raven-haired woman, who was just as beautiful as Declan. Both of them halted as well.

"Yes, imagine that. A toy store having an actual customer at Christmastime. Shocking." The coldness and shift in Declan's voice drew my attention away from the other three people. His handsome features were suddenly hard. But a heartbeat later, he was charming again, his voice warm and pleasant. "Might as well make introductions while we're all here. This is Fred Page, the one who's opening the new bookshop." He gestured from me toward the three individuals. "This is my father, Duncan, my brother, Dolan, and my wife, Daphne."

"That's a lot of Ds." I wasn't sure if it was the residual effect of Declan's stunning appearance or his abrupt shift from warm and inviting to cold and harsh, but whatever it was, I chose to say *that* instead of *hello, nice to meet you.*

Dolan gave a maniacal laugh, the father's brows knitted in an expression which reminded me of Watson in his grumpy moments, and Daphne smiled as she spoke. "That's true. I've often wondered if Declan married me simply because of my name. My mother-in-law's name was Della, believe it or not." She shrugged and patted her flat stomach. "We won't know if it's a boy or a girl until the little one arrives, but I can guarantee you the name will start with D."

Dolan let out another wild laugh. It wasn't exactly off-putting, but a little crazed or something. Actually there was something off entirely. I couldn't figure out what it was. I only knew that the Christmassy cheer of Santa's workshop had morphed into something else. And probably sensing it himself, Watson once again pulled on his leash, this time making it very clear he wanted to go.

"Well...." I attempted to force an easy-breezy tone, but

was fairly certain I failed. "It's lovely to meet all of you." I refocused on Declan, this time not mesmerized by his appearance. "I'm running late for dinner with my family. Mom's making a big spread. I'll drop in before Christmas and find something good for the eight-year-olds."

And once more, Declan was all handsome charm and pleasant voice. "Please do. I'm sure we'll find something perfect for them. It was a pleasure to meet you, Fred. We'll look forward to visiting your store when you open."

"Thank you. I appreciate that." I gave a wave that hopefully encompassed everyone. "We'd best get going. Merry Christmas."

Dolan and Daphne responded as I turned and hurried out the door. I paused in the cool air once more, but this time it wasn't refreshing. Just cold. I glanced down at Watson.

"What in the world was that?"

He didn't bother to respond, only took off down the sidewalk, pulling me with him.

Before I'd taken two steps, loud voices reached my ears, and I glanced through the window, past the toys, to see Declan shaking his fist as he yelled at Daphne. Dolan jumped between them, shouting something as well, though I couldn't make it out.

Duncan's old eyes met mine through the window and clearly told me to mind my own business.

I hesitated despite his stare, wondering what I should do.

With another tug on his leash, Watson made the decision for me.

By the time we got to Mom and Barry's house, we were running fifteen minutes late, and food was already on the table. As Watson and I walked through the door, all ten faces turned toward us.

My stepfather beamed. "Watson! My main man!"

Watson let out a loud bark, sounding more like a Doberman than a corgi, and took off like a shot. For being a little guy, he was strong, thanks to his herding heritage, and nearly yanked my thumb off as his leash trailed behind him. He crashed into Barry, who'd knelt from his chair like a long-lost lover.

My nephews and nieces giggled.

After making sure my thumb was still attached, I gave a little wave as I hung up my coat. "I know I'm second fiddle to His Majesty, but I'm here too. Sorry we're running late."

My tiny mother rose from her chair and hurried to embrace me. "You're never second fiddle, dear. But do hurry over. The Tofurkey stew is getting cold, and you know it only resembles actual meat when it's hot."

Barry glanced up from his love fest with Watson. "Not true." Then he shrugged. "All right, it's probably true. I haven't had meat in a good three decades. What do I know?" He gave me a wink. "Good to see you, sweetheart."

I gave a quick round of embraces to Barry, my stepsisters, their husbands, and their four children before taking my seat beside Mom. Barry was the only vegetarian, and thankfully, for our new weekly family dinners, Mom also prepared a meat dish for the rest of us. Tonight's appeared to be lasagna.

Mom reached toward the pan with the spatula, then hesitated, glancing at Barry. "I almost forgot. Want to do the honors?"

He smiled and held his hands a couple of inches above the tabletop. As one, we grasped each other's hands completing the circle. "Mother Nature, thank you for all the nourishment and gifts you have provided. Thank you for the love and affection of family." His watery blue eyes twinkled. "And with the exception of Watson, who was made for such things, please forgive my family for devouring—" He glanced at my mom. "—what's in your pasta dish again?"

She sighed. "Beef, pork, and veal."

With a shuddering nod, he turned his attention skyward once more. "For devouring a mama cow, a pig, and a baby cow."

Zelda's oldest daughter giggled.

"Blessed be, peace on earth, and namaste." Barry released Mom's hand, signaling for the blessing to be done, then lifted a fork in the air. "Dig in, you murderers."

Even after six years of his marriage to my mother, I still hadn't been able to fully figure out where Barry stood on things. He was an adamant vegetarian, consumer of recreational marijuana, and wore only tie-dye shirts and loose-fitting yoga pants. I knew he was very sincere in his beliefs, but his strange prayer-like times I thought were more for show and to both humor and drive my mother a little bit crazy.

Sure enough, as she scooped a square of lasagna onto each person's plate, Mom gave an eye roll as she announced, "Here's your pig and baby cow. Eat it all or we'll never hear the end of it." She couldn't quite make it all the way through with a straight face, however.

And then the family was lost to the sounds of forks and knives on stoneware.

I also hadn't been able to make up my mind how I felt about our weekly family meals. This was only the third one since I moved to town. My stepsisters and their families had been on a cruise when I first arrived. On the one hand, the meals were somewhat comforting, the laughter and noise of people who love each other, a family. But it was foreign to me and at times felt a little chaotic and claustrophobic.

Dinners as a kid had been just as full of love and affection, but with being an only child, things were much quieter and calmer. Except for when my uncles came to visit. These larger family dinners always triggered an ache at the loss of my dad. Not that it took much. Even though he had passed seven years before, there were times when it felt like mere moments ago. I hoped he was looking down on us and smiling at the love my mom had found, and probably chuckling and shaking his head, knowing exactly how the disorder got under his only daughter's skin at times.

Distracted as I ate, I allowed my attention to wander over Mom and Barry's house, once more finding it both comforting and disconcerting to see Christmas decorations from my childhood combined with ones from Barry's life. The Christmas village that once belonged to my grandparents now spread out around the base of the tree, right next to a plastic elf wearing a fur-trimmed, tie-dyed suit. Barry had gleefully demonstrated how it danced to 'Grandma Got Ran Over by a Reindeer' when its ear was pinched. It was the only time I'd ever seen Watson annoyed with Barry.

A mix of pleasure and ache settled over me at the colliding of worlds. My past intermingled with my present. My childhood mementos that I'd shared with dad now side by side with this new life. Even on my tree at home, in my new-to-me cabin, decorations I'd made with Mom and Dad as a child hung next to corgi ornaments and a porcelain flamingo wearing a Santa hat from Barry.

All in all, it wasn't unpleasant. So many aspects of life crash together during the holidays. Time always seems to fold in on itself.

Coming back to the moment, my focus narrowed on the Christmas tree. Something seemed oddly familiar. Then, it clicked.

I motioned toward it with my fork as I addressed Mom. "Where did you get that garland? I just saw it for the first time today. It's amazing how it constantly changes colors."

Verona's husband, Jonah, angled himself from the other side of the table to look at me. "You must've been in the toyshop."

I nodded.

Before I could reply, Zelda's husband, Noah, piped up. "By next year every store downtown will have it."

Truth be told, I wasn't exactly sure who was Jonah and who was Noah. Even though I knew which husband belonged to which sister, when they weren't seated by their wives, I couldn't tell the identical twins apart. After knowing them for so many years, I supposed I should make more of an effort, but one set of identical twins marrying another set of identical twins just seemed to be asking for confusion, so I didn't feel too bad. At least with Barry's daughters, they were identical in every way except their hair—Verona being a blonde and Zelda a brunette. I was certain one of them colored her hair, but I'd never asked. My money was on Zelda, but, like their father, it wasn't smart to place a bet on anything either of the twins would do.

From the proud look on the brothers' faces, I did the math quickly. "Another one of your inventions?"

They both nodded, and one of them—goodness knew *which* one—explained. "We just took those LED light strips and then made sleeves out of fiber-optic threads, like the ones we used to get at fairs and circuses and stuff. The first one took ages to make, but then we figured out how to mechanize the production. I could have sworn we told you about it a couple of weeks ago."

"I'm sorry. I'm sure you did. I've been so overwhelmed with trying to get my house together and the store ready for inventory that I probably forgot." Even though it was true, it was just an excuse. The twins had made a sizable fortune from their strange inventions. Each one came with endless filming of infomercials. They were nice guys, but it was all they talked about. Their constant string of failed and successful invention attempts blurred together. I doubted even their wives were able to keep it straight. "They're absolutely beautiful. Mesmerizing." Thinking back to what Declan had said, I spoke before I could stop myself. "I would imagine those would be hard to hang. If the fibers break, don't they stick in skin pretty easily?"

They both nodded enthusiastically, not daunted in the least. "That is an issue. One we're trying to figure out. Hopefully we'll have it all sorted by next season. But for now, we put a warning label on the box and the instructions suggest the use of cattleman's gloves when decorating."

Zelda spoke from her place beside Barry, a forkful of lasagna lifted halfway to her mouth. "Once they fine-tune it, the boys are going to make gowns for Verona and me for next year's New Year's Eve bash." She smiled at me guiltily. "To be honest, I'm not comfortable with their impact on the environment, but for a light-up gown, I'm willing to make an exception for special occasions every once in a while."

"I told you I'm not wearing that. It's socially and morally irresponsible." Verona glared at her twin. Though Barry hadn't even learned he had daughters until they were in their twenties, the twins were a testament of nature over nurture. Both of them were female versions of their father's hippie, naturalistic outlook on life. She smiled at me. "However, that kind of dress would look lovely on you, Fred. I bet it would make that long auburn hair of yours positively glow."

I couldn't hold back a shudder. "Goodness, no. I'd look like a walking, talking Christmas tree."

One of my nieces or nephews giggled. Not that I blamed them.

"I still say the impact is low if we only do such things on extremely special occasions. And I'm sure the boys could invent a way to recycle them. If nothing else."

"How is the house coming, Fred?" Barry cut off Zelda good-naturedly. Though Zelda and Verona were identical in nearly every single way, in the few areas they differed, it could be all-out war.

Even though I was with family, I was still uncomfortable being the focus of so many people at one time, but figured it was the lesser of the evils. "Mom was right. It was silly of me to have everything brought out here from Kansas City. I donated to Goodwill over half the things I paid to have driven out here." I gave a partial shrug toward Mom.

"And you're right about not wanting all the things I had with Garrett in this new life. Once I get the store up and running, I thought maybe you and I can go shopping for some new items to replace things the ex-husband touched."

Mom shimmied her shoulders in pleasure. "Sounds wonderful, darling. And I'll buy a new bundle of sage to clear everything out again."

"That'd be great, Mom." The longer she was married to Barry, the more hippie she became. It was rather endearing. I gave a sweeping glance toward my nephews and nieces. "And speaking of shopping, I am still getting the hang of buying presents for you all. I'd really appreciate Christmas lists this year. There was a beautiful assortment of carved wooden toys at Bushy Evergreen's Workshop, but even the owner thought I might want to shop elsewhere for you all."

Before the kids could reply, Zelda sucked in a breath and gave her sister a knowing look before turning back to me. "The owner? So you must have met Declan. Isn't he the dreamiest thing you ever saw?"

"Hey! Your husband is sitting right here!"

I glanced quickly at the twin who'd spoken. If he was Zelda's husband, that meant he was Noah. I made a mental note that Noah was on the right and Jonah was on the left. That would only help me until after dessert.

Zelda waved him off. "Oh hush, you know I adore you. And you're very handsome. But there's two of you, which means you're replaceable. There's only one of Declan Diamond."

I nearly choked. "Diamond? Are you kidding me?"

Zelda looked at me like I'd lost my mind. "No. Why is that strange? I think it's rather fitting for him. He sparkles like one."

"Declan Diamond?" How could she not see this? "I met

the entire family. They all start with Ds." I listed them off on my fingers. "Duncan Diamond, Declan Diamond, Dolan Diamond, and Daphne Diamond, for crying out loud."

"Huh!" Verona smacked her sister's arm. "I never noticed that. Have you?"

Zelda shook her head as both their husbands looked affronted.

Barry chimed in, his voice solemn. "His face might be pretty, but that man's heart isn't."

"Barry!" Mom chided, her tone full of reproach. "That's a horrible thing to say. I know he isn't the nicest man, but—"

Barry shook his head in a rare act of disagreeing with Mom, and doubled down. "No, I mean it. He's an awful human."

I couldn't stop myself. The only aspect I'd inherited from my mother was her hair; everything else, including my curiosity, came from my detective father. And I knew just how rare it was for Barry to speak so vehemently against someone. "Why? What did he do?"

Before Mom could protest, Barry launched in. "Duncan and I went to school together back in the day. I watched him and his wife, the Lord rest her soul, build that toyshop from nothing to a beautiful success. Duncan working his fingers to the bone carving the most well-crafted and artistically sound toys and figures you could find anywhere. They spared no sacrifice for their two boys. Dolan's a little off, sure, but he's got the heart of an angel. Declan would sooner slit your throat than give you a five-dollar bill."

"Barry. Not in front of the kids." Mom tried again, but Barry was on a roll.

He nearly shook. I'd never seen Barry truly angry before, not even when he was falsely accused of murder. "Three years ago that ingrate had Duncan declared incompetent and took complete control of everything. The shop, the houses, the finances, everything. Duncan's little more than a poorly paid, hired hand in the very life he created."

"Granted, I didn't even hear Duncan speak, but he didn't seem incompetent in the few seconds we were together." Despite Mom's protests, I believed every word that came out of Barry's mouth. Especially considering the glimpse I had through the window. "How could that legally have happened? Didn't Duncan fight it?"

Barry shrugged, his anger slipping to an expression of confusion. "I honestly can't say. It still doesn't make sense. Gerald did everything he could, but it wasn't enough against Declan's high-paid Denver lawyer."

I barely caught myself before I let out a groan. "Gerald Jackson was Duncan's lawyer?"

He nodded. "Yeah, and he fought hard. It just didn't work. Duncan lost everything. Declan controls the entire family."

I cast a knowing glance at Mom, but she just shook her head. She knew better than to speak against Gerald Jackson. He was another of Barry's childhood friends. A nice man, I was certain, but a horrible lawyer. Mom wouldn't speak ill of most people, but having been the wife of a detective for so long, she knew incompetence when she saw it.

And poor Duncan Diamond, those grumpy, irritable eyes of his. Surrounded by his beautiful creations, and powerless.

One thing was for sure, Bushy Evergreen's Workshop was about as far from the actual Santa's workshop as you could get.

Thankfully, I'd made plans to meet Katie when she ended her shift at the coffee shop. If I hadn't, I probably would've thrown in the towel around two in the afternoon. As fun as it was to begin to see my dream come together, pushing box after heavy box of books from room to room was a bit back-breaking. Watson managed a good three minutes on the main level with me, and then disappeared upstairs to the kitchen. I figured he was continuing to look for the candy he'd found our first day in the building. That, or he was just letting me know he didn't appreciate being brought back here for another entire day.

At the scheduled time, Watson and I walked into Black Bear Roaster coffee shop just as Katie was hanging up her apron. She gave us a happy wave and elbowed the teenage barista with her elbow.

"Give Fred my employee discount on whatever she wants, please." She motioned toward the restroom. "I'll be right back. Just let me change out of my work clothes."

Knowing it was a mistake to consume caffeine so late in the day, I ordered my normal, a large dirty chai, and opted for a pumpkin scone. Whatever. I'd earned it.

By the time the chai was slid across the counter, Katie

had joined Watson and me once more. Her brown, normally curly, shoulder-length hair had been pulled back into a short ponytail, and she gave me a quick hug and scratched Watson's ears. "Do you mind eating as we go? I've got to get out of here."

I cocked an eyebrow and intentionally leered at her sweater. "I'm not a fashionista by any means, but are you sure you want to go out in public wearing that?"

"Shut up!" She gave me a playful shove on my arm, causing some of the chai to spill, which Watson, being the helpful corgi he was, quickly cleaned off the floor. Katie motioned down at her purple sweater, which had an embroidered polar bear, giraffe, penguin, and mouse, all wearing Santa hats, on the front. "I don't think ugly Christmas sweaters should be relegated to ugly Christmas-sweater parties. It's not right."

I couldn't really say I agreed, but somehow it made me adore Katie just a little bit more. "Even so, why are all the animals stacked on top of each other? Are they trying to see over something?"

"They're stacked biggest to smallest. Like a Christmas tree." Before I could point out that the stacked animals looked nothing like a Christmas tree, she pulled up the hem of her jeans and showed me her mismatched socks one at a time. "The right one is a cranky Christmas unicorn, and the left is the Grinch dressed up like Mrs. Claus."

Katie didn't usually remind me of Barry, but if he ever opted to not wear his tie-dye, this was exactly the sort of outfit he would concoct. "When I agreed to go Christmas shopping with you, despite detesting shopping, I didn't realize I was agreeing to Christmas dress-up."

She waved me off and then returned the favor of wardrobe commentary. "And surprise, surprise—Fred Page and baby-poop colors. Pea-green sweater over rust-colored broomstick skirt." Her eyes narrowed. "The only thing that makes me detest your color palette more is that you actually pull it off. Which shouldn't be possible." She cocked her head and then pulled back my hair in her overly familiar way. "You always have great taste in jewelry, however. You're tall enough to pull off long dangling silver earrings. On me, they would just make me look shorter." She slipped her arm into mine, once more providing Watson with a happy treat trailing behind us as she pulled me toward the door. "Now come on, before all the stores close."

Unlike the night before, though the sun was already setting, the late afternoon had clear skies and was only mildly brisk. The snow which had fallen that morning was still fresh enough on the heaps of cleared-away mounds that ran along the sidewalks to give a pleasant Christmas vibe when combined with lights winding up the streetlamps and making a canopy over the sections of Elkhorn Avenue between the rows of shops.

We passed store after store, with Katie doing no more than glancing through the windows. I couldn't tell if she was looking for something specific, or nothing at all.

"Who are we shopping for, anyway?" I used as benign a voice as possible. After a couple of questions about Katie's family, I'd caught on that it wasn't a topic she cared to discuss. And while I wanted to respect her boundaries, well… I was my father's daughter. I was curious.

If Katie noticed my double intent, she didn't let on. "No one, really. I just enjoy Christmas shopping. I'm going to get my coworkers at the coffee shop some little tacky Estes Park souvenirs, just to be cute or something. And Carla, the owner, is having a baby in February. I haven't had a kid to buy for in years.

So at least there'll be one cute present to get." She grinned up at me, a relaxed expression on her round face. "And I know you hate shopping, so I thought I might help you with your list."

That leading question hadn't garnered much information other than that at some point she'd had kids in her life to shop for. "I don't have a list, but if you want to do all my shopping for me, I'll happily give whatever you decide to buy. Even if it's ugly Christmas sweaters."

"Not a bad idea."

I took another bite of the scone and gave up. Hesitating, I studied Watson's pleading face. He was supposed to be on a diet. He let out a long whimper.

Whatever. It was Christmas. Weakening, like we'd both known I would, I handed the rest to Watson. We paused for the five seconds it took him to scarf it down.

"I really thought having you work at Black Bear Roaster would help their pastry items not to be dry. Every scone I've tried is almost tooth breaking."

"Nothing is made in-house. Everything Carla gets, she orders from a factory in Denver." Katie sighed wistfully. "When I mentioned that I'd be happy to make things at home and bring them in, she about had a conniption. Granted, I know it wouldn't meet health requirements, but it's killing me not being able to bake. It's making me miss working for Opal, as cantankerous as she was. Goodness, at this point I even miss Lois, even with her aversion for sugar. At least she had the sense to make things fresh."

I couldn't help but laugh. "You know you're a baker at heart when murder doesn't bother you as much as prepackaged scones."

Katie shrugged, unconcerned. "Not saying murder is good, but let's be honest. We've all met at least one person we've been tempted to try it out on. But processed food? That's just evil."

I started to make a crack about Katie's sweater and sock combo being evil when I realized we were walking in front of Paws. In a moment of panic, I hunched down to a squatted position and scurried, nearly crab-like, to the other side of the large window. Watson let out a startled yip. Upon reaching safety, I straightened once more, then realized Katie was no longer beside me.

She stood right in front of the pet store's window, staring at me. "What in the world was that?"

"Get over here." I motioned frantically at her until she complied. "The owner has two corgis, and he's desperate to have a playdate with Watson."

Katie glanced back at Paws. "What's wrong with playdates? Sounds like the cutest thing I can imagine. So cute that I might need to find a place that makes ugly Christmas sweaters for corgis, get the three of them together, and voila, I could have next year's Christmas card."

"Number one, something's off about Paulie. He's very nice, but there's something I can't put my finger on. Not to mention he named his corgis after those two eels in *The Little Mermaid* movie." I pulled the strand of hair that had blown in front of my eyes and tucked it behind my ear. "And two, you know that trying to wrangle Watson into a sweater would make Opal seem like an angelic cherub."

"Nah. Watson loves me. But even if he didn't, I'd just distract him with baked goods until I got him dressed." Katie motioned over her shoulder with her thumb. "And while we're listing things, my second point is that I want to see you do that every single year. It's our new Christmas tradition. All five foot ten of you scrunched down and scurrying over the sidewalk in plain view of all the tourists, thinking that somehow *that* made you invisible from the window."

I opened my mouth to argue, but then saw a mental picture of the scene she described and felt my cheeks burn. "Fine. Good point. It was just a moment of panic. Let's move along before Paulie truly does notice me."

"Sweetie, if he didn't notice that display, I think you're safe."

We finally went in a few stores, and Katie picked out horrendous knickknack after horrendous knickknack. Boxes of chocolate-covered caramel balls labeled elk droppings, potholders with scantily clad park rangers on them, and pinecone owls with felt scarves.

"You know, everyone you work with already lives here, right? They won't actually want any of that."

"As if that's the point." After finishing the north side of the street, we'd paused and put the purchases in Katie's car, then began making our way up the south side. When we were directly in front of the Cozy Corgi, Katie held a gloved hand up to the window and peered in. "Wow! Look at all those boxes. You made a lot of progress today."

I'd nearly forgotten why my back was aching. "I did. I think tomorrow's supposed to be a little warmer, so I'll crack open the windows and see if I can air the shop out some. Then maybe I can start shelving the books."

"It's going to be wonderful, Fred. I can feel it." Katie pulled back from the window, and we continued down the sidewalk. "Have you decided what to do with the second story yet?"

That consideration had been playing in the back of my mind all day. "I stopped in at the T-shirt printing place yesterday afternoon. The owner mentioned the possibility of putting my logo on T-shirts, hoodies, and hats and such. I can turn the top floor into Cozy Corgi merchandise. I was sort of thinking it was silly, but after seeing you buy a week's salary worth of junk about Estes Park, maybe I'm sitting on a gold mine and don't even know it."

She shrugged but lacked some of her typical enthusiasm. "Well, that's an idea, I suppose."

"Why? Sounds like you have a thought?"

Katie hesitated, then shrugged again. "No, and I'm sure some merchandise would be cute, but I don't think an entire floor of it would be the way to go." She was distracted for a moment as we passed a pizza parlor. "You know what, I think I'm almost done shopping. Let's make the toy store the final shop and then grab dinner. Sound good?"

"I get to be done shopping *and* eat? I knew you loved me." Plus, I'd get to be inside Bushy Evergreen's Workshop again. After Barry's history lesson the night before, I wanted to see what else I might notice.

"Great. I'll make it fast, and then—" She glanced back at me, her eyes widening, and then a goofy grin spread over her face as she pointed. "We might need to take care of that situation first."

I glanced back to see Watson squatting on the sidewalk, glaring at us for interrupting his privacy. "My fault for giving him the scone." Sliding my purse off my shoulder, I dug through, searching for the waste bags. Then I remembered I'd taken them out earlier in the day. But I'd left them on the counter. We were only a couple of stores down from the Cozy Corgi. I gestured toward the next block. "Why don't you go ahead? I left the bags at my shop. I'll go get one to take care of this and then meet you at the toy store."

"I don't mind waiting."

"No, go on. This means we get to dinner quicker."

"You sure know how to convince a girl, I'll give you that." Katie gave a little wave. "See you in a second."

I paused to let Watson finish his business, and then we hurried back to the Cozy Corgi. The waste bags weren't on the counter. I started to do a quick search of the store, then realized they might've rolled anywhere as I was moving boxes, and with the tourists outside Christmas shopping, it was only a matter of moments before someone's shoe would turn the search into a moot point. I retrieved a large wad of toilet paper from the restroom, locked the shop back up, and rushed toward the ice cream parlor, moving quicker than Watson desired, practically dragging him.

By the time we got there, sure enough, the crisis was over and the damage done. Fearing that Watson's and my unintended victim was now inside the ice cream parlor glaring at us through the window, I hurried away once more, this time, refusing to give in to my new inclination to lower myself like a moron and rush out of view.

Once we were several stores down, I paused to glare at Watson, then reminded myself it wasn't his fault. I was the one slacking on motherly doggy duties. Watson was simply doing what dogs do.

"Well, they didn't kick us out of town when we found a dead body in our shop. Surely dirtying a tourist's shoes won't be the deal breaker."

We crossed the intersection leading to the next block that held my uncles' antique store, Rocky Mountain Imprints, and the toyshop. When we passed Wings of the Rockies, I was tempted once more to crawl past the window. I had to break that inclination and quick! The owner of the wild-bird store and I weren't fans of each other. I hesitated at the door to the toyshop as I had a realization, then muttered conspiratorially to Watson. "We've only been in town a month, and if we count the ice cream parlor, there are already three locations we need to avoid. Maybe they *should* kick us out of town."

Watson simply stared after a second glance toward the door, as if asking what I was waiting for, didn't I know he was cold, and since when did I care about what people thought about us to begin with?

He had a point.

Shoving it all away, I pushed open the door, and we walked into the warmth of the toy store.

We made it about ten steps as we rounded the first tower of toys before halting. It took a moment for the scene to make any sense.

Declan was sprawled on his back in front of the counter. Katie was on her knees beside him, her fingers clawing at the ever-changing-hued garland that was wrapped around Declan's throat.

"Island of Misfit Toys" played in the background.

Watson whimpered.

A sense of déjà vu washed over me.

Another dead body. They really were going to kick us out of Estes Park.

Katie looked up at us, wild-eyed, her brown curls pulled free of the ponytail and whipping around her face. "Fred. Help me."

Her panicked tone broke through my shock. Dropping Watson's leash, I hurried toward her.

"I can't get it off. I can't get it off!" Katie's words were so rushed that they came out in the slur. Only then did I notice the blood on Declan's neck and on Katie's hands. I couldn't tell whose it was.

The garland. Noah and Jonah's stupid, sharp garland.

I changed course midway, nearly twisting my ankle in

the process, and followed the trail of garland behind the counter. I yanked the plug-in out of the wall, causing the flickering lights to die, then glanced at the countertop. For a second, I didn't see what I was looking for, but then I found them sticking out of a cup full of pens. I grabbed the scissors and then joined Katie on the floor on the other side of Declan. "Can you pull it enough to get some slack?"

Katie stared at the scissors in confusion, and then understanding dawned and she nodded. "I think so." She pulled one hand free to make room, then used her other hand to create space between the garland and his neck, sucking in a breath as the garland made fresh cuts.

It was just enough for me to slide one of the blades through. Luckily the scissors were industrial quality, but even so it took forever. I had to practically saw through the layers of fiberglass, plastic, and wire. Maybe it took less than a minute, but it felt like hours as I worked with the scissors as Katie tried to pull the garland evermore loose.

And then it was free.

"Is he alive? I didn't even check. I just started trying to get it off him."

I held two of my fingers to the underside of his jaw and closed my eyes. After a few seconds, I shook my head. "No. We were too—" And then I felt it, barely there. Weak and faint but there. "Yes! He's alive."

Without thinking, I threw myself from the floor and grabbed the phone I'd noticed on the counter, then dialed 911.

Officer Green's pale blue eyes narrowed in suspicion as she glared at me. "Why were you here again?"

From outside the toy store's windows, red light from the ambulance flashed across her face as it drove away, giving her a demonic appearance. To be fair, Officer Susan Green and I didn't have the best history, despite our limited interactions, so maybe it clouded my view of her.

"Like we said, Katie and I were Christmas shopping. We came in the store to purchase toys"—I attempted to keep the *duh* out of my tone, kinda—"for presents."

"Really?" Her cold gaze darted between Katie and me. "Katie Pizzala... Pozl...." She glanced down at her notepad. "Pizzolato."

"You can just call me Katie P." Katie tried for a smile. "Or just Katie, obviously."

Officer Green's lips tightened to such a thin line that I was surprised she was able to speak. "Katie *Pizzolato,* you don't have any family in town. Who would you possibly be buying toys for?" Not giving Katie a chance to reply, she turned to me. "And the youngest kids in your family are eight years old. Are you telling me you're going to buy them an old-time metal top, or some hand-carved wooden blocks?"

I stared at her, impressed, despite myself. "You're very thorough, Officer."

"It's *my* town, Miss Page. I make it my job to be informed." She made a circling gesture with her pen, encompassing the toy store. "And as such, I know it doesn't make any sense for either one of you to come in here to buy toys."

My temper flared, and I barely stopped myself from saying that she was right. Katie and I got bored during our shopping spree and decided to strangle the owner of the toyshop to liven up the holidays.

Luckily, Katie piped up. "Carla, she owns Black Bear Roaster—"

"I'm aware who Carla is, Miss *Pizzolato*."

Katie flinched. "Okay, well, I work there now since—"

"I'm aware of that too, Miss *Pizzolato*. We've already established that I'm aware of what happens in *my* town." Officer Green seemed to be taking a bit too much enjoyment in every ounce of this.

Watson growled, drawing Officer Green's attention.

I took a step in front of him.

Remarkably, Katie just continued, her words coming out in a rush to finish before being cut off again. I had no idea how she wasn't screaming. "Since Carla is my boss and she's pregnant, I thought I'd get a baby gift here."

Officer Green opened her mouth, another argument coming, then gave a reluctant nod. "Oh."

She scribbled something on her notepad, then turned to me again. "And you? Please tell me your family isn't getting ready to produce any more offspring."

Despite my best efforts, I glanced toward some of the still-flashing garland on the shelves behind Officer Green. Instead of giving in to the impulse to add another strangling victim to the afternoon's events, I channeled my father. "Officer Green, we both know that you and my family have a tense relationship. It seems that it might be appropriate to have another officer do this questioning."

"I'm not questioning. This isn't an interrogation. No charges are being pressed. I'm simply taking statements from witnesses." Somehow her sneer managed to deepen. "And as far as another officer, I'm sorry, but your boyfriend is out of town at the moment."

"Branson isn't my boyfriend." While there was definitely an attraction between us, and Branson had asked me out, we had yet to go on a date.

Her eyebrow cocked. "Either way, *Sergeant Wexler* is out of town." She smiled. "I'm afraid you're stuck with me. And I'd appreciate it if we could get back to the issue at hand. An attempted murder is more important than the status of your relationship with my so-called superior."

At that moment, another officer I remembered seeing at my shop last month cleared his throat and interrupted, holding up one of the large wooden nutcracker soldiers in gloved hands. "Officer Green, this was under that giant teddy bear." There appeared to be a red stain on the soldier's blue helmet.

Officer Green's eyes narrowed as she inspected the nutcracker. "Bag it." Then she turned back to Katie. "You still say you heard someone running when you walked into the store?"

Katie nodded. "Yes."

"You didn't see anyone hit the victim with anything? Didn't even see the strangulation begin?"

"Hit the victim?" Confusion flashed over Katie, but she pushed onward. "No. I told you. I came in the store, heard what I thought was running footsteps, and then found Declan on the ground, with the garland wrapped around his throat." For the first time, impatience sounded in Katie's tone. Or worry. I wasn't sure which.

Officer Green glanced down at Katie's hands and then mine. "And yet you're both covered in blood."

I followed her gaze. Somehow in the chaos, I hadn't even noticed. "Declan was bleeding. The garland was cutting into him, and into Katie's hands as she tried to get it off him."

Further disgust. How she managed to have so much was nearly miraculous. "Yes, I'm aware of the garland as well, Ms. Page. One more delight bestowed upon the world from your family."

"You weren't kidding. Even I wasn't aware the garland came from Noah and Jonah. There's no way I can keep track of all their inventions." The level of her knowledge of my family was a bit unsettling. It went beyond knowing her town, as she said. It was clear she'd been spending her time looking for something, some way to make life difficult for us. I didn't bother trying to keep my tone respectful. "You seem a little obsessed with my family, Susan. I don't think that's healthy. You might need to get some help for that."

Not helpful, Fred. Shut up!

Her shoulders straightened, and she took a step toward me. We were the exact same height and roughly the same build. But whereas I'd inherited my father's large bones, I was soft and curvy. Officer Green had turned her build into that of a weightlifter. It took every ounce of nerve I had not to flinch at the sight of her anger.

"Like I said. It's my job to keep this town safe. I know to

keep vigilant. Even if Sergeant Wexler is distracted by... other things, I promise you I won't be." She took another step, close enough that I could smell her spearmint gum. "And on that note, you claim to have arrived late, after Miss Pizzolato supposedly discovered Declan just in time to conveniently interrupt a murder. If you were out shopping with your friend, why weren't you together?"

After too many years with a condescending husband, and then a betrayal from my best friend and business partner who stole my publishing house away from me, I was well equipped to handle being spoken down to by someone on a power trip. Officer Susan Green seemed to always be on a power trip, at least where I was concerned. Once more, an endless litany of things I shouldn't say flitted through my mind and played over my tongue. So many that I had to bite my bottom lip.

"That shouldn't be a hard question to answer, Fred." Officer Green took a final step forward.

Watson growled again, and this time moved in front of me, baring his teeth.

Though I loved him for it, I yanked on his leash, forcing him behind. I had no doubt that given the chance, she would impound him or worse. The thought brought my tone back to respectful. "Watson... made a mess on the sidewalk, and I'd forgotten a waste bag. I had to go back to my shop to get one."

"Oh really?" From her victorious tone, I might as well have admitted I was the one who had attempted to kill Declan. "Can you offer proof that you picked up his refuse?"

"No...." I gaped at her, astounded at this line of questioning. "I... didn't get back in time. Someone had stepped in it."

Her blue eyes brightened for the first time, and she pulled out another pad of paper from inside her vest. "Well, I *hate* to have to tell you, but I will be writing you a ticket. Being a poopetrator comes with a hundred-dollar fine."

The idea that she was standing in the middle of a near-murder scene and worried about giving me a ticket for Watson's mess on the sidewalk should have been enough to make my head explode, but I was so astounded at both the use of her word *poopetrator* and her ability to utter it without so much as a smile that I was only capable of standing there in silence.

It seemed to be the final straw for Katie, however, who finally cracked. "Are you insane? Declan Diamond was nearly murdered, Fred and I barely managed to save his life, my hands are all cut up, we have no idea who was running away, and you're worried about dog poop? What is wrong with you?"

It would've been bad enough for Katie's outburst to prompt Officer Green to lose her temper, but the smile that spread across her face as she turned to look at Katie was so much more terrifying. "Right now, Miss Pizzolato, you are the only one talking about someone running away. Even your friend here can't vouch for you. The most obvious answer is typically the right solution. Perhaps after leaving hazardous waste on city property, Winifred Page accidentally interrupted your murder attempt, and you panicked. That or she's attempting to cover for you. Poorly, I might add."

Katie's mouth hung open, speechless for a few moments. Then she blinked. "That makes absolutely no sense. Why would I try to kill Declan Diamond?"

Officer Green shrugged. "I'm less concerned with the why of the case, Miss Pizzolato, than I am the who." She refocused on her pad of paper and began jotting down something as she spoke. "Tell me again specifically what you hoped to buy when you came into Bushy Evergreen's Workshop."

The questioning continued for another half hour or more. By the time Katie and I were allowed to leave the toyshop, we were both trembling with rage and exhaustion. And I had a newly written ticket shoved in my purse.

We walked in silence until we reached the front of the Cozy Corgi and Katie glanced at the empty store to the right, where *Healthy Delights* was still painted over the window. "I'm so angry right now... It makes me completely understand how Opal died. I could club someone with a rolling pin, too."

I laid my hand on her shoulder. "Well, that makes two more reasons why we're friends. I feel the exact same way, and I know that I shouldn't admit that, but I'm going to anyway."

Katie let out a long shaky breath, and worry warred with the anger in her tone. "Should we be concerned? Officer Green will find any excuse possible to pin this on us. I don't know why she hates me so."

I didn't even have to consider that one. "She doesn't hate you."

Katie scoffed.

"Okay, yes she does. But not because of you. It's because of me. She's detested Mom and Barry for a long time. Her brother owns the magic shop. And Mom and Barry own the property. They're wonderful people, but you know what they'd be like as his landlords. Absentminded, scatterbrained, slow to follow through on everything. And I know her brother has tried to buy the shop multiple times, and Barry always refuses. Susan blames my family for both holding him back and, I think, just for being pains in general."

"Really? That's it? She is trying to pin murder on us just because of that?"

I shrugged. "Partly, yes. But I think there is also just a molecular dislike between us. I noticed it the first time she was questioning me about Opal, and it only got worse when Branson took over. I don't think she likes him, either. And knowing that there's some sort of attraction between the two of us, only makes her despise me more."

Katie sighed and sounded like she'd been awake for a week. "Well, I wish he was here."

"Me, too. Me, too." Branson had told me he was going to be gone a week or so, while insisting he'd take me to dinner before Christmas rolled around. But in the chaos in the toy store, I'd forgotten.

Katie brought my attention back from Branson. "What I don't understand is who would try to kill Declan? He owns a toy store, for crying out loud. You don't get more benign than that."

"Well... actually...." Judging from what Barry had said the night before, and from what I'd seen through the window, I could think of three people who might want to kill Declan. "How about we swing by the hospital to have them take care of your hands, then pick up a pizza, go to my house, and I'll fill you in?"

By the time Katie left, it was nearly nine o'clock. After

hours of speculation and gossip, my anger had abated, but I was still unable to turn off my brain. I settled in the over-stuffed armchair close to the fire, the Christmas tree sparkling from across the room in front of the window, and continued to reread my favorite Jacqueline Winspear novel. Before long, between the warmth of the book, the fireplace, and Watson at my feet, I dozed off.

The buzzing of my cell phone on the arm of the chair startled me awake. The fire was little more than embers, and a chill had entered the room. I glanced at the screen. It was nearly one in the morning, and though the number was unknown, the area code showed it was local.

I hit Accept. "Hello?"

"Fred!"

Katie's panicked voice made me sit up straighter, causing Watson to scurry away as I accidentally kicked out my feet. "Katie! What's wrong?"

"I've been arrested. They're saying I tried to kill Declan."

"What!" In my still slightly fuzzy brain, I wondered if she was kidding, but then I remembered Officer Green's expression. "Why?"

She sniffed. "My fingerprints were on that nutcracker guy they found."

"They were?" I hesitated. "Did you touch it?" Stupid question. Obviously she had if her fingerprints were on it. "And what does the nutcracker have to do with it?"

"I guess so, I must have, right? But I don't even remember that thing. I've never liked those. They're saying he was hit on the head with it, before being strangled, I guess. All I remember is walking in, seeing Declan's body, and trying to get that stupid garland off of him. But maybe... all I can think of is maybe it was in the way so I moved it, tossed it aside. I don't remember. It was all a blur."

I tried not to let my own panic take over. Whatever was going on, it could be figured out. "Okay, where are you?"

"At the police station." Katie's tone said that should've been obvious. "They arrested me. You're my one phone call."

I had to process through that. "Katie, why in the world would I be your one phone call? You should call your lawyer."

"Lawyer?" Katie's voice spiked. "I don't have a lawyer! What normal person has a lawyer? I don't even know a lawyer. And even if I did, I can't afford them. They said they're going to provide me one."

"Oh, Katie." I couldn't hold back a groan.

"What? I can't!"

I knew exactly which lawyer would be provided. Even if there were a slew of them to choose from, both chance and Officer Green would make certain Gerald Jackson would be the one called. "Okay, well, I'm sure whoever they send you is better than nothing. But don't say too much. I'll get you a better one tomorrow, as soon as I can figure out who a better one is." Although *any* lawyer would be a better one. Not that I was going to say that to Katie at the moment.

"Fred, I didn't call to talk about lawyers." Some of the panic seemed to fade from Katie's voice, and she almost sounded relaxed. "I called for you. I need *you*."

"Why? What can I do? I'm not a lawyer."

Again, Katie sounded like the reason should be apparent. "Obviously I can't trust what the police are going to do if Officer Green has it out for me. I need you to work your magic."

"My magic?"

"Good grief, yes, Fred. Your magic! You're the one who cleared Barry's name when he was accused of killing Opal." She softened to nearly a whisper, making me wonder if someone was listening in. "I need you to figure out who did this."

FIVE

After an almost sleepless night, I knew where to start. Even though I was still new to town, I was fairly certain I'd already discovered the biggest gossips among the shopkeepers. Gossip seemed to be the best bet. I didn't know much about Declan or the rest of the Diamond family, other than what Barry had told me, but if he was nearly as horrible as Barry said, I was willing to bet there were plenty of stories about Declan. My first thought was Anna and Carl Hansen, who owned the home decor shop. My initial impression of them had been their business ownership was little more than a front so they could be in the center of the hubbub at all times. But they were down the street and across the block from Bushy's, while the runners-up in the gossip competition were a mere few doors down. So they were the winners.

First things first, though. After a bad night, I needed caffeine. Although, that was really just an excuse. I could sleep twelve hours and still need caffeine to function. As Watson and I walked toward the Black Bear Roaster, I had to admit something to myself. Only part of my tossing and turning had been worry over my friend. There was plenty of that. I hated the thought of Katie spending the night in a cell, hated that she was caught in the middle of another murder drama just a few short weeks after the first. The same could be said for myself, I knew. And I needed to quit thinking of it as a murder investigation. Declan was simply unconscious, not dead. For that matter, I needed to quit thinking of it as an investigation. I wasn't the police. I was an ex-teacher turned ex-publisher turned bookshop owner who was also the daughter of a police detective. That was all.

But that was the other reason I'd been unable to sleep, not just worry over Katie, but a tingle of excitement. The realization made me feel guilty. I shouldn't be feeling anything like that, and not only because of Katie. A man was almost killed, and part of me felt like I'd been handed an early Christmas present. This wasn't a pretty little puzzle I had to put together. It was serious. Life and death. One that wasn't even my job to do.

And yet....

I glanced at Watson as I opened the door to the coffee shop, and he peered up at me, eyes wide and bright. At least one of us was fully rested, if his soft snores throughout the endless hours had been any indication. "Your mama needs therapy or something."

Watson seemed to consider, then flared his nose at the scents drifting our way, and led me inside.

He was right. Might as well focus on the task at hand. And if I was finding enjoyment over what Katie had asked me to do, so be it. Maybe I was simply getting a thrill by trying to help my friend.

Before I could mock myself for that thought, Carla spotted me from behind the counter, gave a big wave, then ushered me over. Despite my caffeine addiction, I'd never met her before, but judging from her expansive belly, I didn't need to be an actual police detective to determine who she was.

"You're Fred, right?"

I nodded. "Yes. And this is Watson. You're Carla."

She flashed a half smile, then leaned toward me across the counter, as much as she was able. "What in the world is going on? I got a voicemail from Katie this morning, letting me know she wouldn't be at work today. I had to drag my ever-expanding girth outta bed before dawn. She said something had come up and she'd explain to me when she came back in." Carla gestured over my shoulder toward the slew of customers. "But everyone's talking about her being arrested for trying to kill Declan Diamond."

For a heartbeat I debated lying, or at least playing coy. I wasn't certain why Katie hadn't just been upfront in the message, but it wouldn't do any good for me to play along at this point. "That's true." I decided to bend the truth, just a touch. Doubtlessly Carla would pass along anything I said, so maybe it would help some of the rumors die down. "She and I walked into the toy store yesterday and found Declan on the ground. Someone had tried to strangle him."

"Strangle?" Carla's eyes grew wider. "I heard that she bashed Declan over the head and he's in a coma."

Good Lord. That sentence alone made me miss the city, where you could wander around for an entire day and not bump into anyone you knew. Katie had been arrested in the wee hours of the night, and already the town was talking about how she was an attempted murderer. How in the world did people know about Declan getting hit on the head? Katie and I hadn't even known that at the time. As soon as the thought crossed my mind, I knew the answer. Obviously Susan Green was enjoying letting *her* town know all about Katie Pizzolato. I leveled my gaze at Carla, making sure to keep my tone firm yet friendly. If I sounded the least bit defensive, I would only make matters worse.

"I can guarantee you, she did not bash Declan over the head. Nor did she try to strangle him. The only thing Katie did was try to save his life, which she did."

"Oh!" Carla gave a tiny flinch and sounded a little bit chastised despite my effort at neutrality. "Oh, well then. That's... good of her." Carla passed a hand over her belly. "I'm glad to hear it. She's a sweet girl, a little odd, but likable, I suppose. A bit evasive when people try to get to know her better, especially around family."

I knew that much to be true. She didn't talk about family even with me. But I hadn't found it too big of a concern. Not everyone had a great family life. Despite our growing closeness, we'd known each other little more than a month. Not enough time to trust me with whatever hurts she might have. That Carla thought she was owed those details as Katie's new boss was nearly enough to make me turn Watson around and head to the other coffee shop clear across town. Then I remembered the quickly growing number of shops I was avoiding. I couldn't add another to the list.

"Well, I can promise you, Katie is not a murderer. And her family life doesn't keep her from being an excellent barista and employee." Might as well go for gold; it might help Katie out when she returned. "Plus, I can attest personally that she's one of the best bakers I've ever known. She could probably triple your business."

From the grimace that crossed Carla's lips, I knew it was a losing battle.

Before she could say anything else, I decided to make my order. It was clear any information I might get from Carla would be of the pure speculation variety. At least the gossip Anna and Carl—and my uncles—dealt in seemed fact-based. “I’m sorry to cut this short, but I really must get going. Would you mind getting me a large dirty chai and one of your pumpkin scones?” Maybe it would be softer first thing in the morning. If not, it looked like Watson would be breaking his diet yet again.

A few minutes later, Watson and I were back outside. I thought I’d hop into my Mini Cooper and drive the two blocks to my uncles’ antique shop, but instead I decided to walk. If I really was going to be digging around, trying to figure out who might have it in for Declan Diamond, I needed to make myself a little more present among the other shopkeepers and definitely stop avoiding them. Even so, when I was close to Paws, I hurried Watson to the other side of the street. I considered it a win that I didn’t attempt another crabwalk.

Before giving Watson the other half of the dry pumpkin scone, I double-checked to make certain I’d put waste bags into my purse. Luckily for him, I had, and he voraciously enjoyed his second breakfast.

I spared a glance into the toyshop as we passed. The door was locked, and the windows dark, like I’d expected. Another wave of guilt cut through me. Regardless of how I felt about Declan, his wife, his *pregnant* wife, had to worry about her husband dying at Christmas. I hadn’t even thought of her in that way—as a wife, expectant mother, someone who loved her husband and was now hurting.

Of course, none of that was true if the other ways I had been thinking about her were accurate. All through the night, I’d speculated on motives for why she might try to kill him. Just from the brief flash I’d seen through the window two nights before, their marriage definitely wasn’t without strife. Then again, lots of marriages were less-than-perfect and didn't result in murder, but maybe the brother who'd stepped between Declan and Daphne? The father Declan had pushed aside and taken his business and freedom? Maybe even a combo of the three?

Well, it wasn't my job to worry about Daphne and how she might be feeling. That was what the rest of her family was for. My job was to try to figure out.... I shook my head at the thought as I pushed open the door to my uncles' antique shop. No, it wasn't my job to find out who tried to kill Declan. But I was going to do it anyway. Katie was right. I'd helped to clear Barry's name and I *would* clear hers.

"Bless my soul, Fred and Watson. My day just got better." Gary smiled at me from where he knelt on the floor with a box of tools open at the base of a lamp. He issued a deep groan as he pushed himself from his knees to a standing position. At over six foot and maintaining the heavy muscles of his pro-football years, even at the age of sixty, he dwarfed me as he wrapped me in a hug. "Always good to see you, sweetheart."

"You too, Uncle Gary." And it was. Even though Gary was my uncle through marriage, he always brought to mind my father, with his deep voice, strong body, and calm, unshakable demeanor.

After releasing me, he gave Watson a quick pat on the head then refocused on me. "You're either here because you decided to get the sofa and lamp for your shop, or you're snooping around trying to help your friend."

If Carla knew about Katie, no part of me was surprised Gary knew as well. "Both, actually. Though any help you might give me on Katie is more important than the antiques, of course."

"No niece of mine is going to say *anything* is more important than antiques." My mom's brother, Percival, rounded a corner in their mazelike antique shop and shook his finger at me. "Even if murder is involved, or attempted murder, in this case." Though he was the exact height as his husband, the two of them couldn't be more different. Percival was a decade older, and his wispy stature was the antithesis of Gary's bulk. He gave me a warm hug, then leaned his face close, pointing to his balding head. "Give your uncle a kiss, darling. We're under the mistletoe."

I had no idea how I'd missed it, but sure enough, he'd donned a headband with a long spring at the center and a sprig of mistletoe bobbing over us both. With a chuckle, I gave him a quick peck on the lips before he bent to pat Watson.

Watson let out a growl and backed up, his wide eyes startled as he stared at the waving mistletoe.

Percival gasped and stood up, offended. "Well, I never. See if you ever get a treat from me again, little one."

And at that word, I could see the war raging in Watson. Kill the alien creature floating above Percival's head or get a treat. To my shock, murder won. Watson growled again, this time showing his teeth.

I pointed toward the mistletoe. "You may want to give him a little space. I don't think Watson's a fan of your headband."

Understanding dawned in Percival's eyes, but he lifted his chin. "Well, he'll have to get with it. Fashion is fashion." He cast an accusatory glance at my salmon-hued broomstick skirt, but uncharacteristically kept his mouth shut. "Thankfully, he's a corgi, and I know he's part super sleuth like his mama, but even he can't reach up here."

"But I wish he could." Gary bugged his eyes out at me. "I've been waiting for that stupid headband to fall apart for twenty years. I'm pretty sure it's going to outlive us both."

Percival smacked Gary's arm but turned his attention to me. "So what's this I hear about something being more important than antiques? You can't tell me that sofa and lamp aren't going to be absolute perfection in your cozy little bookshop."

"No, you're right. I can't. I was just telling Gary I've decided to take both of them. I'm going to put them in the mystery room, the one with the river rock fireplace, like you suggested."

"Well, of course you are, you brilliant woman. You wouldn't make any other choice." Percival smiled in satisfaction. "Now if you'd just listen to me about your wardrobe...."

I laughed, repaying the smack on Gary's arm with one of my own. "I knew it would be too good to be true for you to keep your opinions to yourself."

"Pretty sure a man wearing a mistletoe headband has no room to talk about your wardrobe, Fred." Gary cast a sidelong glance at Percival, then smiled at me warmly. "You look beautiful as always. I think your hair has grown longer. Mountain life must be agreeing with you."

I normally kept my hair a little lower than my shoulder blades, but it had gotten long, especially on the days when it went from curly to merely wavy. And with the lack of humidity, this was happening more than it had in Kansas City. "I think it is. I really do love it here. Despite the crime rate."

Percival snorted. "Darling, I'm afraid we're going to have to blame that one on you. You walk into town, and we have our first murder in years, and now an attempted one." He cocked his head. "Although, I suppose that isn't true. We just didn't know about some of the other murders."

"Speaking of, you said you weren't here just for the sofa

and lamp. So fill us in." Gary motioned toward the sofa that would soon be in my shop. We crossed the space, and Percival and I sat on the sofa, with Gary taking a seat in an ornate armchair at its side.

I unhooked Watson's leash so he could explore and get away from Percival's mistletoe. "That's actually what I wanted from you. To fill *me* in. I only met Declan and his family once, two nights ago. And at first I found him very charming. But by the end, I'd changed my mind. And from what Barry tells me, my second impression was the correct one."

"If your first impression was that the man was a gorgeous, stunning, ravishingly handsome man, my darling niece, then you would be correct." Percival made a fanning motion with his hand in front of his face.

Gary rolled his eyes. "And if your second impression was that he was a selfish, egomaniacal narcissist, then you would also be correct."

"Well, nobody's perfect." Percival shrugged and gave a nod that was probably supposed to come off as wise. "All those things can be said just as truly about endless ugly people. If you're going to be evil, you might as well look good doing it."

"Evil? You really think he's evil?"

To my surprise, though it hadn't been his claim, Gary nodded. And while it was completely in Percival's nature to exaggerate, it wasn't true for Gary. "Why? Because of what he did to his father?"

"Oh, so you do know. Though that makes sense since you spoke to Barry." All humor left Percival's voice as his eyes darkened. "Duncan was never the most cheerful of people. Even as a kid, everyone said he had the soul of an old man. But he was kind, even if a little abrasive. And one of the best woodcraftsman I've ever seen. Besides when he lost Della, having his no-good son steal his business out from under him was the most devastated I've ever seen a man."

"Devastated enough to kill his own son?"

Gary and Percival both flinched, and it was Gary who responded. "You really are your father's daughter, aren't you? No beating around the bush and right to the point."

Percival didn't wait for me to respond. "No. And maybe that's the problem. No matter what Declan did, Duncan could never hurt him, not even spank him. Those two boys were his weakness. Even Della said so. He spoiled them both rotten. I know Dolan's a bit of a strange bird, but he turned out fine despite it all. Declan didn't."

I decided to push a little more. Percival was right. That had been my father's approach—direct and upfront. I knew it wouldn't always work with the people in town, but I wasn't trying to manipulate my uncles. "Then what about Dolan or Daphne? If Declan was so evil, surely both of them had plenty of reasons to want him gone."

Both men shook their heads. Percival's voice stayed serious. "No way would Dolan do such a thing. I've known him since the day he was born. He didn't get his brother's looks or his father's talents, but he got his mother's kind heart. You couldn't ask for a sweeter man. And Daphne?" He shrugged. "Granted, I don't know her very well, but every interaction I've ever had has made me think she truly does have it all. Just as stunningly gorgeous as Declan and as sweet as Dolan. Her only flaw is her husband."

Maybe she decided to get rid of her only flaw. I didn't say that. As trustworthy as Gary and Percival were, it seemed they had a blind spot in regards to the Diamond family. Which, considering the connection went back for almost the past seventy years, at least for Percival, I suppose that made sense. "What about other people? Maybe Declan wasn't evil just to his family."

Gary pointed at me. "And that's what I was thinking. You're onto something there, Fred. I don't know if Declan managed to screw over anyone as royally as he did his own father, but it's well known you can't trust the man in business. He's cutthroat. Which, honestly, has helped the toyshop. The fellow who runs the pet shop tried to open a toy store when he came into town. Declan brought all the fires of hell down around him."

Percival sniffed. "Good enough, I say. There's something not quite right about that guy. He seems better suited to be around animals than children."

Even though there was only one person they could mean, I had to make sure. I'd planned on avoiding the pet shop until a last resort. "Paulie Mertz? The guy who owns Paws?"

Misreading my tone, Percival lifted a finger in my direction. "Now don't get defensive. I know he owns two corgis and all you corgi people stick together, but there's something there, even if I can't put my finger on it."

"I agree, actually. Though I can't picture him going up against Declan, not that I've had much interaction with either man."

"Nah, you've the measure of both of them I'd say. The pet shop guy folded so fast you would've missed the entire thing if you'd blinked." Gary shrugged. "Not that I could blame him. Declan can be an intense adversary if you cross him. He's a snake. Of course, that depends on who you ask. He's charmed most every woman in town. At least those who let their eyes do their thinking for them."

It took me a second to catch Gary's implication, but when I did, a huge portion of the town opened up as possible suspects. "Are you saying he's a bit of a womanizer?"

"A bit?" Percival cackled, his brightness returning. "The man has had so many affairs he might as well run for political office!"

And that would point back to Daphne. Get back at a cheating husband. Though physically, I couldn't see it. Declan was massive, strong, and healthy. Daphne was small, feminine, and pregnant. If he'd truly been hit in the head hard enough to put him in a coma, I couldn't quite picture her managing such a feat. But maybe.... "Were some of these affairs with married women?"

They both nodded.

A cuckold husband would definitely have the motivation. And the strength. Even if I couldn't figure out who it was, maybe I could find something to prove that motivation. Enough to clear Katie's name.

That brought the other reason I was here. "While we're at it, I need some advice. As you know, they have Katie in custody on suspicion of Declan's attempted murder, even though she's the one who saved his life."

"Ridiculous. The Green family have always been a barrel of idiots." Percival shook his head in disgust, and Gary didn't disagree.

I didn't know the rest of the family, and I didn't like Susan Green, but she didn't seem like an idiot to me. If she were, I'd be a lot less worried about her.

"Even so, she's managed to get Katie into a mess. If we were in Kansas City, I'd know who to call, but I don't know here. Who's a good lawyer in town, or even down in Denver who I could trust with Katie's case?"

For the first time, Percival looked utterly confused.

"What do you need that for? I talked to Gerald myself this morning. Told me all about it. He's in Katie's corner."

I spared a quick glance at Gary, who bit his bottom lip and gave a small shake of his head.

Some defensiveness had slipped into Percival's tone. "I know he's a little left of center, but so am I. He's a good lawyer. He'll do right by Katie."

I sighed, knowing that arguing would get me nowhere. "Well, I'm glad to hear it."

It was a marvel to me. I'd seen the good-old-boys-club effect countless times in my life. And as freethinking and liberal as Barry was, I could understand his loyalty to Gerald. I'd expected different from Percival somehow. The three men and my mother had all grown up together; I guess grown up with Duncan Diamond too, come to think of it. Despite her unwillingness to speak ill of most people, my mom was the only one who was prepared to raise doubts about Gerald Jackson's capabilities. But somehow, even with these men I adored, the good old boys club was in effect—binding, and apparently, blinding as well.

Unclear if it showed just how much I adored Katie or if it merely proved I relished playing detective, I left my uncles' shop and headed directly to Paws. I'd planned on avoiding it entirely, unless for some reason it came up as a last resort. I wouldn't call my uncles' story about Paulie a last resort at this point, but it was definitely a lead.

Unlike most of the other stores I noticed when Katie and I were Christmas shopping, as Watson and I walked into Paws, we weren't greeted by the scent of cinnamon, clove, pumpkin, or any of the traditional scents of the holidays. While it didn't seem unclean, it smelled exactly like what it was. And from Watson's perked-up reaction, it appeared he approved. Even with my human nose, I could make out cedar chips, dog food, and the musky odor of rodents. I was certain, to Watson's heightened senses, it was a smorgasbord of scents. And above it all, combined with the manic melody of piped-in "Rockin' Around the Christmas Tree," were the loud screeches of parakeets, the gurgling of fish tanks, and the whirl of hamster wheels.

Before Watson made it to the counter, Flotsam and Jetsam came bounding from the back like overgrown Christmas chipmunks who'd overdosed on coffee beans.

One of them wore a Santa hat with a jingling bell in place of the snowball, and the other had on an elf hat complete with pointed ears. Whichever one was wearing the Santa hat stumbled over a dog toy in the aisle, caught himself, and arrived at Watson a few seconds after the other. Watson stiffened but allowed the two shameless dogs to paw at him playfully and pull on his ears.

Unlike many of the corgis I'd met, Watson didn't have an overly playful nature, nor did he appreciate it in other dogs. Typically, if another dog tried to play with him, Watson would growl, back against my legs, and make it very clear if I didn't get him out of the situation soon, he'd hold me personally responsible for the rest of our existence. However, for whatever reason, if the dog was another corgi, even if he didn't play along, he managed to grin and bear it. Well, not so much grin. Watson had arrived in my life a little over a year ago, and I wasn't certain if whatever life he'd had before had turned him into a little bit of a sourpuss and grump, or if it had been his nature to begin with.

"Fred! Watson!" Paulie Mertz followed the path of his corgis and emerged from the back corner of the store, which was lined with fish tanks. At the sight of him, my mouth fell open, but I managed to catch my reaction quickly enough, or at least I thought so. The small thin man wore a clearly fake Santa beard and elf ears that matched the ones on his corgi. "I've been waiting for you to drop by. Every time I knock on your bookshop, no one ever answers. Even when I've seen your little cute orange car in front of it. I've been trying to schedule our corgi playdate."

"Oh, I'm so sorry, Paulie. Chances are I was either working on things upstairs or getting inventory arranged down in the basement." A complete and utter lie. Thanks to the large picture windows that looked out from either side of the front door, I had noticed Paulie headed my way, and I'm not too proud to admit that I hid—every time.

And at that moment, I quit blaming myself for the crab-walk in front of his window and searched desperately for a topic completely unrelated to corgi playdates, then realized they were plentiful.

"That's quite a beard you have on there. I didn't realize you got into the spirit of Christmas quite so emphatically." Ridiculous thing to say, considering I'd managed to talk to the man for a grand total of ten minutes. Like I knew anything about him.

He offered a yellow-toothed smile. "I can take it or leave it, truthfully. Christmas is little more than commercialism and gross consumption." He offered a self-sacrificing shrug. "I do it for the boys. Flotsam and Jetsam have quite the holiday spirit, as you can see."

Right then, one of them nipped at Watson's nub of a tail. My little grump sat down promptly, utterly failing to tuck what little tail he had away. He glared up at me.

"Yes, they seem to be very much in the... frantic frenzy of it all."

Paulie nodded, seemingly completely unaware of Watson's and my discomfort. "Watson doesn't look like he's in the spirit of things at all. I have a reindeer costume in the back, even have antlers. I can get it so he doesn't feel left out."

"No, don't, but thank you." I tried to keep my voice pleasant. "He'd murder us both."

Paulie furrowed his brow as he inspected Watson. "Yes, I can see that." He bent down to scratch Watson's ears, and though Watson attempted to pull away, with Flotsam and Jetsam trapping him on either side, he was forced to endure Paulie's affection. "You have Ursula's disposition, don't you?" He started to laugh and then broke it off abruptly. "No, you're not evil. More like King Triton. He wouldn't let Ariel have any fun."

I didn't even try to stop myself from looking around the shop to see if he had any of Noah and Jonah's garland hanging about. Somehow I'd forgotten the man's obsession with *The Little Mermaid*, despite his corgis being named after the sea witch's eels.

It was time to pull the trigger, before Watson lost his patience or I began to seriously consider plausible substitutions for the garland. "Sorry to drop in and run, Paulie, but I actually have tons to do today. If I'm to open the store by New Year's, I shouldn't be allowed out of the shop until I get the books shelved."

Paulie perked up, a cheerful expression over his poorly bearded face. "The boys and I would love to help. We're very good workers. We'd get the job done in half the time." His tone changed somewhat. "And with the extra time, we could always grab dinner after."

Luckily, this time I could rely on the truth to set me free. "To be honest, I'm a complete control freak. I want to make sure every book is exactly so-so. I'm afraid by the end of trying to help me, you'd think I was the worst person in the world."

His face fell. "Ah, well, I understand."

There was such sincere loneliness in his tone that I couldn't help but feel bad. Nor could I bring myself to change my mind, whether or not that made me a horribly selfish person.

"Actually I just wanted to pop in—" I couldn't simply lead in with prying him for information. Not after hurting his feelings. "—and get another bag of that dog food you sold me last month. Watson just loved it."

I was pretty certain Watson understood a lot of what I said. But the fact that he didn't throw back his head and howl in laughter proved some things escaped him. The very thought that he would lower himself to eat dry dog food, no matter that it was a hundred dollars a bag, was nearly sacrilege. I'd been tossing some of the dry food out each morning for the chipmunks and squirrels in the trees beside my cabin.

Paulie perked up. "Wonderful! Let me get that for you." Then he was gone. Unfortunately, his two eels... er... corgis stayed behind, not giving Watson a respite.

A few seconds passed before there was a loud groan and a loud bang, followed by more parakeets screeching.

"Fred?" Paulie's embarrassed voice drifted from some unseen aisle. "Would you mind giving me a hand?"

I'd forgotten I'd had to help him the first time as well. Sure enough, when I rounded the corner to the dog food aisle, I found him struggling to pull the medium-size bag upright once more.

"Sorry, Paulie, I should've remembered. Here. Let me give you a hand." Sidestepping Flotsam and Jetsam, who were bookending Watson as he stayed at my feet, I bent down, and in a smooth motion tossed the bag of dog food onto my shoulder.

"I'll, yes. That... works too."

From the embarrassment that once again cut through Paulie's voice, I knew I'd messed up again. The least I could've done was to take one end of the bag and pretend I needed his help.

We crossed back to the counter, and indeed, I could've used his help as the three shifting corgis at my feet nearly caused me to stumble twenty times. And from the occasional soft gurgle from Watson's throat, I knew, whether

Flotsam and Jetsam were corgis or not, our time was limited. I pulled out my credit card and decided to make it fast, after all. I wasn't sure if direct would work on Paulie Mertz like it did with my uncles or not, but it would have to do. "So while I'm here, I'm sure you've heard about what went on with Katie and me last night."

His brown eyes widened, and he nodded, a feverish glint growing in them. "With that Declan Diamond character. Yes, I heard."

There was no denying the glee in his tone, proving what Percival and Gary had said was true, not that I had ever doubted them. But combined with his expression, I finally put my finger on part of the reason Paulie Mertz gave me the willies. What my uncles had said was true, corgi people tended to stick together. Despite our differences, there was some almost unnamable quality that linked us. Something positive. Whatever that thing was, something about Paulie Mertz left me feeling uncomfortable. I almost felt guilty for it, but I'd learned to trust my instincts, even if I couldn't put my finger on why.

I took a heartbeat to make sure my tone stayed neutral. "Yes. That. And it seems like the whole town has also heard Katie was arrested for trying to kill him. And I can assure you, that isn't the case."

This time the glint in his eye was a little less malicious, possibly even holding a level of admiration, though I couldn't tell. "I heard you were the one who found out what happened to Opal. Does that mean you're looking into this for Katie?"

One of the eels accidentally nipped my ankles going for Watson's paw, and I jumped with a little yelp.

Paulie didn't attempt to call them back. Without asking, I snagged three of the large dog bones from the glass jar on the counter, tossed two of them to different sides of the room, and handed one to Watson. Sure enough, Flotsam and Jetsam went running. I refocused on Paulie. "I wouldn't say I'm looking into it. That's not my job, obviously; that's up to the police. I simply own a bookshop." Maybe it was my new perspective associating him with a rat, but the last thing I needed was him going around town saying I thought I was better than the police. "I just happened to hear a rumor about you and Declan, actually."

And with that, all awkwardness seemed to fade away, leaving him cold and hard. "I don't think I like what you're implying, Fred."

"What I'm—" His meaning solidified quickly. "Oh, no. I didn't think you had anything to do with it. I mean you couldn't even—" I started to say couldn't even lift a medium-size bag of dog food, but caught myself, thankfully. "—hurt a fly, I'm sure. You own corgis after all."

And like that, the warmth was back. Not warmth exactly but something akin to it. "Oh, sorry. Honestly, I've been waiting for someone to make that accusation. It's hardly a secret that Declan and I don't get along. I thought we were going to be friends. We were on the same softball league last summer when I moved to town."

"*You* were in a softball league?" I hadn't meant to say that, nor let my surprise slip out.

If he was offended, Paulie didn't let it show. "I was. You should consider joining, especially if Declan's not there. A lot of the shop owners do. Peg and Joe Singer from Rocky Mountain Imprints. Rion Spark, who owns a wedding dress shop, Pete Miller, the glassblower. Mark Green, who owns the magic shop. Even his sister, the cop. It's a great way to meet people if you're new and want to make friends. At least it's supposed to be."

If I didn't already find the idea of playing softball revolting, doing so alongside Susan Green and her brother sounded like a death wish. I didn't want to be anywhere near her when she had a bat in her hands.

Paulie had thrown so much information at me that I had to refocus to get back on track, which was also hindered by Flotsam and Jetsam being finished with their dog bones and once again pawing at Watson. "I hadn't heard about the softball team, but I did hear that you originally wanted to open a toy shop, but Declan... had other ideas."

He snorted. "That's one way to say it. He threatened me if I didn't open a different kind of shop."

"He threatened you? Physically?"

"No." Paulie shook his head. "Legally. Said he'd take me for everything I had. Even though there was nothing in the town ordinances saying there could only be one toy shop in town." He leveled his gaze at me. "Though, there is now."

"Really?" Despite myself, I leaned toward him. "You're saying he has such pull that he got them to change some of the town statutes?"

He shrugged, as if suddenly playing coy. "Estes Park is a great little place. But they like their own. Trust me, you'll find out soon enough, I'm sure. The town council has some very good people on it, so I've heard. But also has a couple who make sure the few natives left do better than the rest."

Now that was news. None of my family had mentioned that. Although, they wouldn't, would they? If it was true, they might not even be aware. Despite my mother being gone for a few decades, she was still a local. I'd had a very easy time with licensure and cutting through the red tape for opening my bookshop. Maybe that was because, even though I wasn't native, I was close enough?

That bit of news didn't have an impact regarding

Declan's attack; he and his family were natives. But perhaps he'd pulled the same stunt with other new business owners in town. And one of them decided to fight back?

Watson let out a loud yelp at my feet and finally gave in and growled, baring his teeth at the two obnoxious corgis. I couldn't bring myself to scold him. In truth he'd done much better than I had. I shoved one of the corgi eels with my foot, drawing attention to me, as I signed the receipt Paulie offered me. "Well, Paulie, despite what it took you to get here, it seems like the pet shop really does suit you."

"Yes, it does." With the smile he gave, some of his rat-like appearance faded again. "Blessing in disguise, unanswered prayers, all of those things. I'm really happy here. At least with the shop."

Again his loneliness was evident in his tone, leaving me uncomfortable and still a touch guilty. I threw the bag of dog food over my shoulder once more. "Thanks for your time, Paulie." I patted the bag. "And for this. We should get going. Lots of work to do."

I'd almost made it to the door before he called out. "What about that corgi playdate? I'm a little busy myself, but I have a bit of time Saturday evening. How about then?"

Proving that I'd inherited just a touch more from my mother than auburn hair, I couldn't bring myself to deny him in his obvious loneliness. "Sure. But it will have to be quick. I simply have so much to do."

The brilliant smile that beamed from him erased all rodent similarities from his appearance, save for his yellowed teeth. "Oh, that is wonderful. I'm so happy. Flotsam and Jetsam will just have the time of their lives!"

"Yes, I'm sure they will." Even as I waved goodbye, I was trying to think of a way out of it. "See you Saturday."

. . .

After tossing the hundred-dollar bag of squirrel food in the trunk of my Mini Cooper, I got two burgers from Penelope's to go, and Watson and I made our way to the scenic area behind the south side of the shops, where the river ran. The city had recently revamped the space to enhance the natural features. They had brought in large boulders to make small mountains on either side of the river, planted large yet charming groves of aspen and spruce—which were currently decked in Christmas lights—and spread the area with limestone paths and picnic areas flanked by bronzed statues of wildlife.

From our picnic table, I could see the back of the block of stores that held my uncles' antique shop. Only in Estes Park would the backside of shops be nearly as charming as the front. Even the alleyways between some of them looked more like rock-and-brick Tuscan lanes, despite a trash dumpster here and there.

Unwrapping the smaller of the two burgers, the one without cheese, I tore it in fourths and laid the pieces at Watson's feet. "You more than earned this, buddy. Diet or not." He'd given me the complete cold shoulder since we left Paws, and as he turned his suddenly happy gaze on me, it looked like I was on my way back to redemption. Although I knew him well enough to be certain one burger wasn't going to cut it. And despite feeling like he understood most of what I said, I hoped he hadn't caught the scheduled playdate. If he had, the next couple of days were going to be full of attitude that no amount of burgers could squash.

Despite the soft clouds covering the sky, the day was bright, and snow drifted lazily. It was cold, but with my down jacket, not uncomfortable. I supposed it would have been smarter to eat inside the bookshop, but after Paulie, I felt the need for fresh air. And I definitely owed it to Watson.

The tourists doing their Christmas shopping were fewer on the backside of the stores, and with the winding paths and semiforested areas, I almost felt secluded in our little Christmas scene.

By the time I was halfway through my cheeseburger and fries, I was nearly human again. Which made me think of Katie. The next stop would be to her. Maybe I would take her a cheeseburger. Though if I remembered Branson's schedule correctly, he was supposed to be back tomorrow. Surely he would get Katie out, since I had little hope her incompetent lawyer could.

Maybe my next stop should be going back home to my computer and searching out lawyers in Denver.

Between the snow, branches of leafless aspens, and my thoughts, I almost missed the movement in the alley several yards away behind the shops. But when I recognized Daphne's beautiful raven hair flowing down her back, I zeroed in on her. She tossed a large bag into the dumpster and then stood, her hands covering her face. Her shoulders shook so that even from a distance it was easy to see she was crying.

My suspicions about her once again made me feel guilty. I'd wondered if she'd tried to kill her husband, and here she was, sobbing. Despite how horrible Declan seemed to be, apparently she loved him. As I considered whether I should go over and offer to comfort her, or move away to give her privacy, she was joined by someone else. Dolan's hair made him just as recognizable as Daphne. His coppery orange coloring nearly glowed through the falling snow.

Proving that he had a gentle soul like I'd heard, he wrapped Daphne in his arms, comforting her. At least she had Declan's family for support. What it must be like to be expecting your first child and not sure where your husband's coma would leave you.... Poor woman.

Just as I was about to turn away, Dolan broke their embrace, pulling back slightly, as he said something to his sister-in-law. And then he kissed her. I jolted from my spot on the picnic bench, causing Watson to startle as well. I instantly began to explain away the kiss. Just a simple sign of affection between family. I myself had kissed my uncle on the lips that very morning. But then Daphne ran a hand up Dolan's back and her fingers stroked through his hair, pulling him toward her, deepening the kiss.

Maybe not the concerned wife after all....

"Katie, we really don't have to do this." I grinned at her over the stack of books, three boxes high, between us. "It's your first day as a free woman. Surely there are more fun things you'd rather do."

She shook her head, curls flying. "No. It feels good to help." She bent, chose a few books from a box, and started arranging them on the shelf. "I got to sleep in this morning, in my own bed, praise the Lord! That's all I really wanted."

"Didn't like the cots in the jail, huh? If I remember correctly, Barry thought they were the height of luxury."

She cringed, then cocked her brow. "Nothing against Barry, but you have met your stepfather, correct?"

I chuckled and shelved some more books for my side of the room. While I was a control freak, when Katie suggested helping with inventory, I couldn't turn her down. We were starting in the main room, though. I was going to keep the mystery room for myself.

"Speaking of elderly white guys, did you call the one I found for you down in Denver? I was so mad I could have strangled Officer Green last night when she wouldn't let me visit you, but it did give me time to research decent lawyers."

Katie hesitated and then shrugged. "No, I didn't. I don't think I need to go down that road. At least Sergeant Wexler made it seem like Officer Green had been an idiot to suspect me. I really think it's over. And I'm saving up to try to get a spot for my bakery, as you know. The last thing I want to spend a small fortune on is a lawyer. After all, there are two empty shops beside you. Maybe one of them will end up being mine."

I'd known it had been Katie's hope. Unfortunately the property had been left to some of Lois and Opal's long-lost family in Oklahoma, who were now squabbling about what to do with their inheritance, so the stores sat vacant.

As I spoke, I kept my attention firmly away from Katie. "I'm so glad that Bran—Sergeant Wexler showed up last night and got you out of jail. I didn't think he was coming back until today."

"Well, it was nearly one in the morning, so technically...." I could feel Katie's gaze on me. "Haven't heard from him yet?"

I shook my head. "No. No reason that I should."

"Right." She snorted. "No need to pretend with me, remember? Nor for you to call him *Sergeant Wexler*."

I cast her a glare.

Katie merely shrugged again. "What? It's true. And let me tell you, he was a real knight in shining armor last night. The way he came storming in there. I had the impression he had barely gotten back to Estes and came directly to the station when he heard about me." Katie's tone was heavy with innuendo. "And we both know he didn't do that for me."

"Of course he did. He's a good police officer. Anyone who knows you knows you couldn't kill someone."

"Sergeant Wexler doesn't really know me, as you are aware, Fred."

"Maybe so, but he's not an idiot. As if in those three minutes it took me to catch up with you at the toy store you went in, entered some state of rage, and attempted to kill a man twice your size, only to have me walk in and you switch courses." Despite my protestations, the thought that I'd been the reason Branson had hurried down to the police station in the middle of the night made my heart do things that simply annoyed me. "It didn't have anything to do with me."

Katie gave another snort but didn't press the issue. She shelved a few more books, and then her tone switched from teasing to irritation. "I didn't tell you. Guess who gave me a good talking-to as soon as I woke up."

I turned to her. "I have no idea. Who?"

"Carla!" Katie bugged her brown eyes at me. "Can you believe it? She said she heard that I got out of jail and wanted to know why I hadn't shown up for my shift this morning."

I nearly laughed, then realized Katie wasn't joking. "You're serious?"

Katie nodded. "Dead serious. And I thought Opal had been a hard boss."

Maybe I'd have to reconsider and start driving the farther distance to get my coffee across town. "You deserve better than that. I sure hope things get cleared away with the stores next door. It would be so wonderful to have you as a neighbor, and you living your dream as a baker. Wouldn't that be perfect? Me in my dream bookshop and you in your dream bakery?"

She paused, giving me a strange look, and when she

spoke, her voice was hesitant. "Actually, about that... I've been thinking—"

She was interrupted by a knock at the door. We both turned, and my heart skipped a beat, betraying me utterly.

"Well, speak of the devil. A handsome devil."

I ignored Katie's jibe, took a breath, and headed over to unlock the door and let Sergeant Wexler in. It'd been a couple of weeks since I'd seen him.

He smiled at me warmly, and for a second, I thought he was going to give me a hug. Probably would've if I hadn't stiffened. "You're a sight for sore eyes, Fred."

Was I? "Oh please, you just returned from a two-week vacation. I'm sure I can't compare to whatever sundrenched beach you were on."

He twisted his lips. "I wouldn't exactly call it a vacation." He stepped the rest of the way in, so I could close the door, and shot another smile at Katie. "Heard you broke out of the big house last night."

"Thanks to you." Katie's smile was easy, and though she found him handsome, it was clear he didn't have the same effect on her as he did on me. "Thanks for coming to my rescue, Sergeant."

He let out an annoyed sigh. "Don't thank me for that. You shouldn't have been there to begin with. Just sorry I wasn't here when you two needed me." Those green eyes flashed toward me again. "Can I help unbox some books?"

Like he had once or twice before, his offer only served to discombobulate me. The men in my family, my father and uncles, Barry, and even my stepbrother-in-laws, were always gentlemanly and kind where their wives and female relatives were concerned. And even though I'd been divorced for many years, I somehow expected to be treated like a servant by any man who wasn't part of my family. I was constantly on guard against it, truth be told.

"That would be great. Thank you. But aren't you on duty? I don't know how the city would feel about their tax dollars for your salary going to getting the Cozy Corgi ready."

With a wink, he walked over to the box Katie was emptying and joined her. "Well, I can multitask. I'm not just here to unbox inventory. I'm here on official police business." He shrugged. "Well, sort of unofficial police business."

Katie straightened. "Please don't tell me you have to take me back in. Even for questioning. If I never see the inside of another police station, it will be too soon."

Chuckling, he patted her shoulder and shook his head. "No. You're good. Although—" He glanced back at me. "—as ludicrous as the situation was to consider Katie a real suspect, I can't completely blame Officer Green for what she did. Did you know the only fingerprints found on that hideous nutcracker were Katie's and the members of the Diamond family? I'm not saying Katie would do such a thing, especially with you being mere moments behind her, but one would expect there to be other fingerprints, don't you think?"

"You did say you found fingerprints of some of the other members of Declan's family. Maybe one of them...." All of a sudden it hit me. Branson had come here, to us, to me. And was discussing facts of the case which he most definitely shouldn't be. "Wait a minute. What's going on here? Why are you telling us this?"

He shelved another book and then turned fully toward me, the emotion in his eyes unnameable. Or at least something I was uncomfortable naming. "We may not know each other all that well, Winifred Page, but I'd bet my badge that the moment your friend was accused of attempted murder, you took matters into your own hands."

I hesitated, trying to determine if I was getting set up. "You made it very clear, Sergeant Wexler, that I was to keep my nose in my own business. Leave the police work to the police, if I recall."

He smirked, the expression somehow making him even more dashing. "And I seem to remember you telling me you don't like being told what to do. And that if you got it in your mind, you could probably solve a case quicker than any of us."

"I don't know if those were my exact words."

Another smirk. "So you want me to pretend you haven't been going around asking questions?"

I wasn't sure how to answer him. I knew my uncles hadn't called to complain. And I was highly doubtful Paulie would either. And I hadn't gotten a chance to ask anyone else. After I'd been turned away from seeing Katie, I'd spent the rest of the evening finding a decent lawyer for her. That had seemed more vital at the moment. "Nobody's called you. You're just guessing."

"I wouldn't call it guessing. I think I've got your number."

"Now you listen here." Katie's voice rose in temper as she rounded on Branson. "Anything Fred might have done, and I'm not saying she's done anything, was to help me. You've pretty much said yourself that the police were making a mistake by arresting me. What do you expect—"

"Whoa, whoa." He held up his hands in surrender. "Number one, I wasn't complaining." He glanced my way again. "And you've already proven to me you have a quick brain and you're a natural. As long as you're not breaking any laws or intentionally hampering a police investigation, I'm not about to stand in your way."

I balked, completely thrown off guard. "You're not?"

Branson smiled, almost gently. "Should I? Is it what you expect, for me to tell you that since you're not a police officer you don't know what you're doing? Or that just because your father was a detective doesn't mean you inherited his innate skill? Or do you expect me to simply tell you to leave it to the big boys? That it's man's work?"

Yes, to all of it. It was exactly what I'd expected. And though I didn't say so, I knew my answer was clear in my eyes.

He studied me for a moment. And while it made my cheeks heat, it wasn't an entirely unpleasant experience. Finally, with Katie glancing back and forth between the two of us, he continued as if nothing had been said. "If you have any information that would help, I'd appreciate it. Like I said, it was ludicrous to think Katie had anything to do with this, given the circumstances, but I can't entirely blame Officer Green—as much as I might like to—given the fingerprints."

Okay, it looked like we were actually going to do this. I swallowed and then began. "You said there were other prints on the nutcracker, those belonging to Declan's family. Maybe it was one of them."

He tilted his head, and I could tell from his expression it wasn't a revelatory thought to him. The corner of his lip turned into a grin. "Very true. But the problem is, the other problem, there were only two types of blood present at the scene. Declan's and Katie's. If another member of his family had tried to kill him with that garland, their blood would be there too."

"Well, I hadn't thought of that." Katie glanced at her

hands, which she'd mentioned were still tender. "There's no way anybody could wrap that garland around his neck and not get cut themselves."

That answer was obvious. "Unless they wore—"

"Hello! Hope I'm not intruding."

I turned toward the voice, and for a moment didn't recognize the woman standing in the doorway. I guess I'd forgotten to lock the door after letting Branson in. The blonde's smile faltered when she noticed Branson and Katie.

"Sorry. I guess I'm intruding. I just needed a break from the shop and thought I'd talk to you about the logo. But I can come back."

And with that, it clicked—the woman from Rocky Mountain Imprints. "Peg. I'm so sorry. In all of the chaos, I'd forgotten all about the Cozy Corgi logo." I turned to Branson and then Katie. "You remember me mentioning that right? Maybe turning the second floor into Cozy Corgi merchandise."

Katie's grimace surprised me, but it turned to a quick smile. "Yes, I do."

"Sounds like a good idea." Branson nodded toward Peg. "Nice to see you, Peg. Everything going well with you and Joe?"

She nodded. "Of course."

"Good. I'll actually be stopping by later this morning. I know you two already gave statements to the police, but since you're right next door and I'm playing catch up, it would be great if I could have a moment of your time. You never know when someone might know something, even if they're not aware of it."

"Sure." Peg shifted a few pieces of paper to her other hand, different products that would be used for the logo, I assumed. "Whenever you want to come down, Sergeant, Joe and I will be ready for you. You're always welcome."

It suddenly felt like four was a crowd. "Peg, do you mind showing the sketches to Katie? Let me finish up with Brans... er... Sergeant Wexler?"

Peg was just as tiny as a pixie, like she'd been before, and just as quick. Her eyes widened at my slip. She cast a quick glance toward Branson. I needed to be more careful. I didn't know Peg, but if she was even half the gossip as my uncles, there would be more fun rumors flying around town by the afternoon.

"Oh, of course. Plus, it looks like you got your hands full here. I have a strong husband back at the shop that I can loan you for a few hours this afternoon if you need to expedite getting all the books unpacked."

Branson snorted. "You're the one who earned all those trophies for the softball team, not Joe."

Pride sparkled in her eyes. "True, but he can bench-press more, so he gets to do all the heavy lifting." Peg refocused on me. "He really wouldn't mind helping."

"Thank you, that's very kind, but I wouldn't dream of imposing." I glanced at Katie. I wasn't sure why she seemed not to like the idea of the corgi merchandise, but I hoped whatever sketches Peg had would change her mind. Likewise, I wasn't entirely certain why Katie's opinion on the issue mattered all that much. I wasn't in the market for a new business partner. "See what you think about them, Katie. Let me finish up with Sergeant Wexler, and I'll be right over."

Reminding myself that not only was I not looking for a new business partner, but neither was I looking for a man. It was easy to forget that while in Branson Wexler's presence. We took a few paces away, and I lowered my voice. "As I was saying, you're right about the blood and that garland, but the attacker could have been wearing gloves, couldn't they?"

"Of course they could've." He grinned. "See, I knew you had instinct."

Though I could tell he was being kind and flattering me, I couldn't keep from rolling my eyes. "Oh, come on, now. Don't be insulting. It doesn't take much instinct to know that if the prints you're looking for aren't there, gloves are probably involved." I cast a glance around him, making sure Peg wasn't listening. Having her potentially gossip about Branson and I would be one thing. Running back to tell her business neighbor that I was accusing them of trying to kill a member of their family was an entirely different one. "But maybe the attacker was a member of Declan's own family. Watson and I"—I motioned upstairs as if Watson's current location mattered in the moment—"saw Dolan and Daphne kissing this afternoon. And not a brother and sister-in-law kind of kiss, if such a thing even exists."

"Really?" His eyes widened, and any level of flirting that had been there left his tone. "Now that is news." He considered for a moment. "That would for sure point to possible suspects. Daphne trying to get out of her marriage, and Dolan in a fit of jealous brotherly rage." Branson squinted at another thought. "Although I just can't see Daphne being able to do that kind of damage. Declan is a big man."

"That's what I was thinking. Although everyone talks about how wonderful and kind Dolan is."

Branson didn't seem concerned by the thought. "He wouldn't be the first one who's tried to kill for his brother's wife." He shrugged again. Then his tone lightened. "Maybe it will all be a moot point soon anyway. From what I hear,

Declan's situation is improving. With a coma, there's never really any guarantee of when the person might wake up, but if and when he does, chances are he'll know who his attacker was. Unless it was a complete surprise, since the impact came from behind. The doctor is hopeful he'll wake soon."

Katie let out a relieved sigh. I hadn't noticed the two of them coming closer to us. "Well, that's wonderful news. I'm ready for this to be behind me." She blushed. "And for Declan to be okay, of course."

Branson chuckled. "I can see why you two get along so well." He gave a quick nod toward Peg but kept his eyes on me. "I know you've got things to talk about. But you and I discussed some things before I left town. I believe Christmas was the deadline, correct?" He gave a wink and a pretend tilt of the hat that wasn't there and strode to the door before turning around and offering a model-perfect smile. "Ladies." And then he was gone.

Try as I might, I couldn't really focus as I looked at the printouts of different merchandise with the Cozy Corgi logo on them that Peg offered. My thoughts instead swirling around Branson still wanting to go out to dinner. To go on a date.

It was so much more stressful than trying to figure out what to put on the second level of my shop or who had attempted to kill Declan Diamond.

EIGHT

"The hoodies with the Cozy Corgi logo on them were really great. The hats were good too." I'd ordered a hoodie from Peg before she left, just to see, and now I studied Katie's expression as she firmly kept her attention on arranging the books. "I thought the shot glasses were a bit too much, though. I'm not sure it's quite the branding I want to go with."

Katie let out a puff of air but gave no further commentary, just reached for another book.

I couldn't say that Katie seemed angry after Peg left, but she wasn't her normal self either. "Do you know something about Peg that I don't?"

She looked at me wide-eyed, startled. "No. I don't think so. Why?"

"It just seems that every time I bring it up, you seem a bit uncomfortable. I thought maybe Peg was another Opal or Carla-type person."

"No, I don't think so." She smiled, but it was clearly forced, as was the ease in her tone. "And yes, the hoodie was adorable, the hats were indeed great, and totally a big fat no on the shot glasses."

Whatever tension was suddenly between us was one

more confirmation about me needing to do this on my own. "Well, I'm glad we agree, then."

Katie shelved another couple of books, then turned to get a better look at me from across the room.

"It's just that I was thinking maybe we could—" Her gaze flicked over my shoulder, out the window, and she flinched. "What in the world?"

I turned around to see what she'd noticed. It only took me a second, and I choked back a laugh. Directly across the street, in the store Cabin and Hearth, Anna and Carl Hanson were openly gaping at Katie and me through their window. Maybe there was a glare, as Anna had both her hands pressed to the glass over her brow. As soon as they noticed me looking back, they both gave a little jump, waved awkwardly, and trundled away. I angled back to Katie, chuckling. "They're not exactly subtle, are they?"

"You think?" She grinned, the tension from before fading. "I know I'm no super sleuth, but my keen intuition is telling me they might want to talk to you."

I considered for half a second. Branson had pretty much said Katie was cleared, mostly, despite the fingerprints, considering she had me as an alibi, so I couldn't pretend I was doing this for Katie. I'd simply be doing it because I was curious, because I wanted to figure it out. There would be nothing altruistic about it from this point onward.

I was okay with that.

I put the book I'd been holding on the shelf and dusted my hands on my skirt—more habit than anything, since the new books didn't have a lick of dust on them. "Do you mind if I go chat with them? As you can see, very little that happens in town gets past them."

Again Katie's grin was genuine. "I'd expect nothing less. And I look forward to hearing what you find out."

"Well then, be right back." I walked over to the counter and grabbed my purse, slung it over my shoulder, and began to head for the door, then remembered Anna's affinity for dogs. Stopping at the base of the steps, I hollered up to the second floor. "Watson! Nap time's over."

A second or two passed, and then a loud yawn made its way downstairs. I could just picture him, stretching out his front paws with his knob-tailed rump sticking in the air. A few more seconds passed, and then the slow padding of his paws sounded over the hardwood.

Katie joined me. "He really likes to take his time, doesn't he?"

That was an understatement. "Just reminding me who's in charge."

"Apparently."

"Want to see the tables turn?" I gave her a wink, and she nodded. I refocused upstairs and raised my voice once more. "Watson, treat!"

The clattering of his paws went from church mouse to herd of elephants in a heartbeat. From our vantage point, Katie and I could see him rush around the edge of the banister, lose his traction on the newly refurbished hardwood floors, his hind legs skidding out from behind him. He managed to catch himself before crashing into the wall, and then tore down the steps, eyes wild with excitement and tongue whipping like a flag from his mouth. He came to a skidding stop at my feet, this time not quite managing on the slick floor, and bumped into my ankles.

Katie nearly doubled over in laughter.

Watson didn't spare her a glance, his gaze traveling from both my hands up to my face, clearly asking what the trick had been.

I tickled the pink spot on his muzzle. "You're an embarrassment to corgis everywhere, sir."

He glowered, whined, and then gave a tentative hop on his front paws, reminding me of the magic word I'd uttered.

"Come with me. We're heading over to see Anna. She has your treat."

Watson piped up again at the word and followed me without argument as we left the shop, crossed the street, and walked into Cabin and Hearth.

The home décor shop was like stepping into a high-end log cabin. Though the place was crowded with merchandise, it oozed comfort, charm, and coziness. But at the same time, it only took a glance to know that every piece would cost a small fortune.

Anna and Carl were standing behind the counter, both furiously studying some paperwork they held between them. If I hadn't known they were there, I might not have recognized them. They were both short and round, Anna with white poufy hair, while Carl was bald and wore glasses. I guessed them both to be in their sixties. The first time I met them, they reminded me of Mr. and Mrs. Claus, but now, they *were* Mr. and Mrs. Claus. Complete with fuzzy red outfits lined in white fur, Carl's cinched by a large glistening black belt straining over his expansive middle, and Anna wearing a frilly reindeer-patterned apron.

I nearly chuckled. They might be grade A gossips, but convincing, they weren't. I decided to play along and not mention the incident at the window, since apparently I was supposed to believe they'd been standing there studying that piece of paper for hours. "Don't you two look simply amazing? I feel like I've just traveled to the North Pole."

The Mrs. Claus version of Anna looked up and played her part so well that she gave a little flinch in surprise. "Oh, Fred, my dear. So nice to see you." The smile she gave me was friendly enough, but it transformed to a thing of genuine beauty when she glanced down at my feet and let out a shrill squeak. "Oh, and Watson!" She smacked Carl on the arm before she hurried around the counter. "Go get him a treat. And put on your beard. How are you going to be Santa without a beard?"

A pink hue rose to Carl's cheeks as he gave me a nod and waddled toward the back room.

Anna reached us in a matter of moments and was on her knees in front of Watson, the red fabric of her skirt billowing out around them. "You just hold on, you little doll. He'll be right back. You'll get your snack."

Watson didn't go hog wild over her like he did for Barry, but whether he actually liked her or considered her a dog treat dispenser, Watson allowed himself to be petted, going so far as to lick her hand.

I was forgotten for the minute or so it took Carl to return. He held out a small brown dog biscuit, which Watson scrutinized for a second, clearly not what he'd expected, but he took it nonetheless.

Anna stood and smacked Carl again, this time audibly. "What is wrong with you? I told you we were saving the dog bones for *Watson.* And you know I give the treats to the dogs, not you." She smacked him again, this time harder. "And you forgot your beard. Again."

His blush deepening, Carl let out an apologetic sigh and left us once more.

Anna shook her head at me, clearly commiserating about how stupid husbands could be. "We only have five of Lois's dog bones left. And I told Carl we were saving every single one for when you and Watson visit. I don't know what we'll do when they're gone, but we'll figure out something."

There'd only been two things Lois Garble had made that anyone liked in her all-natural candy store. One was her hard licorice candy. And the other her all-natural dog bones. In truth, I was a little taken aback. I assumed Anna was like that with every dog, and maybe she was to a degree, but it warmed me a little that she thought so highly of Watson. "That is so sweet of you, Anna."

She waved me off, bending to scratch the top of Watson's head.

Carl was back, large all-natural dog bone in his hand, and a massive Santa Claus beard covering half his face. This time, he remembered protocol, handing the dog bone to Anna so she could in turn offer it to Watson. For his part, Watson was in heaven.

Carl's beard would put Paulie's to shame. "Goodness. You two truly do look like Mr. and Mrs. Claus. It's amazing."

Anna nodded in agreement. "We wear them every year. On Christmas Eve, we go to the hospital and visit all the kids who are there. It's the highlight of our holidays."

It seemed Anna and Carl were full of surprises, and I had vastly underestimated them. I'd chalked them up as being little more than town gossips, which was true, but I hadn't envisioned such kindness from them.

Before I could think of an appropriate response, Anna started in once more, this time directing her full attention on me. "So, tell us all about it. We heard you were there. In truth, I thought you'd come and talk to us before now, but better late than never." She leaned a bit closer, her voice lowering conspiratorially. "We heard there was blood everywhere. Just everywhere. Of course, I said that sounded like nothing more than hype, but that's what we heard."

"No. There wasn't blood everywhere. There was just

some." One of the good things about not actually being a detective was that I didn't have to be overly careful about what information I shared. "There was some due to the garland, but it was mostly contained."

Carl let out a huff, and Anna nodded approvingly. "Those boys came here trying to sell us that garland. I know they're your family, but...." She *tsked* and shook her head. "Who wants garland that you have to wear gloves to hang? Christmas is supposed to be beautiful, not bloody."

I couldn't disagree with her. And since they were the center of the gossip world, I assumed they'd already heard, but I wanted to make certain Katie was cleared all the way around, even in rumors. "Watson had made a mess on the sidewalk while Katie and I were walking to the toy store, so I went back to get a bag and then met her there." I decided to leave out that I couldn't find one, lest she deem me an unworthy corgi mama and closed up the gossip shop. "It was a matter of a couple of minutes, and I walked in and Katie was kneeling there, struggling to get the garland off Declan's neck, cutting herself in the process. She saved his life."

Anna and Carl had both been nodding through my spiel, clearly having heard it all, but stopped at that last pronouncement. "Katie saved his life?"

"Yes. She loosened it enough for me to cut it off, but it was only thanks to her in those minutes before I arrived that it hadn't finished the job." Again, I had no idea how truthful that part was, but it seemed right. And any benefit I could throw Katie's way seemed smart.

Anna shook her finger at Carl. "See, I told you that girl would never be able to hurt someone like that. Even if she did work for Opal."

Carl's eyes narrowed over his fluffy Santa beard. "Actually, what you said was—"

She smacked him again. "Shut up, Carl." She turned back to me. "It's clear you and Katie are good friends."

"That's true we are. She's a lot of—"

"It's also clear that you and that handsome Sergeant get along too."

How long had they been staring at us through the windows? Although, I knew there were already rumors about Branson and me. "He's a very good police officer."

Anna nodded and smiled, clearly waiting for me to elaborate. When I didn't, she blinked, looking slightly annoyed. "Well, I have to say, I'm not surprised. Declan Diamond is a handsome fiend, but a fiend nonetheless. And obviously since poor little Katie didn't do it, my money is on Duncan. If I had a child and they did to me what Declan did to him, I'd string him up by Christmas tinsel as well."

"I've told you a hundred times, there's no way Duncan would ever do that." It was the first time I'd heard Carl disagree with Anna. Before, he'd pretended to be uncomfortable with her level of gossip, though he soon got roped in right along with her, but not full-out disagreement. "Duncan is a family man through and through. He'd sooner strangle himself than one of his boys."

Anna shrugged, nonplussed, causing her massive bosom to heave. "You're entitled to your opinion, Carl. You've been wrong plenty of times before."

He glared. "Well, I think it's terrible to point your fingers at that poor man. Like he hasn't been through enough heartbreak without people in the town he grew up in, has been a vital member of, suddenly accusing him of attempting to kill his own child."

That seemed to be the consensus about Duncan Diamond. But I couldn't help but wonder if it was just another offshoot of the good-old-boys club. If they truly believed Gerald Jackson was a decent lawyer, I wasn't sure how much I could trust their judgment about Duncan, either. But it was clear we weren't going to get anywhere besides a marital squabble if we kept going on that train of thought. I was more curious about what I'd seen the day before.

"I've actually heard quite a bit about Declan having affairs. All the while having a newly pregnant wife at home. If I were her, that would make me pretty angry, wouldn't it you?"

Anna sucked in a shocked breath, and her eyes gleamed in delight. "What? You think Daphne might have done it? Now there's a theory I haven't heard."

Again I thought back to not wanting the Diamonds to hear I'd been gossiping about them, though it was much too late for that now. To keep from confirming or denying, I turned my attention to Watson, who was sprawled happily at our feet, still licking his chops. "That was good, wasn't it, little buddy? It's been a little while since you've had one of those."

He cast a glance at me, clearly annoyed I had interrupted his post dog bone euphoria and letting me know he was fully aware I'd been using him this whole time. I doubted he minded too greatly after having had his favorite treat.

To my surprise, Anna wasn't distracted by Watson for once. "I really must say, that is quite a thought. And quite out of the box. I wouldn't even have considered—"

Anna started sucking in several breaths while snapping her fingers and taking a step back, startling Carl and scaring Watson to take shelter behind my skirt. Anna didn't even notice. She began waving her hands in the air. For a second I feared she might be having a seizure. Then she pointed at me, her tone excited euphoria. "But if you put that together with what happened last night at the Chinese restaurant, that might make perfect sense."

There was a pause, and then Carl sucked in a breath of his own. "Oh! You might be right."

They both looked at me, expecting me to have a similar reaction. When no further comment came, I decided to confess. "I'm sorry. I'm not sure what happened at the Chinese restaurant last night. I was at home looking for a good lawyer for Katie, just in case. And then came directly to my shop this morning."

Carl flinched. "A new lawyer for Katie? Why in the world would she need one? Gerald told me he was on her case."

Anna gave one of the largest eye rolls I'd ever seen and stared at her husband like he was the biggest moron in the world. And for once, Anna and I were on the same page. But I couldn't let her get distracted by Gerald Jackson.

"What happened at the Chinese restaurant last night?"

Anna turned back to me, her gaze increasingly hungry as she grew voracious. "Declan served Daphne with divorce papers last night, right in the middle of the Chinese restaurant, right in the middle of everyone having their dinners. Can you imagine how devastating it must be?"

I waited for the punch line, but none came. "I'm sorry, I don't see how that was possible. Declan's in the hospital." When there was still no response, I added for good measure, "In a coma."

This time Anna's eye roll was directed at me. "Well, of course I don't mean Declan himself, dear. But someone on his behalf. He obviously must have arranged for the divorce papers to be delivered before he was attacked two nights ago. It doesn't matter whether or not he's in a coma. I'm sure whoever he hired to do it either didn't know that he had been attacked or had already been paid so figured he should follow through on the job."

That made sense. Kinda. Daphne had gotten her divorce papers last night. One night after Declan was attacked. And just a few short hours after I'd seen her and Dolan kissing. Maybe they had known it was coming.

"Were you there? Did she seem shocked?"

Anna wrinkled her nose while shaking her head. "Goodness no. We only eat American food. Carl's stomach can't handle anything exotic." She actually reached over and patted his extended belly. "But from what I hear, she sat there stone-cold sober and white as a ghost. Hardly any reaction at all, really. Then she handed it to her brother-in-law. But it was Duncan who lost his temper. Got up from the table, yelling at the poor guy who served the papers. Screaming about how he couldn't do this to their family when they were in the middle of so much hurt." She raised her eyebrows. "Another piece of evidence against Duncan, if you ask me. Losing his temper like that. Right in the middle of a restaurant, in public."

"I'm telling you, Duncan would never be able to do anything like that. He didn't hurt his son."

No, but maybe Declan's brother would. Maybe Declan had found out about their affair and was getting ready to expose it to the rest of the town, or to their father. Or maybe Declan told Daphne he wanted a divorce, and she didn't want to be cut out of the business or the money. Either way, it seemed even from his unconscious state in a hospital room, Declan Diamond was able to cause drama and more pain for his family.

NINE

As I left Cabin and Hearth, my mind mulled over all the different possibilities that could have happened within the Diamond family, including that maybe trying to figure out which one of them had tried to kill Declan was a waste of time. Maybe it had been all three. But I thought Katie had said she'd only heard one set of footsteps running away. I'd have to check.

I was so caught up in the speculation that I'd barely taken three steps from their shop when I crashed into someone.

They gave a loud *oof*, and there was a crash of packages to the ground. Watson's barking went wild.

"Oh, I'm so sorry. That was completely my fault. I wasn't watching where I—" My sight caught up to my lips and caused them to close. Or at least quit making words. I was fairly certain my lips were hanging open.

Leo Lopez stretched out a hand to steady me. "Not at all. I'm sure the fault was mine."

His yellow-brown eyes gazed directly into mine for a second, and then he looked down at Watson.

It was only then I realized Watson's frantic barking wasn't due to the collision but to his excitement. He was on his hind legs, his front paws bashing against Leo's knees. Though we'd only met once before, Watson's reaction to Leo had been the same then, like he was another incarnation of Barry.

Leo bent down to ruffle behind Watson's ears with both his hands. "It's good to see you too, little man. You're a good boy. Good boy." Though his tone had slipped slightly into baby talk, it altered to just a touch of heat, though his eyes didn't look up at me. "You've been doing a good job of keeping your mama safe?"

I forced a laugh I hoped sounded natural. "If by safe you mean eating me out of house and home, then yes. Quite safe."

"Good enough, I suppose." Thankfully Leo continued to lavish attention on Watson, allowing me some much needed time to pull myself together.

I'd moved to Estes Park to restart my life. Be with my family, open a cute little bookshop, and read by the fire every night with Watson at my feet. That was it. I was done with romance, done with men, and done with husbands or relationships. It had been bad enough when I'd met Branson Wexler, with all his classic good looks and muscles poured into a police uniform. To make matters worse, I'd run into Leo Lopez a couple of days later. Another man in uniform, this one a park ranger, and with a face and body nearly the carbon copy of a young Oscar De La Hoya—and at five years my junior, I truly meant young. Having only seen him once, I'd managed to put Leo out of my mind—mostly. Judging from the racing of my pulse, my heart couldn't make the same claim.

With Watson's frantic exuberance abated to merely whimpering adoration, Leo picked up a couple of packages in a bag on the ground before smiling at me once more. "It's good to see you, Fred. It's been a while."

Whereas Branson was several inches taller than me, Leo was only slightly just, making it where his eyes could look straight into mine. And even in the winter light, they glowed like honey. I had to look away as I motioned across the street toward my shop.

"I've been so busy, with trying to get the Cozy Corgi ready to open by January, and getting my cabin situated, that I haven't had a spare moment."

"I know. That's what you said when you texted."

Despite there being no accusation in his tone, I couldn't help but feel a reproach, whether intended or not. Leo had sent me a message about a week after we met, saying he would love to get dinner sometime. At that point, Opal's murder had just been solved, and Branson had also asked me to dinner. Maybe I'd taken the easy way out by simply texting back that dinner would be lovely, but at the moment life was too busy with the shop. Basically, the equivalent of *I'd love to, but I have to wash my hair.* The guilt I felt with him standing before me was irritating. I was in Estes Park for myself, not for a man. Not a policeman, not a park ranger, not for any uniform a tall, dark, and handsome might put on.

"I really am busy." Once more I motioned across the street as if he might have forgotten where my store was. "Even right now Katie's in there shelving books. I really should be helping her."

"You don't have to explain to me, Fred. You don't owe me anything." Another smile, completely unflappable. "I'm excited to see the Cozy Corgi. Like I said, having a bookstore where a taxidermy shop used to be sure makes me happier. I hated that place." His tone grew serious, and he touched my arm once more, differently this time. The sensation wasn't unpleasant. "I did want to thank you again. It hasn't stopped the poaching, but at least one more poacher is out of business."

"You know I didn't actually kill Sid, right? I simply found the dead owl in the freezer."

He shrugged as if the finer details didn't matter. "Well, thanks to you, it was one more clue, even if Sergeant Wexler says it's not related."

I'd noticed before, though only hinted at in slight tone and vague dismissals, that Branson and Leo had a past. And not a good one. I tried to brush it off. "Well, anything to help." I gestured toward his package-laden arms, adamantly not noticing the bulges of muscles as I did so. "Doing some Christmas shopping?"

"Sure am. I'm heading home tomorrow. I just finished my shift at the park and needed to come down here and wrap up the rest." He gestured with his chin toward the other block. "Luckily I'd already taken care of toys for the nieces and nephews. Otherwise I'd be out of luck today, considering...." His smile faltered, and he blushed. "Sorry. That was a callous thing to say. One I definitely don't mean. I did hear you and Katie were part of the reason Declan is still alive."

Interesting how the version changed depending on who I was speaking to. It didn't surprise me this was the take Leo would have. "That's true. It seems he's in a coma, but I've heard he's getting better, so maybe he'll wake up soon and all mysteries will be solved."

Leo cocked his handsome head, a slight dimple forming in his left cheek. "Mystery? You diving into this one too? Like the owl?"

For one embarrassingly long moment, I nearly lied,

fearing I would look foolish to him. And once more my irritation flared, and once more, at myself, not him. "I am. At first I just wanted to clear Katie, but it looks like that's already happened. And now"—I shrugged, unwilling to sugarcoat—"well, now I just want to know."

His smile didn't dampen nor did his eyes show any humor. Instead he nodded in approval. "You're a fascinating creature, Fred Page."

"No, not hardly. My father was a detective. There were times he'd talk cases over with me. And I was married to another policeman for a while, though he wasn't half the officer my father was. Or half the man, for that matter." At that, his eyes widened, and I wondered if I'd announced about the ex-husband to try and scare him away. "I guess you could just say it's in my blood."

He was distracted momentarily by Watson pushing at his ankles with his head once again, and he leaned down partially to give him more affection, but didn't take his attention off me. "Like I said, fascinating creature. And I would know. I spend my days with fascinating and beautiful creatures."

It was my turn to blush, and for the third time, I motioned to my store. "I should get back. I really am—"

"Busy." He winked, and though there was no humor in his voice, it still lacked any accusal. "You know, I've heard that about you." He seemed to consider, for the first time, a little unsure. "I'm done with my shopping. I'd be happy to help you... and your friend out. It would go faster with another set of hands. And then I could say I knew the Cozy Corgi back when...."

Having Branson Wexler and Leo Lopez in my shop within an hour of each other was probably the quickest way to set the old place aflame. Or maybe that was just me. "No, but thank you. I do appreciate the offer."

Though his tone didn't change, there was clear disappointment in his eyes. One that matched how I was feeling. "Well then, I'll leave you to it. I look forward to the grand opening."

"Me, too. If it ever gets here." I hesitated, looking for a good way to change my mind, one a little less obvious than *wait, don't leave, please come over*. I couldn't find one. "Have a safe trip and a wonderful holiday with your family."

"Thank you. I hope you and yours have a wonderful one as well." Leo started to walk around me and then paused when he was even with my shoulders, which brought those golden eyes of his even closer. "And, Fred? It really was good to see you."

I nodded and swallowed. He was several paces away when I finally found my voice and mumbled that it was good to see him too. But I was certain he couldn't hear. Then it hit me. I didn't even thank him for his referral to his friend who'd built Watson's dog run. That would be a great conversation restarter, and maybe we could work our way back to him helping Katie and me. Gritting my teeth, I refused to act on the impulse.

Watson whined at Leo's departure, and it took every ounce of my willpower to not turn around and watch him walk away. Instead I checked for traffic, and then Watson and I hurried across the street and back into the Cozy Corgi.

I expected Katie to hurry over and demand to know what I'd found out from Anna and Carl. Instead she leaned against a half-filled bookcase with arms folded and one eyebrow cocked. "Well, Winifred Page, you've been holding out on me. I didn't know you had *two* suitors."

"I don't. I don't even have one...." Why in the world was I bothering to lie about something so completely obvious to everyone? Whatever, I stuck with it. "I'm here for family, books, and hopefully one day homemade baked goods when you open your bakery. Other than that, men are off the table."

Katie unfolded her arms and started to shake her finger at me.

I cut her off. "And what were you doing watching out the window, Little Miss Nosey? You trying to give Anna and Carl a run for their money? I would've thought better of you, Katie Pizzolato."

She rolled her eyes. "Then you'd be wrong." Her smile grew a little more wicked, and her voice held a touch of singsong in it. "But whatever you want to tell yourself, my friend. You are here for the family, books, and baked goods. Right. And I'm here for the way the lack of humidity makes my lips chapped all the time. It's wonderful."

"You know what, you're a—"

Katie cackled and shook her head. "A truly wonderful and adorable individual. I know."

A laugh burst from me. "Well, that much is true, I suppose."

We ordered a pizza and worked for another hour or so, then separated for the evening. It was clear that despite her sleeping in, Katie was still exhausted from her time in jail. Watson and I drove home, past the new developments of mini mansion log cabins, and wound our way through the forest back to what had been my grandparents' old genuine log cabin. We had just stepped inside, me already envisioning curling up by the fire, when another thought hit me.

I hurried to the kitchen and retrieved a small treat from the corgi-shaped cookie jar for Watson, not that he needed another one, but in prepayment for what I knew would annoy him. "I'll be right back. I won't be gone more than an hour."

As he scarfed down the treat, I hurried outside, locked the door, and jumped back into the Mini Cooper. I wasn't sure whether the hospital staff would let me into Declan's room, but I thought I had a good chance. Since it was well-known I was there that night, and even though some were accusing Katie of trying to kill him, plenty were saying I was the reason Declan was still alive. I couldn't even fully fathom what I expected to find, but something. Even if it was just a gossipy nurse mentioning who had visited or if he'd mumbled something in his coma-induced confusion.

Or, the way my luck was running with handsome men over the past afternoon, maybe I'd walk into his room and he would wake up. Ask to take me to dinner or some such nonsense. Despite myself, the thought made me chuckle. The man might be a womanizer, and he might've been charming when we'd met, but I highly doubted, at least judging from his wife, that tall, broad, and long auburn-haired was Declan's go-to for dinner dates. But I wouldn't have thought it would be true for Branson and Leo either.

Luckily, as I'd experienced before in the police station, the hospital was also a stereotype of small-town life. There were no guards on duty, no front desk to check in, not even on the neuro unit floor, where I knew he was being held.

I walked, unharassed, down the hallway, checking out names written in dry-erase marker under the room numbers. I heard a door slam, causing me to jump, but no one was coming for me, so I continued on. Halfway down the hall, I found it—Room 324, D. Diamond. Glancing around once more, I noticed a couple of nurses at the far end of the hall talking to a policeman, probably a guard who was supposed to be at Declan's door. None of them looked my way, so I stepped inside.

Like every other hospital room before it, the space was nondescript, smelling of antiseptic, and even with the solitary string of Christmas lights hung over the shut window, it was depressing in the dim light. The only sound was the beeping of his monitors and the mechanical wheeze of the ventilator. Somehow, despite wires and tubes seeming to pour from his arms, bandages encircling his neck, and his mouth and nose covered with equipment to keep him breathing, surrounded by all the mundane, Declan looked like a male version of Snow White. Simply waiting for a kiss.

Well, good luck, buddy. From what I hear, you've had more than your share of kisses.

I took a couple of steps closer to the bed, still not sure what I was looking for. There were a few cards on the bedside table, a Get Well Soon balloon, and a small potted Christmas tree pruned from a rosemary plant. There was no blue soldier nutcracker, no flashing garland, no killer's gloves. Nothing.

Just Declan.

"Who did this to you?" I narrowed my eyes at him, daring him to wake up and answer. "And what horrible thing that you did caused you to earn it?"

He sucked in a breath, gagged around the ventilator, and I expected his eyes to open as he answered me. The steady beat of the monitor glitched, the pattern continuing in a staccato rhythm and then changed to one long continuous, uninterrupted beep. I glanced at the heart monitor, just in time to see the jagged red spikes trail off into a flat line.

My own heart decided to flip, and then my feet moved even before my brain told me what to do. I rushed to the door and nearly threw myself out into the hallway. "Help! We need a nurse here! Quick!"

Three nurses were already rushing down the hallway, apparently having been alerted by some system. The policeman wasn't with them. They darted past me, not sparing a glance, and gathered around Declan.

I leaned against the outside of the doorframe. Listening. Less than half a minute later, there were more footsteps, and a middle-aged woman in a lab coat also hurried past me and into the room. A doctor, I presumed.

I could barely hear what they were doing over my pounding heart, over my brain screaming at me to leave, to get out of there. But I couldn't; I was frozen. Stillness was what finally forced me to move. When I noticed the steady beep had been silenced, I realize Declan Diamond was dead. For a heartbeat, I considered staying where I was, but then I pictured Officer Green arriving on the scene. It didn't matter if Branson was back in town or not. I glanced around, noticed the stairwell a few doors down, and took the escape offered.

Even with the snow falling outside my living room window, the sparkling Christmas tree directly in front, the cozy warmth and glow of the fire, the steaming hot chocolate beside the overstuffed armchair, the unread book on my lap, and the softly snoring corgi at my feet, my brain refused to shut down, and my blood seemed incapable of slowing its rapid race through my veins.

I had been in the room the moment Declan Diamond died.

And I'd run.

At least I'd called for help, not that it had done any good. But I'd run.

One second I was stressing over how it would look if one of the nurses recognized me. Dreading Officer Green's reaction to me at the hospital would be nothing compared to her showing up at my door. And the next moment, I was plunged into a crisis of identity. I was Winifred Wendy Page, daughter of Charles Page, the best detective in the entire world, who died in the line of duty. I did not run away. No matter what.

But I had. Maybe I really was just a bookshop owner. Nothing more, nothing less. I supposed that wasn't anything to be ashamed of. But this felt so right, helping Barry, then Katie, then simply trying to put the puzzle pieces together. But this wasn't a puzzle. It was life and death. And as Charles Page's daughter, I should know that better than most.

When the headlights flashed over the living room as a car drove up, then parked in front of the porch, I was almost relieved. At least one of these scenarios would be over—I could quit worrying about whether I was recognized, or stop anticipating the condescending glee in Officer Green's eyes as she took me in for questioning.

It would be done.

Watson leaped up, barking when the knock sounded on the door. I patted his head. "It's okay, boy." Then I stood and walked over to the front door. I nearly just threw it open, but then reminded myself I was a single woman, living alone in a log cabin in the middle of the woods. And it seemed this beautiful tourist trap of a town wasn't quite the safe haven I'd envisioned. I looked through my recently installed peephole and nearly did a double take. Not Officer Green.

I opened the door. "Hey. What are you doing here?"

Branson stomped snow onto the mat, then stepped inside, looking larger than life in his uniform, complete with bulletproof vest and gun holster. He gave me a sidelong glance. "Do you really need to ask that?"

No, of course I didn't. It was a different person than I'd expected, but the result was the same. "Let me grab my jacket, and I'll come with you."

He gave a little flinch. "Come with me?"

"Yes. Down to the station for questioning."

He studied me for a moment, then shut the door. I'd not

even noticed the cold air and snow coming in nor Watson taking a protective stance between us.

"Do you want to go down to the station?"

I considered. Maybe I was reading this wrong. Maybe all my fears had been for nothing. The nurse hadn't recognized me. Why would they, really; I was new in town. Just because a lot of people seemed up on gossip didn't mean everyone was. Maybe Branson was here as a precursor to the dinner he wanted to take me on, though that didn't seem his style. Nor was it something I was comfortable with. But given the circumstances, possibly the better of two options. Well, whatever. I'd been sitting by the fire beating myself up for running away. I didn't care if Branson knew or not. I wanted all my cards on the table. I wanted to feel like Charles Page's daughter again.

"I was at the hospital when Declan Diamond died this evening. I figured that's why you were here."

Branson's lips twitched, and I thought he was going to smile, but he held it back. "Yes. That's why I'm here. I thought I'd have to worm that out of you somehow."

So he had known. "You're not taking me down to the station?"

His brows furrowed, and then he glanced around the cabin. "You've done a lot of work since I was here last. Looks like a real home. It suits you."

"Thanks. It's definitely better. I'm going to replace a few of the things I have now. Start fresh. In fact, I hope—" I realized what we were talking about. "Wait, what are we doing? Why we talking about my house right now?"

Branson shrugged, then the smile did arrive. "Just saying this is a nice place to have a discussion, much better than the police station, don't you think?"

I considered for a moment. "I take it this isn't official?"

Another shrug. "No reason for it to be, I don't think. Unless you had something to do with his death?"

I flinched. "No, of course not. But shouldn't you—"

"Oh, Fred." The smile remained, and Branson shook his head. "I really do have your number. You're a by the book kind of woman. And I'm willing to bet that detective father of yours was a by the book kind of guy as well."

"He was. And I'd like to think that I am."

"Yeah. I can see the condemnation in your eyes. You're actually judging me for *not* taking you down to the station." He gave a little laugh. "I'm not always a by the book kind of guy, Fred. You and I both know you didn't kill Declan Diamond. So why in the world would I bring you down?"

He could see judgment? I hadn't even been aware I felt that. Though, maybe I did. "Well, obviously someone recognized me. Doesn't this need to be on the books in order to be official? Otherwise it will have to happen again."

He sighed, looked around once more, and motioned toward my mug by the armchair. "It's been a long night, Fred. Mind making me a cup of whatever you're having?"

"You want hot chocolate?"

He gave a little eye roll, but his grin grew. "Well, to be honest, I was hoping for something stronger, but sure, hot chocolate sounds great."

I nearly argued for a moment, told him that yes, I did want to go down to the station. Make this official, but maybe he was right. And honestly, I was tired of thinking.

"Fine. Come on. I have a pot simmering on the stove." I turned and headed to the kitchen, Watson at my feet and Branson trailing behind.

He took the same seat at the table he'd sat in the one other time he'd been here as I got a mug out of the cabinet and ladled in hot chocolate.

"I see you truly did decide to keep the tie-dye flamingo curtains, huh?"

They were an eyesore, but were from Barry and my mom. I barely noticed them any longer, and when I did, they brought a smile to my face. "They have character."

"They definitely have something." Branson chuckled as he took the mug from my hands and breathed in the smell of cinnamon and chocolate before letting out a long sigh. "Actually, this is perfect."

I let him have a drink and then decided to push. "So fine, you're not taking me down to the station, but obviously someone recognized me, so fill me in. Why are you talking to me here instead of where you should?"

"You weren't recognized, actually." He smirked a bit. "We'd already taken everyone's reports, and Officer Green was speaking with the doctor, when one of the nurses found me and said she just remembered there'd been a tall kind of redheaded woman who called for help from his room. That in all the chaos she'd forgotten."

"Kind of redheaded woman?" As if that was the point.

"Her words, not mine." He grinned again. "I could go on about the luxurious color of your hair, but I'll save that till after you agree to have dinner with me."

"You're ridiculous." I refilled my own mug of hot chocolate and lifted it to my lips to hide any sort of reaction or blush my body might betray.

"You know, I've heard that before." He set his mug on the table between us. "You weren't technically recognized, but there was only one tall, kind of redheaded woman who would randomly be in Declan Diamond's room around the time he was murdered."

"A fair deduction, I'll give you that. And yes, I was there. I wanted to see if I noticed anything, something that the police missed, or talk to the nurses and see who all came to visit. But—" Branson's words cut through my thoughts. "Did you say murdered?"

He nodded slowly. "So you didn't know that?"

"No. I was barely there any time, but he seemed normal when I walked in, totally fine. All the beeping of the machines was steady. And then they changed all of a sudden, and he flatlined."

Though his green eyes narrowed, I didn't see any distrust there. "You had to have missed the killer by seconds."

"That doesn't even make sense, Branson." I shook my head, trying to think through it. But no one had been there. "There was a policeman talking to some nurses down the hall. He would've noticed."

"He didn't notice you, did he?" He cocked a brow. "Officer Borland isn't the star of the station, let's put it that way."

That much had been obvious. He didn't come running with the nurses. Probably stepped into the restroom or out for a smoke. "Even so, I was in Declan's room. Nothing happened. One minute his heart was beating along just fine, and the next it wasn't."

Branson took another drink, then nodded slowly. "Heart attack. It looks like the lines were tampered with, though. Someone put in a nice little air bubble. Could've done anything. Caused a stroke, respiratory failure, but in Declan's case, a heart attack. Of course, that's all speculation until confirmed by autopsy, but it was clear enough." He leveled his gaze on me, all serious this time. "I know you didn't do it, Fred. I don't want to cause any grief for you or your family after everything that's already happened. If you saw anything, I need to know. Depending on that, we may have to go down to the station and make an official report. But I'll try not to. Do you remember anything?"

"Like I said, Branson, I don't mind being taken down. It's the right thing—"

"I got it, Nancy Drew. You do the right thing. I know." He reached out and covered my hand with his on the tabletop. "Do you remember anything?"

I started to argue but decided it would be pointless. I closed my eyes, picturing the scene. Hearing the beeping of the machines, smelling the disinfectant. I started to shake my head, then heard the pounding of the nurses' feet running toward me, then remembered running away myself, the slam of the door as I booked it down the stairwell and out to my car. My eyes flew open.

"The door."

His eyebrows raised. "The door?"

"Yeah. The door to the stairwell. When I went out, it slammed."

"I don't see—"

"When I got there, before I arrived at Declan's room, I heard a door slam. I didn't think anything about it. But I'm willing to bet it was the exact same door. You're right. I must've just missed the killer."

"That's all you remember?" He let go of my hand and slumped back in the chair.

"It is. But I didn't even remember that to begin with. At least it's proof, well, kinda, that someone else was there."

He shrugged. "True. But not exactly news. Obviously someone was there since they put air in his IV, and obviously, you barely missed them, given the timing. You sure you didn't see anything? A flash of clothing or something, enough to know if it was a man or woman?"

I shook my head again. "No. Nothing. Sorry."

As Branson bit his bottom lip, considering, I tried once more. "We really probably should go down to the station, do this officially. Just in case."

His eyes flashed with just a hint of annoyance. "No. I told you. There's no reason to. It would just cause more paperwork, and then days of Susan foaming at the mouth as she tried to pin this on you. All the while, whoever really did this has more time to get away or cover their tracks. I don't put rules or protocol over results."

He most definitely wasn't the same kind of cop as my dad. It didn't mean he wasn't a good one, just different. And yet, it brought to mind Leo. How he'd had suspicions the taxidermy shop was involved in some of the poaching, and Branson wouldn't give him the time of day. Branson had been wrong on that one, at least it seemed that way.

"I still think—"

Branson stood. "Fred, if you want to go down and make a statement, be my guest." His voice was hard, not unkind, but firmer than I'd heard it. "But I'm not wasting time doing it. Like I said, it would cause more work for all of us. As I told you earlier today, I have faith in your skills. I'd rather you snoop around over the next day or two, trying to find out what really happened, as opposed to trying to convince Susan you weren't the one to give Declan more air than he needed."

I couldn't say I entirely agreed with Branson, but part of me did. Especially the part about being wrapped up in trying to clear my own name for something I didn't do. Something Officer Green most definitely would take it upon herself to prove that I did. Finally, I nodded. "Okay."

He nodded back, only a touch of his warmth returning. "Great. Thanks for the time and the hot chocolate." His expression altered, something flitted across his face that I couldn't name, and when he spoke again, he was himself once more. "Have a good night, Fred. It's always a pleasure to see you." And with that, he left.

Watson was snoring within ten minutes. I'd be lucky to get even two hours of sleep. Not only did I have the revelations about Declan's murder to consider, but my view of Branson was shifting. He definitely wasn't the type of officer my father was, but I couldn't tell if different always meant bad, or if it simply meant different.

As expected, I was exhausted the next day. So much so, I couldn't think clearly enough to even decide who to speak to about Declan. Instead, I opted for continuing to work at the Cozy Corgi. My brain often started to make connections and opened up to new ideas when it was distracted with something else. Plus, the books weren't going to shelve themselves.

By midafternoon, Katie had finished her shift at the Black Bear Roaster and joined me. I filled her in on the night's events. To my surprise, the only thing she reprimanded me for was not taking her along to the hospital.

Katie's theory was that it was a joint effort between Dolan and Daphne to get the controlling brother and cheating husband out of the way. It was just as good a theory as any. "But just think what that would mean for poor Duncan. His oldest son murdered, his youngest son and daughter-in-law murderers and in jail. And him all alone in that toy shop just whittling away." Katie considered for a moment. "Although Daphne is pregnant, so maybe he could raise his grandchild. But he seems too old and grumpy to do that very well."

Somehow I hadn't even thought about the baby. What a

tragedy it would be born into, especially if Katie's theory was correct. "I don't know, I still think Duncan might be responsible. After all the betrayal Declan put him through. I know everyone says he's got a gentle soul and is just a kind old man, but they also say Gerald Jackson is a fine lawyer, so I'm not keen to put too much stock in Duncan's peers' opinion of him."

As I'd shelved books that morning, it was Duncan I kept returning to. I even walked down to the toy store at lunch, thinking I'd go and buy something, see if I could turn the conversation in a way that might give an idea of what they were feeling. "The toy shop is still closed. And I don't have a good reason to show up on their doorstep. But it really did sound like Declan serving Daphne with divorce papers was the last straw for Duncan. Maybe it's what pushed him to go to the hospital and finish what he'd started."

Katie shook her head but didn't look over at me as she used a box cutter to slice through the tape on a new box of books. "I just don't see it. Duncan, grumpy as he may be, is an artist, a creator. He makes toys for children, for crying out loud. You might as well accuse Santa of being a murderer."

"I don't know if I would go so far as to equate Duncan to Santa. You said yourself, he's grumpy. Santa is supposed to be jolly. As much as I hate to admit it, Carl Hanson makes a much better Santa than Duncan Diamond ever would."

She waved off that thought. "Again, Duncan is a creator. He brings things into the world, not takes them away. Even if his creation was used to try and kill his son." Katie shuddered. "I've never liked those nutcrackers. Even less now."

"They are rather creepy, the way their mouths hang open like that. Just waiting to smash something."

"Did you know—" Katie paused and looked over at me, all seriousness. "—that the first wooden soldier nutcrackers were carved by German miners? It was their side job. They would whittle during their free time and sell them on the side."

"You know, Katie, I definitely can't say I knew that."

She nodded emphatically, sending her curls bobbing in a way that had already grown familiar and endearing. "It's true. And they were often given to German children for good luck."

I gaped at her. "For something that creeps you out as much as you claim, you sure know a lot about them."

She raised a finger. "My favorite fact is that some of them were carved to look like politicians who were despised during the day, and weren't really for cracking nuts at all. Of course the people who made them said any resemblance was completely coincidental, but I do think it explains why I feel the way I do. They're meant to be creepy."

"Katie, what in the world...?" And then it hit me, and I burst into laughter. I'd forgotten about one of her quirks she'd told me about. "Oh, I get it! You got sucked into the never-ending hole of facts and trivia about nutcrackers, didn't you?"

She lifted her chin primly. "Possibly."

She really was something. "I don't think Google is your friend. I'm afraid you might dive in and never come back."

"You have your ways, and I have mine. You might think you can solve a murder by talking to all the big gossips in town, but I happen to think research could shed the most light on things." She flinched a little, though I hadn't said or reacted in any way, and then her tone changed, almost wary, but some other emotion was there as well. Maybe... hope? "It's a different topic, but you want to hear what else I researched?"

From the sound of her voice, I nearly said no, afraid of what was coming. "I bet you're going to tell me."

"Well...." Katie took a shaky breath and then turned away from me, focusing on the books once more. "There's lots of studies saying that bookstores are more successful when there's a bakery up top. Something about the smells of fresh bread and cookies and things making customers below buy more."

The change in topic completely threw me off. "What?"

Still she didn't look at me. Her fingers trembled as she retrieved another book. "It's true. I also read that it's considered good fortune to have bookstores and bakeries together." She cleared her throat. "Something about... the alliteration, I believe. Bookstores and bakeries. B and B. You know, for, um, good luck or something...."

And it clicked. The moment it did, I was nearly ashamed it hadn't clicked weeks before. All the hints she'd dropped, even the irritation Katie always showed when I brought up Peg and turning the second floor into Cozy Corgi merchandise. "Katie?"

"Hmm?" She turned toward me, all wide-eyed innocence, but then looked away again quickly.

"Are you wanting to open your bakery upstairs?"

There was a long pause. She seemed to consider, and then she sucked in her breath. "Well, what a thought? Well, I just don't know... is it something you would want?"

It was so ridiculous, and Katie was more nervous than I'd ever seen her, and I couldn't keep from laughing. I walked over to her, gripped both of her shoulders, and turned her to face me. "How long have you been thinking about this?"

"I don't know." She shrugged unable to meet my gaze for more than a moment, then looking away. "Ever since you found Opal. I mean there's already a kitchen up there. It seems to make sense." She grimaced. "I know that makes me awful. I shouldn't have been thinking about such things when Opal had just been killed. But I've wanted this for so long. And it just seems so utterly perfect. You and I get along.... We have a lot of fun together. It could be this great adventure...."

"Katie. I...." It was so out of the blue. A bakery upstairs. In my bookshop. Another business partner.

She pulled away, and though she sounded disappointed and possibly hurt, she didn't sound angry. "Never mind. I know that's not why you're here. You came up to have your own adventure. To be Winifred and Watson. Just the two of you. I don't want to intrude."

I started to speak, to agree, and then to argue, but then the picture started to form. She was right. I had come up here to have my own adventure. To finally make life on my own terms. But I hadn't been sure what to do with upstairs. I'd wanted the bookstore to be small and cozy, not some large rambling houseful. I didn't want to rent it out as an apartment either. But a bakery? Katie had a point. It would make the bookshop smell wonderful. It would be a great business to have together. People would come in for pastries and leave with the book, or they'd come in to buy a book, and then they'd wander upstairs to read it over coffee and cake.

It felt right. Scary, but right.

Branson had been correct. I'd always been a by the book kind of woman. In everything. In my studies, my time as a professor, in my marriage, and starting the publishing house with Charlotte. Until everything hit the fan and I decided to hit Reset and throw caution to the wind. That hadn't been by the book. None of this was by the book. And yet I felt like it was working. Bookstore and bakery. What a perfect combination.

I sighed and sank back against the bookshelf. "You're going to make me gain a thousand pounds, aren't you?" I met Katie's gaze as she looked over at me in surprise. "Just remember, there's already been one dead body up in that kitchen. There can easily be another."

"You mean...?" Katie's eyes widened and her expression shifted from disappointment, to confusion, to awe. "You mean...?"

I laughed and felt a giddy sort of thrill course through me. "I mean, Katie, would you consider opening a bakery in the top part of my bookstore? I've heard studies saying that the smell of baked goods can greatly increase the sale of books."

Katie froze, then jumped up and down, and then jogged in place as she squealed. "Yes! Oh, yes! It's going to be amazing, Fred, you wait and see. Absolutely perfect!"

At Katie's commotion, Watson let out a yelp from upstairs and rushed down to inspect. I shook my head at him. "You've already claimed upstairs as your own. You're gonna be so happy for it to be turned into a bakery. So much for your diet, I won't be the only one gaining a hundred pounds."

Katie's eyes twinkled, and she bent down to rub Watson's haunch. "I haven't told anyone this, but I know the recipe for Lois's all-natural dog treats. I was going to wait and make you a bunch for Christmas. But now I'll make you a new batch every week."

At the word treat, Watson began to whine in frantic anticipation.

I grinned at the two of them. Despite not wanting a business partner, a part of me relaxed. Yes, this was right. And I'd lived enough to know that nothing was ever perfect, but that didn't mean it couldn't be wonderful.

"Well, since you brought up that word, we have to follow through. I'll go get one out of my purse." I headed toward the main counter, then paused, looking back at Katie with another thought. "You didn't really find those studies about bookstores and bakeries online, did you?"

Katie shrugged, all unconvincing innocence. "Well, if you give me five minutes, I can show them to you. You can put about anything you want to on Wikipedia."

"That is just the best news, sweetie." Mom snuggled her birdlike frame against me. There were five of us crowded into a four-person booth, but thanks to her small stature, it was doable. "Oh, that reminds me." She reached below the table, snagged her purse, and began to dig through it. "I made this necklace for Katie. I'd like for you to give it to her." As she spoke, she made a pile of junk on the table. Travel-size bag of tissues, lipstick, seashells, a spool of wire, and a wide assortment of coins and pieces of lint. Finally, she pulled out a long string of clear crystals and beads, with a large smooth stone as the centerpiece. It was a muddy-dark color with a rainbow sheen over it like an oil slick. "This is labradorite. It protects against evil wishes and psychic attacks. I figured she could use it right now. I realize they're no longer thinking she's a valid suspect, but you and I both know that can change on a dime."

Barry leaned over from his spot on the other side of Mom and pulled a matching necklace outside of his tie-dyed shirt. "She made me one too. Except my stone is fluorite. It protects against sorcery and curses."

Mom gave me a knowing glance. "I was going to use

black tourmaline, which is best for all-around general protection, but Barry had other ideas."

"Did you get a witch's knickers all twisted up, Barry?" Percival beamed from the other side of the table as he forked some of the fajita chicken from the sizzling plate he and Gary were sharing. "What have I told you about leaving Myrtle Bantam to herself?"

"Oh, stop." Gary elbowed him in the side. "Quit making fun of Myrtle. She's a harmless little thing."

"Harmless!" Percival screeched. "Harmless? Please don't tell me you forgot about when that sparrow flew into our store and Myrtle saw me try to encourage it back outside."

Gary cocked an eyebrow in my direction. "He was encouraging it with a broom."

"Exactly. A broom is full of twigs and sticks. Birds sit on twigs and sticks. They make nests out of them. They raise their babies in them, for crying out loud." Percival placed the fork on his plate, the chicken forgotten so he could use both of his hands. "She was walking by and then came rushing in with both arms waving in the air, screeching and squawking and clucking like you've never heard before. It was like I was trying to kill the poor thing."

Despite himself, Gary chuckled.

So did Mom, though she swatted her brother. "Stop it. You're being unkind. And Myrtle is most definitely not a witch. She's just a lover of all things with wings and feathers. Even if she does squawk sometimes."

Having been subjected to a Myrtle Bantam squawking tirade myself, I didn't feel overly inclined to come to her reputation's rescue.

The only one who hadn't chuckled was Barry, who now shook the pendant of cloudy blues, whites, and purples at

Percival. "You mock all you want, but there are forces out there that none of us are prepared to deal with. Don't come crying to me when you get cursed."

Percival did a waving motion with his finger encompassing the entirety of Barry. "Honey, you're the one dressed in head-to-toe tie-dye. Which, I hate to tell you, those pants and that shirt clash, which is saying something, considering its tie-dye. If either one of us is cursed, it's you."

Still chuckling, Mom spread her hands out over the table, between Barry and Percival. "Now you two, save some of the drama for Christmas Day. I'm sure the grandkids wouldn't want to miss it."

"It really will be nice to have the whole family together." Gary smiled gently at Mom. "Are you sure the only thing you want us to bring is the sweet potato casserole?"

"Absolutely. Everything else is covered. Verona and Zelda are making the rest of the side dishes. Barry is in charge of appetizers, and I've got the turkey and the vegetarian roast handled." She patted my arm. "And Fred is bringing Katie, so technically, she's bringing dessert."

I wasn't the worst cook in the world, but I wasn't the kind of cook you leave in charge of something for a family gathering. "I offered to bring grilled-cheeses."

She patted my arm again. "I know you did, dear. Bringing Katie will suffice."

"What exactly is in vegetarian roast?" Percival leveled a stare at Barry once more. "Or is that the curse you're trying to guard against?"

As Percival and Barry launched back into exchanging harmless barbs, Mom put Katie's necklace in my hands. "I really do think it's wonderful she's opening a bakery. I bet it's just what the Cozy Corgi needs. I'm so glad you found each other. I do wish she could have joined you for dinner tonight."

"I invited her to come, of course. But she's so over the moon that she wanted to go home and start shopping online for exactly what cooking and baking equipment she'll want to install upstairs."

Confusion crossed Mom's face. "But there's already a kitchen. I thought she could just move right in."

"So did I. But apparently not. While it worked well enough for Opal to make her edibles, it is not going to cut it for what Katie has in mind. It seems she's thinking full-on industrial-bakery-sized—" I had no idea. "—everything, it seems."

"Goodness, sounds expensive." She looked concerned and then shrugged the emotion away. "But I'm sure it will pay off. It's going to be absolute perfection."

"I hope so. She's been saving for a long time. Didn't have enough to open her own place entirely, but she has enough to redo what she needs. I'm glad we went ahead and redid the floors and walls up there. That was thanks to you."

Mom smiled and shrugged away the compliment just as easily as she had the concern. "So glad you're here, darling. I hope this new life treats you better than the old one."

I bent down awkwardly to give her a quick kiss on the cheek. "It already is, Mom. It already is." The truth of those words hit me, surrounded by the older generation of my family, as we were all squished into a brightly painted booth at Habanero's, Barry and Percival still bickering, and Gary simply enjoying the show. Even with the drama since I moved into town, I was certain this was the life I not only needed, but wanted.

We continued eating for a while, the conversation ranging from speculation about the first lawsuit Noah and

Jonah would have over their Christmas garland, to listing the gifts they were getting for the grandkids so no one got the same thing, to their hopes of what would happen to the empty shops next to the Cozy Corgi.

By the time the sopaipillas were delivered, I didn't think I could eat a bite more. But sure enough, I managed, and before long my fingers were sticky with honey.

Mom had just stuffed another bite into her mouth when she looked over and stiffened slightly. I followed her gaze.

Gerald Jackson, who was nearly as wide as he was tall, was making his way from across the restaurant toward our booth. She leaned in to me, uncharacteristically speaking with her mouth full. "Be nice, Fred."

I was a woman pushing forty and yet could still get reprimanded by my mother for not even doing anything. It was like she knew me.

"Howdy there, boys! So good to see you!" Gerald nearly trumpeted over the background music as he reached us.

All three of the men in our booth let out similar sounds of greeting, and there were rounds of handshakes and back-slapping.

When the male camaraderie died down a bit, he tipped his hat in Mom's and my direction. "Always a pleasure to see you, ladies."

I managed a noncommittal nod, and my mother a sweet "You too, of course, Gerald. Happy holidays."

Maybe someday I'd be as gracious as my mother. But I doubted it.

"And to you, Phyllis. I'm sure you're glad to have your girl back."

"That's very true, Gerald. It's nice to have the family together at Christmastime again." And though her other hand reached out and slid over Barry's leg under the table, I was certain that a part of her was also thinking of my father. I often felt he was still watching over us, also pleased that we were all together.

Pleasantries exchanged, Gerald refocused on the men at the table. He started to squat slightly to rest his elbow on the table to be closer, then, finding that difficult, seemed to think better of it and stood straight once more. "Terrible business with the Diamonds. Just terrible." He patted his chest. "Just breaks your heart, all that Duncan has sacrificed and this is where it leads."

It took all my willpower to keep from pointing out that Gerald was the reason Declan had managed to get his father declared incompetent. Having Mom pressed against me probably didn't hurt.

There was a round of agreement from the table. "And then that scene the night before last at the Chinese restaurant." Percival *tsked*. "And to such a charming, beautiful girl like Daphne. After all Declan's years of philandering, she deserved better."

Somehow in the chaos of it all, I'd never passed on to them about Dolan and Daphne. Well, I definitely wasn't going to do so with Gerald Jackson in our midst.

Gerald nodded his agreement with Percival. "That is true, but I take it you haven't heard the latest?" His wild eyebrows rose nearly halfway up his bald head as he leered over his glasses at each man in turn.

All three of them shook their heads. Mom and I didn't bother.

This time, Gerald managed to support his weight with his hands on the edge of the table as he leaned nearer. "Well, with Declan's death, certain things came to light. One of which was he changed his will, less than a week ago, in fact."

Barry, Percival, and Gary all sat silently with their mouths open, waiting. It was Mom who ushered him forward. "Well, do you know how he changed it?"

He looked at her in surprise, like he'd forgotten Mom was there. Then cleared his throat as if uncertain he should continue with the gossip.

It was a good thing the waitress had taken Gary and Percival's sizzling cast-iron fajita plate away. I would have been tempted to smash it over his head.

"Don't worry about Mom and I being delicate, Gerald. We handled things the night Barry was arrested for Opal's murder. All on our own, if you remember." To my surprise, Mom didn't elbow me or anything. Gerald, who acted as Barry's lawyer—and apparently every other man over the age of fifty in Estes Park—had been so late that all the drama had been over, all because he had to drive to his little house in Glen Haven for a bottle of his homemade kombucha.

"Ah, yes. Well...." Gerald blinked rapidly a few times and then once more promptly forgot Mom and I were there. His gaze darted back and forth between Gary and Percival but then finally came to rest on Barry, seemingly judging him to be the most worthy of the news. "As I've been told, the original will left the entire business to Daphne and Dolan. Those two, of course, would take care of Duncan, just as always." He pulled his glasses farther down his nose and leaned in even closer to Barry. "But now, he's left everything, and I do mean everything, to Sarah Margaret Beeman."

"You're kidding! He left it all to another woman?" Percival gasped, startling Gerald. "Now *that's* a scandal!" Gary nodded his agreement.

"Poor Duncan. Poor, poor Duncan." Barry just sounded

sad. "And Daphne and Dolan too. He managed to betray his entire family."

Gerald nodded his agreement. "I don't see how such a thing would hold up in court, but it is Declan."

I couldn't imagine it holding up in court either, although, with Gerald defending the rest of the Diamonds, who knew...

After a few moments in silence, Mom spoke up, her voice timid. "Who's Sarah Beeman? I don't think I've ever heard of her."

"No idea." Gerald shrugged. "That's part of what makes it so confusing. No one knows her."

I did. I almost said so, then stopped myself.

Maybe I didn't. Sarah Beeman. It sounded so familiar. I knew that name. If it hadn't been for the reaction of the others around the table, I would've assumed it was someone I'd met downtown as I was trying to clear Barry or Katie. But if that were the case, all of them would've known who she was. There was no one in town I knew that they didn't. So I must not know her.

But I did know that name. I was sure of it.

And talk about opening it wide for motive. If any of the Diamonds had known about the will, it would definitely be a reason to murder Declan. It seemed their reasons were almost limitless.

I expected to see Katie the following morning when Watson and I stopped in for our daily chai and scone at the Black Bear Roaster. Instead, Carla, looking impossibly more pregnant than the day before, met us with a glare from behind the counter. "Pumpkin spice latte and gingerbread scone like normal, correct?"

She'd waited on me once, hardly enough time to have established a normal order. "You know, I think I'm going to mix it up, be crazy today." I gave her a wink, and the second I did, I felt weird about it. Perhaps I thought it would cheer her up; though why a wink would do it, I had no idea. "How about let's try a large dirty chai and a pumpkin scone."

Carla shrugged. "You got it."

As she made the drink, I glanced behind the counter and only found a thin teenage boy refilling the coffee grinder, probably working during his Christmas vacation. In less than two minutes, Carla was back, sliding me my chai along with a piece of pumpkin bread. I nearly corrected her mistake, then thought maybe she was doing me a favor. I was the one insane enough to keep ordering scones and expecting them to change. "Thanks so much. Ah, I thought Katie would be here."

Carla halted, the credit card I'd given her frozen in midair. "She called me late last night, gave her two weeks' notice. Apparently she's opening her own bakery." She sniffed. "I told her to not bother coming in. She was a weird one, anyway. Although I regretted that decision at five this morning, let me tell you." Carla rubbed her belly.

I paused for a second, waiting for tirade against me and my bookshop, but none came. It seemed Katie hadn't mentioned where she was opening her bakery, and I was grateful.

A minute or so later, and Watson and I were headed across the street to the Cozy Corgi. I took a bite of the pumpkin bread, which was mildly moister than the scones, and tossed Watson a bite when we reached the other sidewalk. We were almost to the store when I realized my dilemma over whether to continue going to the Black Bear Roaster would be short-lived. Soon dirty chais and non-dry scones would be right above my head every morning. The thought felt like a mental cozy blanket pulled up over me. Life was going to be wonderful. Endless caffeine, endless pastries, and endless books.

Dear Lord, I'd be lucky if it was only a hundred pounds I gained.

To my surprise, even after the pumpkin bread was gone, Watson didn't trundle up the steps and disappear to the second floor as normal. Instead he wandered over to the nonfiction section that Katie and I had arranged the day before, and fell asleep in the rays of the winter sunlight pouring through the window. As rare as that was, I knew I should enjoy it while it lasted. As soon as Katie was baking upstairs, I'd never see Watson again.

As I worked on arranging the biography section, careful not to wake Watson, I pondered the implications of Declan leaving everything to the mystery woman. I was of two minds on the situation. It made sense for any of the three remaining Diamonds to be so angry at Declan that they would murder him. But Declan had made other enemies, hadn't he? Even if not as obvious as his family drama, there were other possibilities.

And who in the world was the mystery woman? Everyone knew everything about everyone in a town as small as Estes Park, or at least thought they did. The only possibility I could imagine was that the woman must not be from here. Maybe from Denver or Lyons?

I was nearly done with the third box of books when I realized what day it was. I looked over at a peacefully sleeping Watson as guilt and dread washed over me. Today was the day I'd agreed to the corgi playdate with Paulie Mertz. I was tempted to find an excuse. I was opening a store, for crying out loud. If I could use it for an excuse to refrain from a dinner with a handsome park ranger, I should definitely be able to do it to keep Watson away from Flotsam and Jetsam. But I really just wanted to get it over with.

Katie called around lunchtime, sounding ecstatic about the abrupt dismissal from the coffee shop. She'd gone down to Denver to check out industrial baking equipment in person, as opposed to online, and needed me to get some measurements from the upstairs kitchen.

Then, after a lunch of leftover Mexican food from the night before for myself, and a can of tuna for Watson—how he could tell the difference between canned dog food and canned tuna, I would never know—it was back to work and pondering over who the mystery woman was. It wasn't long before I had a new suspect. Sarah Beeman, whoever she was, certainly had a motive—she was in line to inherit everything.

As the afternoon wore on, pondering Declan's killing gave way to a buildup of dread of the corgi playdate. With less than an hour to spare, I grew more and more tempted to cancel. And with every moment that passed, it would make it ever more rude. I was so caught up in my thoughts that I let out a yelp when the mail was shoved through the slot in the door.

Watson beat me to it, sniffing the pile of mail like he expected either a snack or a bomb, then gave me a withering glare when I walked over and picked it up. It was all junk. How it was possible that a new business, one that hadn't even opened, could get so many catalogs and applications for credit cards was beyond me. I was nearly ready to toss it all into the recycling when I noticed the letter stuck in the pages of a floral catalog.

My skin tingled as I read the envelope: *Sarah M. Beeman.*

The rest of the mail fell from my fingers with a clatter on the floor, and a yelp from Watson. I barely noticed.

Sarah M. Beeman. *That* was why I had recognized the name.

What was the name Gerald had said? Sarah Margaret Beeman.

And as before, the return address was a Denver law firm.

It still didn't make sense, but at least I knew I wasn't going crazy.

I checked my cell, half an hour before I was to meet Paulie. Another second passed and I made up my mind. I grabbed the leash off the counter and patted my thigh. "Come on, Watson. We've gotta make this quick."

. . .

When we reached Rocky Mountain Imprints, we were thwarted. Two burly men were blocking the entrance as they did something to the doorframe. Only then did I notice the glass that made up the center of the door was missing. Repairmen, obviously. I nearly decided to wait, to come back later, but the prospect of being with Paulie and his two crazed corgis while this was on my mind sounded like the epitome of torture. I motioned toward the empty space.

"Sorry to bother you. Do you mind if we pop in for a moment? I hate to get in your way, but I promise I'll be quick."

Though both looked annoyed, one of the men opened what remained of the door and allowed Watson and I to walk in.

"Thank you so much!"

We barely rounded the corner into the store, when Peg saw us. "Oh, hi! So nice of you to drop by. I was planning on heading down to you in a few minutes."

That threw me off. "You were coming to see me?"

She tilted her cute blonde head. "Well, of course, silly. You're the client. Or potential one, at least." She winked, then raised her voice and hollered toward the back. "Joe, sweetie, bring up Fred's hoodie, would you?"

The hoodie! I'd completely forgotten. Peg had said it would be done by today.

She turned her attention back to me. "It came out super cute. I really hope you'll be pleased. I chose a soft brown background. I think it goes nicely with the white lettering."

A man just as large as the two repairmen out front, walked into view from the back of the store and handed Peg the folded hoodie. "Here you go, love." His voice was deep and soft. The picture of them together was somewhat off-putting. Peg so small, and Joe absolutely huge. And where Peg was beautiful in a pixie sort of way, the same could not be said for Joe, in any sort of way. The man was unfortunately homely. He gave me a polite nod, then disappeared back through the racks of T-shirts.

Peg unfolded the hoodie and grinned as she inspected it, then turned it toward me. The size I'd ordered for myself looked nearly like a tent next to her petite stature. And for a moment, all my other concerns vanished, and I sighed. She'd been right. The logo was perfect on the soft brown background of the hoodie. Like on the sign of my store, a fat corgi sat on the top of the stack of four books, with the words *The Cozy Corgi* arched over its head. I reached out and touched the corgi with my fingertip. It was still warm. Joe must've just finished making it. I couldn't seem to tear my gaze away. "Oh, Peg, it's wonderful."

"I'm glad you think so. I really do think they'll be a big seller for you. Especially if you do a variety of products. I know you weren't in love with the idea of shot glasses, but there's other things to choose from." She folded up the hoodie, slipped it into a bag, and handed it to me. "This one's on the house. Wear it a couple days, give it some washes, see the quality of it, and let me know. We'd love to be your supplier."

I was glad she mentioned washing it first. I'd been ready to sign on the dotted line. Bakery upstairs or not, I'd find a place somewhere for Cozy Corgi merchandise. Even if I was the only customer. "Thank you, Peg. I'm sure it will be just fine, but I'll try it out and let you know."

Just then there was a loud crash, causing Peg, Watson, and myself to jump.

A deep voice rumbled embarrassingly from the front

door. “Sorry! My bad. We’ll cut a new piece of glass. It’ll just take a little bit longer.”

“No problem.” Peg called to them and then looked at me with a commiserating sigh. “Business ownership isn’t all glitz and glam, as you’re about to find out. Some kid must’ve hit our front door with a BB gun yesterday, and it’s turned into this big old thing. Expensive, but not enough to turn in to the insurance without our premiums going up. Always something.” She shook her head.

“I know what you mean. When I came up here, I thought I’d spend a week or so and have my shop open. By the time we finally do, it will be almost two months. And that’s still a big if I can get it ready by January.”

She shrugged. “It’s not a big deal if you don’t. You’ll be missing some money during the winter months, but not a ton. Just make sure you’re up and running by the end of May. Our biggest season is when kids are out of school. Then it’s every man for himself. We each have to make enough over the summer to last us the entire year.”

Thanks to the betrayal of my best friend and the dollar amount of compensation I received, even though it wasn’t what it should have been, I didn’t have to worry about sales to the same level as many of the other storeowners. Otherwise, I never in a million years would have opened a brick-and-mortar bookshop. I figured it best not to mention that, though.

“Thanks for the advice. Any insight I can get into operating a store in a tourist town is priceless.” I repositioned the bag with the hoodie in preparation to leave and then remembered why I’d come in the first place. I held the envelope out to her. “Oh, silly me. I almost forgot. I got another misdelivered piece of mail.”

She took it, read the envelope, and her eyes widened

slightly. She glanced toward the back again. Before a heartbeat passed, she smiled up at me. "Misdelivered mail will be the least of your headaches as a business owner, I can promise you." She tucked the letter away. "Thanks for bringing this. And while I don't expect you to handle our mail, if you see any more letters addressed to her, feel free to throw them away."

Odd request. "Who is she? I've met a lot of people in town but haven't met anyone named Sarah Beeman."

Peg rolled her eyes. "That's what I mean. Even small things add up to large annoyances. I don't know who she is. We've gotten letters addressed to her since the time we opened the store. I can only assume she was someone who owned the shop in this location before, or maybe someone who worked here. I don't know." She cleared her throat and glanced toward the back once more. "I tried to find her the first couple of times, and then gave up. I suppose I need to contact the post office and let them know that if they come across any more letters to her to just return them to the sender."

"Well, I know she has to be around here." I wasn't going to share all that I knew, but maybe a tidbit of gossip could loosen the wheels, or trigger a memory that she might tell me later. "The Diamonds next door know her."

She flinched, then shook her head. "They do? I don't think that's true. I asked everyone around when I got that first letter to her. Including the Diamonds. They didn't know."

"That's strange. I'm certain Declan knew her."

Peg just shook her head. "Maybe so. The Diamonds are a wonderful family, but Declan and I never got along." A flush rose to her cheeks. "I'm sorry. I forgot. One shouldn't speak such things of the dead. God rest his soul."

That most definitely wasn't a tenet I lived by, but I nodded along anyway. "No problem." I held the bag with the hoodie up. "Thank you again for this. I absolutely love it. I'm certain I'll want some other things in my store."

She smiled, but not as brightly as before. "I'm so glad. It will be a lot of fun working with you. Do let me know what you've decided, and of course if you have any questions, never hesitate."

With a wave, I turned to leave, but as we approached the door, there was still glass everywhere. One of the repairman looked at me and simply shook his head. I glanced over to Peg. "Do you have a back exit? I suppose I could pick Watson up and carry him over the glass, but he hates it. And I'm covered in enough dog hair as it is. Anytime I pick him up, I might as well be wearing a corgi fur coat after."

"Oh, my goodness. I wasn't even thinking. I'm so sorry." She rushed around the counter and waved me toward her, then pointed to a door in the back that was barely visible through all the T-shirts hanging in the way. "Right through there, sweetie. That's the alley. It leads to the new riverwalk out back." She reached up to pat my shoulder, and then bent to offer a similar gesture to Watson, who scooted quickly out of her reach.

"Thank you. Never mind Watson; he's always a little grumpy. Unless you're my stepfather, and then you're Christmas morning and birthdays all rolled into one." My stepfather *and* Leo Lopez, it seemed.

She waved me off. "Not a big deal. I have a cat at home that is the exact same way. Absolutely worships the ground Joe walks on. I might as well be kitty litter for all she is concerned."

And with a final wave, Watson and I wove our way

through the maze of T-shirts, past another trophy case with a baseball bat leaning beside it, and out the back door. Though the day was cloudy, it was bright, and I had to blink, letting my eyes adjust. Once I did, the alley looked strangely familiar, and glancing behind, the answer of why was obvious. It was the alley that Rocky Mountain Imprints shared with Bushy Evergreen's Workshop. The alley where I'd seen Daphne and Dolan kiss two days before.

The toyshop had still been closed as Watson and I had passed it to get to Peg's, and I was tempted to go knock on their back door. Though what I would ask if somebody answered, I had no idea. If one of them did know who Sarah Beeman was and they were Declan's killer, asking them in an alley wouldn't be the smartest move. And with a jolt, I suddenly remembered Paulie Mertz and his eel-like corgis. I glanced at my cell. We were almost late.

I barely noticed Watson tugging on my leash, until he let out a sharp yelp and a whine.

I hurried over and found him chewing on something on the side of the dumpster. "Watson. Stop it."

He yelped again, but kept right on chewing on his treasure. Probably a sharp bone.

I squatted down beside him, and pulled whatever it was from his mouth. "You are ridiculous. Only you would continue to eat something that's hurting you. Actual dog food, you're too good to eat, but this"— I shook it at him, sparing it a glance —"old work glove is a delicacy all of the sudden." I narrowed my eyes at the glove. There was something red and chunky all over it.

Unperturbed, Watson darted back at the pile of refuse that had fallen from the dumpster and began chomping down on something else.

"Oh, for crying out loud." I yanked his leash away, far

enough to see that he'd discovered a fourth of a pizza. Of course, he'd been attempting to eat a glove because it was covered in pizza sauce. Brilliant. I gave another tug, but Watson was strong enough that when he made up his mind, moving him wasn't a one-handed job. I tossed the glove back by the pizza, and pulled him away, both hands tight around his leash. We were out of the alley before he stopped struggling.

He glared up at me, making it very clear that there would be no corgi cuddles later.

"Give me that look all you want to, buddy. All you did was just make me feel not the least bit bad for you about what's to happen next. I was planning on making you play with Flotsam and Jetsam for thirty minutes at the most. But I think you deserve to have to play with them for an hour."

Even as we made our way to the park, I knew that was one threat I wouldn't follow through on. No way in the world was I spending the entire hour in solitary conversation with Paulie Mertz.

Watson whined the entire two-block walk from the alley to the park. "Complain all you want to. I'm not going to have any sympathy, Mr. Stubborn Pants." The pathetic look he gave me already had me softening, like he knew it would. "Maybe just fifteen minutes with the evil twins, how about that?" Though how in the world I was going to get away with only fifteen minutes without seeming like the rudest person in the entire universe, I wasn't sure.

With one block to spare, the winter night sky opened up and snow began to come down in torrents. I lifted my gaze skyward. "Thank you for the Christmas miracle, Santa." I could blame the Mini Cooper, say that it didn't have four-wheel drive. That much was true, so it wouldn't be a lie. Hopefully Paulie wouldn't know that Mini Coopers came with front wheel drive, and it was doing just splendidly in the mountains so far.

I did a double take when I noticed Paulie and Flotsam and Jetsam at the playground across the street. When he'd suggested meeting at a park, I'd pictured a dog park, or at least a large area with trees, open space, and paths. This was a kids' playground, and a tiny one at that. Though I supposed it was my own fault; he'd clearly said meet at the park close to the intersection of Elkhorn Avenue and East Riverside Drive, down by the river. It was in the middle of shops. I supposed I just hadn't been thinking. Well, one more plausible excuse. Watson needed to run, get out his energy.

I nearly snorted out a laugh at the thought. Watson and I had the same outlook on running. Something dangerous needed to be chasing us, or there had to be a really good meal at the finish line. Other than that, he'd sooner help unbox books than run.

Paulie waved frantically as we crossed the street, like we couldn't see him. Both Flotsam and Jetsam followed suit and bounded at the end of their leashes.

Watson whimpered.

"I know, buddy. I know. Maybe ten minutes."

As we drew nearer, both the corgis crashed into Watson and me, and Paulie pulled me into a hug. In truth, the hug wasn't very effective as he still had a hand on each of the hyperactive dogs' leashes, but I was grateful, as it made it shorter, even if a touch more awkward. "Fred, it's so nice of you to join us for a playdate. I didn't expect you to show up. I've tried doggy playdates with a couple of other dog owners in town, and... well...."

He looked such a combination of embarrassed and happy that I readjusted mentally. Fifteen minutes. A person could stand anything for fifteen minutes, right?

For the life of me, I couldn't think of a thing to say. Watson bashed into the back of my legs, saving me from having to figure it out. Looking down, Flotsam and Jetsam were still bounding up and down, this time frequently landing on Watson's paws. Disentangling myself, I pulled Watson along with me and took a seat on one of the swings.

It took Paulie a few seconds to follow as he untangled his corgis' leashes, offering Watson a brief respite.

"For some reason, I was picturing a dog park or something. I don't know why, I've driven past this a million times, but there's not much space for them, is there?"

Paulie gave a little shrug, and even in the shadowy lights from the cloudy evening, I could make out embarrassment over his face. "Well. I thought you wouldn't show. Like I said, that's happened before. There is a dog park, but it's a farther walk. So I thought we'd meet here, just in case you canceled, not so far to go." His smile brightened. "But the next time, we can meet there." The cheerfulness lasted a total of three seconds, and then his features crashed once more. "No, we can't. Flotsam and Jetsam have been banned from that dog park." He perked up again. I didn't think I'd ever seen such speedy mood shifts. "But you could come to my house. Plenty of room for the dogs to play."

Oh dear Lord, so much for Christmas miracles. One of the other dogs bumped into Watson, he yelped and then growled, which was much sooner than he normally did with other corgis. But a perfect excuse. "Sorry, Paulie. As you can see, Watson really doesn't get into playing all that much. He kinda just eats and sleeps and casts judgmental glances at other dogs and people walking by. That's kind of his thing."

Paulie only looked daunted for a second. "Well, you could come over for dinner." He must've seen the answer rising to my lips, and he rushed ahead. "You could bring Watson, of course. I could put Flotsam and Jetsam in my bedroom. It wouldn't be a problem."

Dinner? And this was why I should've turned this down from the beginning, even if I would've felt guilty. I reached out to take his hand, then realized what I was doing and folded my hand in my lap over Watson's leash. "Paulie.

That's very sweet, and you're very.... That's very sweet. But I want to be clear up front. I'm not looking for dates or a relationship. I have my hands full starting a business. I'm sorry."

"No, no, no!" Paulie waved both his hands, causing Flotsam and Jetsam's leashes to tremble, and setting them both off on a barking tirade. "I didn't mean as a date. Goodness, I know you're out of my league. Plus I hear you and Sergeant Wexler are an item. Course then I noticed you and that park ranger fellow outside of Carl and Anna's the other day, so maybe not."

He'd just thrown so much information at me at once, that again I was speechless. He'd noticed me and Leo? And even Paulie Mertz had heard the rumors about Branson and me? This time I did reach out and put my hand over his, despite my better instincts. "Paulie, it has nothing to do with leagues or anything like that." I pulled my hand back.

He snorted, but it wasn't a sarcastic sound. "Oh, please, Fred. You're so far out of my league, it's ridiculous. But I truly wasn't asking for a date. I know I'm not really supposed to make friendships, but I'm just... lonely. I promise, that's all."

I believed him. He truly did look lonely and sad. And seemed like he was hurting. Some of his words came back to me and struck me as odd. "What do you mean you're not supposed to make friends? What kind of rule is that?"

His eyes widened. "Oh, I didn't even mean to say that. Nothing. I just meant..." I could swear he was searching for something to say, some excuse. "Well, I don't exactly fit in most places. My teeth are stained. I often smell like fish water from cleaning the aquariums. I get nervous and start to sweat, even in a snowstorm, and I frequently get nosebleeds."

There was growling and snapping at our feet, and I leaned forward ready to pull Watson to safety, but it was simply Flotsam and Jetsam playing together, apparently having finally given up on Watson developing a playful personality.

That was a relief.

I turned back to Paulie and placed my hand over his again. "Oh, Paulie. I couldn't tell you were sweating, and I've never noticed you get a nosebleed." As soon as the words left my lips, I realized that I'd addressed the wrong part of his statement. I should've argued against the yellow teeth and the smell of fish tank, but it was too late to try to cover that up. Plus, the man had a mirror. I couldn't exactly tell him his teeth weren't stained.

Even so, he smiled like I'd just paid him the highest compliment.

Despite the truth of his list of social faux pas, it still didn't explain the friendship comment he'd made before. There was something there. But I didn't push.

I checked on Watson again. He seemed to be contentedly licking his paws as he continued to be forgotten by the other two corgis. I refocused on Paulie. "I'm sorry you're having a difficult time. I know it's hard being new in town."

He gave me a knowing look. "You're much newer to town than I am, and you're not making it look difficult."

Just as I was searching for something else to say, Watson let out another yelp, this one sounding like pain, and once more I was ready to pull him back from the others. But they weren't bothering him. He gave his paw a lick, and then yelped again. I reached down, took the paw he'd been licking, and ran my fingers gently around it, feeling the pads. There was nothing, and Watson didn't flinch as I touched his paw, like he would've if there was a thorn or splinter.

His tongue darted out to lick his nose, and he let out another pain-filled yip, sneezed, and then yipped again. He was clearly hurting.

My heart rate shooting up, I whipped off the swing and knelt in front of him. "What is it, sweetie? What's wrong?"

He let out another whimper of pain.

I gently tried to lift his head to see into his mouth, but it was too dark. As I fished in my purse, trying to find my cell, Flotsam and Jetsam crashed into my back like I was playing.

"Boys! Stop!" Paulie stood and pulled them away quickly, then tied them to a leg of the jungle gym, just out of reach, and then he was back. "Sorry about that."

"It's fine." I found my cell, switched on the flashlight feature, and handed it to Paulie. "Would you hold this for me? Angle toward Watson's mouth."

He did, and in the light, I could see just how wild Watson's eyes were. I'd never seen him look like that.

I reached for his muzzle, attempted to raise the lip enough to see his teeth, to see if he had something cutting into him. He yelped in pain again and pulled his head away with a warning growl. I pulled my hand away, and my breath caught as I noticed blood over my fingertips. I looked up at Paulie. "Something's wrong. I gotta get him to the vet. I have to go."

"Of course. Of course." Paulie handed me my cell. "They're closed by this time of night, but they have an emergency number, and I know the vet. Want me to call them and let them know you're on your way?"

Gratitude rushed over me. "Yes, that would be wonderful. Thank you." And then all my attention was on Watson. I took his leash and gave him a gentle pull. He stood tentatively and took a few steps, seemed pain-free, and then sneezed again. He howled in agony, then trailed off to a whimper.

I bent down, scooped all thirty-three pounds of him into my arms, and ran as smoothly as I could to my car.

The veterinarian, Dr. Sallee pulled into the parking lot moments behind me. Though we hadn't met before, he didn't bother with paperwork or formality, which I appreciated. He got the clinic up and running as he asked the expected information-seeking questions. Had Watson had an injury? Had there been some sort of impact? Had he been eating normally? Frequent and regular bowel movements? Was he up to date on shots?

It wasn't until we had Watson on his examining table that he asked the magic question. "Has he gotten into any trash recently?"

"No, of course not." I yanked my hair away that had fallen into my eyes, and felt close to tears. Then it came back to me. "Wait, yes. Probably... less than an hour ago, maybe half an hour ago. We were in the alley behind the T-shirt shop. Watson found leftover pizza."

"Pizza shouldn't do that unless it was rancid. But then he'd be sick, not in pain." Dr. Sallee refocused on Watson. "You're sure his pain is from his mouth?"

"Yes. That's the only place. Nothing's wrong with his feet. He doesn't let on when I touch his belly or anything."

The vet refocused on Watson and reached out to touch his muzzle. Watson growled and tried to get away. "I'll need you to hold him. If I can look in his mouth without him biting me, I will. Otherwise I'll need to figure out a different way. I'd rather not give him sedation since we don't know what's happening."

Feeling like a traitor, I bent over the examining table and fixed Watson in place with my arms and body weight. "I'm so sorry, baby. I'm so sorry."

Watson struggled a little, but actually seemed more at ease with my presence around him. He snarled as Dr. Sallee reached for his muzzle again, but didn't move to bite. Though there was a low grumbling growl radiating through him the entire time, he allowed the vet to lift his lips and inspect his gum.

The vet's voice was low enough I could barely hear it. "He's bleeding, but I don't see anything causing it. Nothing looks infected. But...." He cocked his head and leaned a little closer, then angled his light a different way. "What in the world...?" He retrieved a long tweezer and then was back, once more twisting his head, getting the lighting just right, as if he couldn't quite see whatever it was, and then he darted the tweezers inside and pulled something nearly microscopic and bloody out of Watson's mouth. He held it up between us, his eyes narrowed. "This was stuck in his gums. I'm not sure what it is."

I wasn't either.

After walking over to the sink, he filled a glass with water and then dipped the tweezers inside. He stirred it around, then pulled the object back out and returned it to the light between us. "I still have no idea."

"Neither do—" Dr. Sallee twisted the object slightly, and in so doing, the bright green of the shirt under his lab coat somehow reflected in it and I realized what it was. A shard from Noah and Jonah's garland. "It's fiberglass. It's from Christmas garland."

He looked puzzled but only for a second, and then his eyes grew wide. "Oh, that flashy kind that a couple of the stores have up this year?"

I nodded. "Exactly."

He grimaced. "Nasty stuff." He stroked Watson's head. "Who knows how long that's been floating around in there just waiting for the chance to get stuck. Better check and see if there's some more."

There were. Five other pieces. Three of them embedded, two caught in the folds of the skin of his inner cheek. The doctor also gave me a prescription that would help sweep away any fragments that might have entered Watson's digestive tract.

"Make sure he takes it easy tomorrow. And if you notice any changes at all, give me a call. I don't predict anything happening, not with that medicine, but if there should be any bleeding or he's not eating normally any time over the next three or four days, I want to know immediately. Even if it's Christmas. Strange that he'd get into that."

Watson was asleep on the passenger seat when I pulled in front of the house. After sliding the car into Park, I stared at the twenty feet between us and the front porch. When I first moved to Estes, I was still such a city girl that I let Watson have free rein in the yard, just like I had in Kansas City. Then Leo mentioned how common it was for pets to be snagged by mountain lions and other wildlife, sometimes when right beside their human. Since then, we used a leash from car to cabin. We'd removed his collar at the veterinary office, and the thought of putting it back on with those stupid scratchy pieces of garland possibly in his throat was more than I could bear. But I also wasn't willing to risk him walking by my side, this time of night especially.

I got out of the car, walked around to the passenger side, and cracked open the door so Watson wouldn't jump out if he woke up suddenly. Sure enough, his tired eyes opened and blinked at me. Wedging myself in, I opened the door a little farther, and wrapped my arms around him.

Watson let out an annoyed huff as I lifted him, offered a halfhearted squirm, and then stilled, allowing me to carry him. "Oh, baby. You really don't feel good, do you?" I was going to murder my brothers-in-law.

Once inside, I closed the door with my foot and gently carried him over and placed him by the armchair, intending to light a fire and sit with him.

Watson blinked again, looked around, and then stood. He gave a small stretch, and then padded off toward the bedroom. I followed. He curled up in his dog bed which was directly beside my four-poster. Then he let out a contented sigh.

That made me feel better. If he had an opinion of where he wanted to sleep at that moment, he at least felt well enough to be himself. I lay on the floor, curled up beside him as best I could, and softly stroked his fur. I intended to lull him to sleep, letting him know he wasn't alone. In less than two minutes, Watson glared at me through slitted eyes, gave a little huff, stood, and repositioned to lay the other direction.

Laughing, I placed a quick kiss on the top of his head. "Yup, you're going to be fine."

Even so, I knew sleep was a long way off. If it was going to come at all. The thoughts of fiberglass shards inside of him scared me to death. Thank goodness some had caught in his mouth, otherwise I might never have known until it was too late. I got onto the bed and curled on my side so I could keep watch over him.

I couldn't lose Watson. I just couldn't. He'd quite literally walked into my life at one of my darkest moments since my father's death. Came right up to me, shoved his little corgi forehead against mine as I knelt and sobbed, my hands covering my face. Looking back, it was such a completely un-Watson-like thing to do. From that moment on, things got better. I didn't have any notion that my father had been reincarnated into the form of a corgi or any such nonsense, but I did feel like Dad had given me a gift. A reminder he was watching, that he loved me.

It had been an added bonus that Watson possessed such a strong, and at times obstinate, personality. He was the kind of dog my father would've loved. He wasn't one to try to impress. If anything, he expected the opposite. It was up to the rest of the world to impress *him*. Dad would've liked that quality, and it only made me more certain that he'd picked Watson especially for me.

I couldn't lose Watson.

As I lay there watching him, I realized I was actually a little angry with him, not unlike times I'd felt after my father had been murdered. Those ridiculous moments where I raged at him for having the audacity of getting killed, for leaving me and Mom. And now Watson, so stubborn about not eating dog food, demanding human food in all its forms, had decided to eat the world's most deadly Christmas garland, of all things. It simply didn't make any sense. None.

Maybe if I had anything in my house or the shop, and some of it had broken off and fallen into his food and he hadn't realized... it would make sense. But I didn't have any of it. Maybe at my mother's and Barry's during family dinner? As soon as that thought entered, I let it go. That had been days before. He wouldn't still have pieces floating around in his mouth. It had to be fresh, had to be today.

Maybe it was in the pizza in the alley behind the toy store. They had the garland. Maybe they'd torn it all down and thrown it away and some had gotten into the pizza.

The answer was so obvious, and it crashed into me so hard, that I simultaneously felt stupid and stunned. Not the pizza.

The glove.

I sat up. The large workmen's glove Watson had been chewing on. The one with the red-stained pizza sauce on it.

I drummed my fingers on the duvet as I thought, each new notion crashing like another wave over me. What if it wasn't just pizza? What if it had been blood? I glanced down at Watson. He'd been chewing on the glove. If he'd gotten bits of the garland from the glove, then he just found what Declan's murderer had used to help strangle him.

By the dumpster? It seemed rather careless.

That part didn't matter. I was certain that was what it was. And right behind Bushy Evergreen's Workshop. It was the only thing needed to figure out which one of the Diamonds had killed Declan.

I called Branson. He didn't answer, so I left a voicemail. Then I texted him a few minutes later. I tried to call again.

After ten minutes, I couldn't take it anymore, and I called the station.

There was an answer after one ring. "Police, what is your emergency?"

"No emergency, but I have information on the Declan Diamond murder. Could I speak to Sergeant Wexler?"

There was a brief pause, and the clicking of keys. "I'm sorry, Sergeant Wexler's not on duty. But I'll get you through to the officer in charge of this case." Before I could protest, she put me on hold, and silence filled my ears, an occasional beep let me know the connection was still live. I had a sinking feeling about who was going to pick up. Sure enough, nearly three score of electronic beeps later, Susan Green's voice greeted my ears. "This is Officer Green. I hear you have information on the Diamond case."

I nearly hung up the phone. I had my thumb over the End Call button and then envisioned her tracing the call and how that would look. I lifted the phone back to my ear.

"Yes. I do. I think I discovered the glove the killer wore to be able to use the garland to strangle Declan."

She groaned. "Fred?"

"Yes. This is Fred."

"So you found a glove, huh?" I swore I could hear the eye roll. "Just one? Was this killer doing the moonwalk at the same time as the strangling?"

"Maybe there's two. I didn't check." I was surprised my voice was audible through my gritted teeth.

"Really? I thought you were better at police work than the rest of us. You know, the rest of us who are actually… *police.*"

"I never said that." Watson groaned in his sleep, and I realized my voice had risen. I didn't think I'd ever met anyone other than my ex-husband who could make me so angry so quickly. "May I speak to Branson… sorry, Sergeant Wexler?"

"What's wrong, Fred? Lovers' spat? He finally realize you're just as batty as the rest of your family and refused to take your calls?"

It was her soft chuckle that did it.

I saw red.

"You know what, that's exactly what happened." I ended the call.

Well, that was stupid. She'd just call back and then give me a hard time for hanging up on an officer of the law. How she'd ever earned such a title was beyond me. Although it wasn't, really. Cops like her had been the bane of my father's career.

I waited for her to call back. To my surprise, she didn't.

After a few moments of considering calling her, I pushed the thought aside. Even if she did actually listen to me, I didn't trust her to follow through on it, and if she did, she'd probably find some way to use it against Katie, my parents, or myself.

I could go get the glove. Easy enough. As I started to slide off the bed, Watson gave another moan in his sleep, this one seeming like he was having a pleasant dream.

No, I wasn't going to leave him, and I wasn't going to carry him back to the car. I wasn't going to risk anything happening to him. And chances were, the glove was fine. No one knew I'd seen it, and that alley was on the same side as my shop. Trash pickup wouldn't be for another three days.

Besides, Branson would call back. He'd listen.

Lying there, I nearly vibrated with excitement and nerves. One step closer to figuring out who killed Declan, one step closer to truly and completely clearing Katie's name. And though maybe I should be ashamed of the thought, one step closer to me figuring this thing out. The next thought, I was certain I should be ashamed of. I had a sense of disappointment knowing the glove was going to tell who killed Declan. Through DNA or some such. It seemed a little anticlimactic to me. I wanted to figure it out, not hand it over to science.

My stomach growled, reminding me that I hadn't eaten dinner in all the chaos. Quietly I got up and started making a grilled cheese. Before long, Watson padded into the kitchen, doubtless the smell of buttered bread in the skillet wafting into his dreams. Typically I would've given him some of my grilled cheese, but I didn't want to risk any chance of constipation, just in case he'd swallowed some of the shards. Instead, I simply toasted a slice of bread and gave it to him as I ate my sandwich. His snack was gone in two bites, and then he disappeared back into the bedroom. He was eating as voraciously as normal, another good sign.

My thoughts drifted back to Declan and the Diamonds. I felt like I had missed something. Something obvious. It wasn't surprising that the glove was behind the toyshop. Well, it was, for the killer to do something so careless, but even so, it only confirmed what I already suspected. The killer was right there. But which one? The betrayed father? The brother in love with his sister-in-law? The pregnant wife who discovered her husband was cheating?

Cheating. It was one piece of the puzzle.... Sarah Margaret Beeman.

Maybe she played more of a role than just that of the other woman.

At that thought, I left my crumb-filled plate on the kitchen counter, retrieved my laptop, and carried it back into the bedroom so I could keep an eye on Watson.

I situated myself against the headboard and propped the laptop on a couple of pillows in my lap, then opened Google and typed in Sarah Margaret Beeman. Might as well start with the simple and go from there.

I got nothing relevant, of course. There was an author with the name Margaret Beeman, an actress, a woman who worked with horses, but none close by and of an age that I thought would appeal to Declan. I narrowed it down to Colorado, still nothing.

I tried a couple of people-search websites, but they kept asking questions like—is Sarah Margaret Beeman related to so and so? Has Sarah Margaret Beeman ever lived at this address? Has Sarah Margaret Beeman ever been convicted of a felony? After hitting *I don't know* multiple times, I realized I was wasting my effort. That, and each one of them wanted me to put in a credit card number. Which I would've done if I thought it could help. But I didn't.

Even though I realized I was wasting time at this point,

I also knew I wouldn't be getting any sleep with as fast as my mind was racing. So I went with it. I just typed in Sarah. Like I suspected, nothing helpful came up. Too much came up. Including a list of nicknames. I had no idea women named Sarah were also called Sadie or Sal. How odd.

Odd, but not at all helpful.

Feeling like I was wasting time, I did a similar search on Sarah's middle name, more out of desperation than anything. As with Sarah, Margaret offered up more information than could ever be useful. The third link was to Wikipedia. I hesitated with the mouse over the link. Knowing that if any of my ex-professor colleagues found out I ever clicked on Wikipedia as an actual source, they would quite literally crucify me. Well, whatever. I clicked.

I discovered that Margaret was a French name originally, and then later English. Not helpful or even overtly interesting. But then there was a long list of nicknames. A few of which I had no idea how they could possibly come from the name Margaret. The last one of those was a name I knew. *Peggy*.

I stared at the name, my blood running cold just as the tingling over my skin increased. Peggy was a nickname for Margaret. I couldn't understand why, but there it was in black-and-white. So, it made sense that Peg would be as well.

Peg. Peg Singer. Not quite Peg Beeman, but I knew I'd found it. I was willing to bet Beeman was Peg's maiden name. Those two letters from the Denver law firm to Sarah M. Beeman. Sarah Margaret Beeman. In essence, to Peg Beeman. I was also willing to bet at least one of those had been in regards to Declan's will and the fate of the toyshop and the Diamond family. I'd quite literally handed over evidence to the killer.

Peg had killed Declan.

No sooner had the thought crossed my mind than I shook my head. It didn't make any sense. Why would Peg kill Declan for making her sole beneficiary? An image of her holding up my hoodie, nearly engulfed by the size, flitted to my mind. Peg couldn't have killed Declan. Not only did she not have the motive, but she quite literally couldn't. It would've been like a toy poodle killing a Doberman.

No, of course it wasn't Peg. It was Joe. Joe was every bit as big as Declan, bigger.

Joe had found out about the affair between his wife and Declan.

I texted Branson. *I know who killed Declan. Call me back.*

I woke up to the sun streaming through the bedroom window. I'd fallen asleep on top of the covers, and the computer upside down like a tent beside me. Watson peeked at me, only his pointy ears and chocolate eyes visible as he stood on his back legs, his two forepaws pounding on the mattress as he whined.

"For goodness' sake, Watson. Must you be so demanding every...." The night before came back to me, and I sat up straighter. Doing a little test, I lilted my voice in the same tone I often used when I said treat or walk. "Breakfast?"

Watson let out several deep, excited growls, plopped to the ground, and began to bounce on his two front paws like a bunny in his excited way.

The sight sent such relief through me I nearly cried. I slid off the bed and gathered him in my arms. "You're feeling better! You're really going to be fine, aren't you?"

The bark he gave next was a clear admonition, and he jerked himself free, giving me a side glare, then looking toward the bedroom door and beginning to bounce again.

Laughing, I stood up. "Yes, Your Majesty. Anything you

want since you're feeling better! You name it. Toast, a can of tuna? Prime rib?"

He let out two short impatient yips.

"Twice, huh? I'll take that to mean you want the second choice. Which is good. I don't actually have any prime rib." He pranced at my feet as I walked to the kitchen, nearly tripping me a billion times in the short distance. I don't think I ever enjoyed nearly falling so much.

Watson was almost through with his bowl of tuna when other aspects of the night before returned as well. I rushed back to the bedroom and snagged my phone. There was a message from Verona, and another from Katie. No missed calls, and nothing from Branson.

I called him again. Still no answer.

I considered calling the police. Susan wouldn't be back on duty this quickly, surely. But then I paused. I'd already tried the police. I'd attempted to do the responsible, regular citizen sort of thing. But it wasn't what I wanted to do.

Feeling much, much happier than I should about that, I brushed my teeth, threw on clothes, and pulled my hair into a ponytail quicker than I ever had in my life. I was so wide-awake, I didn't even need to stop at the Black Bear Roaster. Solving a murder was an even better wake-me-up than caffeine.

Still nervous to put a collar on Watson, despite him seemingly being back to normal, I carried him into the car. From his thrashing around, chances were high I was doing more damage than the collar ever would, but the die had been cast. And truly, from the way he was acting, by the time I closed the passenger door and received a murderous glare through the window, I figured the only thing I'd risked was matricide.

Just to make sure I could say that I truly had tried, I

texted Branson. *I know who killed Declan. I'm on my way to get the glove. Call me back.*

I'd just started the engine when I realized what I was forgetting. I hurried back into the cabin, grabbed a gallon-sized Ziploc bag, and then Watson and I were on our way.

When I attempted to pat Watson's head, he sniffed and turned around. Unwilling to give him the last word, I tickled his nubbed tail. He attempted to tuck it away but failed, causing me to giggle, and only dig my hole deeper.

The snow had fallen through the night, and it truly was a winter wonderland. If it had been another moment, I would've paused and enjoyed the sight of the herd of elk, steam rising from their nostrils, as I drove into town. It couldn't have been lovelier. The snow lay heavy on the branches, turning each one into a Christmas tree. The blanketing covered every building, house, and store, transforming Estes Park into a magical Christmas village as the snow sparkled in the glistening morning sun.

I giggled again at the thought, remembering the porcelain Christmas village under my grandmother's tree when I was a kid. How I'd lie on my stomach and watch the battery-powered ice-skaters twirl over the frosted-mirrored pond. Imagining what life would be like in such a magical place. It turned out, pretty murderous. At least much more than one would expect.

I giggled yet again. Watson deigned to inspect me over his shoulder. Clearing my throat, I focused on the road. Something was wrong with me that I was so excited about going to retrieve a murder weapon.

I parked just on the other side of the stream of the newly redone riverwalk. From the spot, I could see the alley that the toyshop and T-shirt place shared. I didn't attempt to pat Watson as I exited the car, though I did crack the windows slightly. He wasn't the only one who could play hard to get. "I'll be right back. You can't come on this one, but I won't be very long."

He'd been crossing the middle console onto the driver seat to hop out just as I closed the door, and once more he glared daggers at me from behind the window.

Swinging my purse on my shoulder, I left the parking lot, made my way over the little wooden bridge that crossed the narrow part of the river, and headed down the winding, mostly cleared, sandstone path. Halfway to the alley, I realized just how cold it actually was, which should have been a no-brainer, considering all the snow, but I'd been so excited I hadn't brought a coat. Whatever. I remembered the plastic bag, no... the *evidence* bag. That was much more important than being warm.

I strolled purposely across the space. There was no one about. And even if there was, I wasn't doing anything other than what people did all day long, every single day.

As I entered the alley, my heart rate increased, just a touch, despite there being no reason for concern. It was morning, bright out, and I wasn't doing anything suspicious.

Right... because I began every morning by digging through people's trash.

Standing in front of the snow-covered dumpster, which the white stuff somehow made look magical, I realized the other thing I'd forgotten. Gloves. Both for the cold in digging into the snow and to avoid my own prints from contaminating anything. Susan's voice mocked in my memory about her being the actual police.

I hated to prove her right, even for a second.

The solution was obvious enough. Retrieving the Ziploc bag from my purse, I turned it inside out, and used it for a combination glove and digging tool.

Thankfully, I didn't actually have to dig through the dumpster. The pizza Watson found had been on the side closest to the back doors. So I started sifting off snow from the right of the dumpster. I wasn't quite sure under which lump of white fluff it would be. The snow might be pretty, but it just turned everything into big, sparkling, indefinable lumps.

I dusted some off, revealing a couple of T-shirts and some broken toys. And then I found the pizza box. I had to be close. Although I couldn't remember once I'd pulled the glove out of Watson's mouth if I had flung it away. I didn't think so. I really should have tried to recreate that scene in my memory before walking into the alley.

I began to dust the snow away a little more frantically, it wasn't like the glove would break if I hit it. Something small and hard went flying and hit the back door to Rocky Mountain Imprints with a loud clank. I froze, waiting.

Nothing happened. I began flinging snow again, though with a little less vigor. An orange yo-yo went flying next, but didn't make any noise other things clattering across the ground. And then, there it was. The glove, now matted with snow and frozen stiff. I wrapped my Ziploc-gloved hand around it, picked it up, and then refolded the bag right side out, enclosing the evidence, and zipped it up in triumph. I looked at it, smiled, and gave a nod of approval. "Gotcha!"

"Fred! What are you doing?"

I jumped and let out an embarrassingly squeaky yelp, as I looked toward the voice. Peg was standing right outside the back door, her hand over her eyes as she squinted at me in the brightness.

My mouth moved silently for a second or two—or maybe an hour, who could tell?—then words came. Like magic. Totally bypassing my brain and all thought processes and spewing out of my mouth. "Watson got into something bad in here last night as we were leaving. I had to take him to the vet. Dr. Sallee suggested that if I could find out what it was, we'd have a better chance of helping him." Look at that. Not only words, but full sentences, good ones too. *Take that, Susan Green!*

"Oh, I'm so sorry, the poor dear." Peg's tone shifted from surprised to sympathy. "I hope it's nothing poisonous. I would just hate—" Her words fell away instantly, and she looked at the bag in my hands, her gaze returning to me, then back to the bag. "Fred, what have you got there?" All sympathy vanished, her tone was as cold as the snow.

Her reaction threw me off. She recognized the glove. Which meant, she knew. Obviously. But... *Peg knew?* "Just some material... um... there was some... ah... pizza sauce on it that he was eating. I thought maybe Watson had swallowed some of this...."

I was fairly certain Susan Green was laughing so hard that Peg was about to ask her to be quiet.

"Fred...." Peg took a step toward me, and I automatically backed one away from her. She paused, staring, and then to my surprise, darted back to the shop.

Relief flooded through me, though I continued backing up, feeling like I needed to keep my attention right where it was.

With a ferocity that shocked me, Peg burst back out the door. Her wild expression made it look like she should be screaming, but she wasn't. Only pure silence as she tore down the three steps, the baseball bat gripped in both hands and raised above her head as she flew toward me.

I spun on my heels and attempted to run, and slipped. Another idiotic mistake, me and my dumb cowboy boots, even in the snow. I caught myself before I fell and managed to move, just in time to feel the air brush past my head from the bat.

I ran, and I could hear her pounding footsteps right behind me. It was a losing game, and I knew it. I wouldn't be able to win a race against a sleeping hippopotamus, let alone little Peg Singer, or Sarah Margaret Beeman, whoever.... I ripped the purse off my shoulder and threw it back behind me, not bothering to look.

She let out a loud yell and there was a crash.

I dared to look back, and sure enough, she'd fallen, though I wasn't certain if it was due to getting tangled in the purse straps or simply hitting a patch of ice. Not that it mattered. No sooner had I glanced than she was getting back up. Peg started toward me, but her bat had skated away.

The tables had turned. I couldn't outrun her, but I could squash that little pixie like a bug.

She took two steps, paused, maybe seeing the expression in my eyes, and then darted back for the baseball bat.

And with that, it was back to running.

Thanks to the few yards she had to go to retrieve the bat, I made it through the trails, over the bridge, and into the car. Once more I was glad to have my burnt-orange little Mini Cooper. As long as the key was on me, which thankfully hadn't fallen out of the pocket of my broomstick skirt, the car automatically unlocked, and I pulled open the door, scaring Watson half to death. I hit Lock and slammed my foot on the brake to start the ignition.

A loud crash against the driver-side window caused both Watson and I to scream. The glass cracked in a myriad of spiderwebs, but didn't break fully. One more hit and it would. I shoved the gear in Reverse and hit the gas. As we pulled past her, Peg swung the bat again, managing to take out a headlight.

As soon as we were clear, I shifted into Drive and stomped on the gas again. I spared a glance in the rearview mirror. To my surprise, I didn't see her.

Just as I reached the end of the parking lot and started to turn onto the street, there was a loud rumble, and a huge four-by-four truck backed out between the cars.

I didn't wait to make sure. Flooring it, I zoomed onto the street, and within half a block reached the main intersection of downtown. Another glance in my rearview revealed Peg pulling out of the parking lot, her truck's rear tires fishtailing. Hitting the gas again, I took a right turn at the lights, praying no tourists were jaywalking and about to get plowed down. Luck was on our side.

For one crazy second, I couldn't think where to go, then for an even crazier one, I decided to go to my house.

Watson whimpered in the passenger seat, and I spared him a glance. "It's okay, buddy. It really is. It going to be okay."

Lies, lies, lies. Of all the injustices I'd done to Watson that morning, this was the only true one.

And then the obvious hit me. The police station. I didn't care if Susan Green was there or not. It could be filled with fifteen billion Susan Greens, and it would still be the place to go. Now I simply needed to outmaneuver a huge four-by-four truck.

No problem. Running, I couldn't do. Drive like I was a stunt double in *The Italian Job*? Piece of cake.

Thankfully the police station was less than half a mile away, so I wouldn't have to truly test my skills for too long. I tore through the next intersection, running a red light, but it was early enough in the day that there were no cars or pedestrians in the way.

My phone rang, lighting up the center display of the Mini Cooper. Announcing Branson Wexler was calling.

Men had the best timing.

I hit Accept on the steering wheel as I whipped around a spot of ice glistening in the sunlight.

"Fred. I'm so sorry. I just saw your messages. What—"

"Shut up!" I was aware of my screaming, and I was also aware that there was no other way I could do it right then. Poor Watson was howling in the passenger seat. "I'm bringing Peg into the station, right now. She's the killer, I think. At least she's trying to kill me."

"What are you—"

"I said shut up!" I could see the police station now, coming up on the left. "I'm almost there. If you're in there, come outside. If not, call them and let them know I'm coming." What a ridiculous thing to say. Like I was going to wait on Branson to come get me from the car, or that he'd have time to call if he wasn't there before I came peeling in.

Peg's engine roared behind us. I spared another glance and saw the massive chrome of her grill growing larger. Another ten seconds and she'd plow right over us.

"Fred, slow down. You're not making—"

"Shut up!" Without a moment to spare, we reached the turnoff to the police station. I cranked the wheel to the left, and was airborne for a second as I hit the curb. Watson let out another loud, mournful howl.

Although probably stupid, I spared a second glance, and saw Peg's truck zoom by, then noticed her making a similar motion on the steering wheel, and the truck began to turn, once again fishtailing and nearly going out of control.

I slammed the car into Park right in front of the police

station doors, managing to dart my hand out just in time to keep Watson seated, then scooped him up, grabbed the glove, and darted from my car.

Branson was saying something over the speakers.

Watson was so frazzled, he didn't even resist.

"Help!" I burst through the front doors of the police station, scaring the officer at the front desk, judging from the cup of coffee that went flying. "She's trying to kill us."

Just as I reached the desk, I turned around in time to see Peg's truck fly past the police station.

I pointed after her and looked over at the wide-eyed officer. "You're probably going to wanna chase her down."

"Merry Christmas Eve Eve." Branson held up his glass of wine between us and waited patiently for the awkwardly long amount of time it took me to realize I needed to raise my own glass in cheers.

"Merry Christmas Eve Eve." I clinked our glasses together, and then we both took a sip. I wasn't a wine connoisseur, but this was better than any I'd had before, full of earthiness and spice. A perfect holiday wine. Considering it was about three hundred a bottle, it should have tasted like gold. It wasn't that good.

Branson set his wineglass down, interlaced his fingers, and propped his elbows on the tabletop. "You seem distracted, everything okay?"

I knew the correct answer was *Yes, I am fine, just a little flustered from Watson and I nearly being run over earlier that morning.* Instead I was honest. "I feel a little out of place. I've driven by here several times, and judging from the outside and the name, I never would've guessed it was so fancy in here." The candlelit interior of shiny dark wood and brushed steel reminded me of some of the more exclusive restaurants on the Plaza.

"Well, I will admit that the name *Pasta Thyme* doesn't

overly evoke a fine-dining expectation." His gaze traveled over me. Not uncomfortably, but only heightening my lack of preparation and appearance. "Trust me, Fred, you're the furthest thing from out of place. You look beautiful."

No, I didn't. The one thing I had going for me was Percival's lessons about dramatic cat eye and a subtle lip gloss. Other than that, I looked like I did every other day. Tangerine peasant blouse, faded turquoise broomstick skirt, and white cowboy boots. At least the boots had silver tips on the toes to match my dangling silver earrings. Thank goodness, I'd managed to actually put on earrings again. I hadn't even done anything with my hair, just left it flowing free, though I was fairly certain I combed it.

Branson, on the other hand, was the epitome of beauty. He could've stepped out of any movie from the fifties. I was on a date with Rock Hudson in a classic black suit, cranberry shirt, and an emerald-green tie. A Rock Hudson, who was evidently truly interested in me and not secretly wondering if I had a brother at home.

No, not a date. After wrapping up with Peggy that afternoon, Branson had called and suggested we get dinner and he'd fill me in on how everything had worked out.

A tuxedoed waiter appeared from thin air with some silver scraper thing and dusted breadcrumbs from the tablecloth around my plate. He didn't have to do that for Branson—none of his crumbs had made a run for it.

Tuxedoed waiter.

Suit-clad Rock Hudson.

In the center of the table was a small yet lavish bouquet of a solitary poinsettia bloom in the midst of sprigs of holy and silver sticks.

Yeah, date. Whether I wanted it to be that or not.

I couldn't bring myself to respond to the 'me looking

beautiful' comment, so I turned things to where I was the most comfortable. "So, she admitted it? Peg was the one who actually killed Declan?"

"She did." If Branson was disappointed in the shift of the conversation, he didn't let on.

"She admitted to both? Attacking him at the toy store and at the hospital?"

"Sure did."

"Huh." Ridiculously, disappointment flitted through me. I hated being wrong.

Apparently my emotions were on my sleeve, and Branson chuckled. "You thought it was her husband?"

"I did. I thought he found out about their affair. And I couldn't imagine little Peg being able or strong enough to hurt Declan to begin with." Thoughts of my poor beat-up Mini Cooper flashed through my mind, causing me to let out a chuckle. "Although, now I understand how she was able to get all those softball trophies. She's got quite an arm."

"That she does." Branson took another sip of wine. "I'm actually surprised that poor wooden nutcracker was in one piece from how hard she can swing. It was no wonder Declan was in a coma."

That part had been bugging me all day. "So why the garland? If she'd already hit him, why stop?"

He tilted his glass of wine toward me. "You've got a sharp mind, Fred. You really do. I asked her that myself. She wasn't able to give an answer. I don't think even she understood it. But my guess is our little Peg Singer, or Sarah Margaret Beeman, doesn't really have the heart of a killer. Hitting someone once is one thing, bashing them repeatedly is another. And though I'm sure she didn't account for that garland to end up so bloodied, using it to strangle is a little less visceral than beating her lover to death. As for what she did at the hospital? She could've smothered him with a pillow, but putting air in his line, she didn't even have to touch him."

It made sense. Although she seemed more than willing to bash me to death with that baseball bat. Then again, she and I hadn't been having an affair.

The waiter returned and refilled my glass of wine. I hadn't realized I'd drank it so fast. It went down smoothly, too smoothly, and I was nervous, not a good combo. I started to take another sip and then pushed it away. I didn't drink very often, which meant I was a lightweight, and I was going to stay in control on this date, or whatever it was.

Somehow the emerald of Branson's tie caused the green of his eyes to nearly glow.

I pushed the wine a little farther away. "And Joe didn't know?"

For the first time, Branson winced. "That was the hardest part of the day. I'll admit, it's difficult to see a man like Joe, one so big and strong, completely break. He was devastated. He didn't know about the affair. Not a good Christmas for him. Discovering his wife had been cheating and that he was married to a murderer all in one fell swoop."

I hadn't even considered that. And I'd thought discovering Garrett's affair and ending our marriage had been bad. At least he hadn't been a murderer or a dirty cop.

I'd have to go check on Joe. Let him know.... Let him know what? That was a stupid impulse. I was certain I would be the last person he'd want to see. "Did she explain why she killed Declan? Why she attacked him to begin with? I can't understand."

Another wince. "Peg remained steadfast for over an

hour in her interview. Wouldn't admit to anything. Then I brought Joe in. Everything fell apart in that moment, for both of them. And fell into place for me." He leveled his gaze on mine. "Affair aside, she loved her husband. She really did. The minute he broke, so did she. And if I had any doubts left about her being able to kill Declan, her fury at him, even still, would have convinced me." He paused as the waiter returned to refill our waters. "She'd tried to end their affair. But Declan wouldn't have it. He was convinced she was going to leave Joe, which, I think had been the original plan, though Peg never fully admitted to that part. That's why Declan was going to leave Daphne. He truly believed he and Peg were going to be together. It seems he was almost delusional about it. That's why he'd done the documents in her maiden name. He was that certain she was leaving Joe. When Peg got the updated version of Declan's will, it was the last straw. It sent her into some sort of rage."

Horror washed over me. "That's what did it? Her reading the will?"

Branson nodded, his gaze concerned. "Yes. Why?"

I took a steadying breath and gripped the edge of the table. "I think I'm the one who gave her that. A couple of letters had been misdelivered to me. It seems that happens all the time. Both of them were from a Denver law firm."

Branson reached across the table, placed his hand over mine, and gave a gentle squeeze. "None of this is your fault, Fred. You just returned the letter to where it was sent."

I realized that of course, but still, it was like I'd placed the nutcracker in Peg's hand.

The waiter arrived, sliding our plates of food in front of us, then grating fresh Parmesan over the tops.

I glowered at my plate of creamy sausage tagliatelle.

The dish had been thirty dollars, and the portion was roughly half the size of a bowl of spaghetti anywhere else.

"You're going to die when you taste this." Branson smiled at me, then plunged his fork into one of his gnocchi. Thankfully he hadn't seemed to notice my reaction.

Following suit, I skewered a thick noodle and swirled it, then took a bite. I shuddered, literally. I glanced down at my plate in shock, then back up at Branson.

"Told you." His grin turned wicked. "All the pasta is housemade. I'm only going to take you to the best places, Fred."

I was speechless, both to his statement and in the pure divine that was happening in my mouth. The wine was most definitely not worth three hundred dollars, but I would've paid thirty dollars a bite, if need be, to experience the pasta again.

Both because I couldn't think of a response to his claim and being completely overwhelmed by flavor, I made some sort of awkward sound of agreement and took another bite. It was just as good as the first.

The next several minutes were lost to the pleasure of food and the discovery of their garlic bread, also housemade, rivaling the pasta. Gradually, thoughts of Peg began to tumble over the exquisiteness of the meal and my nerves around Branson.

"I think the only other thing I don't understand is the glove. Why in the world would she be so careless just to toss it by the dumpster in the alley outside her store?"

Branson chewed a few more seconds, swallowed, then wiped his mouth, though it hadn't seemed to need it. "Katie truly did interrupt her. Peg dashed out the back of the toy store, tossed the glove, and hurried into the T-shirt shop, just in case whoever had interrupted her came into her store to get help. It would've been a fairly perfect alibi." He shrugged and gave an almost sympathetic wince. "But Peg said she went back to find it and couldn't. Finally decided an animal had carried it off. Personally, that's the one part of the story I don't understand. If it were me, I would've torn that place apart. There's no way I would've missed finding those gloves." He shrugged again, just one shoulder that time. "Although, we tore it apart this afternoon, and we never found the second one."

Despite the situation, I laughed a little. "I can see that. I don't know how many times I've lost my keys or my cell phone, and nearly destroyed the house in the search only to find them in the exact place I'd looked countless times before."

"Maybe so, but your keys or cell phone couldn't help prove that you'd murdered someone."

"True." I really could understand that happening. "Just more proof that I shouldn't go around killing people. Something like that would totally happen to me."

Branson snorted, and somehow made the garish noise sound classy. "Really? You have a hit list going that I should know about?"

I shook my head, though Officer Green flitted through my mind. As did my ex-husband and my ex-best friend turned ex-business partner. No, those two flitted away instantly. It was thanks to them that I'd made the choices I did and ended up in Estes Park, and I was grateful for that. It took a little more effort to erase Susan's name from the list, however. "No. I don't commit murders. I just solve them." I couldn't help myself.

Branson didn't laugh. If anything, I could've sworn his gaze grew a little heated. "That you do, Winifred Page. That you do."

I plunged my fork back to the plate, ready to twirl around more noodles, only to discover it was empty. Branson must've seen the disappointment over my face as he laughed. I grinned up at him sheepishly. "Don't you hate it when you don't realize that you're done and go for that last, delicious bite only to discover you've already had it?"

He winked. "Their portions aren't exactly huge. We can order a second round."

Santa help me, but I almost said yes. Then remembered I had some pride. "No, that portion was perfect."

Branson's eyes narrowed. "You're aware I can tell when you lie to me, right?"

"I don't know what you're talking about."

"Sure you don't." He took his final bite, chewed, swallowed, and then needlessly wiped his mouth again. "Dessert, then. They're simple and unfussy, but their tiramisu and cannoli are the best I've ever had."

I could only imagine the price tag on those, and I felt the sting of guilt at realizing how much Branson was going to pay for a night he considered a date and one that I was unwilling to label. But the best tiramisu and cannoli he'd ever had? I couldn't say no to that. And as guilty as I felt about leaving Watson at home, without him here, I wouldn't have to share.

Branson ordered the desserts, and though I couldn't tell what words he was about to say, there was a spark, a change in his demeanor, and I couldn't let him go wherever he was about to go.

"So where were you? I tried to call and text last night and this morning." I smiled to let him know I wasn't angry and tried to include in the expression an apology for stopping whatever was about to happen the second before. "Not that you need to stay by your phone for me, but I truly did try to do the right, proper citizen sort of thing."

What I thought was disappointment flitted across his face, but it was gone quickly, and when he laughed, it didn't sound forced. "You're not attempting to cause me to feel bad for making it possible for this whole thing to go exactly how you would've wanted."

He really did have my number. "I didn't imply anything of the kind, and I definitely didn't say you needed to feel bad. I was merely asking. You just got back from being out of town for a couple of weeks, on a trip you said wasn't exactly a vacation, but not exactly work. Same thing last night and this morning?"

For the first time, he looked uncomfortable, and maybe a touch... panicked? Whatever it was, it was gone in a flash and his easy charm returned. "Yes. Something like that again."

I waited for a second, thinking he was going to continue, then realized that was the only answer I was going to get. Which was fine. He didn't owe me one, especially since we weren't on a date. Even if we kind of were.

But for whatever reason, that hesitation allowed a thought of Leo, his warm, honey-brown eyes, and his deep, soft voice to flash into my mind.

Nope. That wasn't happening either.

"And you're right, Sergeant Wexler. I'm glad things went down just as they did." For whatever reason, it seemed like I was mostly an open book to Branson, so I only hesitated for a second before deciding to ask what I really wanted to know. "Did you happen to run into Officer Green today? I was wondering if she had any... thoughts about the situation."

He chuckled, this time the sound fully heated, and

there was that spark again. "You might be on the right side of the law and have an uncanny knack for solving murders, Fred, but you've got just a touch of wickedness in you."

I shook my head. "Not true. Not at all. Just ask my mother. She'll tell you."

"Then she'd be wrong." Branson once more lifted his glass of wine my way. "And I'm glad of it."

Before he'd finished his sip, our tiramisu and cannoli were delivered. And I discovered that if I'd been willing to pay thirty dollars a bite for the pasta, I'd have to triple that for the desserts.

SEVENTEEN

Watson and I spent Christmas Eve finishing the nonfiction room. Watson didn't so much shelve books as nap, snore, and occasionally beg for treats, but just having him act fully like himself was more than enough help. Katie kept calling from Denver, wanting more measurements on the floor space of the kitchen. I had a feeling she was spending a small fortune—possibly a gargantuan fortune—on equipment. Percival and Gary brought down the Victorian sofa and lamp and arranged them by the river rock fireplace. Even though I hadn't started on shelving any of the mystery books, it was the only confirmation I needed to prove that it truly was going to be my favorite nook in the store.

By the time the sun set at a little after four in the afternoon and the streetlamps and Christmas lights twinkled on outside the window, I finally got up the nerve to do what had been in the back of my mind all day.

Remembering my coat and gloves, and feeling safe enough to not only put a collar and leash back around Watson's neck but also a green snowflake-patterned scarf, we made our way up the street, and with a deep breath, walked into Bushy Evergreen's Workshop.

As before, the smells of Christmas filled the toyshop,

and somehow left me feeling cozy, even though I was intimately aware of what had happened in that cheerful place. The piped-in music played a soft version of "Baby, It's Cold Outside." The only things different were the lack of the sparkling garland and the lack of a handsome man at the counter.

Dolan and Daphne smiled a greeting from their place behind the counter as Watson and I rounded a tall tower of toys and came into view. Both of their smiles faltered for just a second but quickly slid back into place. Dolan's hand was covering Daphne's, and even when I noticed, they didn't pull apart.

"Hi. I needed to do some last-minute Christmas shopping." I couldn't seem to get a handle on my nerves. "Is it okay if I do that here?"

Dolan's smile changed, becoming a little more sincere, and though he would never be a head turner, I could see what everyone had meant. There was such genuine kindness and gentleness, that in truth, he was twice as attractive as his brother. "You'll always be welcome at Bushy's. We're in your debt."

It took me a second to figure out what to say. I most definitely hadn't expected that. "No. You're really not."

Daphne shook her stunningly beautiful head. "Yes, we are. Sergeant Wexler made it very clear that it was you who figured things out. Believe me, we were very aware of what everyone thought had happened."

I made a mental note to thank Branson for not mentioning that I too suspected them of killing Declan. "I lucked into it more than anything." I nodded down at Watson. "Really, it was his penchant for constantly looking for food that discovered the missing puzzle piece. Not me."

The sound of a throat being cleared caused all three of

us to look toward the rear of the store. Old Duncan Diamond shuffled from the back and held something out to me. He didn't smile, and it was clear from his bloodshot eyes that he'd spent countless hours over the past several days weeping. "I thought it was you. I made you this to say—" His voice broke, and he gave a small shake of his outstretched hand.

I took the object he offered, held it up for inspection, and gasped. The carved figurine was less than two inches tall and three inches long but a near-perfect replica of Watson. It was unpainted, but had been varnished a shiny golden brown.

Percival and Gary had filled me in on the gossip when they delivered the furniture. Declan's will had left everything to Peg. But considering the circumstances, Joe had Gerald Jackson give it back over to Duncan. Gerald had handled the paperwork, so of course, Percival and Gary somehow thought he'd worked a miracle.

I stared at the beautiful corgi in my hand and felt my eyes burn. I didn't deserve it. It was clear they felt they owed me a thanks for giving them their life back.

They didn't.

Knowing that if I said anything to Duncan the tears really would come, I knelt and held the figurine out to Watson. "Look, buddy. It's you."

He sniffed it, then gave it a quick lick. For him, that was the height of being impressed.

I stood back up and clutched it to my heart, and though it was a horrible thought, I felt like Duncan had given me something that ensured I would always have Watson with me, forever. My gaze met his, and I attempted to say thank you, but failed.

His lips turned into a small, sad smile.

He understood.

I sniffed and glanced over at Daphne and Dolan, just in time to catch Dolan pulling his hand away from where it had rested on Daphne's flat stomach. And though it was only a hunch, I would've bet everything that the father of Daphne's baby was right there in that shop.

Just when I thought I was going to lose it and actually start to cry, the piped-in music switched, and a version of "Jingle Bells" with dog barks autotuned to match the melody began to play. Watson barked along, loudly and utterly off-key.

And the spell broke, which was both a little sad and a relief.

Daphne smiled, and her voice was soft and content. "I believe you said you had some Christmas shopping to do?"

"We're having to pull the garland from the market. There are over fifteen lawsuits pending." Noah had the audacity to sound baffled as he lamented to Barry while the men set the table for the Christmas meal. Mom and the twins were both cooking away in the kitchen. They'd kicked me out over an hour ago. So, as normal, I was with the boys.

Jonah sounded just as flummoxed. "We even had on the packaging to wear gloves. It's like people don't know how to read."

"Yes, it's the most shocking thing I've ever heard." Percival rolled his eyes and gave a stage whisper to Gary. "Who would ever think Christmas decorations that could double for murder weapons you might find in a game of Clue would ever lead to litigation?"

Looking utterly offended, Noah opened his mouth to retort, but I jumped in quickly. "Could the lawsuits hurt you? Take your homes or anything?" As much as I'd ended up despising that garland, I knew they'd never had any malintent.

Jonah scoffed and waved away the concern as if it was nothing. "Nah. Our insurance is good. And our lineup of products we're launching starting in January is strong enough that even if the lawsuits are more than we anticipated, we'll be fine."

"Well, I loved it." Barry shook his head empathetically. "But we had to get rid of it. Anything that hurt Watson has to go." He turned and squatted down, making eye contact with Watson, who'd been sleeping across the room. "Don't we, boy? You come first, don't you?" Barry's Christmas outfit consisted of a red-and-green tie-dyed tank top with a penguin wearing reindeer antlers on the front, over baggie fuchsia-and-orange tie-dyed yoga pants. I wasn't sure if it was the clashing combination or his hairy back showing from the tank top as he held out his arms toward Watson that caused my eyes to burn.

It seemed that dogs truly were colorblind, as Watson sprang from his nap and launched himself at rocket speed into Barry's arms.

In the corner of the room, by the Christmas tree now decorated with boring everyday garland, my four nieces and nephews played with their new toys, each electronic. They'd been allowed to open one when they arrived, the rest would come after the feast. I almost hated for them to open what I brought. I couldn't imagine any of them were going to be overly excited about all the hand-carved toys they were about to receive. Maybe when they got home, they'd toss them in a chest, forget about them, and in thirty years discover them again and see them as timeless heirlooms. Maybe.

Mom popped her head out of the kitchen, glanced around, then spotted me. "Dear, would you call Katie again? If she's much later, dinner is going to get cold. We're just about ready."

"I called her less than five minutes ago, Mom. She said she would be here soon." Mom was insanely easygoing, except for when she cooked. It was time to eat as soon as it was ready. It was hot and fresh, or not at all. "If need be, we can start before she gets here."

"Never. Not in a million years would we do that to lovely Katie." Mom looked scandalized. She disappeared back into the kitchen, but her voice carried over the Christmas carols playing in the background. "But call her again, would you?"

I was the one who'd opted to move back to be with family.

Acquiescing, I lifted my cell. At that moment, there was a knock on the door. I hurried over and threw it open. "Thank goodness. My mother was about to turn me into your stalker."

"Sorry about that. I just couldn't force myself to quit decorating this morning." She held up a tray covered with a silver dome that had melted snowflakes trailing down its etched surface. She shoved it toward me. "Take this, will you? But don't drop it or make it too off-center, I spent hours on that thing."

"Oh, great. No pressure." I took the tray, which was lighter than it appeared.

Katie shut the door behind her, and hurried over to me. I'd been carrying it to the kitchen, but she stopped me in the middle of the living room. "Here, I can't wait for you to see." Without any warning, she lifted the lid with a flourish and revealed her dessert.

"A gingerbread house! It's..." Confusion flitted through me, then I understood. For the second time in less than twenty-four hours, I gasped and felt my eyes stinging. "Oh, Katie. It's... just perfect."

It was a gingerbread *dog*house, the sides slanted to form a hexagon shape, with an arched doorway in the front outlined in peppermints. Little candies shaped like red balls rimmed the four edges of the house while multicolored, sugarcoated jelly-orange slices framed the outline of the front. A little green wreath complete with red berries of icing hung over the doorway. Snow piled up around the golden foil landscape and on the roof as icicles hung delicately from the edge. A small path curved from the open front door, lined with more red candies and... I cocked my head as one more detail snapped into place.

"Are those dog bones?" Percival sounded scandalized.

A second later Barry let out a gasp of his own and clapped his hands. "They are!"

Sure enough dog bones standing on end made a fence of sorts leading up the curved path and also outlined the edges of the roof.

Gary was nearby and walked over as he let out a low whistle, then gave an appreciative glance toward Katie. "Girl, if that's any indication, you're going to make a fortune in that bakery or yours." He raised his voice. "Phyllis, Verona, Zelda, get out here. You've gotta see this."

"Not if she puts dog treats on her desserts." Though I was fairly certain that Percival had meant to whisper, his comment earned him a swift elbow in the side from Gary.

For once, Mom quit worrying about getting dinner on the table as soon as it was done. And for several minutes, the entire family gathered around the gingerbread doghouse, oohing, aahing, and lavishing endless praise on Katie.

She was as red as any light-up nose on Rudolph I'd ever seen, and looked utterly pleased. "Show Watson. It's in honor of him, obviously."

"Watson." I knelt as I called him over.

As ever, when he knew I had food in hand, he rushed over like he lived to do my bidding.

I held it out to him, close enough that it was on my level, but far enough away that no dog hair could fix itself to the icing.

He stared at it, wide-eyed, gave a sniff, and then lunged, taking out a good fourth of the gingerbread doghouse and several of the dog treat fence posts with one shark-like bite.

The entire family screamed, and I stood quickly, trying to get it out of harm's way as if the damage hadn't already been done. Totally guilt ridden, I turned to Katie. "I'm so, so sorry."

If anything, her smile had gotten bigger, and she beamed. "Good! He liked it!"

Mom gaped at her. "Sweetheart, we all love Watson, but you spent forever on that."

Katie's brows knitted, and she looked utterly baffled as she glanced from Mom to me. "No, that was for Watson. Obviously I'm not going to serve you dog treats." She gestured with her thumb toward the door. "I made decorated gingerbread men, lemon meringue pie, and a pumpkin-carrot cake for the rest of us. It's all out in the car."

"Hallelujah and Merry Christmas, Tiny Tim!" Percival raised his hand in the air. "After a meal that includes a meatless roast, which might be worse than actual dog bones, I'm going to be craving a dessert smorgasbord!" He threw his arm around Katie. "Welcome to the family. You're stuck with us! Unless you used some kind of sugar substitute, then you're out."

A Cozy Corgi Mystery
Bickering Birds
MILDRED ABBOTT

BICKERING BIRDS

A COZY CORGI MYSTERY

Mildred Abbott

"You can do this. You've been preparing for months. This isn't a big deal. You've done plenty of things much scarier." The reflection in the bathroom mirror squinted, obviously not believing the words. I couldn't blame her.

I shook my head, trying to clear it, and attempted to infuse my tone with more confidence. "You were a professor, started your own publishing company, and faced your crazy mother-in-law on your wedding day. This is nothing." The only thing the headshake accomplished was making my auburn hair frizz slightly so a strand became caught on my lip-gloss. I pulled it free. Leaning closer to the mirror, I sighed. A hunk of mascara was stuck in the corner of my eye. After retrieving a square of toilet paper, I fixed that without managing to mess up the half an hour of work I'd done on my face. I was tempted to wipe it all off. I hated wearing makeup, but I knew my uncle would comment if I arrived at my own opening night looking like it was just another day.

With another glare at my reflection, I thought I could hear the Winifred Page inside the glass whisper about how I left my years of teaching behind without looking back, got betrayed by my partner in our publishing company, and had been divorced for six years—negating any sense of accomplishment I might feel from those endeavors.

I straightened to my full five-ten height, squared my broad shoulders, and lifted my chin defiantly. "Well, maybe so, but I've solved two murders lately, and have successfully turned a run-down taxidermy shop into the most charming bookstore in the entire world. I've got this."

Before my mirror twin could offer further commentary, I threw open the bathroom door. In my haste, I nearly stepped on one of Watson's forepaws with my cowboy boots. He chuffed in annoyance but didn't bother to move. A corgi was the official breed of the Queen of England—I'd made the mistake of telling Watson that at some point, and clearly it had gone straight to his head. He was royalty, and he knew it.

"Sorry about that, buddy." I bent slightly and ruffled the ginger fur between his ears. "Although I think it's your fault. You haven't been downstairs to see me once today. But if you're waiting for me outside the bathroom, it means you want something." I stepped around him and went to the main section of the bookshop, Watson's claws clattering over the hardwood floor behind me.

I paused, taking another breath. The sight of the Cozy Corgi finally complete did more to soothe my nerves than arguing with my reflection.

In the early January evening, night had fallen outside the large picture windows, and the gleaming hardwood floors, bookcases, and ceiling nearly glowed in comparison. The bookshop was laid out like a house, with a large center space surrounded by rooms and nooks around the perimeter. A couple of rooms had their own river rock fireplaces.

It was the bookshop of my dreams. Maybe I truly did have this.

A loud metallic clang sounded above the soft jazz piped in over the speakers, followed by muttered curses.

"Come on." I motioned to Watson but didn't bother to look back. "Let's go check on Katie. I'm pretty sure that's where you want me to go anyway."

I walked over to the large staircase in the center of the space and headed upstairs. The appearance of the Cozy Corgi was as wonderful as I had imagined. The aroma of fresh-baked goodness wafted over the entire store—an aspect I'd neither planned on nor wanted, but it seemed like the icing on the cake, or the glossy cover on the book. Something....

In the weeks since Katie had decided to open her bakery on the top floor of my bookshop, the upstairs, originally an apartment, had been remodeled. A couple of walls had been removed, and most of the place was now open concept, with Katie's brand-new state-of-the-art kitchen glistening in all its shiny glass and stainless steel glory.

For a second, I didn't see Katie at the pastry-laden counter, but then her round face topped with her mass of curly brown hair popped up from behind. She let out a gasp. "Oh, Fred! You startled me." Her gaze traveled behind, landing on Watson. "I'm glad he was with you. I just dropped an entire tray of dog bones. If he'd been up here, he would've eaten all thirty of them before I had a chance to scoop them up." She laid a baking sheet piled with dog treats on the counter.

I glared down at Watson. "I knew there was a reason you came to see me. It wasn't for support, but permission."

Nonplussed, Watson trotted past me and plopped down in front of the bakery counter. It still amazed me that Katie had somehow managed to train him to not go into the cooking space. Although, I was certain the amount of baked bribery had something to do with it.

"I can't believe you took the time to make Lois's recipe for all-natural dog treats. It's opening night. The last thing you should be thinking about is Watson."

Katie scurried around the counter and tickled Watson's fox-like ears. "Don't say such a thing. The place is called the Cozy Corgi. Watson is the star."

By way of response, Watson lay, rolled over, and waited expectantly for Katie to rub his stomach.

She obliged.

Watson was one of the most reserved dogs I'd ever met, and there were few people he seemed to go crazy over. Katie wasn't one of the people he adored on principle, but he'd most definitely come to believe she was there to serve him.

"Do you mind if he has one?" She finished scratching Watson and stood, already reaching for one of the massive dog treat bones, certain of my response.

"Goodness knows I've come up here enough times to sample everything you've done today. It would be rather hypocritical to deny him." I spared another glance around the space. Katie's bakery was a perfect match to the book-shop below. Somehow, she'd successfully blended old antique tables with rustic log chairs, and intermingled some of the spaces with overstuffed couches. Despite my claims to the mirror, I wasn't entirely sure I was prepared for my undertaking, but I was certain Katie was. I had no doubt she was born to be a baker.

"You doing okay?" Katie walked over to me, capturing my attention. "You look like you're going to be sick."

"Just nervous. But I'll be fine." I pulled out my cell from the pocket of my broomstick skirt and glanced at the time. "Five minutes. You ready?"

Katie squealed in way of response, threw her arms around me, and pulled me down into a hug. "This is going to be the best night ever!"

"Fred, darling, it's perfect. All of it. Absolutely perfect." Mom reached out and squeezed my hand. "It is you. It's just so you."

"That it is." My uncle, Percival, took me by my shoulders and angled me toward him. "The question is, are you *you*?" He looked over at his husband, Gary, and widened his eyes. "We need to call that handsome sergeant Fred's been dating, let him know someone body-snatched our niece. This woman's wearing foundation and blusher."

Gary rolled his eyes and offered me his kind, bright smile. "You look lovely, Fred. But then again, you always do."

I shoved Percival off. "You are a pain. And I'm not dating Branson. We've only gone to dinner a couple of times."

Barry arrived as if out of thin air, waving one of Katie's ham-and-cheese croissants in the air. "Have you all had these yet? That woman is a miracle worker." My stepfather tore off a piece and tossed it to Watson, who was cavorting at his feet. Barry was one of the few my corgi truly did lose his mind over, even when food wasn't involved. "I left Zelda and Verona up there. I'm pretty sure they're clearing out everything Katie has in stock."

"I have to agree with you. Katie is a bit of a miracle worker. And that says a lot coming from someone who didn't even want a business partner up until a couple of weeks...." My brain caught up with my mouth, and I gaped at Barry before jerking the croissant out of his hands.

Though he looked surprised, Barry shrugged and grinned at me. "All you had to do was ask, love. You know what's mine is yours."

"No!" I shook the croissant at him. "This is her ham-and-cheese croissant. *Ham*, Barry! Ham!"

Mom sucked in a gasp, while Percival let out a near screech of a laugh, causing some of the customers milling about the bookstore to look over at us.

Barry plucked the croissant right back out of my hands. "Nope. She made a batch with meatless veggie ham slices, just for me."

"Oh, for crying out loud." Percival groaned and visibly deflated. "I thought we were finally putting an end to this vegetarian fad."

Mom gave a gentle slap to her brother's arm. "I think after twenty years, we can rest assured it's not simply a fad."

I let the comfort of their bickering fade away to background noise as I watched the people milling about the Cozy Corgi. There was a good turnout. Not only that, people seemed to be lingering. I'd feared they'd take one trip around the store and then leave. But people were spread out over the couches and chairs in all the different rooms, some of them eating Katie's pastries as they perused books.

My eyes stung, and I blinked away tears. Since I'd moved to Estes Park from Kansas City, there'd been several moments of confirmation that I'd made the right decision in hitting Reset on my life. This was another, and a significant one. With my family present, my dog at my feet, my new best friend baking her heart away up above me, and countless books around me, I was in heaven.

A squeeze on my hand made me glance over to meet

Barry's watery blue eyes, which sparkled knowingly at me. He didn't need to say a word.

"I know you told Percival you're not dating the handsome sergeant, but I thought I might draw your attention to him walking through the door." Gary's low rumbling voice was warm against my ear as he leaned closer. "You'll probably want to greet him before he comes to us."

I let go of Barry's hand and winked in thanks at Gary. Lord knew what humiliating thing Percival would say if Branson Wexler walked over.

Though we'd been out two or three times over the past month, seeing him out of his police uniform still threw me off. At forty-two, and with the physique of a man a decade younger, Branson's handsome features were even more noticeable in his designer everyday clothes. He gave me a quick, warm hug and pressed his lips to my cheek. "Looks like you've got a smashing success on your hands, Fred."

Though pleased, I shrugged off the compliment. "They're mostly here for the baked goods." I could feel my family's gaze at my back. No chance Percival had missed that kiss. Percival *or* my mother.

"No false modesty needed here. You've bragged multiple times about being better at solving murder cases than half the police force, I'd think you could admit to making one stellar bookshop."

I nudged his chest playfully. "Brag? I don't brag." I pulled my hand away when I realized I was flirting. Good Lord. I was flirting. I cleared my throat. "You seriously do need to go upstairs and try Katie's baking before it's all gone."

"This won't be the last time I drop in, Fred." His green eyes gleamed, although maybe it was the reflection from the stained-glass lamp nearby. For a heartbeat, his expression faltered, and I thought he looked nervous, though that was an emotion I couldn't quite picture on Branson Wexler. It was gone almost as soon as it arrived, whatever it was. "I don't want to intrude if you have plans with the family, but I thought maybe I could take you out to a celebratory dinner when you're done. Maybe go back to Pasta Thyme?"

A mix of disappointment and relief flooded through me in equal measure. "I'm sorry, Katie and I are going to dinner afterward. But you read my mind. That's where we're going. I've been craving it ever since you took me there."

His eyes narrowed, playfully this time. "Well, I'm glad it's Katie you're going with. Otherwise I might get jealous of someone else eating with you at the place we had our first date."

"Oh, that's...." *Date!* He'd said date. Sure we'd gone out for dinners, but that was what we called it—going out to dinner. Not going out on a date. And we for sure hadn't labeled things as a first date or a second date. If that was what we were doing, then technically we'd had our third date a week ago. And granted, I hadn't been on a date in nearly fifteen years, but if what I remembered from third dates was still true, we most definitely hadn't been on one.

Branson's low chuckle brought me back to the moment. "You're rather ravishing when you're flustered, Fred Page."

Ravishing? I was many things, many good things, actually, but ravishing wasn't one of them. I'd never been *that* girl. And at nearly forty, I most definitely wasn't *that* woman. On good days, maybe I'd pass for pretty. But most of the time, I'd fall in the category of healthy and approachable.

Another laugh. "Yep. Being flustered is a great color on you."

As I tried to think of a response, any response, and in

any possible language that would come out of my mouth, sensible or not, I glanced around the Cozy Corgi, seeking desperately for something to distract. When my gaze landed on it over Branson's shoulder, relief didn't begin to come close to what I was feeling.

And the it, wasn't an *it* at all. Leo Lopez walked through the front door of the bookshop. Unlike Branson, Leo was still in his uniform, clearly having just gotten off his shift at the Rocky Mountain National Park. The tan fabric of his park ranger outfit did nothing to hide his physique either, even with the bomber jacket he wore over it. Although, to be fair, his physique made more sense, as he was almost a decade younger than Branson. His brown eyes lit as his gaze landed on me, and he strode forward with a wide brilliant smile.

Probably noticing I'd been distracted, Branson turned, and at the sight of Leo, he stiffened.

For his part, Leo broke stride for a second, and his smile transitioned from one of genuine beauty to something a little more forced. Unlike Branson, Leo didn't hug or kiss me when he joined us. "Congratulations, Fred. The place looks amazing, like I knew it would." He gave a slight nod of acknowledgment to Branson. "Wexler."

"Lopez." Branson returned the nod. If it had been any other two men, and any other situation, I would've laughed at the ridiculousness of them nodding oh so formally. It was such a male thing to do. Almost like two bighorn sheep I'd seen on a drive in the park the other day, each circling and measuring each other. With any luck, Branson and Leo wouldn't end the evening with a skull crushing head-butt.

Although, with the elevated tension, I wasn't entirely sure how true that would be.

"Thanks for coming by. So nice of you to take the time."

I found my voice more out of desperation to break the moment than anything else.

It worked. Leo drew his attention back to me, the smile more genuine again. He pulled something out of his pocket, paused, and I could see the war raging internally. Then he held out a small box. "This is for your housewarming... er... grand opening." He cleared his throat, and I recalled Branson saying I was ravishing when I was flustered. Apparently that quality was going around. Leo shoved the box toward me. "It's not much."

"Thank you, Leo. You didn't need to do that." Impossibly, Branson stiffened even further as I took the gift. "I have no idea what the etiquette is for anything like this. Should I open it now?"

"Whenever you want." Leo shrugged. "Like I said, it's not much."

More to have something to do with my hands than anything, I pulled the thin red ribbon loose and lifted the small lid. Despite my internal promise to attempt to sound both pleased and neutral, I sucked in a genuine gasp of pleasure. I glanced up at him and then back to the silver earrings before lifting them into the air. Each one had three pounded-silver corgi silhouettes connected by tiny silver hoops. They glistened in the light.

Leo shrugged again. "I've noticed you really like dangly silver earrings." He motioned to the pair I had on. "I figure these are like them, except with little Watsons."

"I love them. They're perfect." I put them back in the box and closed the lid. "Thank you." I felt like I should hug him or something, but stayed where I was. Suddenly I prayed Barry would hurry over and say something ridiculous, no matter what it was. Or Percival, even if it was some horrid comment about me needing to choose between two handsome men. Or knowing Percival, telling me there was no reason to choose between two handsome men—that I should take them both.

And for crying out loud, Watson and I were here for mountains, family, and books—not men. I wasn't supposed to care about glistening green eyes or honey-yellow brown ones either for that matter. And I most definitely was not supposed to be stuck between two men, feeling awkward and self-conscious and oddly guilty—though I'd done nothing wrong—on the opening night of the Cozy Corgi. That wasn't the plan.

I slid the box into my pocket, then reached out with both hands and gave Leo's and Branson's forearms a quick squeeze simultaneously. "It is so wonderful for both of you to come. I simply can't thank you enough. However...." I glanced down at my feet, expecting to find Watson there, then remembered that Barry was nearby so I might as well be chopped liver. I saw the two of them exactly where I'd left them. Barry was lavishing affection on Watson, while the other three members of my family had been joined by Barry's daughters and their families.

The entire group was watching the fiasco that was my life. I slapped my thigh. "Watson. I promised you one of Katie's treats! I completely forgot."

At the word *treat*, Watson sprang to attention, and his gaze darted between Barry and me.

I might've smiled at Branson and Leo as I headed away, but I wasn't sure. I slapped my thigh again, this time hard enough it stung as I angled around my family and toward the stairs. "Come on, Watson. Treat!"

Thankfully the promise of a second of Katie's all-natural dog bones won out, and Watson headed in my direction.

Percival cocked an eyebrow as I slid past him, teasing thick in his tone. "Fred, I don't mind getting Watson his treat. I don't want to take you away from anything."

"Don't you dare." I offered him a glare and a shake of my finger, then made a hasty escape up the stairs.

True, I'd faced two different killers since my move to Estes Park the previous November. I knew some people considered me brave. Doubtlessly, that image would be shattered if they knew I was stuffing my face not simply because Katie was a master baker but because I was waiting for a farewell text from Leo or Branson. Honestly, I didn't care which one left. But I was certain neither would walk away without some sort of goodbye.

By the time I received Leo's parting message and braved returning downstairs, I'd devoured a ham-and-cheese croissant of my own—this one with ham from an actual pig—and polished off one of Katie's lemon bars for dessert. Never mind that the two of us were going to dinner in a matter of hours. Of course, Pasta Thyme had small portions, despite the expensive price tag, so I didn't feel too guilty about it. Watson received another dog bone as payment for allowing me to use him as an escape. He opted to stay close to Katie as opposed to returning downstairs with me. I couldn't blame him.

I felt a little guilty but texted Leo back, thanking him again for the earrings.

He didn't respond.

I couldn't blame him for that either. I was the one who'd abandoned him. But it wasn't my fault both he and Branson had decided to pursue me for some stupid reason. Nor was it my fault they were both stupidly attractive and charming in their own ways. And it most definitely wasn't my fault my brain seemed unable to function properly when I was around either one of them.

Thankfully it was my family—and not Branson—who waited for me when I arrived on the main level. However, they were only waiting to say goodbye.

After watching them go, I glanced around, trying to spot Branson. I couldn't. Maybe I'd been wrong and he'd left without a farewell. I was okay with that too.

Relaxing somewhat, I wandered around the bookshop, chatting with customers. Most people didn't seem like they were there to buy anything, more to check out the grand opening of the Cozy Corgi. I knew part of the draw was coming into the place where Opal Garble was killed. That was fine. Book sales would come later. And even if they didn't, part of the blessings of being betrayed by my ex-business partner was ending up with enough money from the buyout that I could keep the bookstore running as long as I wanted. Provided I didn't develop some lavish lifestyle, including going to Pasta Thyme for too many dinners.

I fell more in love with my bookshop as I saw it through the eyes of those exploring it for the first time. I would change nothing about it. The lighting was perfect, the furnishings managed to strike a balance between well-crafted yet not ostentatious, and the entire environment truly was cozy. My affection for the bookshop continued to grow as I walked into my favorite section—the tiny room in the back left corner that I'd reserved for the mystery genre. It also happened to be the space with the largest river rock fireplace, which was little more than embers at the moment. And there was Branson, sitting on the ornate antique sofa, looking at a book by the light of a Victorian lamp.

The fact that I was relieved he hadn't left without a farewell betrayed my emotions. When I spoke, I was pleased my voice was steady. "What are you reading?"

He smiled up at me and presented the cover. *The New Exploits of Sherlock Holmes*. "Will you hate me if I confess I can't stand mystery novels?"

His statement took me aback, and I blinked. "You know.... Kinda, yes." I managed to laugh. "All right, maybe not *hate* you, but how in the world can anyone dislike mystery novels? Especially a police officer?"

He shrugged. "It's like being at work. Why would I want to read that? Spend all day solving cases, then come home to read about someone else doing it?" He shook the book. "Plus, Sherlock Holmes is a little bit arrogant, don't you think?"

"Give me that. You don't deserve to touch it." I snatched the book from his fingers, and though I managed another laugh, part of me was a bit offended for some reason. And in truth, my estimation of Branson Wexler went down a tick. My father had been the best policeman I'd ever met, and he'd devoured mysteries by the truckload. His favorite being all things Sherlock Holmes. "Surely you've realized you're in the mystery room. I'm not certain you even deserve to sit on the sofa or enjoy the fire."

"I stumbled on a land mine, didn't I?" He chuckled, and unless I was mistaken, heat seemed to glow in his eyes. "Although, I suppose I should know better. Your dog is named Watson, for crying out loud. Obviously you like Sherlock Holmes novels."

"Charlotte and I had done an open call for submissions for books similar to Sherlock Holmes at the publishing company right around the time Watson came into my life. It was kismet." And though Charlotte's and my business partnership had dissolved, Watson had lived up to his name on a couple of different occasions already.

"Well, he's pretty cute." He stood and lifted the book from my hand again. "I'll put this up for you. And who knows, maybe over dinner you can convince me about the charms of reading mystery novels." He flashed a hopeful smile, but it faded as something caught his attention over my shoulder.

I turned to see.

"Myrtle and her disciples." His voice was cold, more so than I'd ever heard it before.

I hadn't been sure what I was looking for, but at his words, I saw Myrtle Bantam. I was about to ask what he meant by *disciples*, and then figured it out. Maybe I didn't have my sidekick Watson with me, but I could put two and two together on my own at times. A crowd of people stood around Myrtle, each of them wearing rather hideous army green vests covered in various patches. I returned my attention to Branson. "You call the members of Myrtle's birdwatching club her disciples?"

He didn't look at me when he responded, keeping his narrowed eyes on the small group. "Yeah. They do her bidding. Drive the police force crazy, constantly accusing someone of poaching. It's every other week that there's a new suspect they're convinced has the police hoodwinked. Sometimes they turn in each other." He looked at me then, a partial smile returning. "She even has twelve of them. I'm not kidding."

Okay, even I had to admit that was a little funny. And I wasn't entirely surprised at Branson's reaction. Part of the conflict between him and Leo was because of Leo's insistence that the previous owner of my shop had been a poacher. Branson hadn't given his claims any credence, and Leo had been right.

"Do you mind if I leave this with you?" Branson handed the Sherlock Holmes book back to me. "And will you call me a coward if I request to escape through the back door? I don't have it in me to deal with that lot this evening."

Despite being relieved to see him, after our conversation about mystery novels, I was ready to see him go. It probably said horrible things about me that I would find someone wanting because they weren't in love with my favorite genre of literature. "Of course not. You know that Myrtle and I don't see eye to eye on everything either. And I appreciate you coming to the opening night. It is very sweet of you."

"Thanks for understanding." This time his smile was genuine, and he gave me another brief hug and a quick kiss on my cheek. "Congratulations, Fred. The Cozy Corgi is truly spectacular. See you soon." And with that, he was gone.

Time to focus on my bookshop and the potential customers instead of a love life that I didn't want to have anyway. Even so, at any other time, I would've had a similar reaction to Branson's at the sight of the bird club and go out of my way to check on other customers before going to Myrtle. It wasn't exactly bad blood between us, but she hadn't taken to me questioning the shop owners about murder when my stepfather had been accused. I'd kept my distance since then.

The group wasn't hard to find, nor were they in an unexpected place. There was another small nook, half of which was devoted to books about nature and wildlife, and the other half to photography. Steeling myself, I crossed the bookshop, smiling as I passed customers who caught my eye, and approached the group. Though not as tall as me, Myrtle was crane-like. She had a willowy figure, bordering on bony, and her white spiked hair was reminiscent of feathers. To top it off, she had a tendency to flap her arms when she spoke, and unfortunately also had a propensity to sound like she was squawking. She truly was bird in human form. The fact that she owned Wings of the Rockies, a wild-bird store, and led a bird-watching club, seemed the most natural thing in the world.

"Hi, Myrtle." I gave a little wave, feeling awkward as I drew closer. "And everyone else. So glad you all could come by the grand opening tonight." Two familiar faces caught my eye among her disciples—Branson's term of Myrtle and her ornithological friends truly did seem apt. "Carl, Paulie, I didn't know you two were members of the Feathered Friends Brigade." I scanned the other faces that turned in my direction. "Is Anna here?"

Carl grinned and hurried over to hug me. We'd never hugged before, but it seemed it was the thing to do at grand openings. I hadn't been aware of that fact. "No, she uses my time at the club as her girls' nights. She said to send her regards"—he pulled out a dog bone—"and to give Watson one of these." Carl and Anna owned the home furnishing store right across from the bookshop, and Anna was obsessed with Watson.

I took the dog bone. "Thank you. I'll make sure he gets it. Right now he's upstairs hoping to get more of Katie's baking, I'm sure."

"I'm the newest member. I joined recently." Paulie, who owned the pet shop, also gave me a hug. "Congratulations, Fred. The store is beautiful."

Carl gave me a knowing glance over Paulie's shoulder. "One of our members moved away, so we had an opening."

Paulie was relatively new to Estes Park and not very well liked. I was glad he was starting to find his place, maybe.

Myrtle cut off the greeting by thrusting a large hardback book in my direction. "Care to explain this?"

I took the heavy book out of her hand, instantly regretting my decision to come over. It seemed I was destined to make a bad impression on Myrtle, no matter what I did. I glanced at the cover. "Oh, yes. I remember ordering this one. Have you looked through it? The photographs are stunning. The birdcages span the past two centuries. My favorites are the ones from the Victorian times." I pointed to the cover, which showed an example of just that. I caught Carl give a quick shake of his head, couldn't understand his meaning, and kept speaking. "There are some that look like entire homes, complete with rooms. Like genuine houses for birds."

"A genuine house for birds is a nest in a tree, Miss Page." As Myrtle's voice rose in volume, so did her propensity for sounding birdlike. A rather stunning pin of a swallow glinted on the scarf at her neck. "Unless, of course, you're talking about a belted kingfisher who uses holes in the ground, or the gyrfalcon that nests in the cliffs of the Arctic." She thumped the book with a bony finger. "I can promise you that none of them live in wire birdcages, especially ones designed to look like evil little houses. It's bad enough in regular cages, but in a contraption like that, there's not even a speck of room for a bird to spread its wings and fly more than an inch. Tell me, Fred, how would you like to live in such a torture device?"

I couldn't bring myself to look away from Myrtle, though I could feel the attention of the entire lower level of the shop staring at us. "I... honestly never thought of it like that. I suppose from that perspective, these cages aren't all that charming."

Myrtle stomped over to the shelf and pulled out another book. She readjusted her peacock-feathered purse on her shoulder. "Now this one is appropriate. A bird-watcher's guide. If you manage to read it, it talks in length about the cruelty of domesticating birds." She smacked it on top of the other book. "Maybe you could take the time to read the books in your own store."

My temper flared, not entirely uncommon, but I managed to rein in my tongue before I said something I'd regret. *That* was unusual. I had to take a shaky deep breath before I allowed myself to respond. I'd promised myself I was going to do everything possible to make a good impression on the other storeowners of Estes Park; it seemed important we support one another. And if I had to eat crow to do it, I would. At least a little. "I don't have time right now, obviously, but if you'd like to arrange something later, maybe you could come down one evening and we could go through all the books on birds together. Let me know if there are some that might be harmful to birds, or make suggestions about others you think should be in here."

Once more I noticed Carl's eyes widen, and he gave an appreciative nod.

For her part, Myrtle's mouth fell open, and despite the tension of the moment, I couldn't help but think she looked like a young featherless bird in the nest hoping its mother would drop a worm in her gaping beak. Clearly she hadn't expected such a response.

Well, that made two of us.

"I will most definitely make time for that." Myrtle's voice had come back to a more reserved tone. "I very much appreciate your willingness to be educated on the subject." She smiled, the first one I'd ever seen from her. "Will tomorrow evening work?"

I started to shake my head, then envisioned another outburst. I wanted the town talking about the charm of my bookstore, and the perfection of Katie's delicacies when they mentioned the grand opening of the Cozy Corgi, not a screaming match between Myrtle Bantam and Winifred Page. And I supposed I might as well get the torture over with. "Tomorrow would be perfect."

Once again, surprise flitted across Myrtle's features, but she caught herself quicker this time. "Wonderful. See you then." Her gaze flicked to the door and then upstairs. "You know, it smells wonderful in here. Maybe the Feathered Friends Brigade should sample what little Katie is offering. Maybe we could start having pastries at our meetings."

There was a murmur of agreement from her disciples. And once more, proving I had a long way to go before I finally acted my age, they sounded like little chicks chirping after their mother hen. Even so, I appreciated the gesture. "That would be lovely." My grandmother's voice echoed in my mind, reminding me to kill my adversaries with kindness. "Please tell Katie when you go upstairs that everything your group has tonight is on the house."

"We'll do that." She gave a sharp nod, walked away, and lifted her hand over her shoulder and snapped her fingers. Sure enough, nearly as one, her disciples followed, Paulie giving a little wave as he passed.

There was one straggler who caught my arm and paused in place. "Don't let her push you around. Everyone thinks Myrtle Bantam is all about the environment, bird activism, and philanthropy, but I promise you, she's in it for the power. Nothing more."

I met the man's hard gaze. I hadn't seen him before. He was middle-aged and rather nondescript, but the anger in his eyes was almost alarming. "Well, I'm not sure about all that, but I know that I'm especially passionate about my corgi, and I assume Myrtle feels the same about birds." I considered myself a very good corgi mama, but I had no doubt I couldn't hold a candle to Myrtle's passion. Probably about anything.

He shook his head. "No. It's not about the birds. It's about power. The woman is an insane tyrant."

I couldn't imagine what power she got from leading a bird club, although she did seem in control of most of her members, but I had to admit she did seem a touch insane. I had no idea what to say to the man.

"Don't get on her bad side. I promise you. She'll—"

A large hand seemed to arrive out of nowhere and dropped onto the man's shoulder, silencing him. "Henry, would you care to join the rest of us for some pastries?"

I glanced toward the voice and met the gaze of another rather nondescript man, though I guessed this one to be around sixty as opposed to middle-aged. He smiled, lifted his hand from Henry's shoulder, and held it out to me. "I'm Silas Belle I don't think we've had the pleasure of meeting."

I shook his hand. "Nice to meet you. I'm Fred."

"I know. We're actually neighbors."

My little cabin was out in the woods, so much so that when I was in it, I felt the rest of the world had faded away. Then I remembered the new development of

McMansions that had popped up on the road leading back into my woods. It was a stretch to call those my neighbors, but I supposed they were the closest thing I had to it.

For a second, it threw me off that Silas knew where I lived, but then I remembered that I was no longer in the city. In this small town, everyone knew everything about everyone else. Doubly true about the woman who moved into town, opened the bookshop, and helped solve two murders.

"Well, thanks for dropping by, *neighbor*." It was a silly thing to say, but at this point trying to find anything sensible seemed like entirely too much effort, or simply impossible.

"Anytime." Silas gave another smile, then turned to Henry. "Dessert?"

Henry flashed me a glance that said he hadn't been done ranting but followed as Silas led him away.

I watched them go. And to my relief, as they walked up the steps, Watson passed them on his way down. He spotted me as he reached the bottom and scurried over to be petted. Kneeling, I scratched both his sides, eliciting a small cloud of dog hair. "You knew I needed you, didn't you, buddy?" This night definitely had not gone how I'd envisioned. The bookshop truly was perfection, but.... People were much more complicated than any Sherlock Holmes book could ever be. Suddenly I couldn't wait to have a quick dinner with Katie and then go back home, light a fire, and read a book with Watson at my feet.

"Oh my goodness!" A loud screech caused Watson and me to stiffen, and I looked toward the voice. A large blonde woman towered over us. "This must be the corgi that your store is named after? Wilbur, right?"

"Watson, actually. From Sherlock Holmes. Wilbur was

the pig in *Charlotte's Web*. Though, with the bakery upstairs, it's only a matter of time."

As the woman knelt to pet him, Watson shot me a glare. Maybe because he'd understood my jibe, or because I was clearly expecting him to allow a stranger to pet him. Or more likely, both.

Well, whatever. It was opening night, might as well make it awkward for both of us.

"Can you believe this? We've only been open for a hot minute, and I already have my first catered event." Katie beamed at me, and her excitement was so genuine I almost felt guilty for the negative things I'd been thinking. "And if they like them, maybe they'll have me do this every week. At least that's what Myrtle mentioned."

"Katie, there's no question they're going to like what you make. Your baking is perfect. Always." I shifted the large box of pastries to my other hand, managing to readjust the handle of Watson's leash without dropping anything as I reached for the front door to Wings of the Rockies. "My guess is that you'll get so many offers for catering events you're going to have to start turning them down."

Katie walked through, carrying twice as many pastries as me, a tweeting chime sounding overhead. "You know, I'd be okay with that. I was already thinking I might need to hire an assistant."

I waited for Watson and then followed her through the door. I was about to say I'd been thinking the same thing about the bookshop, but my words fell away as thirteen faces turned to look at us. I'd been in Myrtle's shop once before, and it had been a mishmash of birdfeeders, birdhouses, books, and countless things I couldn't identify. But it had seemed rather informal. Apparently that wasn't true on the nights the Feathered Friends Brigade met. The center of the space had been cleared, and rows of chairs had been set out, all facing a large pull-down screen. Myrtle stood in front, between the two rows of chairs, with her arms outstretched, having obviously been interrupted in midsentence.

Her gaze flicked to Watson, and her lips thinned.

The two of them hadn't exactly bonded the night before when Myrtle came to inspect my supply of bird books, but there hadn't been any open hostility either. From either of them. And things had gone smoother between Myrtle and myself than I'd anticipated as well. I'd not even thought twice about having Watson tag along to the bird club. It seemed that had been an overestimation on my part.

If my hands hadn't been full, I would've checked the time on my cell. "I'm so sorry! I was under the impression the meeting got started at seven." Katie and I had arrived with fifteen minutes to spare, or so I'd thought.

"We like to get started early." She motioned to a cleared spot on the counter close to the cash register. "If you'll place those there and then find a seat, we'll continue."

Katie and I arranged the pastries quickly and then looked toward the group. There were no chairs. The man from two nights ago stood, hurried over to a closet, and got two more folding chairs out for us. Surprisingly, I was able to remember his name by the time he brought them over. "Thank you, Silas."

"Of course! Glad you all can join us. It's rare we have visitors unless we're actively seeking enrollment."

"Which we're not. We are currently full." Myrtle gave what I thought was supposed to be a smile. "But we do consider it a part of outreach to have visitors. One never knows what might spark a passion for ornithology in someone." She waited for Katie and me to take our seats. "We were getting ready to start the awarding of badges. It's always one of the first orders of business." I could quite literally see her debating how much she wanted to explain. It seemed Myrtle was feeling gracious, or maybe she and I had bonded more than I'd realized the night before. "We have five categories for which members compete for honors." She numbered them off on her fingers as she listed the categories. "Having experiences with the rarest bird, with photographic evidence of course, while obviously not infringing upon the bird's space. Capturing sounds of rare birds. Having raised the most money for conservation for the week. Demonstrating impressive ornithological knowledge. And an adept ability at replicating birdcalls without the aid of electronic assistance."

"I always get that one!" Carl grinned and waved a chubby hand in our direction, earning himself a glare from Myrtle.

Myrtle cleared her throat. "If we're done with interruptions, I assume it's safe for me to commence." She didn't wait for a response. "Did anyone travel this week and have any images to share with the club?"

"Like we don't already know." The mutter was low enough that I thought I was the only one who heard, and I dared to look over. Henry met my gaze and rolled his eyes.

"I spent a couple of days last week traveling over southern Australia." Silas stood and walked toward the front, handing Myrtle a flash drive. He continued speaking as she put it into her laptop. She clicked a few buttons and an image of a little green bird with blue wings appeared on the screen. "The orange-bellied parrot was quite captivating, so much so that I nearly extended my stay simply to spend more time watching it in its natural environment."

The quiet groan to my right at Silas's announcement was once again too quiet for most to hear, and I didn't need to look over to see that Henry was having another reaction.

"Don't forget to announce what camera you used to capture that image, Silas." A handsome younger man spoke from Katie's left.

Silas let out a good-natured laugh. "Of course, Benjamin. For this trip, I took my Nikon D500 DSLR. It did a perfect job, as you can see."

Benjamin halfway stood, addressing the club. "Remember that all members of the Feathered Friends Brigade get ten percent off all camera equipment at my store."

"Benjamin! We've talked about this. I'm not running an advertising group here." Myrtle's lips thinned further to a near birdlike point, and then she motioned to Silas. "Sorry for the interruption, please continue."

Silas began listing different facts about the orange-bellied parrot as well as details about where he stayed for his two days in Australia. Katie leaned close to me, her curly hair tickling my cheek as she whispered, "He traveled all the way to Australia and only stayed two days? Who can afford that?"

Myrtle cleared her throat and cast a glare in our direction. I didn't respond to Katie, she obviously hadn't noticed the gathering of mini-mansions on the way to my house. From the looks of them, several of the occupants could afford such a trip. Especially those whose mansions weren't all that mini. At the end of his speech, once Myrtle was assured no one else had any images to share that they thought might outdo Silas's, she handed him a brightly colored badge. It seemed to match at least ten other badges already affixed to his vest.

Next came the badge for captured sounds. A middle-aged woman named Alice also handed Myrtle a flash drive, and then a moan-like chirp filled the space. She too gave a little speech about whatever bird was making the noise, but instead of listening, I was distracted once more by Henry's reaction. Making sure Myrtle's attention was fixed on Alice, I glanced around the group. It seemed Henry wasn't the only one annoyed. And when Alice was awarded a different badge, judging from her vest, it was once again clear she was a common recipient of that particular achievement. As she spoke, it seemed obvious she wasn't as confident in her facts as Silas had been. I couldn't help but wonder if Alice was cheating somehow, though I couldn't imagine Myrtle allowing such a thing to occur in her club.

A man named Owen won the badge for raising the most money for bird conservation over the previous week. It was the second badge on his vest. Even so, Henry let out another quietly disgusted sound. The man seemed to despise everyone in the club. It didn't make any sense for him to be there. I dared another glance. There were no badges on his vest.

"Now for my favorite part of the evening, we will see if anyone can earn the badge for knowledge of our feathered friends." Myrtle clicked a few buttons on her laptop, before diving into her first question.

Beside me, Katie shifted in her seat in apparent anticipation.

"We'll start with an easy one." As she spoke, Myrtle's voice took on the tone of the teacher and sounded the least birdlike I'd ever heard from her. "True or false, an ostrich sticks its head in the sand because of fright."

Before anyone could respond, Katie's hand shot up into the air so hard that she nearly threw herself from the chair.

Myrtle flinched, her eyes widening. She swallowed, like she was debating what to do, and then she offered a forced smile. "Normally nonmembers don't participate, as they are not eligible to win badges, but we'll make an exception this time. What say you, Miss Pizzolato?"

"That is false."

Myrtle's smile turned a little more genuine. "You are correct. Although that is a fairly sensible response. In truth—"

"They stick their head in the ground to look for water."

I turned to gape at Katie, shocked and a little impressed that she'd interrupt Myrtle Bantam. It was like being back in grade school and the class know-it-all dared to correct the mean substitute teacher.

For her part, Myrtle didn't seem offended in the least. "Very true! I must say I'm impressed. Though the next won't be quite so easy." She checked her computer screen. "The bassian thrush has an unusual way of—"

Katie's hand shot in the air again, this time causing Myrtle to look annoyed. "They use flatulence to lure out their prey. They aim at where they suspect the worms will be and... well... fart...." Katie blushed. "It disturbs the worms, causing them to make their location known."

Myrtle blinked, and several of the members turned to stare at Katie.

Almost begrudgingly, Myrtle nodded. "True enough. Although in the future, I appreciate being able to finish the question." She didn't wait for a response before launching into the next. "There's a bird that dyes its feathers, much like many of you dye your hair—" She flinched as Katie's hand jutted skyward once more, but kept going. "They do this by staining their feathers with red mud. What is this particular bird species?"

Katie waved her hand, and Myrtle looked around at the other members of the club, clearly hoping one of them would save her. No one did. With the sound of defeat, she gave a nod in Katie's direction. "Yes, Miss Pizzolato?"

"It's the lammergeier, more commonly known as the bearded vulture. And it doesn't start that particular behavior until around the age of seven years old."

Everyone, me included, gaped at Katie.

She shrugged. "Well, they do."

Just as I was wondering what other levels of savant knowledge my new best friend possessed, I realized what had happened. As Myrtle checked her screen again, I leaned into Katie. "You entered the Google wormhole about birds last night, didn't you?"

She looked at me like that was the dumbest question anyone had ever asked. "Well, of course I did. I knew we were coming here. I wanted to be informed."

I loved that Katie was such a peculiar woman at times.

"This is our final question. I must say, I'm curious if any of the actual Feathered Friends Brigade will be able to get anything correct this evening, or if you all will be shown up by our caterer." Seeming a little shaken, Myrtle sighed. "This particular species is being driven almost to extinction through poaching because of its red ivory bill." She didn't bother to look surprised as Katie's hand shot up again. Although she did seek the faces of her club members with a desperate expression. Finally her gaze landed on Silas. "Surely you know this."

"I believe I do, yes. But I'm fascinated." Silas nodded but smiled at Katie. "Tell us, Katie. Can you prove to be as much of an expert on birds as you are at baking?"

This time, Katie's cheeks were a vibrant red as she spoke. "It's the helmeted hornbill. And on the black market, their beaks are more expensive than elephant ivory."

"Well done!" Silas clapped, and within a couple of moments, the rest of the group joined in.

Katie looked like she was in heaven.

"She's cheating. Her friend is looking things up on the phone and whispering to her." Henry stood, glaring at Katie and me in something akin to hate. "You two will fit in perfectly here."

To my surprise, both Carl and Paulie stood up, but it was Paulie who spoke first. "Fred would never do that! She's the most honest and kindest person I know. There's been no one in town who's been nicer to me than her."

Guilt cut through me at his words. I did consider myself fairly honest, but I hadn't always had the kindest thoughts about Paulie.

Myrtle clapped her hands, surprisingly able to make quite a loud noise, considering how thin and bony they were. "None of this! Not in my club. Ever!" She pointed at Henry. "Keep yourself under control, or I will expel you from the club and we will have an opening after all. I will not warn you again."

Henry turned every bit as red as Katie had moments before, looking like he was about ready to burst, but then, to my surprise, sat down and clasped his hands together in his lap.

Myrtle glared at him a few extra seconds, then motioned for Katie to come forward. "As I said, nonmembers are excluded from earning badges, but—" She unfastened a pin similar to the ones I'd noticed her wear the past two nights, this one in the shape of a hummingbird. "—take this."

"Oh no, I can't. That's much too nice. I wasn't trying to win anything."

Myrtle thrust the pin into Katie's hand. "I insist. And the next time we have an opening in the club"—she cast a quick glare at Henry—"you have a standing invitation to join."

Katie squeezed back into the seat beside me, most uncomfortable. "I was trying to enjoy the quiz. I wasn't attempting to cause drama."

"I know. There seems to be some other dynamic going on here besides you being good at trivia."

Myrtle cleared her throat, casting an annoyed glare in my direction, and then continued. Next came the badge for birdcalls. I inspected Katie's new pin as multiple people stood and made strange noises. I was thankful for the distraction of the pin as I found it rather embarrassing to hear adults attempting to sound like birds. As for the pin, it was beautiful—and obviously expensive. The casing was silver, and the details were crafted in a mosaic of glossy stones. Myrtle must truly have been impressed to offer such a reward. By the time I handed the pin back to Katie, Carl was accepting his badge for the best birdcall of the evening.

The rest of the meeting was entirely comprised of what equated to be a sermon from Myrtle. And if I hadn't already been convinced, Branson's descriptor of the group as Myrtle and her disciples, was proven accurate. She spoke with as much fervor about conservation, ending poaching, and being on guard for the signs of it in and around Estes and the national park, as any sermon of fire and brimstone I'd ever witnessed, not that I'd heard that many.

As she spoke, I studied the twelve members of the group, trying to understand why they were there. I couldn't see the appeal, they seemed like they had signed up to be led by a dictator, one who liked to hear herself speak. Henry's words came back to me from two nights before—claiming that Myrtle was power-hungry. From what little I'd seen, I couldn't disagree with him, despite her generosity toward Katie. But that made it even more confusing. Henry clearly didn't like what was going on in the group. I thought his annoyance had mainly been directed at Myrtle, but it seemed to be at nearly everyone in the club. So why be a member at all?

From what I knew about Paulie, it made sense, sad as it was. He was hard to be around and awkward to an extreme. As a result, he was desperate for relationships. I wasn't surprised he would be willing to put up with nearly anything to try to fill that void. But the rest, I couldn't imagine. Carl was a little odd to be sure, but he and Anna were the center of the gossip chain in Estes Park. He wasn't lacking for friendships. I didn't know any of the other members personally, maybe most of them were lonely like Paulie, or maybe they were genuinely passionate about birds. I supposed they would have to be to sit through something like this on a weekly basis.

Personally, I couldn't fathom it. Even if the group was about corgis, or specifically about Watson, for crying out loud, I would never subject myself to such an experience more than once.

Myrtle must have some odd draw or power I couldn't see. Something more than badges about birds was going on here. Surely.

The meeting ended, and everyone gathered around the pastries, bragging about Katie's skills, with equal measure of her bird knowledge. Several of them came up to me to give Watson attention. I was impressed with his begrudging willingness to allow all the strangers to fawn over him. My poor little guy was getting used to it after the few days at the bookshop. When there was a break in the attention, Henry made his way over to us. I might have been willing to play nice on the opening night of the Cozy Corgi, but I wasn't going to do that again, and I prepared to tell him so. To my surprise, he grimaced as he approached, and he gave an apologetic shrug. "I'm sorry, Miss Page. Sometimes my temper gets the better of me. I'm so used to people cheating in order to get badges that I jump to conclusions."

I looked around expecting to see some other member over his shoulder having encouraged him to apologize, like a mother would to a child. There was no one. "Thank you, Henry. I appreciate it. And I can promise you that neither Katie nor I cheated. Katie's simply especially fond of trivia, of any variety. Give her five minutes on any topic, and she'll become an expert it seems. It's a skill I can assure you I don't have."

Henry nodded and seemed unsure what to say. Then he appeared to steel himself and met my gaze. "If the rumors are true, you have a good relationship with Sergeant Wexler, is that right?"

I could tell we were heading into dangerous territory. "I'm new in town, so I'm getting to know a lot of people at the moment. But Bran—Sergeant Wexler and I have a lot in common. My father was a policeman."

He nodded like that made sense. "That's great. Maybe you can get him to listen to us sometimes. He refuses to follow up on any leads we offer about people we know are poaching."

It took all my willpower to refrain from pointing out that he'd just accused Katie and me of cheating at a trivia game. It seemed a little much to expect a policeman or anyone else to give him much credence. "If that's happening, it's awful. Maybe it's something Leo Lopez can help you with." Even as I said it, I felt guilty for throwing Leo under the bus. "Do you know him? He's a park ranger."

"Yes, he's one of the good guys. He doesn't always take us seriously either, but more than anyone else." His eyes lit. "In fact, he's leading us on a moonlight snowshoe next week in hopes of spotting some owls. You should attend."

I couldn't imagine anything I would rather do less than attend another meeting of the Feathered Friends Brigade. "I doubt that will work out. Having opened the bookshop, I'm afraid every ounce of my time is spoken for."

Henry looked disappointed, though I couldn't imagine why. "Well, if you change your mind, bring Katie along. I'm sure Myrtle will allow you to attend as long as she's there. But don't bring your dog." He cast a disapproving glance at Watson. "Although I suppose I shouldn't tell you to bring Katie. Clearly Myrtle would like nothing more than to kick me out and put her in."

Even though I knew it was rude, I couldn't keep from asking. "Henry, I hope you don't mind me saying so, but you seem rather miserable here and as if you don't like a lot of the people in the club."

He shrugged.

I took that as an agreement. "Then why attend?"

Some of the heat returned to his voice, though I couldn't tell if it was anger or merely passion. "Despite what others might think, the Feathered Friends Brigade is not about the badges, taking trips to see fancy birds, or making friends. It's about protecting nature, about rescuing species of birds on the edge of extinction, about raising money for conservation. About making the world a better place." He leaned closer, his voice barely more than a whisper. "And there is a saying about keeping your friends close and your enemies closer. That's exactly what I'm doing. And I will get the Feathered Friends Brigade back on track and weed out those who corrupt what it stands for. Even if I have to take down Myrtle to do it." He nodded and pointed a finger in my face, almost hitting my nose. "Mark my words, I'm going to expose the people in this club for exactly what they are, the cheaters, those who don't care about the birds at all, and even the poachers among us."

Over the next week, two things became clear.

The most important was that Katie and I needed to hire at least one person apiece. Even though the winter was the slow season, neither of us could keep up. Granted, I had it easier than Katie. At most, I simply needed to step into the restroom and leave customers unattended for a few moments. She had to get up at four in the morning to begin baking and then serve customers all day. She was wearing herself out.

The other thing was that attending the Feathered Friends Brigade had stoked Katie's competitive side. Between discussing new ideas for recipes and attempting to use inspiration from the literary themes in the bookshop, Katie talked incessantly of wanting a vest filled with trivia badges. I wasn't entirely certain if the sleep-deprived bags under Katie's eyes were due to how hard she was working at the bakery or how long she spent on Google before going to bed.

Katie's new obsession, combined with a text invitation from Leo, had me strapping on snowshoes for the first time in my life. Under the moonlight, as snow drifted down, I couldn't help but envy Watson his coziness and warmth back home. He'd made it very clear as I left him behind that he was irritated, but little did he know he was getting the better end of the bargain.

Leo led the fifteen of us through the moonlit forest over a relatively flat and easy trail that led to Bear Lake before pausing at the water's edge to turn and address the group in a low voice that carried without disrupting the serenity. "I know I don't have to tell any of you this, but as we split up, stay with your buddy, and remember to be as still as possible. The chances of spotting any nocturnal birds while we're tromping around is low, but especially so if we're talking."

I let his words fade away, distracted as a cloud moved above and moonlight washed over his features. He made quite the picture in his park ranger uniform, bomber jacket, and fleece hat and gloves, standing in front of the iced-over lake, snow-covered mountains at his back, and winter forest surrounding him. He looked utterly comfortable and totally capable. I'd been a little surprised at his text, especially after the way I'd abandoned him on the opening night of the Cozy Corgi. Part of me had wondered if Katie had put him up to it—one more nail in the coffin to get me to attend. If she had, it worked. His invitation had been the deciding factor.

"Again, I know none of you need to hear this, but I'll say it anyway. No flash photography. It disturbs the wildlife. And I know everyone's hoping to see a Mexican Spotted Owl, but as you know, they tend to stay in the southern parts of the Rocky Mountain National Forest. Only occasionally will they wander this far north."

That particular species had been the reason Leo and I had first met, when I'd found a frozen owl in the deep-freeze of the shop. It ended up being the proof Leo had needed that the previous owner had been involved in poaching. Although, considering he was already dead, it was too little, too late.

Leo tapped his watch. "We will meet back here in an hour. Reception at this location is decent, and each of you has my cell number. Call me if there's any problem. If all else fails, shout." He flashed a brilliant grin. "Good luck!"

The members of the Feathered Friends Brigade dispersed, all nearly silent. I supposed that was a prerequisite for adequate bird-watching. Leo nodded at Myrtle as he passed her and headed to Katie and me. "How are you two doing? Neither of you have snowshoed before, correct?"

"It's not too bad." Katie shrugged. "I did some research about snowshoeing last night and found a website that suggested different stretches to help get ready. I'm feeling pretty good."

I threw my arm around her shoulders and gave her a quick squeeze. "Of course you did."

Leo chuckled but then turned his attention to me. "And you? I imagine these mountain winters are hard to get used to."

"I can't say I'm used to the elevation yet or hiking in the middle of the night through snow, but as far as the cold, it's not nearly as intense as Kansas City."

"Good. I'm glad you're adjusting." He looked a little nervous. I knew how he felt. We'd already resorted to talking about the weather. "Do you two want to go off and search the woods on your own, or would you like me to accompany you?"

Before Katie or I could respond, Henry hurried over and grabbed Leo by the arm, and though he attempted to whisper, temper was clear in his tone, and his words certainly carried. "I'm glad I caught you without the others around. I was wrong before. About Roxanne." He cast a glance at Katie. "She was the trivia queen, at least before you showed up." Without waiting for a response, he turned back to Leo. "She isn't the poacher. It's Owen. I'm sure of it this time."

"Okay, Henry." Though Leo sighed, his tone was patient. "Let's do like we have every time before. This isn't the place for it. Give me a call tomorrow, and I'll listen to whatever proof you think you have."

"*Think* I have?" Henry's whisper turned to a hiss. "Don't you start acting like that cop. Already making up your mind about me before you've even heard what I have to say. I don't *think*, Leo. I *know*." He gave Leo's arm a shake. "And I know that Owen is the poacher."

Proving she was as adept at moving silently as a park ranger, Myrtle suddenly joined our group, fury visible in her eyes, despite the night shadows. "Enough of this, Henry. You've got to quit accusing people in the group of poaching. We are all on the same side. Every one of us is committed to protecting our birds. All of us. I'm not going to continue to have this conversation with you."

"Oh yes, Myrtle, queen of us all." All attempt at whispering left Henry's voice. "You like to pretend you're all high and mighty, so perfect. But you know about the cheating that goes on. And yet you continue to give badge after badge after badge. While those of us who actually play by the rules get nothing. Like anyone can trust anything you say."

"How dare you speak that way about Myrtle." During the exchange, I'd not noticed Silas at Myrtle's side. And though he did whisper, there was no wavering in his voice. "Do you know how much this woman has done for conservation, how much money she's raised? Where would any of us be without her? How can you even suggest that—"

Myrtle raised her hand, quickly touching his arm. "Thank you, Silas, but I can defend myself." She addressed Henry, and for once there was no birdlike squawk to her voice. It was cold, hard. "I'm done with warnings, Henry. *You're* done. You're out of the group. As soon as we get back tonight, hand in your vest. Your membership is suspended."

Henry had murder in his eyes. "Of course, Myrtle. Three weeks after membership fees are collected. After you make clear that ten grand is nonrefundable, now you kick me out? You've been looking for a reason." He laughed as he ripped off his vest and threw it at Myrtle's face. "You are a piece of work. And I'll bring you down. I promise you that."

Silas took a step toward him, but Myrtle shot out her arm once more, stopping him.

Henry whirled and headed into the forest.

Leo reached for him. "Henry, calm down. It's not safe to go out there by yourself right now."

"I'm as adept in these woods as you are." Henry shook him off. "And you're as bad as she is. Already making up your mind that you know better than me. Mark my words. Owen is the poacher. I'll prove it."

As Henry stormed off, Leo started to follow him, but Myrtle stopped him. "Let him go. Henry is wrong about many things, but he can take care of himself. And from the outbursts I've already seen from him, following will make things worse. For both of you."

Leo hesitated, glanced down at the solitary trail in the snow that led to where Henry headed, then gave a slow nod. "You're probably right."

Without any more concern in her tone, Myrtle turned

and addressed Katie. "There's an opening in the Feathered Friends Brigade. It's yours if you want it."

"I... um...." Katie looked at Henry's footprints, then back at Myrtle. "Um... membership is ten thousand dollars?"

"Yes." Myrtle nodded. "Annually, of course."

"Oh, yes, naturally." Katie licked her lips. "May I... let you know?"

"Certainly, dear." Myrtle gestured toward the forest. "I'm going to attempt to find my first Mexican Spotted Owl this evening. Wish me luck." She and Silas headed out.

Once the pair was out of earshot, Katie turned to face Leo and me, her expression aghast as she met my gaze and then Leo's. "Ten thousand dollars? A year! As if that makes any difference. It wouldn't matter if it were that much for the rest of the century. Who has that kind of money?"

"Well, it is Estes Park. Half of the residents are stinking rich, and the other half of us barely scrape by." Leo shrugged. "However, in this case, I'm thankful for the fee. Every dime of it goes toward preventing poaching. And not just for birds."

That price tag was rather astounding and unexpected. And while I didn't fall into the barely scraping by category, I couldn't imagine paying ten thousand dollars to be in any kind of club, even if the proceeds did go to a worthy cause.

"Well, that part is good, I suppose." Katie grinned at me as she shook her head. "I no longer want a vest filled with bird trivia badges." She slipped her arm through Leo's. "Lead on, Smokey Bear."

Leo let out a guffaw, and somehow managed to still stay quiet. "New nickname?"

"Not overly original as far as names for park rangers go, I know. But whatever." Katie linked her other arm through mine. "Come on. If we have to be out in this godforsaken cold without the hope of getting any badges, the least we can do is enjoy a private tour. Make it interesting, Smokey."

Leo didn't attempt to make it overly interesting. He didn't need to. He filled in some quiet facts here and there, but mostly, he let Mother Nature speak for herself. He led us through the trees, twenty yards or so away from where we'd been, before he stopped and smiled at us. "Now, listen. Don't move anything besides your head. Listen and watch."

Katie giggled but settled in quickly enough.

After a minute or so, I nearly forgot the two of them were there. I'd visited Estes Park since I was a kid, seeing my mom's family a couple of times a year. But somehow, I'd forgotten exactly what the Colorado mountains were like. Even with the brightness of the full moon, with the clarity of the air and sky, the swirls of the starry galaxies above our heads twinkled down upon us, mystical against the dark silhouettes of the trees and the craggy peaks that surrounded us.

In the silence, the night came alive. A soft wind swept cold fingers across my cheek and dislodged some snow that had piled up on the leafless branch of an aspen, causing it to tumble down like a waterfall. The crackle of underbrush sounded close to my feet, though I couldn't see anything, not even the trembling of the undergrowth.

My eyes continued to adjust, helped along by the reflection of the moon over the snow, allowing me to see farther through the dense forest, illuminating boulders scattered among the trees.

A louder rustling sounded to our right. I turned to look, expecting to see one of the members of the Feathered Friends Brigade. Instead a bull elk stared at me from less than thirty feet away, its seemingly limitless pointed antlers forming a crown above its head. On its own, the sight wasn't that unusual. The elk in Estes Park were nearly as tame as dogs, often wandering through the main streets. But as glorious as that was, it didn't compare to seeing the majestic creature in its kingdom, undisturbed by other people. It huffed a steaming breath and then moved on, only then did I notice another five or six farther back in the trees.

Katie let out a quiet contented sigh. I agreed wholeheartedly.

I'd traded my old life for one filled with books, family, and magic. I hadn't expected that last one.

A high-pitched scream cut through the night, breaking the spell. The heads of every elk straightened, and then as one, they disappeared into the trees.

A second scream split the air. Leo, Katie, and I exchanged a brief glance, then like the elk, moved as a unit, though we ran toward the sound.

As we moved, we could hear others running through the forest, all headed in the same direction as us.

No more screaming came, but as we drew closer, we were led by the sounds of a woman close to hyperventilating.

We entered a small clearing and saw Alice and an older woman standing over a dark shape on the ground.

A few steps closer, and thanks to the moonlight, the snow, and my adjusted eyesight, the dark shape took form. Henry lay on his back. His eyes stared sightlessly up into the trees. A gaping wound sliced across his neck.

Though they were always helpful when I needed to know something, I had to admit, I'd at times thought judgmental things about Anna and Carl and their propensity for gossip. Sometimes even about my uncles as well. Within half an hour of opening the Cozy Corgi the next morning, I was taking back every negative thought I'd had. You didn't have to go looking for gossip as a storeowner; it came to you. And judging from the vast number of people wandering through the bookshop to head upstairs to Katie's bakery and how few were returning back down, I had the feeling we were going to be the new hub.

Once more thinking I needed to bring on an employee to handle the cash register, I left my post and wandered up to the bakery, Watson following grudgingly along.

I had to eat my words about Watson as well. I would've been willing to bet everything I owned on him never being back in the bookstore again once the bakery was in full swing. I'd not taken into account the vast number of people who would linger in the charming space Katie had created. It turned out that as much as Watson adored food, he valued avoiding countless hands on him even more. He was always underfoot in the bookshop. Which, I had to admit, pleased me greatly.

Katie noticed Watson and me arriving at the top of the stairs, and she cast me a wide-eyed glance before turning back to her customer. I hadn't quite grasped how many people had not yet come back down to the bookshop. The place was filled. Though there weren't many, every table, sofa, and chair were occupied, and people huddled in little groups whispering excitedly.

I started toward the counter, but then, to my surprise, noticed Carl gesturing emphatically a few feet away. He must've felt my gaze as he looked over at me at that exact moment, brightened, and waved me over before turning back to his audience. "Ask Fred, she was there. Henry lay there in the snow, throat sliced open like in a horror movie."

I started to confirm, but felt strange about it, so I changed directions. "Carl, what are you doing here? I can't believe Anna allowed you to leave her by herself in Cabin and Hearth."

He looked at me like I was an idiot, then gestured across the bakery. "She's getting us another tart. We saw everyone coming over here, so we closed the shop. Didn't want to miss the excitement."

Apparently I hadn't completely misjudged Carl and Anna's propensity for gossip after all. And strangely, that felt soothing.

As if hearing her name, Anna shuffled over and shoved a plate with the pear tart toward Carl, then plunged a fork into her slice of chocolate cake. She smiled at me, glanced down, then returned the fork to the plate with a clatter and shoved it in my direction. "Hi, Fred, hold this." She sank to the floor, her gingham skirt billowing around her as she squealed and reached toward Watson.

I swore he grimaced, but he knew one of his favorite treat dispensers when he saw her and allowed the fawning to happen.

Carl took a bite of his tart and groaned in pleasure, then gestured over his shoulder with the fork toward Katie, speaking with his mouth full. "You landed a goldmine with that one, Fred."

"That I did."

"I'm betting it's a matter of weeks before you put the Black Bear Roaster out of business."

I grabbed his arm. "Don't say that! We are not in competition with the coffee shop. There is enough business for both of us." The Black Bear Roaster had been the only coffee shop downtown until Katie opened. The owner wasn't my favorite person in the world, and she couldn't serve a moist scone to save her life, but I didn't want that notion of us trying to put them out of business to start getting around town.

With a final pat on Watson's head, Anna stood and retrieved her cake. "Don't be ridiculous. Of course you're in competition with Carla. And you're going to knock her socks off."

"No! I don't want—"

"So what's your version, Fred?" Anna cut me off with her mouth as full as Carl's. "I'd say you'll have a much calmer account than my husband. This is the first time he's seen a murder. By this point, it's got to be almost boring to you. I swear, you moved to town, and people start dropping like flies."

The couple Carl had been talking to nodded enthusiastically. I didn't believe I'd met them before, but I offered an uncomfortable smile. "I... ah... don't know if I would put it like that exactly. And...." I glanced over Carl and Anna's shoulders and pointed toward Katie as I raised my voice. "Of course, I'll be right there." I tried another smile, this time at Carl and Anna. "Sorry, Katie needs me. Enjoy your breakfast." Without worrying if I had been convincing or not, I headed toward the counter, even though Katie hadn't even been looking in my direction.

Katie noticed me when I was a couple feet away and grinned. "Perfect timing. Fred, I want you to meet Sammy." A short woman turned to offer me a greeting, a broad smile on her round face, and I halted. I could've been looking at Katie's twin, or at least her sibling. They even had the same mess of curly brown hair. "Sammy is a baker. She graduated culinary school at Christmas and came home to spend a few months with her family. I'm trying to talk her into being my assistant. Even if only for a few months until we get settled."

I shook the woman's hand. "Nice to meet you. It would be great to have Katie get some help. I need to start looking for some myself."

"Nice to meet you, too. Absolutely love your bookstore. It's wonderful." Sammy broke the handshake and attempted to trap a curl behind her ear, it sprung free the second she dropped her hand. "And from the looks of things, I'll be getting a great experience. You're crazy busy."

She even sounded like Katie. It was a little disconcerting. "Well, that's true, but I'm willing to bet it'll die down after a day or two. People are excited or something after last night's events."

"Are you kidding?" Katie scoffed. "With you around, the adventure never stops. Give us another few weeks and eventually you'll find another dead body."

"Not you, too!" I think for the first time in our friendship I gave her an irritated glare. "This doesn't have anything to do with me. And you were with me, remember? Neither of us discovered Henry's body. That was Alice, and...." I snapped my fingers trying to remember the other woman's name. "Lucy."

Katie shrugged, like that was a minor detail. Then she turned back to Sammy. "Just wait and see. Give Fred a week and she'll be able to tell the whole town who killed Henry. She's the best detective the town's got."

I wondered if Anna and Carl would loan me the key to their store so I could hide in there for a while. "Katie, don't be ridiculous. I own a bookshop. I'm not a detective. There's no reason for me to get involved in this. None of my family or friends have been accused of murder."

Again Katie waved me off like I was being ridiculous and somewhat daft. "Like that matters."

I wasn't about to admit I'd had similar thoughts as I'd fallen asleep the night before. Playing over the interactions I'd noticed at the bird-club meeting, it wasn't hard to imagine half of those people wanting Henry dead. It seemed like I'd heard him accuse most of the bird-watchers of some form of foul play. That probably got a little old, to say the least. I hadn't noticed anything interesting about Owen, but I doubted he felt too kindly toward Henry after being accused of poaching.

I gave my head a shake, clearing the ridiculous things I was thinking. But too little, too late. Katie shook her finger in my direction and grinned. "I know that face, Fred." She winked at Sammy. "Mark my words, by the time you get your first paycheck, Fred will announce who killed Henry." She turned back to me, opened her mouth to say something, and then her eyes widened. With a grin, she pointed over my shoulder. "I'm pretty sure *he's* not here for my baking." I followed her gaze and found

Branson standing at the top of the steps, observing the packed space. From his expression, clearly Katie had been right.

"It was nice to meet you, Sammy. Sounds like we might be seeing a lot more of each other." I glared at Katie once more. "And you, don't go making things worse. There's enough gossip going around. I'm not getting involved."

She shrugged. "Whatever you say, Winifred Page."

After giving her a final glower, I turned, and Watson and I headed over to Branson. "Hey. Need some breakfast?"

He shook his head. "No, thank you. I'm here to talk to you, actually." He pointed down the steps. "Maybe we can go downstairs, have some privacy?"

"Of course."

He turned instantly and headed to the bookshop. I followed, Watson at my heels. I'd not caught even a glimmer of flirtation in Branson's eyes or in his tone. He had to be there for professional reasons.

As we got to the bottom of the steps, the front door opened, two women walked in, crossed the bookshop, gave a friendly nod in our direction, and headed up to the bakery. A glance around revealed that Branson and I were alone. "It's a good thing Katie opened the bakery upstairs. Otherwise all the books would be bored not getting to see anyone walk past them."

"I'm sure that will change. Your bookshop will do fine. At least once tourist season begins." Branson attempted a smile, but it didn't reach his eyes. For some reason, he seemed nervous again. He reached down to scratch Watson's head, but Watson ducked out of reach. "Not the cuddliest of dogs, is he?"

"No, never." It wasn't true. He went completely gaga over Barry—and Leo, for that matter. "I can tell you're not here to talk about Watson or the bookshop. What's going on?"

He didn't hesitate further, which I appreciated. "Obviously, I heard about what happened last night. We've been out at the murder scene all morning."

"And what? Has Officer Green determined that I was the one who killed him somehow?" I forced a laugh. Neither Branson nor Susan Green had been the officers to arrive at the park the night before, but Officer Green made no secret of hating my existence. Her doing such a thing wouldn't surprise me in the slightest, though I couldn't picture Branson going along with it.

"No, of course not. You're not involved this time. Not even as a witness. You've already given your statement as to what you saw, but you weren't even the first on the scene." Again, I had the impression he was nervous. "That's why I'm here, Fred, to let you know that, for once, you're not involved. None of your family is. None of your friends or anyone you're close to. I... didn't want you to worry."

"I know that. I wasn't worried. I was teasing about Susan, mostly." I started to laugh, but then I had a thought, one I knew with certainty was spot-on before I spoke. "But that's not why you're here, is it?" I tried to keep my voice neutral. "You're not concerned about me being worried. You're making it clear that I'm not involved, or more precisely, to keep my nose out of it."

He grimaced. "I didn't say that. Don't put words in my mouth. I would never word it like that to you."

Despite my efforts to keep my tone neutral, I placed my hands on my hips and narrowed my eyes. "So that isn't why you're here, then? You're okay with me putting my nose in it?"

He narrowed his eyes right back at me. "Why would you put your nose in it, Fred? It doesn't involve you."

Anger flitted through me, even though I'd been saying the exact same thing mere moments ago upstairs. "If I recall, the last time someone was killed in Estes, you gave your blessing for me to figure it out. And I did. Mostly."

"You were trying to clear your friend's name. I wasn't going to tell you no. But again, Henry's death has absolutely nothing to do with you. You need to stay out of it."

"I'm fairly certain I've made it clear that I don't like being told what to do." I knew it was ridiculous, and maybe even childish, but I tilted my chin and met him straight in the eyes, even if I did have to look up slightly to do it. "And I had absolutely no intention of getting involved."

He nodded, looking relieved momentarily, and then his green eyes narrowed once more. "*Had* no intention of getting involved?"

"Just what I said. I had no intention of getting involved." In the back of my mind, I could hear my mother chiding me for acting like a spoiled brat. But I could also hear my father laughing. "You're the one who came here, Sergeant Wexler. *You* came to *me*. I'd say you're the one trying to get me involved."

He rolled his eyes and crossed his arms over his chest. "Really? You're going to take that route? You're better than that, Fred."

"Am I? You think after a couple of dinners that you have me all figured out."

For a second he looked like he was going to argue, but then he shut his mouth and glared. Watson let out a soft warning grumbling in his throat, and Branson glanced down, then returned his attention to me. "You have skill, Fred, you do. And like I've told you before, you have your father's innate instincts." His tone had grown placating, but hardened again. "However, you own a bookshop. Stick to selling books for this case. Let the police do their job."

"I had no intention of...." My mind caught up with Branson's words. "What do you mean *this* case?" *Why this case? What's different about it?*

Once more I could swear Branson seemed flustered, but it was such a quick flash I couldn't truly be sure. "I already made that clear, Fred. *This* doesn't involve you. Your stepfather isn't accused of murder, neither is your friend and business partner. The only thing it has to do with you is that you happened to be in the same forest when Henry was killed. If somehow that makes you a suspect, then I suppose that would also be true for Katie... and Leo."

Watson whimpered at Leo's name.

Granted, Branson truly had hit one of my biggest triggers right on the head. After I left my marriage, I swore I would never be told what to do again, especially in a way thick with condescension, so maybe my haze of anger was coloring my perception. I was sure it was. Well, whatever. "Was that a threat? That if I don't listen to you then the police attention might turn toward Leo?"

"Don't be hysterical, Fred."

I laughed. It was that or punch him in the face. "Call me hysterical again, Branson, and I'll make sure to demonstrate to you what that word truly means."

"Now who's threatening?"

I opened my mouth to retort, but shut it again. He had a point. And even if he didn't, there was no good way for this to end if we kept going. As much as I hated to admit it, he was the policeman. I couldn't see him doing something as petty as arresting me or charging me with anything, but unlike him, a few dinners together didn't make me feel like I had the full measure of Branson Wexler. Which this conversation made more apparent. "Thank you for dropping by. I'm not sure if you noticed, but things are quite busy upstairs, and currently, Katie is the only paid person on staff dealing with the madness. I have work to do."

"Fred...." His voice softened, and he reached for me.

I took a step back.

Branson dropped his hand, but his voice lost all hardness. "I'm sorry. I really am. I know I handled this wrong."

For one disgusting moment, I nearly said it was okay, that I understood, and on the one hand, I did. He wasn't wrong. He was a policeman, a sergeant. *I* sold books. There was no other request he could make that would make any more sense, and I didn't care. "Yes. You did."

"Again, I'm sorry." He attempted a smile. "But even though I handled it poorly, I need to know that you understood."

"This is your way of fixing it? Implying that I don't understand simple English?" Okay, even I had to admit I was being petty at that point.

"Fred." His tone held a hint of warning.

"Yes, Sergeant Wexler. I heard your words, and I understood them. Thank you for checking."

He tilted his head, and I was certain he was about to ask me to clarify. That it wasn't enough to say that I understood, but that I would comply.

Maybe not an unreasonable request from a police officer to a civilian. But one that might prompt a second murder in this space in the span of a couple of months.

Seeming aware of that fact, he gave a sharp nod. "Very well. Glad we understand each other. And I am sorry that I've ended up offending you."

At least that much was different from my ex-husband.

Although at this point, it wasn't nearly enough of a difference to matter. "I need to get back to Katie."

Another nod. "Have a good day, Fred." He glanced down. "You too, Watson."

I glared after him, watched him walk out the door and then out of sight past the large windows.

He was right. I knew that. And I was willing to bet Branson had done what my father would have if he'd been in a similar situation. Although I'd like to think my dad would've handled things smoother with a woman he cared about. And I truly did think Branson cared about me.

I also knew that in some way, I was being childish. I wasn't simply going to find out who killed Henry because Branson told me not to, but that was part of it. I couldn't pretend to care too much about Henry's death. It was horrible for anyone to be killed, but outside of getting to witness the body firsthand, it didn't feel any more personal than a story on the news. And, like Katie had implied, part of me had already been mapping out what might've happened. Maybe that would have been enough to get me involved. Probably so. But either way, Branson had made my choice perfectly clear.

I knelt and lowered my forehead to Watson's as I ruffled his flanks. "Want to go for a walk in the snow, buddy?"

I spent the rest of the day helping Katie in the bakery. By the time noon arrived, Sammy had on an apron and was officially employed by the Cozy Corgi bakery. And by closing, I'd managed to sell a whopping three books.

Leaving Katie to explain the ropes and her vision for the bakery to Sammy now that they weren't bombarded by customers, I loaded Watson into my burnt-orange Mini Cooper and drove to my little cabin in the woods. As we passed the new McMansion development, I wondered which house belonged to Silas. Even considered attempting to find out so I could see if he wanted to go along. He seemed calm and capable, and since he was an avid birdwatcher, was obviously observant. I knew it wasn't smart to go hiking in the woods alone, even if I had a dog. The other option was Leo, but there'd been enough romantic conflict for one day.

Within half an hour, I was bundled up in winter gear, having traded my broomstick skirt for snow pants. I attempted to put a scarf on Watson, but he wasn't having it.

I was relieved it wasn't Leo at the ranger station as we drove through and entered the national park. Within another twenty minutes, we arrived at the small parking lot at the beginning of the hikes that started with Bear Lake. Though it was a little after six, the sun was already gone and the sky nearly nighttime black, but it was brighter than the night before. Not a cloud to be seen, the moon full and glowing.

I checked to make sure I had a water bottle, my cell, and a flashlight. Then Watson and I took off.

Though not overly playful, every once in a while, Watson enjoyed being in the snow. I hadn't figured out the difference—half the time he acted like the white stuff was the biggest annoyance in the world, and the other half, like on this occasion, as if he was a five-year-old kid eating at Chuck E. Cheese's for the first time. Not even minding being on a leash, Watson buried his nose in the thicker piles of snow by the trail and bulldozed through as we walked, reminding me of the old Disney cartoons of chipmunks burrowing under the ground and leaving a trail behind them.

I hadn't been sure I'd be able to find the location where Henry was killed, but that part turned out to be easy. Maybe I should've expected it. There hadn't been fresh snowfall that day, and while many trails and footpaths criss-crossed all around Bear Lake, it was clear where the most traveled path was. It had been walked over so much in the hours since the murder that most of the snow was gone, revealing the dirt and rock beneath.

No police tape marked the scene. I had been prepared to walk right past it, mentally sticking my tongue out at Branson as I did so, but it seemed the police had gathered everything they needed. Surely they'd searched the entire area. So not only was I being childish, I was also being ridiculous, thinking I'd find anything they hadn't.

The spot where Henry's body had lain was mostly

clear, with patches of snow here and there, and a small amount of bloodstain still visible.

For a second, I considered releasing Watson from his leash and giving him free rein to use his powerful dog nose to find things I couldn't see. But Leo had warned me when I first met him that it wasn't uncommon for mountain lions and coyotes to snatch family pets right out of the yard, even with people nearby. I might want to prove that Branson couldn't tell me what to do, but not at the cost of risking Watson.

We traipsed over the area for probably half an hour, Watson clearly most interested in the site of the killing. All the smells. But neither of us uncovered anything other than displaced rocks and broken twigs in the underbrush.

By the time a quarter after seven rolled around, I was freezing. It seemed colder than the night before, but maybe that was simply because I wasn't distracted. I was about to give up, when I remembered Leo's directions to Katie and me from the night before. I leaned against a large barren aspen and closed my eyes, letting the stillness of the evening blanket me. Like before, for a few minutes I heard nothing, and then it changed, slowly. Again, the wind was the first thing I noticed, with the rustle of branches overhead. Then Watson's breathing and his quiet footfalls as he padded around me. After a few more heartbeats, I heard scampering through the twigs and scraggly plants near our feet.

Then a quiet chirp.

I opened my eyes. At first I didn't see him, but then he moved. A mountain jay, its shiny black head glistening in the moonlight as it pecked at the ground where Henry had been killed. I didn't let myself think about what he might be pecking at.

Maybe he sensed my attention, because he looked over

in my direction and tilted his head. He then hopped a few feet farther away. Though jays were almost as common as pigeons in the city, I paused at his beauty, the rich blue of his feathers visible even in the dim light. He hopped several more yards, still inspecting Watson and me every couple of leaps, and then came to rest a short distance from where Henry had been killed. He began to peck the ground below another tree. He pecked again, and something glinted in the moonlight at his feet. Another chirp, another peck, and then Watson rushed toward him, moving so fast his leash slid off my wrist and dragged after him through the snow.

"Watson!"

He didn't listen, and the bird flew away before Watson was even halfway to it.

Watson stopped where the bird had been pecking, and I finished my rush to him and snatched up his leash. "What in the world are you doing? Trying to get eaten? Since when do you chase birds? Or play, for that matter?"

Watson gave me an unapologetic glance and then sat down in the snow with a huff.

A chirp from above made me glance up, and I found the jay looking down at us from a branch overhead. He was clearly mocking, though whether his judgment was aimed at me or Watson wasn't so obvious.

Remembering the flash I'd noticed as the jay had been pecking away at something, I searched the ground. I found several rocks, limitless pinecones, and just as many broken twigs and branches. Then, half-buried in snow, it caught the moonlight.

Slipping off my glove, I reached down and picked up the cold metal, then wiped the snow off against my jacket before lifting it to the light.

A silver pin. Similar to the one Katie now owned. It was

a strangely-shaped bird with glistening greenish brown stones acting as feathers. I had no idea what type of bird it was, not that it mattered. I didn't need to know the bird. I already knew *whose* it was, which was much more important. Though I didn't think I'd seen this exact pin on her, it matched the style of ones Myrtle wore.

Watson whimpered in anticipation as I knocked on the apartment door. He sniffed all around the base and looked up at me in excitement. That made one of us. I was torn between feeling nervous and wondering if I was being stupid.

Leo opened the door and cut off my concerns. Actually, Watson's frantic barking was probably what cut off my thoughts. Leo attempted to say hello to me, but wisely lavished his attention where needed most by dropping to both knees and giving Watson the belly rub of his life.

"You're going to find corgi hair in the most random places in your apartment for weeks now." I stepped past the two of them into the warmth. "Welcome to my life."

Leo grinned up at me, looking nearly as happy as Watson. "Small price to pay for getting love lavished like this."

That was true. I wasn't one of those who thought because a dog liked someone it meant they were a good person, or that dogs innately knew if people were evil. I'd be willing to bet Watson would forgive an intruder two minutes after murdering me if they had a big enough dog treat. But on the whole, I figured it was a good sign when my little grump was accepting of someone.

To my surprise, when Leo stood, shut the door, and led us into his apartment, Watson reclaimed his spot by my side, managing to pad along without tripping me. Though he kept his adoring gaze on Leo.

"Welcome to my home. It's not much, but better than some." He motioned toward the kitchen. "Would you like a drink? I'm not a big alcohol kinda guy, but I have water.... And maybe some pink-lemonade mix."

"Pink-lemonade mix?" I couldn't help but laugh. "I don't think I've gotten an offer for that since I was ten."

He shrugged. "It's pretty good. Nothing but sugar, but it brings back good memories."

Talk about a different experience from the three-hundred-dollar bottle of wine Branson had ordered for our first meal together. Chances were high my class level put me at more of a pink lemonade kind of gal. "I'm okay, thanks, but if you don't mind a bowl of water for Watson?"

"Of course. Be right back."

As Leo headed to the kitchen, I took the time to inspect his apartment. I wasn't sure if it was because Leo was younger or just a stereotypical man. The space was clean... spotless, but there wasn't much to it. The furniture seemed more for complete convenience than any aesthetic design. There were some pictures scattered here and there of people I assumed were family, but little else to make the place feel homey.

Leo was back in less than a minute, set a bowl at Watson's feet, and then motioned toward the couch. "Want to fill me in? You sounded a little flustered."

I sat on the edge of the couch closest to Watson, and Leo took the other side, leaving an empty cushion between us. I decided not to clarify the "flustered" comment. Better let him think my discovery on the moonlight hike had affected me. In truth, I'd been torn about calling Branson to show him the pin, but figured it would end in another argument. Leo seemed a more natural option, though for some odd reason, part of me felt guilty for dragging him into it.

I opted to cut to the chase and pulled the pin out of my pocket. "Watson and I did a little snooping around where Henry was killed last night. We found this."

Leo lifted the pin from my hand, his honey-brown eyes going wide. "Myrtle's."

"Yeah. That's what I thought too. I don't know if I've seen her wear this exact one, but it's definitely her style."

"You know, I can't say that I have either. But she has a ton of them." He inspected it again. "It's a kakapo. Native to New Zealand and critically endangered."

"Well, that definitely sounds like a bird Myrtle would care about."

Leo gave a halfhearted shrug. "I don't think there's a bird in existence that Myrtle doesn't care about." He chuckled softly. "She's nearly as concerned about those already extinct as she is the ones we have now." He twisted the jewelry, a sad expression crossing his face. "You found this where Henry was killed?"

I nodded. "A few yards away, but basically, yes." For some reason, the next thought hadn't entered my mind until that very moment. I wasn't sure how I missed it before. "A mountain jay found it for us. Seems fitting for Myrtle, doesn't it?"

He chuckled again. "That it does. Although if you are thinking what I think you're thinking, it would be kind of sad that a bird, of all things, would be Myrtle's undoing."

I wasn't sure what I was thinking anymore. So many possibilities had flitted through my mind on the drive over that I couldn't land on one in particular that seemed to make sense. "You know, when I picked it up, that's where I went instantly. That Myrtle must've been the killer, or at least been there when Henry was murdered. But the pin wasn't the murder weapon, and it wasn't right where he lay either. By the time the police got there, the entire Feathered Friends Brigade had all stomped around that area. It could have easily fallen off her coat."

That realization had bothered me the night before as well, once I got home. I was a policeman's daughter. The least I could've done was a better job at securing the scene. Of course, I also realized on my way over to Leo that I'd messed up again. I'd picked up the pin with my bare fingers and removed it from the scene. Though, in my defense, it had already been cleared and was no longer a crime scene. Either way, my prints were all over it, as were Leo's now.

"I take it you're investigating Henry's murder?"

I paused for a second, trying to determine if I'd heard judgment in Leo's tone. I didn't think so. "I don't know, honestly. I don't have a reason to. No one I know very well or care about is under suspicion. I'm probably being stupid." I couldn't bring myself to admit to Leo that at least some part of it was simply due to Branson telling me that I couldn't. Though, that honestly wasn't the largest part.

An expression crossed Leo's face that I couldn't name. Not nervous, but... something.... Finally he licked his lips and narrowed his eyes. "I know you and Branson are close. So please don't take this as a slight against him, but I haven't had the best experience with the police department in this town." He winced. "Maybe that's not fair to single him out. I've had a few interactions with him, to be sure, that haven't gone well, but the same is true for many of the other officers. It's not just Branson. Every concern I've had about poaching was dismissed. You finding the owl was the first breakthrough we've had. And I know the members of the bird club have had similar experiences."

"Well, yes, but you can't blame Branson for that. I've attended two functions with them—including the blowup at the opening night of the bookshop, three—and every single one involved accusations against its own members. Granted, those were all from Henry, but it's hard to take it seriously."

It was easy to see the walls beginning to form behind Leo's eyes.

I rushed ahead to try to stop the damage I'd accidentally done, and in so doing reached out and touched his thigh briefly without meaning to. "I didn't say that to defend Branson. We had a disagreement about all of this. And I've seen enough to know that even if the Feathered Friends Brigade brought the entire case solved on a platter that there's so much bad history between the bird club and the police department, they probably wouldn't even give it a second thought." A twinge of guilt bit at me for betraying Branson, which was ridiculous. I wasn't betraying him, nor did I owe him anything.

The walls crumbled just that easily. "Yeah. Exactly." Leo laughed again, the ease truly back. "Don't get me wrong, I can't entirely blame Branson or the police. There's a limited number of times you can experience the cry-wolf effect before you quit listening. Even me—Henry was trying to tell me his thoughts on the poaching that very night. I didn't listen. Not that it means he was right this time. But when you accuse everyone under the sun, at some point, maybe you finally land on the right person."

I sat up a little straighter. I'd not thought of it like that. "So you're thinking maybe he truly did know the poacher this time, and that person killed him."

"Maybe. Though I can't see the poacher in that group. Most of them genuinely have a strong passion about birds.

There's a couple, like Paulie, who I think are just there for the social aspect, but that's rare."

Excitement buzzed through me, and if there'd been any question whether I was going to continue, that faded away. "Who was the last person Henry accused? Owen, right?"

He scrunched up his nose as he thought. "Yes, I believe so. Two days before had been Roxanne, and last week he was accusing Myrtle again." He held up the kakapo pin once more, as if seeing Myrtle's face on it. "The two of them had a strained relationship. Or at least Henry had a strange relationship with her. One minute she was nearly like a savior to him who deserved worship, and the next she was a traitor who was using the club for her own gain in power."

"What do you think?"

He came back to the moment and grinned at me, his fondness clear. "Interviewing witnesses, Detective Page?"

"Oh, sorry. I didn't mean to treat you like that."

Leo laughed and shook his head. "I'm teasing. Well, kinda. It's a good look on you." At that moment, Watson leapt from the floor onto the cushion between us.

"Watson! Get down. You're not at home."

Though he glowered at me, he started to oblige, but Leo placed his hand on Watson's head.

"As long as he's not breaking rules from your house, it's fine with me. I kinda love the little guy. Although, how could I not? I rarely get such rock-star treatment. Basically it's just Watson and my mom."

My heart warmed suddenly, though I couldn't quite say why. I focused on Watson instead. "Fine. Enjoy the couch. Try not to completely cover the cushions in your fur."

In way of response, Watson rolled over on his back, accepted belly scratches from both of us, and made a Watson-size cloud of hair billow around the three of us.

Leo grinned over at me. "He's not exactly subtle, is he?"

"You have no idea." I offered a grimace. "Maybe he gets that from me. So, I believe you were getting ready to tell me your thoughts about Myrtle?"

He laughed again, and I realized I was getting used to that sound. "She's a trip, to be sure. And I wouldn't completely disagree with Henry. She likes her power and being in control, but I honestly don't think it's about her. She's obsessed with birds, but not owning them or collecting them like so many. She wants to save them." He started rubbing Watson's paws. I was pretty sure the earth had stopped moving—Watson didn't let anyone do that. "But if I'm being honest, I have to fully admit I have a blind spot where Myrtle's concerned. It's rare for people to feel as passionate about animals as I do, or in Myrtle's case, even more so. At times it can feel like there's a handful of you trying to make a difference. And she is. She's trying to make a difference. So I can't see her in a bad light. The only reason I could ever picture her killing somebody was if she found out they were poaching her birds."

I sucked in a breath, and Leo looked over at me. "Maybe that's it exactly. Maybe Henry was the one poaching and he spent all his time accusing everyone else. What's that saying? The lady doth protest too much? He wouldn't be the first one to try such a thing."

Leo shrugged. "Maybe. Although he was pretty passionate about birds as well. Perhaps he's the kind who liked to collect them? I can't say. In a lot of ways, he was as crazy as Myrtle about it all. But there is something with Myrtle that lets you connect. Whatever that thing is, it was missing with Henry."

Both our gazes traveled to the pin on the sofa by Watson.

Leo picked it up once more. "You going to take this to Branson?"

"I suppose I have to. Although I don't know how he's going to handle it. He made it very clear to keep my nose out of it this time."

Leo considered for a moment. "I can take it. Say that I found it when I went back to the scene. In fact you can take me there now and show me exactly where you found it so I can show him. That way you're not in danger of being shut out of the case or getting in trouble."

And look at that—he brought up one of the very options I'd been considering on the way over. Words I hadn't been sure how to bring myself to ask. Now I didn't have to. He offered it up like the easiest thing in the world.

And as the words left his lips, I knew my answer. I prided myself on being Charles Page's daughter. No child of his would lie about a murder investigation. "No. But thank you. That's something I'll have to do myself. I can handle him."

And once more Leo's lovely laugh filled the space between us. "Oh, Fred, I have no doubt of that. I can't imagine anyone you can't handle."

The last time Watson and I had entered the police station, we were running for our lives. Technically, I was running and Watson was in my arms, a position he detests. One might think once a location became a safe haven there was no way it could ever be anything other. But nothing about walking through the front doors of the police station this time came close to feeling like relief.

After my last conversation with Branson, I could already feel my temperature rising. I wasn't breaking any laws, wasn't impeding an investigation, and it wasn't my fault that I'd done a better job of detective work than the entire police department since I'd moved to Estes. And I was done being told what to do.

After I held open the door for Watson and glanced toward the front desk, another surprise flitted through me. Officer Green was talking to the policeman at the desk, who I believed was the same gentleman Watson and I had burst in on the last time we were there. And upon seeing her, a twisted miracle happened. I was glad it was Officer Green and not Branson. I never would've dreamed of that happening in a million years.

As always, when Susan Green looked at me and

sneered at Watson, I could swear I heard Miss Gulch promising threats, followed by, *and your little dog too....*

"Hello. Good to see you, Officer Green." I nodded toward the other policeman but didn't attempt to recall his name.

Susan flinched, confusion washing over her features. Neither of us had ever said it was good to see the other. From our first meeting on, there'd been nothing but hostility. And while I considered her the bigger perpetrator, it went both ways.

"Winifred. It's good to...." Clearly unable to say the words, she turned her solid bulk to look at me full-on. "Are you needing police assistance?"

This was going better than normal as well. I pulled the pin from my pocket and started to close the distance to the counter but was jerked up short by Watson's leash. Looking back, apparently some snow had fallen off his fur and he was having a little snack on the go. I gave a pleading yank to his leash, and he huffed, clearly affronted, then with narrowed eyes took a final lick of the melting treat and uncharacteristically followed directions.

Officer Green's sneer was more pronounced as I turned back. Her pale blue eyes clearly revealing that she would spit-roast a corgi if she got the chance.

Okay, maybe this wasn't going better than normal.

"Watson and I found this on our—" I cleared my throat. "—moonlight walk through the national park. I thought maybe this could be important evidence."

Susan didn't reach for the pin—simply studied it for a second, glared at me, then repeated the pattern several times. After a moment, Officer What's His Name stretched out his hand for it, only to have Susan grip his wrist and shove his hand away.

I should have been upfront. Although in my defense, there was no way I could've played this out that would've ended pleasantly.

"Moonlight walk through the national park, huh?" She finally took the jewelry, studied it for less than a heartbeat, and then gave me the cold ice of her stare once more. "You know, Miss Page, normal people don't traipse back through the woods alone in the dark, even with their guard dog that's more the size of a fat hamster, and parade through a crime scene that's less than a day old." She smiled, sort of. Whatever it was, it wasn't a smile at all. "Of course, I should've stopped when I said *normal* people."

I cleared my throat again, and to my surprise once more, I decided that I preferred this interaction to anything I would've had with Branson. Susan and I weren't exactly cordial to each other, but neither of us were expected to be. "You've got me there, Susan. One thing I've never claimed was being normal. And this wasn't exactly at the crime scene; it was several yards away. And… there was no tape."

"Right." She looked like she was enjoying herself finally. "Because you don't see walking through yellow police tape like somehow crossing a finish line."

I started to object, but the description was apt. One I wouldn't have thought of, but she was spot-on. Especially this time, with my desire to solve it before Branson or anyone else.

Officer Green held the pin up between us. "You know, Fred, while not overly impressed with your attempts to play Nancy Drew, at least with the evidence you found at Christmas, you had the sense to put it in a Ziploc bag. How much show-and-tell did you do on this little ditty before you brought it to me? Should I expect to find half of the town's fingerprints on it?"

I nearly pointed out that I most definitely did not bring it to *her*, but I reminded myself that I was a thirty-eight-year-old woman, and there was no reason to return to schoolyard cattiness. "I'll agree with you there. I wasn't thinking clearly when I picked the pin out of the snow."

She leaned forward, barely enough to be decipherable, but I could feel the hunger in the action. "Goodness. That's embarrassing. Wasn't your daddy a police officer?"

It didn't matter that we were in a police station, nor that she would happily throw Watson and me into separate cells in the back. Susan had hit a nerve, and she was about to see the unleashed fury that all redheads share, no matter what the shade, when Sergeant Wexler appeared as if by magic from the hallway beside the counter.

"Fred. I thought I heard your voice." Branson smiled at me like our last interaction hadn't been tense in the slightest. He even went so far as to walk around the counter, squeeze my arm gently, and pat Watson, who allowed it to happen for about two whole seconds. Then he refocused on me, his handsome face easy and approachable. "What brings you in?"

Officer Green didn't give me the chance to respond. Leaning over the counter, she thrust the pin between us. "Our local busybody bookshop owner brought us the evidence we need to crack the case of who killed crazy man Henry. And due to her considerate nature, she didn't want us to spend police resources fingerprinting the thing, so she passed it around town."

Though Branson winced at Susan's tone, his green eyes cooled, then hardened. Despite myself, I straightened a little under the weight of his glare. "I thought I made myself clear, Fred. You said you understood."

His voice was low but not low enough that Susan and

the other officer wouldn't be able to hear. For his part, the officer who was nameless had the grace to look uncomfortable. Susan appeared to be experiencing Christmas for a second time a few weeks later.

Well, if Branson wasn't going to have this conversation in private, I wasn't about to cower. I straightened to my full height. "You're right. I did say I understood, but I didn't agree to anything. And if we're pointing fingers...." I demonstrated by pointing my finger at the pin still in Susan's hand. "It's a good thing I did. As your department had already scoured the area and seemed to overlook something."

He didn't so much as miss a beat, not even to look at the pin. "So please tell me how to do my job, Fred. What would you like me to do? Doubtless you've deduced that the pin is more than likely Myrtle Bantam's. Do I take it to her and ask if she shoved it into Henry's throat before the knife? Do I assume it's hers because, out of all the people the officers found traipsing around the dead body when they arrived, she is Henry's killer? Or perhaps only the killer would be fool enough to drop some perfectly placed clue for you to stumble upon?"

"My guess is that her dog found it. Isn't he the real detective? After all, he found the candy that cracked the case when Opal was killed." Christmas had indeed come for Susan Green. I knew there wasn't any love lost between her and Branson, but clearly she couldn't help herself. "And it was him that got a craving for pizza which led to the most heart-stopping car chase through town that's ever happened with people who weren't on mopeds."

Branson flashed her a look, one that said to be silent, but that was all. He turned back to me and folded his arms. "Well? You obviously don't respect what we do here, nor me requesting nicely for you to let me do my job. So you might as well tell me what to do next."

Once more, my indignation flared. I decided to leave with as much dignity as I could muster. "I've never told you how to do your job, Sergeant Wexler. And if I thought you weren't able to do it, I wouldn't have brought you the pin, which was apparently overlooked at the site. What you do next is up to you." I turned to leave, hoping Watson wouldn't stop at the puddle that was between us and the door.

"No more moonlight strolls, Miss Page. Otherwise it might be considered police interference."

I didn't look back at Susan. I knew if I did, I genuinely would lose my temper. "Last I checked, the national park belongs to all people, *Miss* Green."

Thankfully Watson decided the puddle was beneath him. Not only wasn't he tempted to eat it, but decided he was too good to walk through it. He took the wide way around, and then we walked proudly out the front door.

Things weren't quite as hectic at the Cozy Corgi the next morning. Even so, there was a decent rush for coffee and pastries, but it seemed more people simply wanted breakfast than gossip about the latest murder. I didn't even get to talk to Katie very much, no more than to fill her in on the previous night's events. She was still busy between customers and training Sammy.

Strangely, I was a little sad about Sammy. Obviously Katie and I both needed help, but it had been nice adjusting to our store with only the two of us. Although, even upon the second meeting, I was blown away that Katie had somehow managed to find her doppelgänger. It was uncanny.

That was a quality I most definitely was not going to look for when I decided to hire someone for the bookshop.

It had been at least an hour since I sold a book, or since anyone had done more than wave as they made the trek from the front door to the stairs leading to the bakery. I studied Watson as he slept in the rays of the sun pouring through the large windows. He'd claimed a spot closer to the front door than I would've predicted, now that we had people coming and going. He was surrounded by books and looked so charming there, his orange fur shiny, the hardwood floor gleaming, with the backdrop of rows and rows of novels.

That was one more reminder of why I was in town. Not to get my heart dashed by Branson Wexler, *which was not happening*, nor to have it comforted by Leo Lopez, *which was not happening either*. I was here for the Cozy Corgi and to enjoy life.

Well, I was going to do just that—even if I did have to keep reminding myself.

I wandered into the mystery room, picked up a reprint of Agatha Christie's *A Body in the Library*, and plopped myself down on the sofa in front of the fire. From where I sat, I could look over my shoulder and see Watson napping away, could still hear his soft snores.

Yes, this was why I was here. And with the soft sounds of chatter, clink of dishes, and hum of machines joining the heavenly aroma wafting from above, it was even better than I'd pictured.

I barely made it three chapters in before Katie appeared in the doorway. "Fred! There you are."

I shut the book and started to stand, but she motioned for me to stay where I was, then plopped down beside me.

She sighed and dragged her fingers through her hair, leaving trails of flour or icing behind. "I needed a break, and I wanted to tell you the gossip." She glanced around the base of the sofa. "Where's Watson?" Without waiting for a reply, she glanced over her shoulder and chuckled. "Working hard, I see."

At that moment Watson let out a quiet little bark and his paws twitched.

"I'm pretty sure he's either dreaming about especially large dog treats when he does that or possibly dreaming about another nap."

"Sounds about right." She turned back to me. "I might be tired, but even this, simply being able to walk downstairs and talk to you for two minutes is an improvement. Sammy is going to be worth her weight in gold."

"I'm sure I should follow your lead and start looking for someone to help me out in the bookstore, not that it's been an issue today." I shook my head at the thought of an assistant without a single thing to do. I'd have to find someone who didn't like mysteries so they could read in a different room and leave me to my sofa, lamp, and fireplace in peace. "Perhaps I should worry about selling books before I hire someone."

Katie patted my knee. "Don't feel bad. Books are a different thing than pastries. People need sugar every day. But when they need a book, they'll come here." She leaned closer to play-whisper, "Well, forget about Amazon for the moment." She winked. "At least when the tourist season arrives, you'll be busy."

I wasn't going to admit that I wasn't overly worried

about it. Simply sitting here by the fire reading was about as perfect as things could get. "So what's the gossip?"

Katie's brown eyes widened. "Well, Benjamin was upstairs. He's the one who owns the camera shop down the way. He's a member of the Feathered Friends Brigade, remember?"

"Yeah, the handsome young one who seemed like he was making a sales pitch."

She nodded. "Exactly. I kinda think that's why he's there. He's tenacious, I'll give him that. He tried a sales pitch on me and Sammy, saying that we needed a high-quality camera so we could post photos of all the pastries online, to bring in more customers." She gave a dismissive wave with her hand. "Like I have time for that. And that wasn't my point." Before launching in again, she glanced around to see if anyone had wandered near as we spoke, a laughable thought considering no one was in the bookshop. "Well, according to Benjamin, the police brought Myrtle in for questioning this morning. I'm still not clear on how he found out about it so quickly, but he said he drove straight there and told them that she was with him at the exact same moment Henry was killed." She narrowed her eyes. "Which I suppose could be true. Honestly, I lost track of time when you, Leo, and I were watching the elk, but the last I'd seen of Myrtle, she was with Silas, not Benjamin. Though, I don't remember seeing Benjamin much at all. I mean, obviously he was there, but I never saw him around Myrtle."

I wished I'd been upstairs devouring another pastry I didn't need instead of reading by the fire so I could have judged Benjamin for myself. "You got the impression he was lying?"

She shrugged. "No, not necessarily. It doesn't match what I remember, but again, there's nothing for me to remember—we split up, and then the three of us saw some elk." Another shrug. "Plus, not that I know Myrtle, obviously, but I can't see her and Benjamin chatting it up. You know what I mean? I don't think he's a true bird lover like the rest. I kinda think he's there to sell camera equipment more than anything about birds."

"I had a similar thought, actually, but at the tune of ten thousand a year, is that intelligent advertising?" Camera equipment was expensive, so maybe he only needed a few sales a year to make it up. "What'd he say about Myrtle? Did he know how the police questioning ended up?"

"That's what I'm getting at. Benjamin said as soon as he heard about them taking Myrtle in, that he drove straight there and let them know that they were together."

"So with him as her alibi, they couldn't hold her. Especially if all they had on her was the pin I told you about earlier."

"Exactly." She cocked an eyebrow and gave an excited grin. "So, I was thinking you and I should leave Sammy here, and we can go up to Wings of the Rockies and get Myrtle's version."

"You're determined that I'm going to play detective on this, aren't you?"

Katie rolled her eyes. "No more than you are, and don't tell me otherwise. I know you and I haven't known each other all that long, but there's one thing I'm certain about—Winifred Page doesn't let a man tell her what she can or cannot do, even if that man happens to wear a badge."

As so often was the case in my conversations with Katie, I was reminded of one of the many reasons I loved her so. "I'm sure I shouldn't admit it, but you're right. I can't say I'm certain my father would approve of going against another officer's wishes, but I'm not letting this go." At the thought, I started to stand to head straight to Myrtle, but then logic took over and I sat back down. "However, if you'll remember, it was Myrtle Bantam who called and complained about me when I was trying to clear Barry's name. Basically told Branson I was harassing the storeowners. I can't imagine a conversation with her going well right now, especially if she knows I'm the one that turned in the pin. And while I don't think Branson would tell her that, if she came in contact with Susan Green, I guarantee you that would get passed on."

Katie let out a little growl. "Dang it! I suppose that makes sense, but I really wanted to go talk to her."

Now *there* was a thought. I sat up straighter, excitement flooding back. "That's a brilliant idea. She loves you. If you had ten grand, you'd be in her club right now. I bet you anything she'll talk to you."

Katie looked nervous. "Without you? You want me to go? Without you?"

This time I was the one who squeezed her knee. "Don't be silly. We both know all you need to do to get her talking is to spend five minutes on Google looking up facts about that kakapo bird and chances are you won't leave her store until closing."

"Brilliant!" She pulled out her cell and began typing away. I was certain she would be an encyclopedia about the endangered species within half an hour. "What will you do while I'm talking to Myrtle?"

No use pretending I wasn't going to play detective again. "I think I'll wake Watson and go to gossip headquarters. Luckily, I don't have to do any research to get Anna and Carl talking. And for once, with him being part of the club, it'll be some firsthand knowledge."

Watson seemed to forgive me for disrupting his nap when he realized we were walking toward Cabin and Hearth. He'd come to equate the store with his favorite dog treats instead of the home furnishings and high-end log furniture it sold. Apparently it didn't matter that Katie was now making those treats in large quantities right above our heads. Watson went from sulking and sluggish at the end of his leash to bouncing on his front paws as we walked through the shop's doors.

If I'd been feeling guilty about ignoring the police edict to leave well enough alone, or wondering if I was disappointing my father as he looked down on me, all such notions fled when I approached the front counter of Cabin and Hearth.

Not only were Anna and Carl present and accounted for, but they were flanked by my uncles. With so much natural talent for gossip gathered in one place, the home furnishing store might've been a front for a new tabloid publication. It was like the universe was flashing the green light saying, "Here you go, Fred, figure it out. Solve that murder, and show that handsome police officer that he can't tell you what to do, even if it is his job." Okay, maybe that wasn't exactly the message, but I was going to take it that way, regardless.

I nearly laughed as the four of them turned as one to look at Watson and me. Then for a second, it didn't so much seem like a miracle provided from the gossip gods as much as stumbling into a nest of hungry vampires. The look in their eyes was ravenous. So much so that I took a step back. Watson whined, but I wasn't sure if he felt the same intensity in their stare or if he was begging for a snack.

"Hi, guys." I managed a wave. "What are you all up to?"

"Talking about you, naturally." Blunt as always, Percival left the group, grabbed my hand, and ushered me to join the others.

Anna and Carl were on the other side of the counter, and I took my place between Gary and Percival, closing the circle. Watson nudged his head against the back of my calf. I ignored him.

Anna reached across the counter and grasped my hand. "Perfect timing, dear. We were going to come find you in a few minutes. Fill us in."

"Fill you in on what?" Even as the words left my mouth, I wasn't sure why I bothered.

Percival rolled his eyes, but Anna used her other hand to pat mine. "None of that. You're the one who took Myrtle's pin to the police last night, and then she was brought in for questioning this morning. So, fill us in."

"How do you all do that? Did you install surveillance cameras in the police department?" I narrowed my eyes at Gary. Though he could hold his own, he was the least natural gossip of the four. "I'm sure Branson didn't tell you, and I know Officer Green hates you and Percival nearly as much as she does me, since you're part of the family." I turned to Anna and Carl. "Is she your in? Do you two have a special relationship with Susan that I'm not aware of?"

"We never reveal our sources, dear." Anna released my hand and patted her poufy cloud of white hair while managing to look dead serious. "And you came to us, remember? Don't pretend you're not here hoping to finagle some details from us."

Percival snickered. "You can act like you don't want the gossip, Fred. But you come by it naturally. It's in the Oswald blood, even if your mother isn't especially good at it. Maybe it skips generations or something. And while it took a different form, your father was good at it too. It's what made him such a great detective." He nudged my shoulder with his. "So give in, favorite niece of mine, and dish."

I did. Filling them in on Watson's and my moonlit hike, finding the pin, my interactions at the police station, and what Benjamin told Katie.

Percival threw his long arm over my shoulder and squeezed. "Oh, darling, I'm so sorry that there's already trouble in paradise between you and that handsome sergeant. Don't give up hope. We can rope him into being part of the family yet."

Gary patted my arm comfortingly but leveled his dark gaze at his husband. "I don't think that was the point of the story, Percival." He gave me a wincing smile. "But I am sorry about that, too."

Carl ignored them. "Benjamin told the police he was with Myrtle when Henry was killed?" For once, his words weren't laced with the enjoyment of a scandal, but sounded more like actual confusion. "That's odd."

All eyes turned toward Carl.

He straightened at the attention, seeming pleased. "Well, that isn't quite how I remember it that evening."

"She couldn't quite explain why, but Katie didn't completely buy Benjamin's story. Something seemed off." I knew I'd come to the right place. "What do you remember from that night?"

Settling into the role of center of attention, Carl leaned against the counter and propped his weight on his elbows. "Well, in full disclosure, I was a bit distracted that evening. Ever since Paulie joined the Feathered Friends Brigade, he's seemed insistent that he and I become BFFs. So I spent a good chunk of the night avoiding him, which is rather like a full-time job. But I teamed up with Roxanne, who has the most badges for her trivia knowledge about birds. After a few minutes, we ran into Raul and Lucy."

Anna interrupted by reaching across the counter once more and touching my arm. "You know Raul, don't you, Fred? He owns Pasta Thyme. Where you and Branson went on your first date? I heard you had a very good bottle of wine."

"What?" Percival went ultrasonic, eliciting a sharp whimper from Watson. He wheeled toward me. "You didn't tell me that? You made it sound like you simply grabbed a meal a couple of times. You didn't say it was at Pasta Thyme or that there was wine involved." He snapped a hand on his jutted hip. "That isn't a meal. That is a *date*. I had no idea things were moving so expediently." He waggled excited eyebrows at Gary. "Can you imagine the gorgeous great nephews and great nieces those two will give us." Before Gary or anyone else could respond, Percival's expression crashed into disappointment, and he looked back at me. "Oh, I forgot. You two are already having problems. We need to figure that out."

I couldn't even think of how to respond to any of that,

and I looked to Gary for help. He simply shrugged. "What do you expect, Fred? You have met your uncle before."

He had a point. I refocused on Carl. "You said that you teamed up with Roxanne and the two of you bumped into Raul and Lucy. Right?" Maybe we could get the show back on the road.

He nodded emphatically. "Yes, exactly. I do think Raul genuinely cares about birds, even if he doesn't have any badges, and he's very committed to the cause. But Lucy...." He waffled his hand back and forth. "I'm pretty sure she's there for discounted bird feed from Myrtle's store."

"Discounted bird feed?" I gaped at him. "She's paying ten grand a year to be in a club for discounted bird feed?"

"Well"—Carl shrugged—"a discount is a discount."

All four of the older generation nodded, and I realized I had gotten pulled off track, again. I shook my head, trying to clear it, only to have Percival gasp and reach toward my ears.

"Are these the earrings Leo Lopez gave you at the grand opening?" He twisted the dangling chain of corgis, causing me to adjust the angle of my head to keep it from pinching. "They are! Well, you truly are a niece of mine. I couldn't be prouder. Romancing *two* handsome men." He reached behind my back and swatted at Gary. "Our great nieces and great nephews might be of the Hispanic persuasion. We'll be so cutting-edge."

Gary cocked a judgmental eyebrow, then cast me a withering glance. "He said the same thing to me at our proposal. If we hadn't been together for over twenty years, I'd have been fairly certain he was with me because I was black, not actually because he loved me."

Percival's expression changed once more, and he turned

wide eyes on me again. "Oh no, I just thought! You're thirty-eight, Fred. Better get moving."

I sighed, not sure if I should laugh or cry. "Goodness, the four of you together are a lot to handle. If we could try to stay on track, and not worry about the ticking away of my childbearing years, and get back to the case. Besides, I have Watson. If you have a corgi, who needs a kid?"

"Watson!" It was Anna's turn to suck in a gasp as she threw her hands in the air, as she was prone to do. "Oh my heavens, I was so caught up in the excitement I didn't even notice my favorite little man." She ran from behind the counter and smacked Carl's arm, another thing she was inclined to do. "Go get him one of the treats. Quick."

Knowing there was no reason to protest, I settled back and watched the fiasco. Anna rushed from behind the counter, all heaving bosom and gingham material billowing around Watson a she threw herself at him while Carl lumbered to the back to retrieve the treat.

Percival and Gary had never seen Anna with Watson before, as they kept casting wide-eyed stares over my head at each new promise of devotion and declaration of adoration that Anna lavished on my corgi.

Finally Carl returned, and knowing his role, handed the large all-natural dog treat to Anna so she could, in turn, present it as an offering to Watson.

And Watson, as *he* was prone to do, once receiving his treat, rejected further physical adoration and waddled to a large four-poster log bed, squeezed underneath, and relished his treasure.

Anna watched him contentedly for a few seconds and then returned to her place behind the counter. "So, Fred, quit dillydallying and fill us in."

I managed a smile before looking back at Carl. "I

believe it was you who was filling us in. What did you see about Benjamin that made you think he wasn't with Myrtle?"

"Oh yes! I almost forgot." I couldn't say I blamed him for that. He nodded, licked his lips, and then launched in once more. "So, like I was saying, Roxanne and I were looking for the Mexican Spotted Owl and ran into Raul and Lucy." To my surprise, there was no further commentary about the new players. "I was a little annoyed they wanted to join us—it makes it a lot less likely to find the bird you're looking for with more people traipsing around—but I think Roxanne has a secret crush on Raul, never mind that he's married."

Anna opened her mouth to comment, but I beat her to it. "And then the four of you ran into Benjamin?"

Carl nodded. "Why, yes. Exactly." He seemed impressed I'd put two and two together. It wasn't so much that, as simply trying not to spend all day in Cabin and Hearth without ever getting back to the matter at hand. "The four of us were milling about, Lucy constantly stubbing her toe on something or other and making noises, when I saw Benjamin and Petra talking to Owen and Silas. They were doing a better job than my group at being quiet, but from the expression on their faces, it looked like they were having a heated conversation."

I thought maybe I'd heard wrong. "You saw Silas with them?"

He nodded again.

"And you didn't see Myrtle with Silas?" The last time Katie and I had seen Silas, he'd been with Myrtle, and Benjamin was nowhere to be found.

Carl seemed to consider, his eyes narrowing. "No, I don't think so."

So Benjamin wasn't Myrtle's alibi, like Katie had expected, nor was Silas like I'd figured. Granted, if I was remembering all twelve of Myrtle's disciples, that left only Alice, Pete, Paulie, and Henry unaccounted for. And Henry ended up dead. So either Pete, Paulie, or Alice had a chance to get Henry alone, or it was Myrtle. "How long was it before you heard Alice scream?"

Carl shrugged. "I'm not sure. Maybe five minutes, maybe ten or more. My group didn't join theirs. In fact, Roxanne and I ended up splitting from Raul and Lucy. We kept going farther back into the forest. Roxanne was convinced she saw the owl hopping from tree to tree, so I followed along. It turned out to be another mountain jay. How in the world a woman so good at bird trivia could mistake a jay for an owl, I'll never know."

Five to ten minutes, or more.... Anything could happen in that time. The people Carl's story truly cleared were Roxanne and himself.

Anna smacked Carl's arm again. "Well, that doesn't help at all. What a waste of time that story was!"

Carl gaped at her. "Well, I didn't say I solved the murder. I said I didn't see Benjamin with Myrtle."

"In that amount of time, Benjamin easily could have teamed up with Myrtle. What good did telling us all of that do?" Anna sounded thoroughly disgusted.

He pointed at me. "She asked."

Another thought hit me. "Wait a minute, Carl. You said that Lucy and Raul were together."

Carl glanced at Anna's hand before nodding.

"Well, like before, anything could've happened in the time you and Roxanne split up with them, but when Leo, Katie, and I heard the scream, I'm fairly certain we were the first ones on the scene. And Lucy and Alice were the only ones who were there." I thought back, trying to recreate the image. Maybe that wasn't true. Maybe Raul had been there as well, off in the shadows, out of sight.

Carl rolled his eyes. "As much as I can't stand Alice, the woman is no murderer. Obviously I don't have proof of that, but she just isn't."

That was similar to how I felt about Myrtle. "Why can't you stand Alice?"

"I *earned* my badges. Every single one." Carl tapped his chest as if he was wearing his vest in counting the badges. "I practice my birdcalls religiously."

"I can attest to that." Anna grimaced. "Twenty minutes a day." She smacked the glass countertop. "Twenty. Minutes. A day. Twenty! Of the most horrid squeaking and squawking noises you've ever heard, outside of Myrtle herself, that is."

Percival snorted. "You got that right. That woman can squawk with the best of them. Maybe that's how she killed Henry."

"You don't like her because she got on to you for chasing that bird with a broom." Gary shook his finger at Percival as he would a naughty child. "Just because the two of you don't see eye to eye doesn't mean she's a murderer."

I tried to rein it in before I lost complete control once more. "What do you mean, Carl? How does Alice get her badges?"

"She cheats!" True indignation crossed his features. "The woman never travels. Ever. So how did she get a recording of the kakapo screeching? The bird is in New Zealand."

"Maybe she went to the zoo, or got it off YouTube." Gary sounded like he was trying to be helpful.

Carl apparently felt otherwise, judging from his stern

expression. "That would still be cheating, though, wouldn't it? A badge for capturing bird sounds is only valid if caught in the wild. Nothing in captivity, and you have to capture it yourself. Same is true for the badge for having the most photos." He shook his head.

Gary tried again. "Well, I know Alice has a son who's going to school to be a sound designer for movies. Maybe he makes them for her."

"That is still cheating!" This time, he smacked the counter, only to receive a second smack from Anna.

"You're going to break the glass." She smacked him a third time.

"So Henry's accusations of people cheating were true." Maybe whoever killed him didn't do so because he accused them of poaching, but simply was one of the other cheaters. It seemed a rather drastic reason for murder, but for people willing to pay ten thousand a year to be in a club, maybe not....

"Henry accused everyone of everything." Carl scoffed. "He even accused me of cheating on my sounds, saying that I had a recording in my pocket and was opening my mouth while I hit Play. Horrible man. But when you accuse everyone of everything, you're bound to land on the truth every once in a while."

Yes, I'd heard that logic about Henry before as well. But still... some of Carl's words replayed in my mind. "Wait a minute. Did you say Alice got a badge for having the sound of a kakapo?"

"Yes, I did. But she's gotten badges for sounds of lots of birds. But that one was the most infuriating, since that's Myrtle's favorite bird."

I gaped at him. "The kakapo is Myrtle's favorite bird?"

"Oh, yes." Carl was all seriousness. "She loves all birds,

but none of them as much as a kakapo. Which, I can't blame her. They are rather fascinating creatures. But if you're going to cheat, it's a little gross to go that extra mile toward brown-nosing the teacher, basically."

"Hold on." Percival reached out and grabbed Carl's arm. "Are you telling me Myrtle Bantam's favorite bird is called a kakapo. As in caca and poo. Her favorite bird is named after two types of poop?" He threw back his head and nearly peed himself laughing.

At that point, I knew I'd completely and utterly lost any chance of getting more actual information from any of them.

I checked my cell as Watson and I stepped back out onto Elkhorn Avenue. No text. Either Katie was still talking to Myrtle, or she truly had been sucked down the Google hole of random kakapo trivia. I glanced toward Myrtle's store at the other end of the street. I was tempted to go there. If Katie was already talking to her, then the ice would be broken. If nothing else, maybe I could get her to accidentally let slip what happened after she and Silas had left us that night. Although with my luck, I'd say something to irritate Myrtle and damage any relationship Katie was managing to build.

No, I needed to trust that Katie knew what she was doing.

The thought of Katie made me realize that the two owners of the Cozy Corgi bookshop and bakery had abandoned their store to someone who'd worked there for less than a day.

I glanced at Watson. "Sammy is pretty much a creepy clone of Katie, which means she can handle just about anything. We're good, right? It's not like anybody was buying books anyway."

Watson flicked an ear in my direction.

"Exactly. She's got it all under control. We'll drop by Myrtle's and see... no. No, we won't." I motioned toward the other end of the street. "We'll go to Alice's candle store, see if we can get her to talk about cheating. Though how I'm going to do that, I have no idea." With the sun sinking lower, the January afternoon was getting cooler, and I adjusted my mustard-hued scarf a little closer. "Okay, decision made, let's go."

Watson followed and let out a little bark as we neared the end of the block.

I turned back to him and found Watson staring at the door to Black Bear Roaster. Despite devouring his dog treat from Anna, Watson was doubtlessly picturing the countless too-dry scones we'd purchased there before Katie had opened the bakery. "Oh no, we're not going in there. I'm sure Carla is furious at whatever business Katie's taking away. Besides, you don't need another parched scone, do you?"

He whimpered.

We had a staring contest for a minute. I lost, as always. I wasn't sure why I bothered. Admitting defeat, I shielded my eyes with my hands, and pressed against the window, trying to see if Carla was behind the counter. She wasn't. Feeling better, I started to pull away, and then noticed someone waving. Carla, holding a baby, sat at the table by the window, less than a few inches away from where I'd smashed myself against the glass. I jerked back, then offered the most awkward wave in the history of waving.

I glared at Watson. "This is your fault. You and your love of bone-dry baked goods. It's not like I can walk away now."

For his part, Watson gave a little hop as I reached for the front door, but looked thwarted when I paused by the first table to the right. "Carla. It's so nice to see you." Suddenly I remembered the baby in her arms. "Oh, you had your baby." I leaned closer. He wasn't the cutest of babies, but newborns rarely were. "He's adorable!"

"This is Shayla, and she's a girl." Carla simultaneously shifted baby Shayla in her arms, exposing her ever-growing belly, and motioned to the woman I'd not even noticed sitting across from her. "She's Tiffany's little girl, and I still have one more month until I'm due."

"Oh!" I attempted a smile toward Tiffany. "Well, Shayla is absolute... perfection." I cleared my throat. "I don't want to take up your time. I'm sure you're busy. We just came in for a coffee and a scone."

Carla's eyebrows shot so far up they were hidden behind her blonde bangs. "Really? Can't you get that at your store? Are you already tired of Katie's inferior baking?"

At any other time, I would've defended Katie with every ounce of fire my long auburn hair bestowed upon me, but I'd already stuck my foot in my mouth too many times in the matter of ten seconds. "Nope. Just had a craving for chai, and Watson loves your scones."

Figuring out that heaven was near as I said his name, Watson gave another little hop.

At that point, I was certain Carla would never be able to find her eyebrows again. "Your *dog* loves my scones?"

Synapses stopped firing as I tried to figure out if it was better to make a purchase or throw myself out the front door. "Watson has a very discerning palate."

And with that, I turned and led Watson to the counter, instantly knowing that I'd chosen the wrong option. Even so, I ordered a dirty chai and a blueberry scone.

I could feel Carla's eyes drilling into my back. Perhaps it didn't take the kid two hours to make the chai, but it sure felt like it. Maybe it wasn't too late to run out the front door.

As I waited, a conversation wafted through the buzzing in my brain. "I'm telling you, there's nothing to worry about. They don't have anything on Myrtle."

At Myrtle's name, I turned around, and apparently not only had I lost the art of having an intelligent conversation with someone without accidentally being insulting, but I'd also forgotten how to not be obvious.

"You gotta quit calling me. She's going to be—" The man was sitting at a nearby table, and his words fell away as our eyes met.

It took me a second to put a name with his face. And when I did, I gave a little wave. "Hi, Owen." Well, look at that. It appeared I'd outdone myself on the world's most awkward wave. I was on a roll.

His expression brightened instantly, and he didn't lower the phone as he spoke. "Fred Page. Imagine running into you here." He glanced at Watson, but didn't offer comment. "Awful business the other night. But I heard you found a pretty little pin to turn in to the police." Though his lips formed what I thought was meant to be a smile, I felt a chill.

"You know, I heard that rumor, in fact—"

The barista cut me off, thankfully. "Large dirty chai and blueberry scone for Fred, on the counter."

I glanced back at the voice, and, for some stupid reason, gave a third wave to the teenage barista. "Thank you!" I'd never meant those words more. I gave a brave attempt at a smile to Owen, without meeting his eyes. "Well, that's me. Watson and I should be off. Nice running into you." I whirled, and practically dragged Watson across the floor as I scooped up the chai and the scone and booked it out the door. I didn't stop until we were two stores down.

Watson let out a huff, clearly affronted.

"Don't give me that attitude. You're the reason I went in there, remember? That was all your fault. All of it. Granted you didn't lift up both my feet and shove them in my mouth and down my throat, but still." I let out a sigh. "Seriously, what was that? Sometimes I wonder if Barry is secretly my real father." I shuddered at that thought and started to hand the scone to Watson, then remembered he'd just had a large all-natural dog treat. I'd given up on the diet I'd placed him on the month before. He'd lasted a whole ten minutes on it anyway. Even so, I broke the scone in half and handed a portion to him. I took a bite of the other, discovered the scone was still as dry as the Sahara, and despite my hatred of wasting food, tossed it in a nearby trash can.

I stood there, stunned, sipping my chai, hoping the caffeine would take effect and reset my brain. Someone was worried about Myrtle, and apparently was repeatedly calling Owen about it. Maybe it hadn't been simply one person responsible for killing Henry. Maybe it had been three. And maybe I was completely wrong about my gut feeling about Myrtle.

Watson finished devouring his scone, and looked at my empty hand, clearly expecting the other half.

Before I could remind him that I would be a horrible corgi mama if I allowed him to overdose on sugar, Owen stepped out of the coffee shop and, miracle of miracles, walked in the other direction without even looking our way.

Even so, I wasn't going to press my nonexistent luck, and I hurried toward Alice's candle shop, though I wasn't sure there was any point after overhearing that conversation. At least Watson and I were off the streets and out of Owen's possible view.

There was a chime as we entered Mountain Scents.

Alice, and an older Asian woman, both looked my way from the counter, straightened, and offered smiles that clearly stated I'd interrupted their conversation. When Alice spoke, her tone was entirely too cheerful. "Fred! And Watson! Petra and I haven't seen you since the hike the other night. I'm still shaken up about it."

For some reason, I hadn't recognized Petra as one of the members of the Feathered Friends Brigade. She nodded and found her voice. "Yes, we were talking about how awful it was. Poor Henry."

Though I didn't have a specific reason why, my gut told me they were lying. Although, maybe I was thrown off from my interaction with Owen and prone to suspect everyone at this point. "Yes, it was quite shocking." I took a sip of my chai, trying to figure out what to say, and then gave the cup a dirty look.

Alice laughed, this time the sound seeming authentic. "It's all the candles." She waved her hand in a circular motion in the air, encompassing the hundreds upon hundreds of candles in the store. "All the smells at once change the taste of nearly everything. I don't notice it anymore, but when I first opened, I thought it was the best diet plan I'd ever had."

Thank goodness Katie had wanted to open a bakery in the top floor of the Cozy Corgi, and not a candle shop. "That's kinda fascinating. I'll try not to take too much of your time so my chai doesn't get cold before I can drink it without it tasting like lavender." For some reason I thought that would be a joke, but it fell flat.

"You should try owning an ice cream parlor. I gave up on diets thirty years ago." If Petra was attempting humor, it felt as flat as mine had.

The three of us stared at each other awkwardly, and I

could feel Watson's judgment. And I had to admit, by that point, it was well deserved.

"Did you come in for a candle?" Though she smiled, Alice seemed as ready to get the show on the road as I was.

This had been a mistake. At least so soon after my interaction with Carla and Owen. I needed time to process through things. And to remove my foot from my mouth, where it seemed stubbornly affixed. I decided to be honest. I wasn't capable of pulling off anything else convincingly at this point. "No, I actually came by to talk about the other night. I was wondering what you ladies noticed in the forest." I shrugged at Petra. "Well, I didn't know you were here, but that was the luck of the draw. Two birds with one stone, I suppose."

Both of their eyes widened again, and it took me a heartbeat to realize that I'd received confirmation that my foot was indeed still in my mouth. One does not reference killing birds with stones to ornithological-obsessed people. Especially when one of their own had been murdered.

"Sorry. You know what I mean." That was doubtful. At this point even I didn't know what I meant anymore.

"Aren't the police investigating Henry's death? I did hear that you found one of Myrtle's pins at the scene, but aren't they taking it from there?" From Alice's tone, I was certain there was going to be a call to the police as soon as I walked out the door.

I attempted to skate around that question. "It's just that... Katie is thinking about joining." Turned out I was wrong. The truth wasn't going to cut it. And even as I continued, I knew the lie would fall flat, as everything else had. I should dial Branson and hand them the phone to get it over with already. "I know that Katie is an adult and able to make her own decisions, but for some reason, I feel protective. And I don't know if joining a club where someone was murdered, most likely by someone in that club, since we were the only ones up there, is the best idea. So... I thought I'd ask you, as two other women, how safe you feel."

They stared at me.

"Well, you know, with all the talk of poaching and everything. I don't want Katie to get mixed up in something." I should've followed Alice and Petra's lead and kept my mouth shut. "If there is a poacher turned murderer in the group, I don't think it's a good idea for her to join."

"Poacher?" Petra flinched, her gaze darkening. "You know, maybe it's bad to speak ill of the dead, but you shouldn't give a word Henry said a bit of credence." For a second it looked like she was about to launch into a sermon, then she sniffed and gave an apologetic glance toward Alice. "You know, I've been gone from the ice cream parlor too long as it is." She hurried past Watson and me with another glare and out the door.

I'd not meant to hit a nerve, or even to imply anything, but it seemed as far as Petra was concerned, I'd done both. And it felt like it was more than me sticking my foot in my mouth. I focused on Alice, hoping I'd not already managed to shut her down. "Sorry, I know I interrupted yours and Petra's conversation. I can come back later if you'd like."

Alice hesitated, and when she spoke, her words were slow and deliberate. "Fred, you are always welcome in my store. But I'm not sure what you're looking for here. I sell candles, that's it. In my spare time, I enjoy bird-watching and gathering with like-minded people. I don't have any clues to give you."

"No, I told you, I'm here because...." I let the words fade away. It was pointless. And even though I knew anything else I could possibly say would also be pointless, this was clearly the one chance I would have. Once I walked out the door, I was certain she really would call the police, and probably never speak to me again. So, once more, I tried for the truth. I reminded myself that I was Percival's niece, so I opted for the blunt truth.

"Honestly, Alice, you're right. I am here because of Henry's murder. Henry, as Petra demonstrated, made a lot of enemies. Constantly accusing other members of the group of cheating or poaching, and who knows what else." As I spoke the truth, some of my confidence came back. "In talking to other people who are in the club, your name came up as someone Henry was right about." I nearly stopped there but decided to push a little further, milk the chance for everything it had since it would be my last. "It seems his accusations about you cheating to earn your badges were true." Though the next part was speculation, I decided to take the risk. "Some are saying that you've gotten your son involved in your cheating. That he's provided you fake recordings from the school in Denver where he is studying to work on sound in movies."

"It's bad enough you imply Petra might have something to do with Henry's death." All timidness fell away, as did any hint of friendliness in her tone. "But don't you dare bring my son into this. He was not in those woods that night."

I flinched, completely thrown off. "I wasn't saying he was, Alice. Simply that he's helping you cheat to earn your badges."

"So what?" She sneered, her lips curling over her teeth, reminding me of what people said about mother bears. I'd not meant to threaten her son, but it seemed she was taking it that way. "They're a few badges. Pieces of embroidered fabric. Nothing to kill someone over. If you want to go around accusing other people, then I suggest you talk to Benjamin, ask him how he helped Silas get all his." She began to walk around the counter, and despite being several inches taller than her, I backed up in the face of her fury. "How dare you think that my son or I would murder someone for a bunch of stupid badges." She thrust out both her hands at me. "Get out of here. You and your dirty little dog. Get out of my store."

She didn't have to tell me twice.

The shelter of the Cozy Corgi was in sight when I noticed Katie hurrying down the sidewalk from the other direction, her eyes bright with excitement. I bypassed the entrance to the bookshop to meet her, having to pause a moment to pull Watson away from the front door. He was either ready to get in from the cold or simply tired of seeing his mama make a fool of herself.

Katie grasped my hand as we met, and her voice was breathless. "How did things go for you? Any luck?"

I winced. "Judging from your expression, I'm guessing you had a better go of it than me. Why don't you start? You were with Myrtle for quite a while."

"Well, I probably spent longer researching that kakapo bird than I truly needed to, but I'm glad I did. Mentioning it to her was like opening Pandora's box." Though still excited, her giddy smile softened slightly. "You know, I genuinely like her. Granted, she's a little obsessive and strange, but so am I. Personally, I think both of those are redeeming qualities."

I rather thought so myself. And despite Myrtle's and my tense relationship, the more time I spent with her, the more I liked her as well. Although after hearing Owen's phone call, I wasn't sure I could trust my gut. "I hope you're right. But what did she say about Benjamin?"

"Well...." Katie hesitated for a second. "She was careful about what she said regarding Benjamin, honestly. I couldn't get a good read on why. She wouldn't say that she wasn't with Benjamin when Henry was killed, but she didn't say that she was either."

"What does that mean?" A large man bumped into my shoulder without apology as he tried to step around Katie, Watson, and me. I motioned toward the wooden bench affixed in the sidewalk close to the street. "Actually, why don't we sit? I know there's not too many tourists wandering around downtown, but we're still kinda in the way."

Katie followed me to the bench. After glaring for a few seconds, Watson curled up underneath, between our feet. "I think it means she wasn't with him. But she's not exactly going to tell me that, is she? Not if Benjamin is her alibi. And not if she feels protective of him."

"So, between what you felt when you spoke to Benjamin and now with Myrtle, and combine that with what Carl told me, I think we can safely assume Benjamin is indeed lying to cover for Myrtle." At Katie's confused expression, I remembered I hadn't filled her in yet. "Oh, sorry. Carl suggested that he saw Benjamin with other people in the woods. Although, there was a gap in time that doesn't make what he saw very helpful. But combined with what you're feeling, I'd say it's accurate."

"But I still don't think Myrtle killed Henry. Maybe Benjamin is just trying to protect her or her reputation, not helping her get away with murder."

I filled her in on what I'd overheard from Owen's phone call.

Katie looked less certain. "Whoever he was talking to is

worried about the police having enough evidence to pin on Myrtle?"

"It seems that way, if I understood what he was saying. Granted, it was one side of the conversation, but it seemed pretty clear." We had to be missing something important, although the simplest answer was that Myrtle was the one who killed Henry. Even if I didn't understand why. "I think I've been assuming that the reason Henry got killed was somehow connected to the poaching. It doesn't make sense for someone to kill Henry over his accusations about cheating over badges, even if he was obnoxious and abrasive." I relayed the interactions I'd had with Alice and Petra. "Whatever's going on, I think there's a lot more to the Feathered Friends Brigade than weekly meetings and badges. Though I can't tell if it's one big thing that everyone's in on, or whether several different secrets jumbled together ended up getting Henry killed."

Katie's expression darkened as I told her about what Alice said regarding Benjamin and Silas. "It sounds like we can definitely assume there's a lot of cheating happening, if nothing else. Not to mention that Henry wasn't half as crazy as he seemed. And if Benjamin is willing to lie to the police to cover for Myrtle, I'd say Alice's accusation is not too far a stretch."

"I agree."

"Oh, I forgot." Katie smacked her thigh. "It was the very first thing Myrtle said to me, but I was more taken aback by how she responded about Benjamin. She says the kakapo pin wasn't hers. She had never seen it until the police showed it to her during questioning."

That made absolutely no sense. "Really? I'd swear it's the exact same style as the one she gave you."

Katie nodded. "It is. She said that it was done by the

same artist who creates her pins. A Native American artist in Santa Fe."

"She honestly expects people to believe she collects those pins yet doesn't have one of her favorite bird?" Maybe I was reading Myrtle wrong.

"According to Myrtle, she hasn't earned it yet."

"She hasn't *earned* it?"

"No." Katie shook her head, and her tone softened. "It's kinda sweet. Or something. Myrtle only allows herself to get pins of birds she's interacted with. She's never seen a kakapo in real life. She's saving up for a trip to New Zealand to visit a sanctuary for them. She was going to get the pin after that, sort of like a reward, I guess, or memento."

It was plausible, I supposed, but still.... "A woman who charges ten grand a year to be part of a bird club doesn't have enough money to take a trip to New Zealand?"

Katie shrugged. "I think that simply proves she's not mismanaging the money. She's dogmatic about raising funds to save birds, Fred. I don't think one penny goes to anything else. Even the check she used when she paid for me catering the other night was from her personal account. Not the bird club or her shop."

Though it was hard to believe, if the pin truly didn't belong to Myrtle, that did change things. It seemed too much of a coincidence for someone else to simply be wearing one of Myrtle's style of pins, losing it, right by the scene of Henry's murder. Although, if they were attempting to frame her, why didn't they put it closer to the body?

"Hey! There you two are!"

Katie and I both looked toward the voice, and saw Sammy leaning out the front door of the Cozy Corgi.

"What in the world are you two doing? I'm dying in

here. I'm having people bring books up that they want to buy to the bakery, but I have no idea what I'm doing."

Katie sprang up. "I'm so sorry! I'll be right there."

Sammy slammed the door without any further response.

Katie grinned at me. "Did you hear that? People are buying books."

"Apparently, all it takes is for me to not be there." I stood, and we took a few paces toward the shop, when I paused. "You know, if you don't mind handling things for a little bit longer, I think I should go talk to Benjamin right now. If my instincts are right, Alice has already called the police, telling them I'm harassing her or something. And it's only a matter of time before Branson shows up. I don't want to miss my chance." I held out Watson's leash. "Would you take him with you? I'm pretty sure if we go anywhere else, he'll murder me in my sleep tonight."

"Of course. Good idea." I could tell from her expression that Katie was disappointed she wasn't getting to go to Benjamin as well, but she took Watson's leash. "Come on, buddy. I've got a dog bone with your name all over it."

I started to object as they walked away; he'd already had two sizable treats in the past hour. But he'd probably earned it. And I could give him the equivalent of a doggy salad that evening to compensate.

Yeah, right. Only if I truly did want to get murdered in my sleep.

I started to check my phone, figuring I'd already missed a call from Branson, then decided to leave well enough alone. That way I could claim genuine ignorance if it all blew up in my face. As if feeling him hot on my trail, I glanced around. The coast was clear, so I hurried down the sidewalk toward the camera shop.

. . .

As I entered Shutterbug, Benjamin noticed me instantly. He was demonstrating a camera that looked about a foot long, to a couple of customers, and his spiel faltered. He swallowed and then forced a smile and continued showing the couple the features of the camera.

My heart sank a bit. This wasn't going to go well. I hadn't even had a chance to put my foot in my mouth, and he already looked one step away from kicking me out.

I considered leaving. Why waste more time, or possibly have one more person making complaints about me to the police? But it felt like my only chance to talk to him.

His gaze flitted my way as he closed the sale and began to ring up the customers. Benjamin looked on the verge of bolting.

For him to be having such a strong reaction, someone must have alerted him that I might show up. Maybe Alice had called him the minute I left. However, I doubted it. The way she'd told me about him helping Silas cheat hadn't felt like she cared enough to warn him. If it got any attention off her and her son, she might happily throw Benjamin under the bus to do it. Maybe Owen had called.

I worked my way closer as they finished up the transaction, hoping it would make it less likely Benjamin would turn and hightail it out of the store. I nearly choked when I heard the final price of the camera equipment they bought. It suddenly made a lot more sense why he might pay ten thousand a year if he had a steady stream of camera sales from the bird club. Although it seemed to me once a person bought a camera, they were probably done for several years, if not forever. But maybe they were now like cell phones, with constant updates and endless demands to have the newest and best in technology.

As soon as the customers were gone, Benjamin turned to me. Though younger, there was something about Benjamin that reminded me of Branson. Nearly as handsome, and I got the feeling, typically as charming. Though it seemed he hadn't quite mastered that aspect yet, at least when nervous. Maybe give him a few years. "I heard you were making the rounds."

That was all the confirmation I needed. "I'm simply trying to figure out what happened." This time I opted for a combination of truth and fiction. Or at least an exaggerated version of the truth. "I'm the one who found Myrtle's pin, and I feel responsible. I don't think she's a killer, and I'd hate for something I did to implicate her if she's innocent."

His shoulders sagged in relief. "It won't. She was with me. Haven't you heard? I talked to the police this morning. Myrtle's probably at her store right now."

I leveled a gaze on him that I'd used during my years of being a professor when I was certain a student was lying about why they couldn't complete a project or had been caught cheating. "Benjamin, everyone knows that's not true. Well, not the police, *yet*; give them time. But like you said, I've been making my rounds. Your name has come up more than once." I moved a little closer, drawing up to my full height, not necessarily to look threatening, just authoritarian. "About several things."

Like it had with my students, the move worked. "Several things?" His voice squeaked.

"Yes. One of which is that you were seen with other people at the time of the murder. With Petra, I believe. Not Myrtle."

He licked his lips but didn't speak. The wheels in his

brain were turning so quickly I could nearly see them behind his eyes. In that moment, Benjamin seemed even younger than I'd thought, and I decided to use a touch of intimidation. "I don't know how much you know about me, but I'm fairly close to Sergeant Wexler, and my father was a detective. I've seen how this plays out many times throughout my life, Benjamin. It never ends well when you're lying to the police."

"What happens?" His eyes got so wide, I almost felt guilty. Benjamin shook his head, as if realizing what he'd said. "Not that I was lying."

"The thing is"—I leaned against the counter, this time trying to take on a motherly tone—"it's kind of like with your parents when you're a kid. When you're caught, things go easier for you if you're honest about it as opposed to continuing the lie. That only makes things bigger and bigger."

"But this wasn't a bad lie. Myrtle wouldn't kill anybody. She didn't."

His admission was so sudden that it nearly threw me off, and it didn't even seem he'd realized what he'd implied. "Then who did, Benjamin? If you know Myrtle didn't commit murder, who did?"

"I don't know!" He threw up his hands. "I really don't. But Myrtle wouldn't do that. Maybe I wasn't with her, but she wouldn't kill anyone."

"So you were simply trying to protect Myrtle?"

He swallowed. "Yeah."

His hesitation was long enough to let me know he was lying, again. "Tell me the truth, Benjamin. Who told you to be Myrtle's alibi?"

"He did it because he loves her. He couldn't handle seeing her taken into custody." Benjamin's words were nearly slurred in his panic. "And it's not a crime, at least not a bad one. He and I are both certain that Myrtle wouldn't kill anyone."

"Who, Benjamin? Who's in love with Myrtle?"

"Silas." He looked at me as if the answer was obvious, and then his eyes widened once more, finally realizing how much he'd shared. "I swear, Fred. It really is okay. Silas loves her. He was trying to protect her, and you said yourself, you know Myrtle would never do anything like that. I'm not lying to cover up a murder. Just to... protect the innocent."

I was so thrown off at the revelation that Silas was having a relationship with Myrtle that I nearly lost my train of thought. I wasn't even sure why the couple seemed like such an odd pairing to me, but they did. For whatever reason, I couldn't picture Myrtle in a relationship with anyone. But I could think on that later. I'd cracked Benjamin. I needed to keep pounding, as uncomfortable as it was, to see what else I could get. "Speaking of Silas, I also heard that you assist him, and maybe even some other members when they require certain photo work done to help them earn badges."

At that, he relaxed, and waved me off. "That's not a big deal either. Silas really has seen all those birds. I simply doctor the photos a little bit. That's not cheating."

"Doctor them? If Silas has seen the birds, why doctor the photos?"

For whatever reason, that question changed everything. Benjamin straightened, and his eyes grew cold. "I think I've said too much to you the way it is. This isn't your business. And no harm has been done. Myrtle wouldn't do that. If I thought she could kill someone, it wouldn't matter what Silas offered. I would never cover for a murderer. Ever."

Whether he was right about Myrtle or not, I heard the truth in his words, but I caught something else as well. "Why? What did Silas offer you to cover for Myrtle?"

He flinched, and I thought he was about to crack again, but he didn't. "Nothing. I didn't say he did. I was... saying that it wouldn't matter what he *might* offer. I wouldn't cover for a murderer."

"Benjamin, I think it's in your best interest if you're completely honest right now. What did—"

"No." Benjamin shook his head. "I think you need to leave. And if you believe that Myrtle is innocent like I do, like you said you did, you'll leave it alone." The way his voice quavered at the end led me to believe he was more worried about the police showing up to talk to him about his lying than he was about Myrtle.

For the second time in less than an hour, I walked back out into the January afternoon after being kicked out of another store. The shadows were growing long, and the charming little downtown suddenly felt ominous.

It was too much at once. The phone call I'd overheard from Owen, the revelation that Silas and Myrtle were in a relationship, Petra and Alice's reactions, and the constant confirmation that most of Henry's claims were true after all.

My cell vibrated in my pocket, and I pulled it out.

A glance at the screen revealed the call I'd expected. Just a little later than I would've anticipated.

I hesitated with my thumb hovering over Branson's name, then hit Decline and put the phone back in my pocket. I had to figure things out before I spoke to him. All I needed now was him lecturing or threatening, and not only would I lose my temper, but I might miss my chance to try to arrange the puzzle pieces in a way that made sense while the information was clear.

As my phone began to buzz again, I knew what Branson's next step would be. Ignoring the cell entirely, I hurried back toward the Cozy Corgi. I should pick up Watson before Branson showed up at the bookshop. I probably wouldn't go home either, as he'd likely show up there as well. Whatever. I'd figure that out later. Right now I'd grab my corgi, hop in my car, and avoid the police.

Branson called and texted nearly ten times in the next half hour. I started by driving randomly around Estes Park, then realized I had a high chance of accidentally running into him as he drove to the Cozy Corgi or to my house. So Watson and I made our way into the national park. It was a stunning night for a drive to clear my head, and I highly doubted he would look for me there.

Though I still couldn't picture Myrtle as a murderer, she truly seemed the most likely of suspects. She was the founder of the club, a group with a limitless supply of secrets and cheating. Her story about the pins to Katie was rather sweet and something I could see someone with Myrtle's disposition doing, but all fingers pointed to her. The solitary reason to believe otherwise was my gut instinct. And as much as I'd learned to trust my gut recently, I didn't believe it was infallible.

If it had been Myrtle, I highly doubted she'd acted alone. There were too many secrets in the club for it to come down to one person. But then again, that was another gut feeling without much basis in anything substantial, besides endless rumors and gossip and accusations. Which in the Feathered Friends Brigade, seemed like it led to getting killed if you talked about them too much.

If nothing else, it seemed Owen had a reason to cover for Myrtle. And Silas as well. I wasn't sure what deal Silas had struck with Benjamin, but I was certain the kid hadn't done it out of his own pure heart. Though I did believe he wouldn't cover for Myrtle if he truly thought she'd killed Henry. But there I went again, nothing but gut instinct to back that up, and I'd had even less interaction with Benjamin than with Myrtle.

Then there was Alice and Petra. Surely Alice wouldn't kill someone because they knew her son was helping her cheat to get badges. And I couldn't imagine what secrets Petra might be keeping, but she'd been so clearly uncomfortable in my presence. They both had. Although, maybe that was more about me than about either of them.

Atypically, Watson wasn't curled up napping in the front seat, but sat up tall, which put his gaze right at the edge of the passenger-side window, allowing him to see the dark silhouettes of the snowy trees as we passed. Maybe he'd enjoyed the snowy moonlight hike the night before and hoped we were going to do it again.

The night before... had it only been twenty-four hours ago? It felt like days. I'd talked to so many people and been kicked out of so many stores. I chuckled at the thought, causing Watson to glance over with a look that asked, "Why is my mother such a nut ball?" before turning back to stare out the window.

And in those twenty-four hours, and the whirlwind of questions to everyone, all I had to show for my effort was alienating myself further from Branson, and Susan, for that matter, not that it took much. That, and a whole bunch of loose ends that didn't seem to lead anywhere.

When my phone rang again, this time from an unknown number, I'd had enough. Keeping my eyes on the road, I hit Accept and lifted the phone to my ear. "Seriously? It's not enough to harass me from your own number, now you're trying to trick me?" Even as I said the words, I heard the ridiculousness of them. The trick had worked. Though maybe not so much a trick as him simply knowing at some point my temper would take over.

"Winifred Page?" The voice was not Branson Wexler.

"Oh... sorry." I couldn't believe I could still speak after shoving my foot in my mouth on so many occasions in one day. Surely this had to be a record. "This is Winifred. I thought you were someone else. Sorry about that." Then I realized it might not be Branson, but I had no idea who I was talking to. "Speaking of, who is this?"

"Silas Belle." There was laughter in his tone. "Sounds like you're having a harassment issue. Might need to call the police about that."

I pulled the phone back and looked at the screen. That had been an odd thing to say, an oddly apt thing to say, letting me know that Silas knew exactly what he was talking about. I brought the phone back to my ear once more and focused on not letting the wary sensation I felt sound in my voice. "Not a bad idea. What can I help you with, Silas?"

"I hear you've been all over town today, asking a lot of questions about Myrtle and the club." Impressively he was able to say the line without losing an ounce of warmth.

If he could be blunt, so could I. It seemed pointless to deny anything. Doubtlessly, Benjamin had called him. Alice, I wasn't so sure of, but possibly. "That's true. I have."

"Anything you want to ask me, Fred?"

My heart began to pound, and for an insane moment, I

glanced at the rearview, expecting to see headlights trailing me. I wasn't in a horror movie, however. And unless Silas had a ton of forethought, he hadn't put a tracker on my car or my phone. "Yes, actually." I swallowed, then barged ahead. "I don't know what you used for motivation, but I do know that you convinced Benjamin to be Myrtle's alibi."

There were several heartbeats of silence, and when Silas spoke again, some of the warmth had faded, but he didn't sound necessarily angry. "It seems money talks only so far to Benjamin. I probably shouldn't have put such a large task in the hands of a man so young and inexperienced." He chuckled. "No offense to your grilling tactics, I'm sure."

I wasn't certain if I should be worried that he'd admitted it so easily or if it implied Myrtle truly was innocent.

Silas didn't wait. "I don't know if this is a conversation that's best over the phone. How about we meet in person? We're neighbors, after all. Would you like to come to my house, or should I come to yours?"

I waited for the punch line. There didn't seem to be one coming. "Silas, you might be the nicest man in the world. I don't know. But I promise you I'm not such a fool that I would go to someone's house, in the dark, to talk about this."

"Bring someone. I promise you there's no malintent on my end." The warmth was back, and he almost sounded nonchalant. Which only proved he was very much in control. "Bring several someones if you want. My singular request is that they not be law enforcement. I don't have any intention of admitting to them that I encouraged Benjamin to fake his alibi for Myrtle. And I believe after you hear me out, you'll understand why."

"And why can't we do this on the phone?" As if

answering my own question, I drove through a thick grove of trees and the line went static for several moments.

Once the connection cleared, Silas continued speaking in his calm voice. "Deception is easy over the phone, Fred. If I'm going to convince you to not tell the police about my arrangement with Benjamin, I need you to believe me. And if I truly meant you any harm, I wouldn't have admitted it over the phone. You could drive straight to the police right now and fill them in, which is your right. But I hope that you won't."

He had a point, although that point could easily be simply to make me more willing to fall into his trap. I debated mentally, and as if he could hear me thinking, Silas didn't speak, giving me time to process.

I didn't think I had a ton of weaknesses, not anymore. Sure, my temper got the best of me every so often, and I could get flustered at times. And having a bakery right above my head was proving to be as problematic as I thought it would be for my diet. But hands down, my biggest fault was one of my biggest strengths. And even if I knew the saying *curiosity killed the cat*, I needed to have my fix. That curiosity craved to be satiated. "Fine."

As expected, Watson went positively wild when we pulled up to Leo's apartment. Leo was waiting in the parking lot. During my brief phone call with him, I requested for us to use his Jeep, less chance of accidentally running into Branson or Susan if they were scouring the area for me. Which, judging from the calls I was still getting from Branson, I imagined they were.

Leo held the door open for me as I scooped Watson into

the Jeep, and then he hurried around to the driver's side and hopped in. In another second or so, we left the apartment complex and were heading toward my side of town.

"Gotta say, this is fun." Leo grinned his handsome smile at me as he looked away from the road for a second, child-like pleasure written across his features. "I feel like I'm in a Hardy Boys book."

I couldn't help but smile back, partly because I knew exactly the thrill shooting through him. "Actually, I think you're in a Nancy Drew book at the moment."

"Works for me." He tilted his head but didn't look back this time, keeping his gaze focused on the road. "Although, I'm pretty sure they did a few crossovers where the Hardy Boys teamed up with Nancy Drew. They were double digests, twice as long as the normal ones."

I gaped at him. "You read the Hardy Boys and Nancy Drew? You like mysteries?"

"Of course I did! And who doesn't like mysteries?"

And that answer was all the confirmation I needed to know I'd made the right choice. Not that I'd questioned that choice to begin with. First and foremost, no matter how curious I was, I wasn't going to show up at Silas's house on my own. Nor was I going to call Branson. And not just because Silas had asked me not to. Leo had a relationship with Silas and all the members of the Feathered Friends Brigade. He would put Silas—hell, and me—at ease. And he'd also be better able to tell if Silas was being honest, since he had past experiences with him.

We weaved our way around the new developments of mini-mansions at the base of the mountain, nestled against the forest that held my cabin. The houses were beautiful and elaborate. And they felt completely out of place in

Estes Park, like a portion of the rich suburbs had been plopped down among the pines.

We found the house number Silas had given me and Leo let out a whistle as we pulled into the driveway. "I knew the man had money, but he's got the biggest house on the block."

"You'd think with all that money, he could've afforded to build a custom cabin or something, as opposed to buying in Stepford."

"I knew I liked you." Leo flashed a smile but was smart enough to make it brief, then exited the Jeep.

I followed suit, grasping Watson's leash after I lowered him to the concrete.

Silas met us at the door before we even needed to ring the bell. "Well, well, my favorite ranger, Leo Lopez." He stuck out his hand, and the two men exchanged a handshake. He followed by giving me the same gesture. "Smart choice, Fred. Not alone, and someone that I know and trust. No wonder I've heard you're quite the detective."

My gut had been telling me lots of things the past several days, but it didn't help me out a lick with Silas's direct approach. I couldn't tell if he was letting me know he was aware of what I was doing to put me at ease or hint that he was several steps ahead.

The interior of Silas's house was as much of a mansion as the outside. He led us through a massive entrance with a sparkling chandelier hanging from a vaulted ceiling and past a formal dining room. Watson found some scent he loved on the floor in front of a closet door and required a tug on his leash to follow us. We continued into a kitchen-living room combo as big as my entire cabin. And like the housing development didn't fit the aesthetic of my little mountain town, neither did the interior of Silas's house. It reminded me of some of the home tours I'd taken in the Kansas City Plaza. Everything was black, cream, and tan, and decorated with glass and steel. Fine, I supposed. I'd been impressed during the home tour, at least. It all seemed luxurious and modern. But it felt wrong here, somehow. Like it expected the mountains to adjust to it instead of trying to blend in to the rugged wilderness mere feet away.

Leo grimaced or winced here and there, barely noticeable, but he was clearly having a similar response. That changed when we entered the large living room. He sucked in a quiet breath and walked over to a wall that could've been in a museum, filled with golden-framed canvases, each displaying a colorful bird. "These are spectacular. I feel like I'm stepping into a National Geographic." He let out a self-conscious laugh. "If the National Geographic was on Fifth Avenue."

"Thank you." Silas crossed the room and stood beside Leo, admiring the art as well. "It combines my two great loves, ornithology and photography." He cast a glance my way. "I've spent a small fortune on photography equipment. Benjamin is very accommodating." He chuckled. "More than a small fortune, I suppose."

I was surprised at the sudden mention of Benjamin—it looked like we were starting. I'd wondered if Silas would be as direct in person as he had been over the phone. It seemed so. "Is that why Benjamin was willing to lie when you asked him to? Because you're such a great customer?"

Leo flashed me a wide-eyed look, clearly asking what I was thinking taking such a direct approach.

For Silas's part, he didn't even flinch. "No. Although, I'm sure that partly came into play for him. But, no. I paid

Benjamin to say that he was with Myrtle. That time it had nothing to do with photography or cameras, or birds, for that matter." He left Leo's side, crossed the room once more, passed me, paused to pat Watson's head—who gave a half-hearted attempt at ducking away—and then pulled three wineglasses from a cupboard. "What can I get you? Are you two more red or white fans?"

He was so nonchalant that either he was crazy or truly had no worry that once we heard his story we'd believe him. Either way, it threw me off. And maybe that was the point.

"Thank you, Silas, but Fred and I aren't here for a drink." Leo moved from the wall of pictures and came to stand beside Watson and me.

"Well, let me know if you change your mind." Silas opened a bottle of red and poured himself a glass. He continued speaking as he got a small bowl and filled it with water and set it on the floor near Watson. "I'll be direct with you both. Like I told you on the phone, Fred, I can't stop you from going to the police and ruining Myrtle's alibi, but I hope that you will understand why I did what I did and respect my decision enough to let it stand. I don't know who killed Henry, but I have my suspicions. And even if those are wrong, I can guarantee you that Myrtle had absolutely nothing to do with it."

Two huge sofas made up most of the seating possibilities in the living room, one against the far wall and the other at an L-shape position, partially separating the living room from the kitchen space. Silas sat on the one next to the wall and gestured toward the other for Leo and me.

For a moment, he looked nervous for the first time. No... not nervous... I couldn't quite put my finger on it. Almost... in pain. His brown eyes met mine, then he glanced back and forth between the two of us, and finally settled on me. "I love Myrtle. I've been in love with her for years. She's the most amazing woman I've ever known. Her passion, dedication, and purity of heart and one-track mind. She is powerful and amazing. She would never harm another creature, even of the human variety." He swallowed, the pained look persisting. "That's why I paid Benjamin to be her alibi." He gestured around his house. "As you can see, I'm used to getting what I want. I've traveled the world several times over for my love of birds. I met Myrtle on a trip in Costa Rica on just such an expedition, and she blew me away. My life changed the day I met Myrtle Bantam. So you can't blame me if I'm willing to do whatever it takes to make sure she is safe, even if it means paying someone to lie for her. And you can understand why I might be a little bit worried that the story might crack somewhere and she'd get blamed again."

"You love her so much that you would cover for her even if she killed someone?"

Silas barely spared Leo a glance. "Don't be ridiculous. You know Myrtle; she didn't do this."

"I don't think she did it either, but sometimes people surprise us. And surely lying about it will only end up making her look guiltier." Leo's tender voice sounded like he was talking to a heartbroken teenager. It seemed he believed Silas's story of love. "Wouldn't it be better to simply let the police do their jobs?"

"It's a nice thought, but you don't really believe that, do you, Fred?" He looked to me though Leo had asked the question. "The whole town knows that you cleared your stepfather's name, and then your business partner." He cocked an eyebrow. "And here you are again. This time not even trying to clear someone you love. Simply not trusting the police to find the truth."

I couldn't think of anything to say but to agree. Before I needed to respond, Silas refocused on Leo.

"I only know Fred by reputation. But you I know, Leo. How have the police done with the bird club so far? Have they believed any of our theories about the poacher? Have they attempted to investigate? Have they even listened to you?"

Leo was struck as dumb as I was.

Silas looked back at me. "I admire you, Fred. You take matters into your own hands, and you protect the ones you love. I do that as well, though my manner in doing so is a little different. Maybe mine seems lazy to you, throwing money at things instead of investigating, but we each have our strengths. If anybody should understand what I'm doing, it's you."

I studied him, attempting to let my instincts and my brain work in tandem. I felt like they were. I believed him. Completely. From the look in his eyes and the sound of his voice, I had no doubt he loved Myrtle. And looking back, though I hadn't noticed it at the time and the actions weren't overt, the way he'd stood close to her, came to her defense. Always ready if she needed anything. As far as his way of going about it? I understood that too. Maybe it wasn't the way I would do it, but the result was the same. Though I would argue not as effective.

The bottom line was that my gut, as well as those of several people I trusted, told me Myrtle was innocent. And nearly every other person I'd spoken to dismissed the idea that Myrtle was capable of murder. The same had been true for Barry, and then again for Katie.

I was certain Myrtle wasn't going to break the pattern.

I couldn't blame Silas for what he was doing, even if I wished he'd chosen a different way. I nearly said as much, when another thought hit me. "If all that's true, Silas, I still don't understand why you would need to pay Benjamin to lie. Why not do it yourself? There'd have been no chance Benjamin would crack, like he did, and you could be her rock-solid alibi."

"I can't." Silas glanced away then, and a blush flared to his cheeks. When he finally looked back, though he couldn't meet my eyes as directly as before, I still believed him. "Myrtle doesn't know how I feel about her. And at this point, she can't know. It took months after I moved here for her to even speak to me. She thought I moved here for her, which I had, but it wasn't something she wanted. Myrtle doesn't want a relationship. Even her friendships are little more than an outreach for her passion of birds. It's an obsession. A lovely one, but an obsession nonetheless. One that leaves room for little else." He met my gaze again, holding it, and I could see the genuine desperation in his eyes. "She can't know. If she thought I had these sorts of feelings for her, she would cut me out. I don't think she'd let me be in the club anymore. If I was her alibi, she would ask why. I don't think I could do a good enough job of convincing her. But with Benjamin, she won't understand why, but she would never think of him loving her, not like she would if I'd proclaimed to be her alibi."

I glanced at Leo. And if I was reading his expression correctly, he believed Silas as well. Part of me wanted to ease Silas's worry, promise him I wouldn't tell Myrtle, but I wasn't going to jump quite that far. Still, I had every intention of keeping Silas's secret. I turned back to him, trying to keep my voice neutral. "You said you had some ideas of who might've killed Henry. What are they?"

Though I made no promises, I could see relief in Silas's eyes, and his shoulders relaxed. He sat back, sinking a little farther into the sofa. "They're nothing more than ideas. While I'm sure about Myrtle's innocence, I'm not sure about much else. It was Alice we heard scream. Seems like a good plan to me. Kill someone and be the first on the scene, screaming, crying, and shaken. Henry accused Alice of cheating, which I know she is, but still. He let it go for a few months, and then he returned, accusing her of cheating, then accusing her of being the poacher. My other thought was Paulie. I don't have that good of a reason to think it was him, other than he strikes me as a rather slimy little rat. And I know he'd been knocking on Henry's door—" He gave a sardonic chuckle. "—both literally and figuratively, trying to be his friend. The guy's like a little leech. Maybe Henry got tired of it, said something that hurt Paulie's feelings, and Paulie snapped." Silas shrugged. "They're speculation. In truth, while I was nervous to hear you were looking into things, I'm also glad of it, Fred. Whatever quality it is that helps a person figure out these kinds of things, I don't have it. You do, apparently. I can keep Myrtle out of jail with a fake alibi, but you can fully clear her name. Any resources you require, all you need to do is ask."

I thought I heard him wrong. "You want me to keep snooping?"

"Of course I do. Figure it out."

I hadn't expected that. I'd been saving the next question, planning to use it as my ace in the hole, to see if it would shake him at all. Now was the moment. "What about Myrtle's pin? I found it a few yards away from where Henry was killed."

Silas winced, the question clearly bothering him. "That wasn't Myrtle's pin. She only gets those when she's been with that bird species in the wild. Seeing the kakapo is her biggest dream. She'll get there one day, but she won't allow herself to have that pin until she does." He shrugged. "Again, I don't have an explanation, and for the life of me, I can't even come up with a plausible theory on that one. But I know it wasn't Myrtle's."

That fit perfectly with what Myrtle had told Katie, so either it was the truth or Silas and Myrtle were in it together. Though it felt like the truth.

I played my final card, which I'd been holding back, and motioned toward the wall of birds. "There're rumors that you cheat on your pictures."

He studied me again, then finally cast what I thought was an embarrassed look toward Leo. "I love Myrtle, and I'm as passionate about conservation as she is, but I'm not quite as strict as her thinking. Some of the birds I visited in other countries were in captivity. Not by poachers or anything like that—by people who had one of the native birds as their pets, or they were held in a local zoo. Benjamin adjusts those photos when that happens so they look like they're taken in the wild. That's all. Obviously I don't care about the stupid badges. But it gives me one more connection to Myrtle."

"Silas, just because someone lives in whatever area you're visiting, doesn't mean they have the bird legally and they're not poachers." Leo sounded somewhat aghast. "It would be no different than if we'd spotted a Mexican Spotted Owl the other night, captured it, and put it in a cage."

Silas shrugged at Leo. "Sorry. That's what I mean. I'm not quite as strict about these things as Myrtle. And I'd appreciate it if you keep that aspect of my story from her as well."

Leo looked like he was about to argue, but I had a

feeling it was more about the birds and less about Myrtle. Which was fine, but he could do so on his own time.

"Silas, I'm not making any promises about what I will or won't say, both to Myrtle or the police. But I will consider what you said."

For a second, Silas seemed about to argue or push the point, but then he nodded. "Guess that's all I can expect." His eyes brightened. "But at least, if you decide not to listen to my request, will you let me know in advance? Especially if you decide to tell Myrtle?"

I hesitated, barely. "Of course."

Leo cast a surprised glance at me, but I ignored it. I was lying. If for some reason I felt I needed to tell Myrtle, there was no way I would tell Silas first. I could explain that to Leo in the Jeep, but it seemed the best course of action to placate Silas.

Silas took a sip of his wine, and then stood and dusted off his pants. "Thanks for listening to me. And, Fred, I meant what I said. If you need anything at all that can help you figure this out, let me know. Any sort of resources you might be lacking, I'll get for you. Whatever it takes to clear Myrtle's name."

"Thanks. And let me know if any more details come to you or things you think might help."

Watson had fallen asleep on the plush rug that sprawled between the couches, and he gave an annoyed groan as I woke him. Once more as we walked past the closet between the living room and the formal dining room, Watson whined and sniffed around the hardwood floor close to the doorway.

"I dropped a pan of prime rib the other night on the way back from the dining room. Apparently I didn't get it all cleaned up as well as I thought I did." Silas leaned down and ruffled Watson's fur, then glanced up at me. "I have a couple of scraps left over, if he'd like some. Seems mean to tempt him with such smells and leave him wanting."

"No, that's totally fine. But thank you. I appreciate it. He's had more than his share of calories today, trust me." I had to pull Watson's leash twice to get him to oblige, but with an irritated glare, he followed Leo and me out the door.

Branson was waiting for me as Watson and I pulled up to my cabin. And showing that he was every bit as stubborn and obstinate as I was, he hadn't taken shelter in his police cruiser, but sat on one of the log rocking chairs I'd gotten for my front porch, despite the cold. Or maybe, in spite of it.

Taking a moment to fasten the leash back onto Watson, I mentally told myself to stay calm, keep my temper in check, and play my cards close to the vest. No matter what Branson might say, I wasn't ready to share the information I learned from Silas simply to prove a point.

Watson growled as we approached the porch, and Branson stood, his tall, thick mass forming an imposing shadow. "Calm down, Watson. I love that you're protecting your mama, but I promise, she's always safe with me."

It had been a couple of months since he'd said something similar to Watson. It made me want to go back to that night. Although, I suppose we were about to. He'd arrived at my cabin to tell me to stay out of the case on that occasion as well. This time, though, I didn't think we were going to end up having grilled cheese sandwiches and chatting at my kitchen table.

As if proving my point, Branson's voice was cold when he spoke to me—not unfriendly necessarily, just distant. "Don't get all riled up, Fred. I'm not here to lecture. Although, would it have killed you to return even one of my calls or texts?"

"I didn't check them. So technically, I couldn't return them." I managed to make my tone less irritated than I felt.

To my surprise, he chuckled. "An attempt to ask forgiveness instead of permission?"

I shrugged as I unlocked the door. "You already denied your permission, and if you recall, I didn't ask for it." I opened the door and unhooked Watson's leash, and he scampered in from the cold.

"Don't worry, Fred. I'm not inviting myself inside. It's clear you would rather me not be here." Branson took a couple of steps across the porch, then stopped an arm's length away. I could swear he almost sounded hurt by the fact.

That annoyed me, and I turned on him. "Can you blame me? When I was looking into things about Declan's murder at Christmas, you gave me your full support. Even seemed impressed with what I was able to do, but on this one, you're acting like I'll mess everything up."

"I know that you realize I'm a police officer, Fred. Technically I'm not supposed to share any information with civilians or let them investigate. Even if I want to."

"Yes, of course I know that. But I don't care." I leveled my gaze on him. The night was bright, but under the porch eaves, we were in shadow. "Your department keeps messing it up. Again. Myrtle didn't kill Henry. I don't have proof of that, not yet, but I will."

He chuckled, and I nearly bit his head off, but he saved

himself by speaking quicker than I could voice my temper aloud. "That's why I called. If you'd checked your messages. It wasn't Myrtle."

And that dumped an avalanche of snow on the fire of my fury. "What?"

He stepped a little closer still, his smile softening. "Despite the pin, Myrtle wasn't the killer. We have someone else in custody."

"Who?"

He sighed. "Fred, you know I can't...." Another laugh. "Oh, who am I kidding? Paulie Mertz."

I took a step back. "Paulie Mertz? That doesn't make any sense." Though I remembered he was one of two people on Silas's list.

"Now, please don't claim we've got the wrong person again." He raised a hand. "Let me save you the trouble of telling me that you have some sixth sense about this. I can promise you. We got our guy this time. We received an anonymous call that Paulie had illegal birds in his possession, and sure enough, he did, in the back room of his pet shop. It seems Henry had been threatening to expose him. So not only did we find the killer, we found our poacher. That should make Leo happy." There was accusation in that last line. But it was gone in an instant. "That's all I wanted to tell you, Fred."

I couldn't find words. Both for Branson once more giving me details of the case and because this wasn't right. Just like with Myrtle, I knew Paulie hadn't done this. Paulie was an example of when my gut had been wrong. Like everyone else, he'd struck me as rather strange and creepy, and desperate to an uncomfortable level. But he helped me when Watson had gotten into something dangerous right before Christmas, and I thought I'd seen past the hurting and desperate man who came across so off-putting. I even thought I might start to like him.

Branson stiffened. "Well, I guess that's all I wanted to say. Clearly you're not ready to move on, and I don't blame you." He truly did sound rather hurt. "I am sorry, Fred. I hope we can repair things." He gave a little nod and then walked off the porch and toward his car.

Another thought hit me, and I called out to him. "Wait."

He looked back hopefully.

"What about Paulie's dogs? Flotsam and Jetsam? Do you need someone to take care of them?" Paulie had two corgis, two hyperactive corgis that Watson would most definitely never forgive me if I allowed to come into our house, let alone stay for a while.

Branson's shoulders slumped slightly. "No. They're fine. The veterinarian, Dr. Sallee, is taking care of them." With another nod and a small wave, Branson disappeared into his car and drove off into the night.

"I can't believe you spent all morning baking, the rest of the day with customers, and then come home and bake for yourself?" I stared at the mess strewn over Katie's kitchen counter. She seemed much more haphazard when baking at home. "You're a sick, sick woman, Katie Pizzolato."

"And don't I know it!" Katie tore off a bit of sliced ham, and for the twentieth time in the past half an hour, tossed it to Watson, who was waiting aggressively at her feet. "As soon as you called asking to spend the night, I had to bake. We're having a slumber party. We need snacks."

"Snacks would be popcorn and M&M's, something easy, not your ham-and-cheese croissants."

Katie grimaced. "If you're going to consume that

amount of butter and sugar, you might as well make it worth the calories." She tore off a bit of sliced cheese and popped it into her mouth. Watson whined in disappointment below her. "Sorry, buddy. I'm not completely selfless. I need some too." As she layered the ham and cheese and rolled the croissants, she cast more serious glances in my direction. "I'm glad you thought to give me a call, Fred. I imagine you're right. I doubt Silas had any ill intentions against you, but it's unsettling with him knowing where you live."

I made it about fifteen minutes after Branson left. I'd already changed into my pajamas and had a kettle of tea on the stove, ready to settle down in front of the fire and read, when Silas's voice on the phone telling me he knew where I lived crept in. The way he'd said it hadn't sounded threatening in the slightest. But in the middle of a dark woods, as the night grew deeper, and after multiple murders in such a short time, I wasn't sure if it was my gut speaking to me, or simply irrational fear, but I decided to go with it and called Katie.

"I'm probably being silly. Plus, according to Branson, it's all over. They caught the poacher and murderer all in one fell swoop."

Moving on to her next croissant, Katie *tsked*. "Please. You don't believe that any more than I do. Paulie's a strange little man, and rather uncomfortable to be around, but he didn't do this."

I agreed, but I was a little desperate for confirmation. "How do you know?"

"I have no idea." Katie shrugged, completely unconcerned. "I just do. So do you."

That I did. And maybe that was part of why I'd come to Katie's. For some reason, it seemed a little more dangerous, or something, to have the wrong person in jail for murder as opposed to no one. "Who do you think the murderer is?"

Katie didn't look up at me that time, keeping all her attention focused on the pastry. "I don't know. It sounds like you believe Silas loves Myrtle. And all his actions seem to make sense through that filter. I still don't think Myrtle did it, but I don't know. It sounded like Owen kind of gave you the creeps when you overheard him on the phone at the coffee shop this morning."

"He did. That's true. However, I was also completely flustered from making a fool of myself in front of Carla, but there was definitely something there. Though we've heard barely any rumors about Owen. Lots of cheating from Alice and Silas, but nothing about Owen."

Katie looked at me seriously. "Unless you take Henry at face value. Wasn't Owen the one he was saying was the poacher? He told Leo he had proof this time."

"I thought of that. Could simply be bad timing. To be accused of poaching and then Henry gets killed. Or it could be something more. Henry finally found the real poacher and paid the price." It made sense, and it didn't feel wrong either. But neither did it necessarily feel right. "Maybe I should go talk to Owen tomorrow. Although, I don't know anything about him. It's not like he owns a store."

Katie stilled. "If you find him, I want you to take me with you. Or Leo, or Branson, even Sammy. Somebody. With all the names flying around, and the wrong people getting arrested, something about this feels a little more dangerous this time."

"More dangerous? You were the one who stopped an attempted murder a few weeks ago. *This* feels more dangerous?"

Katie considered, shrugged, and returned to the pastry. "Yeah, it does."

We continued tossing ideas back and forth, though none felt substantial, and ended up talking about Sammy as Katie debated whether she should bring her on full-time or if things would slow down at the bakery after the newness wore off. Soon the heavenly smell of butter, cheese, and bread filled the kitchen. It was almost as comforting as a good book.

As Katie took the croissants out of the oven to cool, she grinned over at me. "All right, go get into your pajamas, and I'll put on mine. You can't have a slumber party in real clothes."

"You're serious? A slumber party? Don't you have to be up at the crack of dawn to be at the bakery?"

Katie grimaced at the thought. "Spoilsport. Well, whatever. I want a slumber party. I was thinking of having a Harry Potter movie marathon, but maybe instead we should settle for an episode of something on Netflix. I suppose we should get *some* sleep."

"That does sound fun, how about—"

She held up her hand, cutting me off. "No, no murder mysteries. We get enough of that in real life. Try again."

"But I was thinking—"

"Nope." She smiled but narrowed her eyes at me. "You're cut off. No more thinking about murder, either in Estes or any other place on the television. I made the food; I'll pick the show." She headed toward the bedroom to change into her pajamas as she called out over her shoulder, "Oh, I know! We can watch *The Great British Bake Off*."

Not a bad choice. I liked that show, but I couldn't let Katie get the last word. "Seriously? I talk too much about murders, but you're allowed to dive into more baking?"

She didn't even bother to pop her head out of the bedroom door. "My house, my rules. Now shut up and get in your pajamas. I wish we had a pair for Watson."

Katie and I ended up watching three episodes of the baking show. And at nearly an hour a piece, we were up well past midnight. Though I slept on her couch, I didn't even hear her get up and head off to the bakery. When I finally woke at seven, she was gone, probably for hours and hours. I had no idea how she did it. Although I'd forgotten the luxury of having a doggy door and a dog run for Watson. He'd woken me three times during the night. Two of which were nothing more than him wanting to leave the house. As a result, I was dragging.

Once home, I made breakfast for Watson and myself, then got ready for the day. After a shower and half a pot of coffee, I almost felt human again. When I got to the bookshop, I'd go upstairs and get a dirty chai and whatever Katie had baked fresh that morning.

It had been a rough couple of days. I deserved a second breakfast.

Knowing full well how it would end, I drove past the Cozy Corgi, and on to the next block, to see if Myrtle was in. Nothing more. Simply to check.

Right.

There were some stores closed for the season, but the

ones that weren't were already open, including Wings of the Rockies. It was still early enough that there was plenty of parking, so I pulled my Mini Cooper into a spot across the street, attached Watson's leash, and hopped out.

As I crossed toward her store, I realized I should be acting like a business owner. I wasn't a detective. I owned a bookshop. And currently there were at least one or two bakers in the upstairs of that bookshop and absolutely no one where the books were. I needed to hire someone.

I negated that thought as I opened the doors to Myrtle's store and allowed Watson to walk in ahead of me. There was no reason to hire someone—I wasn't always going to be solving a murder. This would be the last one. How many people could die in Estes Park, anyway? At least of murder.

Myrtle was on a ladder, affixing a copper birdfeeder to one of the ceiling beams. She looked even more like a crane than normal. "Fred. I figured I'd be seeing you today." She unwound a wire and slid the birdfeeder free. Taking it down, apparently, not putting it up. Twisting slightly, she bent and dangled the birdfeeder from the ladder. "Would you mind getting this for me? As soon as I got up here, I realized it wasn't one of my smartest ideas. But I was already up."

"Of course!" I dropped Watson's leash and hurried to her, reached up, and took the birdfeeder. It was heavier than it appeared.

Myrtle made her way down the steps. She seemed a little shaky. After she reached the bottom, she held out her hands for the birdfeeder. "Thank you."

I sucked in a gasp as Myrtle's eyes met mine. She'd aged a decade.

A blush rose to her thin cheeks. "And I thought maybe the mirror was lying. Guess not."

I considered telling her she looked fine. But she'd already read my face, and she'd looked in the mirror. The damage was done. "Are you okay?"

Myrtle laughed weakly and walked to the counter to set the birdfeeder down. She turned back to me, raking her fingers through her silver hair. Instead of its normal product-induced spike, it was a short fuzzy mess. Her eyes were bloodshot and red-rimmed, with painfully heavy bags. And still she trembled. "One of my brigade was murdered, I was taken in for that murder, and now another member of my brigade has been arrested. One who I don't think committed the murder." Her bottom lip quivered. "Which means one of my Feathered Friends is not only a murderer, but is free and willing to let someone else take the fall."

It wasn't the reaction I'd expected. I'd anticipated anger or at least irritation when she saw me. I reached for her arm, but stopped short of touching her, letting my hand fall back to my side. "I'm sorry that my turning in the pin caused you problems. Katie said that it wasn't even yours."

She shrugged like it didn't matter and leaned against the counter. "I don't blame you for that. It was the right thing to do. If the police had done their job better, they would've found the pin. Although, I do know there was a lot of snow up there. So either way, whether by their hand or yours, I would've been the natural suspect."

The door chimed, and an older man began to walk into the shop.

Myrtle closed her eyes as if trying to find strength, then leaned around a display of field guides and shook her head. "No, sorry. Not today. At least not right now. You should go shopping somewhere else."

He flinched. "But I—"

"I said no!" Myrtle let out one of her signature squawks, but this one was filled with panic and exhaustion.

I went over to the man, took him gently by the shoulder, and led him out the door. "Go to the Cozy Corgi. Tell the baker that Fred is giving you a pastry on the house."

He scrunched up his nose. "Who's Fred?"

Must not be a local. "I'm Fred."

"A woman named Fred." His nose became even more scrunched. "Well, Fred, I don't need a pastry. I'm needing some birdseed for—"

"She said no. I'm sorry." And she was probably getting ready to tell me the same thing the longer I took with the man.

"Well, of all the—"

He sounded like he was going to launch into a diatribe, so I stepped back into the shop, but couldn't bite my tongue fast enough before shutting the door. "On second thought, don't go to the Cozy Corgi. Go to the Black Bear Roaster instead. Try one of their scones." I shut the door and locked it.

"I didn't think I liked you when I first met you." Myrtle gave a quavering smile, and there was a hint of laughter in her voice. "But I've had Black Bear Roaster's scones. They're awful. You might be okay." A hiccup of a laugh exploded, then a real one, and then she burst into tears and sank to the floor.

"Oh, Myrtle." I rushed to her and attempted to put my arm around her, but she shrank away. I sat close, helpless, and had no idea what to do.

Watson padded over, his leash dragging behind him. He nudged his cold, wet nose against her hand, like he did with me when he determined I wasn't giving him enough attention.

I started to shoo him away, afraid what Myrtle's reaction would be. Afraid she might even swat at him. To my shock, still crying, Myrtle moved the hand he'd nudged to his head, and after a moment, her other began to slowly stroke his side. Watson pressed up against her thigh and rested there, allowing himself to be stroked.

Watson had come to me from out of nowhere. It was the fifth anniversary of my father's death, and I was sobbing at his gravestone, alone. And then Watson was there, curled up at my side, and he sat with me until the tears dried. When I got up to leave and he followed, I'd almost been surprised that he was real.

I put up flyers and announcements online about a lost dog. No one ever responded. I decided he'd been a gift from my father. Something to help me in my grief. It had been five years and many days my grief seemed as bad as the first. After Watson, things got better.

Watching Myrtle continue to stroke Watson, I was both touched by his atypical compassion and experienced a bite of fear. That somehow, when I got up to leave the store, Watson wouldn't follow, wouldn't want to go. That maybe he wasn't a corgi at all, but some chubby, furry, short-legged angel that stayed with people as they were hurting but then moved on when they were better.

Ridiculous.

But as Myrtle's tears began to dry, I couldn't keep that worry at bay.

After a few more minutes, Myrtle sniffed, reached above her to retrieve her peacock-feathered purse, and pulled out a tissue. Then she gave several honks as she blew her nose. She sighed a shaky exhale and patted Watson's head before looking over at me. "Good dog you got here. I'm more of a bird person myself, in case you didn't know."

Though wavering, her smile was brighter that time. "But he's a good dog." She gave another pat and pulled her hand away.

Without hesitation, Watson stood, trotted around her outstretched legs, and took his place beside me.

I looked into his brown eyes. *You know, don't you? Both what I was worrying about and what I need right now.*

Watson let out a long sigh, one that almost seemed annoyed, then stretched out by my legs and plopped his head in my lap.

I felt my eyes sting in gratitude, and I stroked his bristly orange-and-white fur.

"Sorry about that. I feel like a fool." This time Myrtle's smile was simply embarrassed.

While refusing to break physical contact with Watson, I refocused on Myrtle. "No reason to be sorry."

"You believe that I didn't do it, don't you?"

"I do." I nodded and chuckled. "Of course, that doesn't mean that you didn't, but I don't think you did."

She nearly laughed. "Yeah, you're a little annoying, but I like you. I like you." She patted my leg, and to my surprise, made no move to get up, leaned back against the counter and seemed to deflate impossibly more. Though the tears appeared gone. "I have made a mess of things, Fred. I thought I was doing right. I really did."

I hesitated, almost wondering if she was about to make a confession, but I didn't think that was what she meant. "How so?"

She blinked several times. It didn't look like she was going to answer, but then she took a deep breath and launched in. "I don't like people very much. But I understand them, part of why I don't like them. I was looking for a way to do as much good as I could for the birds. I couldn't do it on my own. So I made the club. Twelve spots, because people like things that are exclusive. I made it expensive, ridiculously so, because people like things that are expensive. If I'd made it only a thousand dollar annual fee, people would've balked, but ten grand?" She laughed and winked at me. "Ten grand means it's expensive and doubly exclusive. And that's one hundred and twenty thousand a year that I can use to help save birds." Another laugh. "You know one way people are like birds?"

I felt like I was talking to a bird in human form every time I spoke to Myrtle Bantam. I figured it best not to say that. Though she'd probably take it as the highest form of compliment, come to think of it. "I can't say that I do."

"They are like starlings. Starlings love to steal and collect things. Fill their nests with worthless shiny trinkets." She tapped the badges on her chest. "I have twelve starlings who pay a lot of money to be special. Even if they have to cheat to make themselves feel that way."

I supposed it was a confession of sorts. "So you did know there was cheating."

"Of course I did. Don't you remember, I said I understand people. Why I don't like them overly much. But"—this time when she tapped her chest, I got the sensation that she was pointing deeper, past the badges—"that proves I'm human too, doesn't it? That I know about the cheating, and that I honestly don't care. Like the club matters, outside of raising awareness and making money to protect as many birds as I can. To me, the ends justify the means. So what if Alice has her son make bird sounds? Big deal if I've caught Roxanne sneaking a peek at my notes for the meeting beforehand and getting her trivia answers? It's a couple of people cheating. Maybe there is more that happens. The only two I'm sure of are Silas and Carl."

I wondered if Silas possibly had a more special place in Myrtle's heart because of that belief or not. And I also wondered if it made me guilty that I knew the truth and wasn't planning on telling her.

She didn't give me the chance anyway. Myrtle grasped my knee, startling Watson, but he placed his head back in my lap. "See what I mean? I've created a club, filled it with people who are willing to pay to feel special, to cheat to feel special. I let it keep going, because the ends justify the means. So maybe"—tears brimmed in her eyes once more, but they didn't fall—"maybe that makes me responsible for Henry's murder, even though I wasn't the one who committed it."

I shook my head. "No. I don't believe that. Not for a second."

She scowled.

"I mean it, Myrtle. Sure, maybe there're some things that aren't exactly on the up and up about your club, but your reasoning makes sense. And even if those badges and the drive to feel special cause a few people to cheat, that's a far cry from murder."

Myrtle licked her lips and nodded slowly, like she wanted to believe it.

I wasn't sure how long her openness would last. Maybe she had decided she liked me, but as she said, she clearly wasn't a people person. Just because she wasn't going to call the cops on me every time I walked into her store, didn't mean she was suddenly going to be a bosom buddy. I needed to use the moment while I had it. Myrtle wasn't the only one who sometimes believed the ends justified the means. And if taking advantage of Myrtle's atypical openness helped free Paulie and led me to the true murderer, that was more than worth it.

I waited till her eyes met mine. “You don’t believe Paulie killed Henry?”

“No.” She sneered. “He’s a little chick rushing around at the feet of all the other chickens in the barnyard, simultaneously trying to get their attention while hoping not to get stepped on. He didn’t kill Henry or anyone else.” She cocked her brow. “He also doesn’t have poached birds in his store. Maybe he didn’t know they were there or simply didn’t know they were poached illegally. Paulie is one of the ones not here for his love of birds. Though he likes them well enough. He needed friends and is willing to pay for them. He’s hardly the only one. Not everyone is here for the birds. Pete is looking for time away from his wife and kids, and a bird club is one of the few things his wife will allow him to do on his own. Benjamin’s trying to sell cameras. Alice is attempting to fill the void her son left when he went to college. Roxanne likes to feel superior and special. Raul is the same as Pete. And Lucy... well, Lord knows why Lucy does anything.” Myrtle shook her head, and sadness seemed to overpower her guilt and worry for the first time. “So you see, Henry was one of the very few who truly cared about the birds. Now the bird club is outnumbered by people who are here for other reasons. I’ve only got Silas, Petra, Carl, and Owen.”

I latched on to Owen’s name. “Really? You believe that Owen is truly here for the birds?”

Myrtle gave me a rather shocked expression. “Why? What have you uncovered? I don’t know if I can take much more.”

“Nothing.” I debated how much to say but decided I might as well be direct. “Honestly, I don’t know anything about Owen. But he was the last one Henry accused of being a poacher.”

She rolled her eyes. "I love that Henry was dedicated to the birds, but he was an idiot. He accused everyone of everything. He was right about some of them, obviously. But more often than not, he was wrong. Owen was simply the latest person to be accused." She shook her head again. "Owen wouldn't be involved in poaching. He has only two badges, because of all of them, he does the one thing that matters. He pays *twenty* thousand a year to be in the club, simply to help the birds. More than anyone, he's here for that. And he's responsible for updating the computer system and putting in information when we spot rare birds and documenting when we notice things that are strange in the park." She narrowed her eyes as she thought. "Honestly, at times he makes me uncomfortable, but the same could be true for me. A lot of us in the club are rather... different. I can't say that Owen would or wouldn't be capable of murder. But he wouldn't be involved in poaching. The birds are much too important to him. He simply wouldn't do it. He was used to Henry's accusations. We all were. So even if I'm not sure if Owen could kill someone, there was no reason for him to kill Henry just because he was being accused of being the poacher once more. Nearly everyone had been accused at least three or four times of being a poacher by Henry, Owen included." She took a deep breath, and I could see Myrtle begin to come back to herself, growing both stronger and distant once more. "I have no idea why Henry was killed. But it wasn't because he accused one of the other members of cheating or being a poacher. I can promise you that."

The miracle of miracles happened after I spoke to Myrtle. Watson and I returned to the Cozy Corgi, and both of us did our jobs. I sold books, and Watson allowed a select few to pet him and then napped at his favorite spots in the sunshine.

Oh, and I had a second breakfast. A tart covered in blackberries and cherries. While Katie's baked goods were so far ahead of those offered at Black Bear Roaster they might as well have been different classifications of food entirely, she hadn't gotten the knack of the cappuccino and coffee machines quite yet. Her dirty chai had a lot to be desired. I discovered, on the other hand, that Sammy did have the knack. I'd been considering returning to the Black Bear Roaster simply for caffeinated beverages, if for no other reason than to attempt to maintain an amicable relationship with Carla. After tasting Sammy's dirty chai, however, I decided I could wait for another day. Then I remembered how intensely awkward our last conversation had been. Maybe waiting for more than another day would be prudent.

By one in the afternoon, I was relieved of having to act like a responsible adult, as winter descended on the town once more and the customers stopped showing up. Katie and Sammy used the time to get a jump on the following day's prep work, and I opted to read.

I settled in with my book on the sofa, the warmth of the fire on one side, the light from the dusty-purple fabric of the Victorian Portobello lampshade above me, and the glow of snow flurries out the front window creating such a cozy environment, a person would think that murder could never happen within a hundred miles. And with the spicy aroma from Sammy's dirty chai wafting around me, I decided I was in heaven. The sensation was doubled when Watson let out a long yawn from his nap, stretched his little legs in front while his nearly tailless rump arched in the air, then he padded to the main room, through the fantasy and science fiction room in between, curled up at my feet by the fire, and fell asleep again.

As I read, following as Miss Fisher solved the murder with more panache than I possessed, the details of Henry's death whirled around in my mind. That was just it, actually. I didn't have any details about Henry's death. His throat had been slit on a snowy night in the woods, surrounded by fourteen other people—most of whom he'd accused of multiple crimes and driven crazy. As far as hard evidence went, I had none, save for the kakapo pin. The only thing I knew for sure was that neither Katie, Leo, nor I had killed Henry. Nor the small herd of elk we'd been mesmerized by. Other than that, it didn't seem as if anyone had an actual alibi for the moment he'd been murdered. The ones who did, weren't trustworthy. I added Carl to the list; I did trust Carl. Which meant Roxanne was cleared as well. And my gut told me that Myrtle was innocent, as well as Paulie. But that was it. Everything else was a convoluted mess.

No wonder Branson told me to keep my nose out of it. Although, they weren't doing much better than me. They had brought in two different people for the murder, neither of whom had killed anyone. If my instincts were correct.

No sooner had I doubled down my effort to concentrate on the book, the front door of the shop opened, and I turned to see a tall figure bundled in a fur-lined parka.

He pulled his hood back as he searched the store, and then he found me. Benjamin.

I started to get up, but he motioned for me to stay as he hurried through the rooms toward me. As he walked, he slid off his parka and then joined me on the sofa. A few clumps of snow fell onto the fabric. I tried not to think about that. Gary and Percival had just refinished it. Hopefully snow wouldn't do any damage, but I was the one who put it in the shop. It would hardly be the last time snow got on it.

Watson shifted as Benjamin sat down, but simply repositioned and fell back to sleep.

As Benjamin turned his wide eyes to me, once again I realized how young he truly was—twenty-five at the absolute oldest, but probably a few years younger. Rather impressive that he owned his own camera shop at that age, come to think of it. I wondered what his story was. "You're dating Sergeant Wexler, right?"

I balked a little and sat straighter. I hadn't anticipated that question. "No. I don't think I am."

Those wide eyes narrowed slightly. "You're not sure?"

I considered that for a heartbeat. "No, I'm not, which probably means that I'm not dating Sergeant Wexler." I attempted a smile. "Wouldn't you say?" At the admission I felt a tingle of disappointment, or loss, some sense of unpleasantness I couldn't quite label. A bit of relief, too.

"Oh." Benjamin's expression fell. "Okay then. I thought you two were close." It looked like he was about to leave.

"Why do you ask? It seems like you were hoping Sergeant Wexler and I were dating for some reason?"

His fingers drummed quietly as he clutched the fabric of his coat. "It would've been good to have an in with someone at the police station." He seemed to consider, glanced at me, and apparently didn't find what he was looking for as he shook his head. "This was a mistake. Sorry. I'll let you get back to your book."

I grabbed his arm without thinking. "We've been on a couple of dates. And...." Good Lord, I couldn't believe what I was about to say. But I needed to know why Benjamin was here, and like Myrtle and I had spoken about that morning, the ends can sometimes justify the means. "He was at my house last night. We talked for a while. We might not be dating necessarily, but I think we're... something."

He searched my face again. "You think he'd listen to you, like if you thought someone deserved a break, maybe he'd take your word on it?"

I thought that depended on the day. There were times I felt nearly certain he would, though none of those days had been lately. But still, I focused on those positive occasions as I answered. "Yes, I do. He did when Katie was accused of trying to kill Declan." At least that much was true, mostly.

Benjamin nodded slowly but was still perched on the edge of the sofa, ready to flee.

"Fill me in, Benjamin." While the stern professor routine had worked on him before, it seemed the young man now needed more of a motherly tone. Not an angle I had a lot of practice at. "It's clear something is eating you up. Obviously you know the right thing to do is to say whatever it is, or you wouldn't be here. If you're worried about

Branson getting involved, I promise you I'll put in a good word."

"Okay." He still teetered on the edge of the sofa, but he nodded slowly. "I know Paulie didn't have anything to do with the poached birds. He didn't even know they were there."

While not exactly a revelation, I felt a sense of relief and vindication that my gut had been right. Mine, Myrtle's, and Katie's. "You do?"

Benjamin nodded and sighed in frustration. "I don't like the guy. But he doesn't deserve this. He's enough of a mess the way it is."

Suddenly I remembered who I was talking to, and I allowed some of that authoritarian professor past to slip back into my tone. "Is someone paying you to do this? Like they did with Myrtle?"

He snorted, then laughed. "For Paulie? Who would do that?"

He had a point.

"No, no one is paying me. In fact...." Benjamin twisted and glanced out the windows, then seemed satisfied and turned back around. "Me saying this is going to ruin a lot of things. A lot."

"You know who killed Henry?" The words slipped out before they'd even fully formed in my mind.

"No." Benjamin looked insulted. "Of course not. I told you before, I wouldn't cover for a murderer."

"Sorry." I brought what I hoped was a motherly tone back into my voice. "Then what's going on? How do you know Paulie didn't have anything to do with the birds?"

"Because, even though I don't know who killed Henry, I do know who's doing the poaching. At least, I think."

"You *think* you know who's poaching?"

He nodded and glanced at the windows once more.

He might honestly think he didn't know who the murderer was, but Benjamin was obviously scared. Which to me, meant he probably did know who the killer was, even if he didn't quite realize it. I reached out again and lightly touched his knee, bringing his attention back. "Who do you think is doing it, Benjamin?"

Once more, he studied me for a long time, clearly debating. From how serious he was taking it—he looked like he was debating jumping off a cliff—he must be fairly certain. He let out a long, heavy sigh. "Owen. I think. I only know of one illegal bird he's been involved with, but maybe he's done more."

Owen. The name was almost like a relief, after the way he'd looked at me when I overheard him on the phone the day before. Then I remembered Myrtle's claim about him a few hours ago. The one person in the group who paid double the membership fees to help the birds. "Are you sure? Myrtle thinks he's trustworthy."

"Like I said, I don't know if he's *the* poacher, the one the entire bird club seems obsessed with. He might not be, but I know he's done it once. And given what Silas asked me to do for Myrtle, I'm betting this is connected. No way Paulie has the backbone to be involved in poaching. The man jumps at his own shadow."

I agreed with Benjamin's assessment, but it still didn't make sense. "Why don't you tell me what you know? The whole story."

This time, he didn't hesitate before he began to talk; apparently having made up his mind, it was final. "I was paired up with Petra on the hike the other night, not for any real reason other than how it worked out. While we were in the woods, we ran across Owen. Petra pulled Owen off to the side but wasn't as quiet as she thought she was. She was mad, telling him that the bird he'd gotten her was sick. That she hadn't paid good money for a sick bird. She was starting to lose her temper, but Owen told her to be quiet and they'd discuss it later."

I replayed his story, trying to put the pieces together and needing more details. "Did Petra actually say that Owen procured an illegal bird for her, or simply that she bought a bird from him?"

Benjamin looked at me like I was daft. "Owen doesn't run a pet store. Why would he be selling a bird to Petra?"

Fair question, but it still didn't necessarily mean it was poaching or even that the bird was illegal. "What does Owen do?"

He shrugged. "No idea."

"Did anything else happen? Are there any other details, even if you think they're not important?"

"I don't think so. Petra was definitely mad as we walked away, but she wouldn't talk about it. Not that I asked any questions. Wasn't much longer before Alice screamed and everybody came running."

One more bit of proof, however thin it was, that Henry had been right about Owen.

Maybe Henry had been nearby during the exchange, had heard, then confronted Owen about it.

"Doesn't necessarily clear Paulie, but maybe it gives enough reasonable doubt." I slipped back into professor mode once more. "You definitely should tell the police this. Maybe if they know it's Owen who they're looking for, that will help prove Paulie had nothing to do with it."

"I know. That's why I want you. Chances are, somehow, it'll come out that I lied about Myrtle. I need you to have my defense with Sergeant Wexler."

Maybe if I handed it directly over to him and didn't try to get more details on my own, Branson would listen to me. Although, I wasn't sure how much I was willing to go to bat for Benjamin. I thought he was telling the truth, but the only thing my gut told me about the kid was that I couldn't fully trust him. "I'll do my best." I pulled out my cell before Benjamin could object and tapped Branson's name.

He didn't answer. I didn't want to leave a voicemail in case that startled Benjamin. Instead I called the police station. A voice I didn't recognize answered and asked if I was in the state of emergency. "No, I have some information about some possible poaching going on. I'd like to speak to Sergeant Wexler, please."

Benjamin flinched, realizing that I was on the phone with the police station instead of directly to Branson, and I covered the mouthpiece of the phone to whisper to him. "It's fine. He wasn't answering his cell. It's still Branson. And if you bolt, it'll make you look guilty."

The dispatch put me through.

Branson answered on the second ring. "When they said you were calling, at first I thought it was because you'd forgiven me. But apparently you have information about a case?"

I was a little surprised he'd been worried about me being mad. But I didn't have time to focus on that. "Benjamin is with me at the bookshop. And no, I didn't go snooping this time. He's got a story for you about a possible poacher, one that may prove Paulie is innocent."

Branson hesitated, probably thrown off by me not responding to his question about forgiveness. "Benjamin has information about a poacher?" His voice was cold suddenly. Clearly hurt, or something, that I called him for professional reasons instead of personal.

"Yes."

"Okay, be right there."

It took nearly twice as long for Branson to get to the Cozy Corgi as I'd expected, and by the time the police cruiser pulled up in front of the shop, Benjamin was pacing the floor. To my surprise, Branson hadn't come alone. Officer Green came with him, and from both their expressions, it was clear they'd been arguing on the way over. Branson attempted a smile as they entered the shop, but it fell flat.

Susan glowered as he leaned close enough to me to not be overheard.

"Sorry. I was planning on talking to the two of you here, but Susan got wind of it and apparently we're going to do this by the book. She made a whole scene of it. Sometimes I'm not sure if I'm the superior officer or if she is." He turned to Benjamin. "You're not under arrest. I'm simply going to request you come with us to the station. You can even follow us in your own car if you'd rather. We'll take your official statement there."

Benjamin looked at me in a panic, then back at them. "Is Fred coming too?"

Susan snorted. "Is she involved in this case, or part of what you witnessed? Something more than simply being nosy, obviously."

He shook his head, and Susan grinned. Branson's features darkened.

I watched from the window with Watson at my feet as Benjamin got in his car and followed the police cruiser out of sight.

"Well, look who it is." Leo grinned as he opened his apartment door, and though his tone was teasing, his eyes had a flash of heat. "It's feast or famine with you, isn't it?"

Watson let out a happy yelp and reared upward, bashing his forepaws into Leo's knees.

As with every other interaction they'd had, Leo gave in to whatever Watson demanded, sinking down onto one knee and rubbing Watson nearly silly, like he was a joyful little puppy inside of the cantankerous old soul that he was.

Watson loved it.

I stepped around them and shut the door, glad to be out of the cold. "Thanks for letting me come over. I wasn't sure if you'd be available when I called."

"Today is one of my days off." He finished lavishing affection on Watson and stood. "You're always welcome, but you said you had news. Gotta say, I'm curious." He motioned toward the sofa where we'd sat before. I'd not even crossed the room before Watson raced past me and leaped onto the couch, automatically taking the center spot.

"Well, Watson feels at home." Leo sat down beside him, and instantly began stroking his fur as he waited for me to begin.

I sat and didn't waste any more time. "Benjamin came and saw me. And he left with the police probably less than half an hour ago."

Leo jerked, startling Watson. "Sorry, buddy." He started petting him again and refocused on me. "Benjamin? *Benjamin* killed Henry?"

"No. He wasn't arrested. He went in for questioning. He kinda volunteered. He thinks he knows who the poacher is."

This time Leo went stone-cold still.

A phone vibrated over on the kitchen counter. I motioned toward it. "You can get that if you want."

"Are you crazy? Like I care about the phone right now." Leo's eyes were wide, and he was pale suddenly. "I know there's more than one poacher, but we've not been able to pin anybody in forever. Who did he say?"

That was why I'd come to see Leo in person. I knew how big this was for him. And maybe some part of me was looking for an excuse to see him. Possibly, but I wasn't going to consider that aspect. "Owen."

"Owen?" A laugh burst from Leo, but it trailed off quickly, his expression growing serious once more. "You're serious?"

I nodded. "Yes. I called Myrtle before I came over here. She and I talked earlier in the day. She doesn't believe it. She thinks Benjamin's lying. Which, he seems prone to do."

Leo didn't speak for a little bit, and his gaze grew distant, but his fingers never quit dragging through Watson's fur, a pile beginning to grow in the crease of the couch cushions.

I started to ask if he was okay, then thought better of it.

"Owen. I never would've considered Owen. Nobody in the bird club would, except Henry, and he suspected everyone. Which, if Owen is the poacher, would've made things pretty easy on him." Though his eyes were narrowed, I could already see he was accepting the possibility. "What proof did Benjamin have?"

"Apparently Petra bought a bird from Owen, and now the bird is sick. Benjamin heard them arguing about it the night of the snowshoe hike."

"Petra?" One of his hands left Watson and touched his heart. He looked wounded. "She's crazy about birds. I can't believe she would do that." Leo shook his head and mumbled to himself. "I bet it's a forest owlet."

"A forest owlet?"

"Yeah, cute little thing from India. Critically endangered. She's nearly as obsessed with them as Myrtle is with the kakapo." Leo sank back into the cushions, finally breaking contact with Watson and looking utterly devastated. "Right in front of my eyes. This whole time. Right in front of my eyes."

"None of this is confirmed. I'm not telling you this so you'll beat yourself up." I reached over Watson and gripped Leo's forearm. "And even if it is true, you're not a member of the bird club. You're only there occasionally. You've got the entire national park to think about. Myrtle does this full-time, and she's as shocked as you are. The last we spoke, she didn't believe it. About Owen or Petra. She barely let me finish before she cut me off. I wanted you to know, but I also thought with the new information and you knowing the members of the Feathered Friends Brigade much better than I do, that maybe this news would trigger something for you. Can you see Owen as the poacher? And if so, as a killer? Or Petra?"

He laughed again. It burst from him in an almost crazed

fashion. "Petra? Can *you* picture Petra murdering someone?"

The idea of the little Asian grandmother slitting a man's throat in the woods did seem a little farfetched, but you never knew. "She wouldn't be the first little old lady who's killed someone in the past couple of months."

Leo sobered. "Well, that's true. But no, I can't see Petra doing that. I also can't see her being a poacher. If she is involved, then maybe she's nothing more than a buyer. It happens sometimes. People love a certain animal so much that they can no longer love it from afar. They have to possess it."

"Sounds like a bad romance. At least a bad one-sided one."

"It's a pretty apt description." Leo shook his head again and sighed, sounding utterly defeated. Then he put his hands on his knees and shifted to a standing position. "I found the canister of pink-lemonade mix so I made a pitcher. Want a glass as we see if we can figure this out?"

I couldn't hold back a chuckle. "You know, that sounds pretty good."

Leo walked around the couch, through the small living room, and into the kitchen. I watched as he pulled the pitcher from the refrigerator and set it on the counter by his phone. He picked up his cell, his eyebrows creasing, then glanced my way. "I have a text from Myrtle."

I stood instantly and made my way over to him. No way was that a coincidence.

"Myrtle says she thinks she knows who the poacher is. She wants me to come to the shop and see what she's found." Without waiting for a response, he tapped the screen and lifted the phone to his ear. Several seconds passed before he lowered it. "She's not answering."

My skin prickled, but I ignored it. "She could be with a customer."

Leo glanced at his cell. "It's almost five. She could be." His honey-brown gaze lifted and met mine. A few more moments passed. "Should we go to her?"

"If you don't, I will."

Leo grinned.

The sun was setting by the time we parked in front of Wings of the Rockies. The snow was thicker than before, and the downtown was empty of people. Leo waited for Watson and me to exit the Jeep and then hit Lock. There was still an Open sign in the window, and the three of us walked in. The chimes chirped overhead like always, but the store was silent.

Watson growled in the back of his throat.

Leo and I looked at each other. My skin prickled once more.

"Myrtle?" Leo's loud voice caused Watson and me both to jump, and I instinctively threw out my arm, as if he was in the passenger seat and we were about to wreck.

I shook my head. Maybe I was being silly, but I could feel it. All three of us could. Something was clearly wrong.

We made our way through the store, glancing behind little nooks and crannies as we walked, and then behind the counter. There was nothing. No one.

I glanced at Leo. "Try calling her again."

He did. After a couple of silent seconds, we heard the sound of songbirds in the distance. Leo motioned toward the door in the back. "Over there. That's her ringtone."

We walked to the door, and I suddenly wished we'd brought a weapon of some sort.

Leo threw open the door and cursed. This time he held out his arm. "You don't need to see this."

I stepped past him and into a large room. Over half of it was simply storage and merchandise; the other side was a makeshift office. Desk, computer, shelves of books. In front of the desk, lying in a pool of blood on the floor was Owen. Like Henry in the forest, his eyes were sightless. I could see two knife wounds, and it was easy to tell which one had killed him.

Watson growled, but I didn't try to shush him.

Leo started to walk over to Owen's body.

"Leo, what are you doing?"

He paused and looked back. "I need to check and make sure he's not alive. Maybe he—"

"No, he's dead. Don't touch him. Don't check." I was surprised at the steel in my voice. It didn't quaver in the slightest. Although this was my fifth dead body in three months, and by that point, I should be perfectly clear I wasn't the fainting type. "It'll mess up the scene. And possibly get you brought in as a suspect."

For a second he looked like he was going to argue, but then he didn't. "No Myrtle."

I'd forgotten. "Call her cell again." No sooner were the words out of my mouth than I saw it. "No, never mind. It's on the desk." The phone was lying on a stack of papers, but Myrtle's peacock-feathered purse was on the ground, the contents strewn over the floor, beside a gun I'd not noticed before. "I don't think Myrtle did this, and I don't think she left willingly."

Leo followed my gaze and nodded. "Call the cops?"

"Yeah." I nodded. "I'll do it."

Branson answered. "Don't tell me you have another

witness or person with information." He sounded stressed, but there was a slight playful teasing in his tone.

"A dead body, actually. At Wings of the Rockies."

There was a heartbeat. "Are you serious?"

"Unfortunately, yes."

"Myrtle?"

I shook my head again, then realized he couldn't see it. "No. Owen."

"Owen?" His voice shot up, clearly shocked.

"Yes. And I'm pretty certain Myrtle's been taken against her will. At least her phone is here, and her purse is spilled all over the place."

"I'll be right there. And Fred?"

"Yeah?"

"Don't go anywhere, and don't touch anything." I could almost see him roll his eyes. "The last thing I want is to have to waste time trying to keep Susan from locking you up because your fingerprints are on something."

"Got it." I ended the call and looked at Leo. "They're on their way."

He grunted, but seemed unable to tear his eyes from Owen.

I grabbed his arm. "Come on. That doesn't mean we need to wait in here."

We started to leave the office, but Watson was stretched to the end of his leash, growling quietly at a file cabinet.

I started to call him and force him to come, then thought better of it. I spoke to Leo, though I didn't glance back at him. "Hold on." I walked over to Watson, and felt Leo behind my back as I knelt down.

Watson continued to growl.

Ridiculously, I feared he'd found Myrtle's body. Preposterous, since there wasn't room. At first I didn't see what had caught his attention, and I had to adjust my position to better see between a stack of boxes and the file cabinet, and then I saw the glint of silver. Carefully, I used the hem of my skirt as a glove and pulled it out.

"A knife." Leo put his hand on my shoulder.

A large knife. Obviously what had killed Owen, judging from the freshness of the blood on it. Though I couldn't imagine why it was there.

Leo sucked in a breath. "Fred, look." He leaned forward, pointing at the knife, but stopping short of touching it. "There's a kakapo inlaid on the handle." He pulled his hand back. "It must be Myrtle's."

I started to nod and then stopped. "No. It's not Myrtle's." I stood and looked Leo full in the face. "Though I bet I know where Myrtle is, or at least who she's with." This time I did have to pull Watson to get him to move and headed toward the door. I glanced back at Leo, who was fixated on Owen once more. "You coming with me?"

Despite his pale face, a flicker of a grin played at his lips. "You know it."

We were nearly across town when Branson called.

In the haste, I'd forgotten all about him and nearly hit Ignore. Then realized we were more than likely going to need the police for the upcoming situation. "Hey, sorry I—"

"Where are you?" He sounded furious. "I told you not to leave."

"I know who took Myrtle. Leo and I are headed to his house right now."

"You're what?" His voice rose nearly an octave, then crashed to a whisper. "You're with Leo?"

"Yes, the two of us were going to go talk to Myrtle, and that's when we discovered Owen's body."

Leo cast a sidelong glance at me, then refocused on the snowy road.

"Either way, I told you not to leave. And you have no business going on a rescue mission. I don't need you getting killed too."

"I won't." There wasn't time for this. "We're almost there, and I'm not stopping now. They might not even be here, but it's probably a good idea for you to head over." I filled him in on where we were headed. Branson sputtered indignantly the entire time.

We pulled into Silas's driveway, and Leo slammed the Jeep into Park. "All right, stay here. I'll be right back, hopefully."

I gaped at him. "What do you mean, stay right here?"

"If we're right, which I'm sure we are, Silas killed Owen less than half an hour ago. We don't need to add another victim."

He started to reach for the door handle, but I cut him off. "And what are you? Are you not a people—er person? Or does being a park ranger make you somehow invincible?"

"Fred." Unlike Branson, Leo's voice wasn't patient, just pleading. "I don't want you to get hurt."

"Well, good. That makes two of us. I don't want to be hurt either." I could feel my nostrils flare, and my temper began to take over. "Nor do I want you hurt. And chances are that both of us are less likely to get hurt if we go together."

For a second, I thought he was going to continue to argue, but then a grin began to form. "Fine. You're probably right. You can come."

Despite the fact we were more than likely sitting outside the home of a killer and getting ready to go confront him, I laughed. "Excuse me, did you just give me permission?"

"No, I was—" He blushed. "Sorry. Didn't mean to do it that way. I simply want you to be safe."

"We've covered that. Let's do our best to make sure the other stays safe, all right?" I glanced back at Watson. "I'll be right back."

We hurried up the sidewalk, got to the door, and I turned to Leo, unable to keep a smile from forming. "Okay, I didn't plan this part out. What do you think? Break a window, ring the doorbell, go around the house and look for unlocked doors?"

He considered for a second and then answered in a tone that was more of a question. "Ring the doorbell?"

"That's kinda what I was thinking." I pushed the doorbell. "This is insane." Even so, I held up my hand to the etched glass oval on the front door and peered in. A large blurry form moved through my field of vision from farther back in the house, in the living room, if my memory served. "Ring the bell again, Leo."

He did.

The large form returned, silhouetted against the light of the room behind him. I was sure it was Silas, and he stiffened when he saw me pressed against the window. He dropped whatever he'd been carrying and pushed it to the side, then to my surprise, strode toward the door. I jerked back on instinct but then forced myself to look again, checking his hands. So many things I'd not considered. His hands were empty, and I pulled back once more.

"I don't think he's holding a gun, but that doesn't mean he doesn't have one somewhere nearby."

"I don't have a gun, but I do have a crowbar in the back of the Jeep."

I spared him a glance. "I don't think you have time to go get it, and it's probably best not to show up looking like we're ready to attack. For all he knows, we're here to talk about what we discussed before. Nothing else."

"Yeah." Leo sounded skeptical. "I don't think that's how this is going to go."

I didn't either.

But there was no more time to consider or predict. Silas opened the door, not wide but enough to make me wonder if maybe he wasn't sure why we were there. "Fred, Leo." He was wide-eyed and pale. Probably in shock. "Now is not a good time."

Even before I said it, I knew it was pointless. "I've given some thoughts to what you requested. About keeping your feelings about Myrtle secret from her. I talked to her this morning; she was a complete wreck. I think maybe hearing that someone loves her might help."

He laughed softly, a crazed smile forming on his lips. "She knows." He started to shut the door. "You should leave now."

I put my hand up to stop it, and Leo took a step closer. "That's not going to work, Silas." I decided to go with the direct approach again. It seemed more effective most of the time. "I want to see Myrtle. Have you hurt her?"

Silas flinched and relaxed his hold on the door, allowing me to nudge it open a little more. "I would never hurt Myrtle. Ever."

"What about Owen? Or Henry?"

Silas cast his wild eyes on Leo. Maybe that had been a little too direct. "I need you to leave, Leo." He straightened, squaring his shoulders, and his voice grew hard. "I don't want to hurt you. I like you." His gaze flicked to me. "Both of you. But I will hurt you, if you don't leave right now."

"Silas, we have to see Myrtle." I tried the same mothering tone I'd used on Benjamin. The aggression was growing thick and needed to be cut somehow. "I only want to know she's okay."

"I already told you, I would never hurt her." Silas started to slam the door, but Leo barged past, knocking me a little off-balance, and plowed into Silas.

I steadied myself on the wall of the porch, and watched as Leo and Silas were airborne in a weird embrace through the doorway, then crashed to the hardwood floor, causing the chandelier to shake and send a rainbow of fractals over the scene. Silas let out a cry as the back of his head hit the floor.

Leo repositioned quickly, straddling Silas and managing to secure both his wrists to the ground.

Silas began to buck.

Leo looked like he was bull riding for a moment, then pressed harder on Silas's wrists and dug his knees into Silas's ribs. "Don't struggle, Silas. I don't want to hurt you either, so don't make me."

Silas stilled.

For just a heartbeat, I was so thrown off that I stared. I might've expected such a move from Branson, but not from Leo. From all our interactions, and Katie's constant reference to him as Smokey Bear, that was exactly how I'd begun to see him. Some big, softhearted teddy bear.

There was nothing reminiscent of a stuffed animal as he glanced over his shoulder. "I've got ropes in the Jeep. Get them, please."

I nodded and rushed toward the Jeep, slipping on a patch of ice on the walkway but catching myself easily. I almost laughed when I realized Leo had managed to say *please* as he pinned a murderer to the ground. The Jeep was unlocked, and I threw open the back door to find a huge assortment of equipment. The crowbar was there alongside an axe, and several coils of ropes. At least he was still teddy bear enough to not request the axe.

Watson peered over the back of the seat, whining pitifully.

"Sorry, buddy, be right back. Everything's okay." I grabbed the ropes and hurried back to Leo, who still had Silas secured.

"Tie up his right wrist." Leo carefully slid his hands down Silas's forearm, making room.

I wedged the end of the rope under Silas's hand, and looped it, before starting the knot. I had a flash like an out-of-body experience as I worked. As if I was spying on us from the chandelier, I could see the three of us on the ground and marveled as I expediently tied rope around a man's wrist. Surely it should be disturbing that I didn't even hesitate.

From out of nowhere, Watson bounded through the door. He let out a ferocious bark, and as his hind foot caught on the doorjamb, he stumbled, plowing into Leo's side.

It wasn't much, but it was enough. Leo's grip on Silas loosened, and my hands were fixing the knot, leaving less pressure on the rest of his arm. As Silas swung a fist through the air, the rope slapped across my face, and his fist smashed into Leo's temple.

Though Leo let out a yell, he managed to hold on to Silas all the same, but Silas used the momentum of his swing to force a roll. He was unable to do it completely, and he and Leo ended up on their sides. With a startled yelp, Watson darted out of the way, then realized Leo was in trouble and rushed back in to bite Silas's ear, instantly drawing blood.

Silas howled and swung again, this time at Watson. Still having the rope in my hand that was secured to his wrist, I threw myself backward from my kneeling position yanking the rope as hard as I could.

There was a snap, and another yell.

"Freeze!"

I yanked harder at the rope, eliciting another scream from Silas.

"Fred! I said freeze."

I wasn't sure who I thought shouted the first *freeze*, but it startled me when I looked over to see Branson and Officer Green both pointing their guns at Silas.

I froze but didn't lessen my hold on the rope.

Watson growled, still tugging on Silas's ear.

"Fred. You can unfreeze enough to remind Watson he's a corgi not a German shepherd." There was a hint of laughter in Branson's tone.

I hesitated to release the rope, fearing Silas would take a swing at Watson, but then I noticed the unnatural angle of his arm. He wasn't going to be doing anything to Watson. I supposed I'd done that.

Releasing the rope, I slid an arm under Watson's belly and pulled him from Silas.

He snarled, then realized it was me and settled.

"Good boy," I whispered in his ear as I ruffled his fur. "You're my good, brave boy." I'd made plenty of jokes about Watson killing me in my sleep. I was going to have to reconsider those. I hadn't known he had it in him.

"You too, Lopez. Let him go. We've got it from here."

In a matter of minutes, Branson and Susan had Silas handcuffed and read him his rights. Susan kept her gun trained on him, even after he was handcuffed, which had sent Silas into fits of howling. She glanced at me occasionally, and I wondered if she was considering pointing the gun somewhere else.

Branson turned to us. "Myrtle?"

I shook my head. "As you can see, we didn't quite make it past the doorway."

He snickered. "I almost wish we'd been a couple of minutes later. Dislocated arm, chewed up ear... any longer and the guy might've been total dog food." He glanced around, his eyes wide as he took in the mansion. "If she's here, we've got a lot of rooms to search."

"No, I know where she is." I motioned toward where Watson was sniffing in front of the door, the same one he'd smelled before. This time there was the key and the lock. "For some reason, I don't think that's a closet."

Branson headed over, twisted the door handle, and looked in, then let out a low whistle.

Watson rushed past him.

Leo and I both hurried to follow, and I could see the objection rising to Branson's lips as we neared the door.

"Sergeant Wexler." Susan's voice froze us in our places. "These are civilians. They need to stay here."

"You know, Susan." I didn't think I'd ever heard Branson's voice sound so cold. "It's time you remember that you're outranked." He stepped through the doorway, gun drawn, and gestured with his head for us to follow.

I gave a mental thanks to Susan, certain Branson was letting us follow simply because she'd told him he shouldn't.

The reason Branson had whistled was instantly clear the moment Leo and I looked in the doorway, and we turned to stare at each other before going in.

Indeed, it was not a closet, but a long set of stairs. But that was where the comparison to anything house-like stopped. Every step we took brought us into a new world. And with every one, we left the winter wonderland of Estes behind and entered a hot and humid rainforest.

The ceilings were at least twenty feet high, though maybe taller. It was hard to tell with the large growths of trees and vines covering the space. It looked like it went on forever. The ground was dirt, rock, moss, and different sorts of vegetation. A small stream babbled through the center. And sitting on its bank, looking completely dazed and in shock was Myrtle. Her hands and feet were bound, and there was a bruise forming on the side of her face, but other than that she looked no worse for the wear. Beside her, Watson pressed against her, barking at us like we couldn't see them. And above everything, were birds. Countless birds. Parrots of every color imaginable, finches, and doves, and all sorts of songbirds I didn't have the names for. And then I realized it wasn't only above us, but everywhere. Behind Myrtle and Watson, a peacock strode between the trees. All sorts of birds—some I recognized, others I didn't—wandered about, a few of them playing in the stream.

We were all rather shocked, and it took us several moments frozen at the base of the steps before we entered the world and rushed to Myrtle's side.

Ten minutes later, police were scouring the house, and Susan and another officer had taken Silas away.

We'd started to bring Myrtle up, but she begged to stay where she was. So after getting her a glass of water, Leo, Watson, and I sat on the bank of the indoor stream with her, while Branson paced, asking endless questions.

"You're certain Owen was the poacher?"

Myrtle nodded. She seemed more herself every second, and she didn't appear to be closing off like she normally did, though she never met any of our gazes. She was constantly looking everywhere, every once in a while gasping at the sight of a new bird she'd not noticed. "Yes. After I spoke to Fred this morning, I made a surprise visit to Petra. What Fred said was true. Petra admitted she'd got the bird from Owen."

"An owlet?"

Branson cast Leo an irritated glare for interrupting, but Myrtle answered him anyway.

"Yes. One that's not doing very well, I'm afraid." Her eyes tracked a red macaw that let out a screech and landed on a branch over our heads. "And then I started checking the books. Owen helped me with a lot of the financial stuff for the club. Honestly, I'm not sure what it means, but something was wrong with the notes. I don't think money was missing, but there was also documentation of where we spotted rare birds nearby, which makes sense, but also some states over." She shrugged. "In and of itself, not a big deal, but considering what I'd seen at Petra's, it made me wonder."

"We'll need to take those books as evidence, Myrtle. More proof of what Owen was up to." Branson made a note in his pad.

"Maybe you can finally put a stop to the poaching ring that's been going on." Leo cast a hard stare at Branson. "It's not one person. Owen might be part of it, but he's merely a part. We've got a poaching ring going on in—"

"Don't get carried away, Leo." Before Leo could respond, Branson refocused on Myrtle. "What did Owen say to you?"

"I was at the shop with Silas. When I found the books, I called him to see what he thought." She finally looked away from the birds and glanced at Leo. But only for a second. "I texted you while Silas was there. I wanted your input as well. Silas was saying that I was reading into the books too much. That Owen wouldn't do such a thing." Her gaze grew distant, seeming not to focus even on the birds anymore, probably lost to the recent memory. "Then Owen showed up. He'd heard about Benjamin being taken in for questioning, and Petra had called him to let him know that I knew about the owl. He came there to kill me. He and Silas started arguing. Owen was saying that I knew too much, that I couldn't live. Silas kept telling him that I could be trusted and that we were going away soon anyway." She shivered. "Owen pulled a gun and was going to shoot me, but Silas... stopped him."

All of us were still.

"So that means Silas killed saving you." I took her by the hand, keeping my other on Watson. The last thing we needed was for him to decide to do a replay of a bird chase. "So he's not a murderer, at least not in that sense."

"Yes, he is." She turned sad eyes on me. "He killed Henry. That wasn't Owen."

"Why?" Leo sounded truly shocked.

She shivered again. "Because of how he spoke to me. The way Henry screamed at me that night in the woods. I was the reason. Silas told me like he thought I would thank him." She gestured around the rainforest. "He made this for me. So he said. A place for me to visit when I lived with him one day." She took a shaky breath, and I thought she was near tears, but none came. "All of these birds are poached, at least most of them, taken from their homes and brought here—no matter how beautiful it is, it's still a cage. *For me.* He committed this atrocity for me." She shrugged again. "I guess Owen did it, technically. He's the one who got the birds for Silas, but it was Silas's money that made it happen. For me. How could he ever think that I would want this?"

I squeezed her hand. "This isn't your fault."

She spared me a glance. "I don't know about that. Maybe if I'd paid more attention to the people around me. The ones I trusted the most are responsible for the very thing I hate. I had no idea Silas felt for me the way he did.

Maybe if I'd realized, I could've ended it before his obsession grew."

"It's still not your fault, Myrtle." In a strange way, I could see, partly, why Silas would think Myrtle would like this place. If I didn't know the ugly part about the poaching, even I would've loved it, and I didn't have any great affinity for birds. They were fine, beautiful, but I was much more of a dog person. This was like stumbling upon a bit of magic. But for Myrtle, it was nothing more than a cage.

"I still don't understand why your pin was near where Henry was killed." Branson's voice wasn't necessarily hard, but it didn't seem like he fully trusted her yet.

"I've told you. It wasn't mine. It was Silas's."

He looked like he was about to argue, so I jumped in. "I think that's true. The knife we found, which we didn't touch, has a kakapo on it, just like the pin. I think because it was Myrtle's favorite bird, it became Silas's way of having her close."

"Silas told me that was his one mistake." She motioned toward the treetops. "If you look on the kitchen counter, you'll find two plane tickets. For ten months from now. Silas said he hoped I would fall in love with him within the year. He bought us plane tickets to New Zealand so I could finally see a kakapo. He said that since I knew early, he'd try to move up our reservations. And he had the pin made for me. He was going to give it to me there. He claimed he carried it with him everywhere."

Branson continued asking question after question. Still distrustful. But every answer she gave was solid.

Finally it was time to go. Myrtle stood with us and looked around. At last tears fell. "May I have a little time down here, by myself? I know they shouldn't be here, and I'm going to do everything I can to make sure every single one of them returns to where they came from, but I have never seen so many birds, so many different kinds of birds, in one place."

Branson started to shake his head, but I caught his eye. After a few seconds, he gave a nod. "Of course, Myrtle. We'll be upstairs. Join us whenever you're ready."

SEVENTEEN

Snow fell through the night and continued into the next morning. I watched from the bakery window as large crystalline flakes floated over downtown. Estes truly was the most charming little town, if you overlooked the recent murders. Carl shuffled through the front door of Cabin and Hearth with a broom and dusted off the sidewalk in front of the store. I'd have to pop in at some point during the day and fill him and Anna in on all the details. Goodness knows they'd earned it. Maybe I'd invite my uncles down to do it all at once. In the distance, the sun shone brightly on the mountains, promising that the snow was short-lived.

"What I don't understand is how the two of you were in Silas's house and couldn't hear all those birds. My grandmother had a cockatoo when I went to live with her. That thing drove me absolutely crazy, all that screeching and squawking and hollering." Katie bugged her eyes. "And that was just one bird."

I came back to the moment, focusing on my friend and business partner. "You went to live with your grandma? How old were you?"

She stiffened slightly. "I don't know, twelve or something." She waved me off. "That's most definitely not interesting. Not near as interesting as a killer with a jungle in their basement."

I never pushed too far into Katie's past. She'd tell me one day when she was ready. I was certain there was something there. But if she was never ready, that was fine too.

Leo finished chewing a bite of his ham-and-cheese croissant before answering. "That room was basically a fortress of its own. Soundproofed, completely insulated. If nobody realized what was going on, Silas could've had Myrtle down there for the rest of her life, and no one would've ever known. There was no way she could've escaped. What we thought was a closet door was as thick as a vault. I can't imagine how much that place cost to build. Or to simply keep going. I'm surprised the energy company didn't raise a stink over the heating bill alone."

I bent down, reaching under the table to scratch Watson's head. "But you knew, didn't you? You smelled something. You knew there was something good in that room."

"I was thinking about that last night as I fell asleep." Leo glanced under the table as well, smiling at Watson before looking back at Katie and me. "As good as a dog's nose is, I can't imagine he would've been able to smell through that door. That seal was impermeable. My guess is he was smelling where Silas's shoes had been, or something—when he would walk up from the basement."

"Any of you want refills?" Sammy gestured at me as she walked up to our table. "I know you want another dirty chai. I think you have a drinking problem."

Katie swatted at her, shooing her away. "You were not hired to be a waitress. You're not getting paid enough to be a waitress. You're a baker."

Sammy chuckled but lifted her eyebrows in a questioning manner at me as she walked away so Katie couldn't see her.

I smiled and nodded. I could do with another dirty chai. Sammy seemed nearly as comfortable in her role of baker as Katie, almost like she felt a sense of ownership. I hoped that was a good thing.

Katie reached over and took a piece of my bear claw but spoke before she popped it in her mouth. "I feel horrible for Myrtle. To have members of her club be involved in that. I'm sure she's devastated. What's going to happen to Petra?"

"I'm not sure." Leo shrugged. "She's not in jail or anything, but purchasing a poached animal could come with jail time. My guess is she'll get a hefty fine."

I hadn't even thought of her that morning. I turned to him. "What about the owl... sorry, owlet?"

He grinned. "Dr. Sallee is keeping her for the time being. I'm betting he'll get her back into shape. The bigger issue is figuring out where all the other birds came from. And how long they've been gone. If it's safe to send them back, or if they've been too domesticated. Unfortunately, I figure most of them will end up in zoos. Which isn't necessarily a bad life, by any means. But—"

"Still a cage, as Myrtle would say." I hadn't meant to interrupt him, but the words that sprung from my lips brought a bit of melancholy. "That's going to be hard for Myrtle."

"It will be. But don't feel too bad for her. Myrtle's getting something out of this." Leo's eyes brightened. "She has that round-trip ticket to New Zealand. She'll finally get to see a kakapo in real life."

Katie gaped at him. "She gets to keep the plane ticket?"

"Yeah, it wasn't purchased illegally. In fact—" He grinned at me. "—I can't say I'm much more of a fan of

Branson than I was before. He's still dismissing that there is a poaching ring. Claims that he bets Owen was the one responsible for what we'd been noticing in the park. Which is ridiculous—he was part of it, but for sure not all. However, I think I'm starting to convince Officer Green, so maybe she can influence him."

"Susan?" I couldn't believe my ears. "She actually gives you the time of day?"

He winced. "I know she's horrible to you and your family. But she's one of the few in the department who will listen to my concerns."

How strange. I wouldn't have predicted that.

"It sounded like you were getting ready to say something good about Branson, though. What'd he do?"

Leo looked at Katie in confusion, and then his expression cleared. "Oh, right. I forgot. We were talking about Myrtle. I brought up Silas's plane ticket to Branson. We're betting the way Silas feels about Myrtle, he'd be willing to make the calls and get Silas's plane ticket switched to her name. If it works, she'll have two trips to New Zealand."

What a strange turn of events. "Silas would do that for Myrtle. Maybe it was love."

Katie had taken a bite of her almond croissant, and crumbs flew as she nearly choked. "Sure, if you call complete obsession, killing people who insult you, and building a rainforests to lock you in *love*."

"Okay, you have a point. A very good point." I laughed at her expression but shook my head. "It's a sweet thought, but I'm willing to bet Myrtle will trade in those plane tickets and use the money for the birds here. She won't use this experience to go see her kakapo. It would ruin it for her."

"Yeah. I bet you're right." Leo's smile faltered. "Didn't think of that."

I patted his arm, but switched the topic. "You weren't the only one thinking about things last night. Myrtle told me that Owen was paying double the annual fee. Do you think he was doing that to avoid suspicion?"

"Partly, yeah, I do." Clearly Leo had thought about this as well. "But honestly, that's one more reason I think it's clear we've got a ring happening. One poacher isn't going to be making that amount of money, at least not enough to throw twenty thousand at a bird club annually. But, yes. It kept suspicion off him, mostly, and gave him bigger access to Myrtle's resources, which aren't small. The police have the books now, so I can't get my hands on them, but someday. I bet those files will show how much Owen was using the bird club for the very thing it stood against."

Another motion outside the window caught my eye. Paulie and his two corgis had joined Carl in the fight against the snow-covered sidewalk. Flotsam and Jetsam looked to be ecstatic at the snowfall, though they were ecstatic—insane rather—about everything, and had Paulie slipping and tripping between the slick concrete and their rapidly weaving leashes.

Leo popped the last bite of his ham-and-cheese croissant into his mouth just as Sammy brought my dirty chai. Katie scowled but didn't say anything. After he finished chewing, Leo stood. "Well, I need to get to the park. Thanks for breakfast. See you ladies later."

I smiled and gave him a little wave as Katie lifted what was left of her almond croissant in a salute. "See you later, Smokey Bear."

As Leo walked away, Watson let out a yelp and rushed toward him.

Leo turned around, laughing, and knelt to one knee as he lavished affection on Watson. "I'm sorry, buddy. I'm so sorry. Bad park ranger, bad. How could I forget my favorite little man?"

Sammy had gone home over an hour before, and Katie and I were closing the shop. She'd just turned off all the lights upstairs and paused by the counter as I was putting the finishing touches to the books. "Pretty good day, huh?"

"Yeah. Funny what happens when I'm here to do my actual job. Sold over twenty-five books today."

"Wow! Almost like a real bookstore." She winked.

"Kinda." I laughed. "Of course, every single one of them was either a mystery or a book about birds."

"Estes loves its gossip. Now, if the next murder corresponds to a book genre, we're set."

"Don't say such horrible things. We're not hoping for murder."

She cocked an eyebrow but didn't give any further commentary. "Want me to hang out till you're done?"

"No, thank you. You gotta be exhausted. I won't be much longer." I walked around the counter and gave her a hug. "See you tomorrow?"

"Better believe it." Katie broke the embrace and walked toward the front door, giving the sleeping Watson a little wave before she left.

Another ten minutes, and I'd finished with the books and straightened the shelves of the few books we'd sold. Twenty-five wasn't that bad, at least by comparison. With the upstairs lights off, the bookshop truly was exactly how I'd envisioned it. It was perfect. The homey smells of the bakery above had already permeated the lower floor, making it even better than I'd dreamed. With a yawn, Watson stretched, stood, then padded over to me.

I gave him a quick scratch behind the ears. "No need to get up. I think we should hang out for a little bit. We spent all this time making this place exactly how we wanted, let's enjoy it. This time, without feeling guilty about being annoyed when a customer comes in."

Watson followed me to the mystery room and curled up under the sofa as I lit the fireplace and turned off all the other lights except the Victorian lamp. I slid a mystery off of one of the shelves, one I'd been meaning to read for ages, and curled up on the sofa. I opened to the first page but paused before I dove in, taking a second to enjoy the crackling fire, the soft glow created by the pale purple fabric, the comforting presence of my furry best friend nearby, and sighed.

Silas had attempted to make a haven for Myrtle. One that was everything she detested. I'd made my haven myself. Watson and me.

The fire popped again, and Watson let out a very undignified snort in his sleep.

My haven was perfect.

Recipes provided by:

2716 Welton St Denver, CO 80205
(720) 708-3026

Click the links for more Rolling Pin deliciousness:

RollingPinBakeshop.com

Rolling Pin Facebook Page

KATIE'S SHORTBREAD LEMON BARS

Crust:

1/2 cup butter
1/4 cup powdered sugar
1 cup flour

Filling:

2 eggs
1 cup sugar
2T lemon juice
Zest from 1 lemon
2 teaspoons flour
1/2 teaspoon baking powder
1/4 teaspoon salt

Directions:

1. Preheat oven to 350 degrees. Cream butter and powdered sugar. Stir in flour and spread the mixture over

the bottom of an 8 X 8 cake pan and pat down. Bake 10 to 12 minutes or until lightly browned.

2. While crust is baking, prepare lemon filling. Lightly beat eggs, then stir in sugar, lemon juice and lemon zest. Stir together flour, baking powder and salt. Stir into egg mixture. As soon as the crust is done baking, pour mixture over the crust. Put it back in the oven and bake until the filling is set and just beginning to brown. About 20 to 25 minutes. Put the pan on a rack and when completely cooled, cut into squares. Remove the lemon bars from the pan and sprinkle them with powdered sugar.

KATIE'S GINGERBREAD

Ingredients:

3 cups flour
1 teaspoon baking soda
¾ teaspoon cinnamon
¾ teaspoon ginger
½ teaspoon allspice
½ teaspoon cloves
½ teaspoon salt
4 ounces butter
¼ cup shortening
½ cup brown sugar
2/3 cup molasses (7 ounces)
1 egg

Directions:

1. Sift all dry ingredients together, set aside.

2. Cream butter, shortening, and brown sugar until light in color.
3. Add molasses and combine.
4. Add egg. Be sure to scrape edges of bowl between each addition.
5. Add dry ingredient in three stages. Be sure to mix well between each addition.
6. Chill dough for about an hour.
7. Preheat oven to 375.
8. Roll out dough and cut to desired pattern for gingerbread house.
9. Bake for about 15 minutes until firm.
10. Assemble cooled gingerbread pieces using royal icing and candies of your choice.

KATIE'S HAM & GRUYERE CROISSANT

Ingredients:

- 2 pounds and 8 ounces bread flour
- 1 ounce salt
- 4 ounces sugar
- 1 pound and 12 ounces water
- 1 ounce of yeast
- 2.5 ounces butter

Butter to roll in – 1 pound and 10 ounces - softened and formed into 9" X 9" square. Place in refrigerator but don't let it get too firm. (This is separate from the 2.5 ounces of butter for the croissant mixture.)

Directions:

1. Put yeast and water in bowl to activate yeast.
2. After yeast is activated, place all other ingredients in

bowl and with dough hook attachment, stir until combined. Continue kneading with dough hook for 10 minutes.

3. Place dough in bowl and cover with plastic wrap. Place in warm spot and let rise for about 30 minutes until doubled in size.

4. Punch down dough to deflate gases. Store in cold place until ready to use. Pull butter block from fridge and let get close to room temperature.

5. Roll the dough into a 14" square with the middle being thicker than the edges.

6. Place square of soft butter on the dough and fold edges of dough over butter until completely covered. Put in refrigerator until both butter and dough are the same temperature.

7. Take dough from refrigerator and roll out to a rectangle shape. It should be three times as long as it is wide.

8. Fold the dough into three sections. Fold right side in first to cover the center third and then fold the left side to cover the folded right side.

9. Place dough in refrigerator for 2 hours. Remove and roll out to a rectangle size and fold over once in half.

10. Repeat steps 7-9.

11. Roll dough out to a large rectangle about 1/8th of an inch thick. Cut into two strips lengthwise.

12. Cut into even triangles with a pizza cutter or sharp knife.

13. Place piece of sliced ham and small amount of shredded Gruyere on each triangle. Starting with the wide end, begin rolling towards the point.

14. Place on parchment-lined baking sheet and place in a warm humid spot to let rise.

15. Brush with egg wash (2 eggs whisked with 1 Tbs water). Bake at 350 degrees until dark golden brown.

AUTHOR NOTE

Dear Reader:

Thank you so much for reading the first collection of the Cozy Corgi Cozy Mystery series. If you enjoyed Fred and Watson's adventures, I would greatly appreciate a review on Amazon and Goodreads. You can review the collection, each book individually, or, even more wonderfully, both! Please drop me a note on Facebook or on my website (MildredAbbott.com) whenever you'd like. I'd love to hear from you. If you're interested in receiving advanced reader copies of upcoming installments, please join Mildred Abbott's Cozy Mystery Club on Facebook.

I also wanted to mention the elephant in the room... or the over-sugared corgi, as it were. Watson's personality is based around one of my own corgis, Alastair. He's the sweetest little guy in the world, and, like Watson, is a bit of a grump. Also, like Watson (and every other corgi to grace the world with their presence), he lives for food. In the Cozy Corgi series, I'm giving Alastair the life of his dreams through Watson. Just like I don't spend my weekends solving murders, neither does he spend his days snacking on scones and unending dog treats. But in the books? Well, we both get to live out our fantasies. If you are a corgi parent, you already know your little angel shouldn't truly have free rein of the pastry case, but you can read them snippets of Watson's life for a pleasant bedtime fantasy.

Much love, Mildred

PS: I'd also love it if you signed up for my newsletter. That way you'll never miss a new release. You won't hear from me more than once a month, nobody needs that many newsletters!

Newsletter link: Mildred Abbott Newsletter Signup

ACKNOWLEDGMENTS

A special thanks to Agatha Frost, who gave her blessing and her wisdom. If you haven't already, you simply MUST read Agatha's Peridale Cafe Cozy Mystery series. They are absolute perfection.

The biggest and most heartfelt gratitude to Katie Pizzolato, for her belief in my writing career and being the inspiration for the character of the same name in this series. Thanks to you, Katie, our beloved baker, has completely stolen both mine and Fred's heart!

Desi, I couldn't imagine an adventure without you by my side. A.J. Corza, you have given me the corgi covers of my dreams. A huge, huge thank you to all of the lovely souls who proofread the ARC versions and helped me look somewhat literate (in completely random order): Melissa Brus, Cinnamon, Ron Perry, Rob Andresen-Tenace, Anita Ford, TL Travis, Victoria Smiser, Lucy Campbell, Sue Paulsen, Bernadette Ould, Lisa Jackson, Kelly Miller, Gloria Lakritz, and Reg Franchi. Thank you all, so very, very much!

A further and special thanks to some of my dear readers and friends who support my passion: Andrea Johnson,

Fiona Wilson, Katie Pizzolato, Maggie Johnson, Marcia Gleason, Rob Andresen- Tenace, Robert Winter, Jason R., Victoria Smiser, Kristi Browning, and those of you who wanted to remain anonymous. You make a huge, huge difference in my life and in my ability to continue to write. I'm humbled and grateful beyond belief! So much love to you all!

ALSO BY MILDRED ABBOTT

-the Cozy Corgi Cozy Mystery Series-

Cruel Candy

Traitorous Toys

Bickering Birds

Savage Sourdough

Scornful Scones

Chaotic Corgis

Quarrelsome Quartz

Wicked Wildlife

Malevolent Magic

Killer Keys (Coming Jan. 2019)

-Cordelia's Casserole Caravan-

New series beginning Spring 2019

Made in the USA
Thornton, CO
05/14/23 20:21:31

2ca510a8-7eb7-4d49-802c-e6b92dfb6211R01